PENGUIN BOOKS

THE SURVIVORS

Elaine Feinstein is the author of *Mother's Girl*,
The Border, and *All You Need*, a biography of the
Russian poet Marina Tsvetayeva, *A Captive Lion*,
and the translator of the *Selected Poems of Marina
Tsvetayeva*.

ELAINE FEINSTEIN

The Survivors

PENGUIN BOOKS

PENGUIN BOOKS
Published by the Penguin Group
Viking Penguin, a division of Penguin Books USA Inc.,
375 Hudson Street, New York, New York 10014, U.S.A.
Penguin Books Ltd, 27 Wrights Lane,
London W8 5TZ, England
Penguin Books Australia Ltd, Ringwood,
Victoria, Australia
Penguin Books Canada Ltd, 2801 John Street,
Markham, Ontario, Canada L3R 1B4
Penguin Books (N.Z.) Ltd, 182–190 Wairau Road,
Auckland 10, New Zealand

Penguin Books Ltd, Registered Offices:
Harmondsworth, Middlesex, England

First published in Great Britain by Hutchinson & Co. (Publishers) Ltd.,
an imprint of Hutchinson Publishing Group, 1982
Published in Penguin Books 1991

1 3 5 7 9 10 8 6 4 2

LIBRARY OF CONGRESS CATALOGING IN PUBLICATION DATA
Feinstein, Elaine.
The survivors/Elaine Feinstein.
p.   cm.
ISBN 0 14 01.4848 5
I. Title.
PR6056.E38S87   1991
823'.914—dc20   90–45025

Printed in the United States of America

In memory of
Fay and Isidore Cooklin,
Rose Feinstein and
David Feinstein

February 1914

1

Two families. Two ways of life. And one city, Liverpool, planted on marsh and meadow. A city made by Irish traders first, and then slavers and shipowners, and at last a city of merchants and brokers, who put down their own great mercantile slabs. The town hall. The Liver building. Lime Street Station.

Only the wreckage of that city remains. Smashed-in windows and boarded shops on Scotland Road. Peeling interiors in Upper Parliament Street. Long before petrol bombs fired the Rialto, you could gawk into the huge bay windows open along Princes Road. Whole streets looked as if the sea itself had washed over the crumbling houses.

Once there were cotton bales and cones of grain on the docks. Massive stock brick warehouses, tobacco factories, soapworks. The pier head glowed red and yellow with electric cars. Liverpool bustled with energy from Lord Street to Brownlow Hill. In those days, Liverpool was a city of confident men.

Solomon Gordon and Abram Katz.

Solomon Gordon was a man of some financial substance, and he dressed fastidiously.

His clothes suggested an Englishman of the professional class, perhaps with a thriving solicitor's office. He was small, sandy-haired and clean-shaven, and everything about him was careful, from the starched triangles of his white collar to the fob-watch on his waistcoat and the single rose-cut stone in his tiepin. He was a narrow, fierce man, without an ounce of fat on his body; a glass-merchant, with a warehouse off Scotland Road.

Abram Katz had no money whatsoever, and his coat was worn and much mended.

Nevertheless he had his own kind of physical assurance. He was a powerfully built man, with a healthy colour in his face, and lines of cheerfulness round his eyes. His untrimmed red beard jutted out over his collar without apology. Gordon would have placed him without difficulty as a Jewish immigrant, probably from southern Russia.

And Abram would have eyed Gordon with speculation. Not because he admired wealth. In his experience, money came unpredictably at God's will, and disappeared in the same fashion. But because of another bond between the two men.

Another city. Odessa.

There were a great many Jews from Odessa in Liverpool.

Every evening Solomon Gordon locked up his warehouse with great care, picking his way fastidiously over the muddy cobbles to check the heavy catch on the store-yard gate. It was a ritual he had no intention of delegating. A man who expected a city without savages deserved to be robbed.

There was nothing Solomon despised more than people who relied on luck. The same failing led them to be satisfied, in business, to accept the approximate. Solomon was an accurate man. It appeared to be a rare passion. In twenty years of trade, he had never stopped marvelling at the rarity of precise minds. Most people hated to say yes or no if they could dodge a little. Worse, they lived on their own self-deception. They believed their own boasting, like crank aviators, hoping to fly on their own euphoria. How could he not overcome such helpless dreamers?

As Solomon walked towards the public house on the corner of the street where he took the tram, he often recognized one or two of his workmen pushing their way into the pub, and wrinkled his nose at the smell that came from it. He liked a drink, in cold weather; but he found beer a long, bitter drink that left a man sloppy and belching. He loathed the smell of it; and the men who stood on the corner, too, though they did not alarm him.

Solomon liked the city. He liked its rain, and its stone

buildings, and the flagstones that went yellow underfoot when it was wet. It was a solid, northern city, commercial but imperial, rich and unromantic. It suited him. Yet as he walked with neat steps away from his place of work, the first prickles of rancour disturbed him. When other men hurried home, Solomon felt a sullen reluctance to do so. Da, his children called him. Or the Old Man. And he knew they feared him as strangers did, and fell silent when they heard his feet on the steps that led up to his front door. Well, he was used to that. He travelled in a poisonous fume of that sudden, dulled stillness. It was almost as if he stunned as he approached, like an insect. He did not complain of the results. Who wanted a house full of idle, giggling children? But he knew they understood nothing of him. He knew they were unwilling to learn from him, and rage filled his blood as he thought of it.

It was his wife's doing, of course: though he reckoned to treat her well. Didn't he have a woman to wash and clean for her? If she chose to cook, it was for her own purposes. He understood what she was up to well enough. He had never promised her love, so she took it, as greedy women will, from her children instead. As he walked, Solomon imagined her standing, heavily built as a duchess, with her arms in the flour rolling pastry on the bare scrubbed wood. And he knew her womanly spirit bound all his children's love to herself alone. It was her spirit that filled the house. From her warm body came certainty and security like sweet unguents, that would suffocate him if he let them, but there was no fear of that. Like everything gentle and tender, his presence dried them up. He had only to put a foot over the threshhold to have it wither. But in his absence his wife's soul spread through the house on waves of sweet floor wax and enwrapped them all. All the lilac and lavender smells were her doing; like the polished silver on the white cloth, round which three pairs of eyes would be seated waiting.

Solomon did not explain to them that it was his hard work their lips were eating. Whatever he could have said, they would only taste her love; her pastry might be made with fat and flour bought with his wits and vigilance, but it was still

11

her love they tasted. If they could have crept out of his critical eye altogether they would have escaped him, but he would not allow that. They had to be educated to survive in his world. So he forced them to answer him to the point, bullied them with sharp questions, until, recently, he had at least begun to see their round eyes narrow to his own shrewdness. He wasn't a cruel man. He couldn't let them evade him, because he knew they would find evasion was an impossible strategy once they were grown up. He didn't bother to explain.

It was not that he wanted to be loved by them. Solomon found what most people meant by love a soft, enfeebling emotion. Another weakness. He'd given it up altogether, along with the pickled herrings and spade boards of Odessa, at fifteen when his mother died; he had cut it out of his soul then with the memory of her sweet dead face, seen one moment after death, before it was covered from his sight for ever. And even then he'd felt, mixed with the pain of her dying, another strange emotion to which he could not yet put a name. Later, when he married, he at last learned to identify the new feeling. He recognized it had been relief. Relief that the need to protect what could not be protected was over because he hadn't made the mistake of marrying for love.

Solomon had married very much above himself. His wife's father was of Dutch extraction, settled in England for some centuries, and proud of his connection with the Sephardi congregation of Liverpool. Solomon guessed, correctly, that their ties with the better-known families were looser than they would have liked; but he was not much concerned with such matters. His wife, Elsa, took more pride in her mother's Hungarian relations. She had brought him a substantial dowry including fine lace, linen, and old silver. She had a calm, flat face and fair complexion, expressed no interest outside her own household, and was not a romantic girl. All this pleased Solomon.

He failed to recognize her only real ambition.

Solomon lived in Bootle because it was convenient. The sour sights of Irish poverty in Scotland Road did not disturb him; there were broad avenues, too, and his own house stood in a trim road lined with trees. It was not a Jewish neighbourhood. There were no corner shops selling sour cucumbers or beigels or white cheese, and no families nearby spoke Yiddish. Solomon missed neither. He had no wish to find himself back in that babbling intimacy; no desire to know his neighbours' life closely. He would exchange a nod of polite acquaintance with the Scottish engineer who lived next door when they met in the street. But he looked for no further friendship. He had no wish to anglicize himself, even if it had been possible. He had not changed his name. 'Gordon' had been, to Russian ears, recognizably Jewish; and it was only an amusing accident that gave it Scots connotations in Liverpool.

One evening, in February 1914, Solomon put the key to his own lock and sensed the whole family behind the door; and something inside him pleaded, not yet, not yet. But he disciplined the voice. There was something afoot, he knew that. Something he'd heard the previous day in his wife's voice; an anxious wheedling. There had been something odd in the way the children soberly waited for their ladle of soup, with their eyes fixed on him, too. It was something they wanted, or something they were concealing from him. Either way he would have to work wearily to hook it out on to the surface, where it could be examined. What was it? Another three weeks' visit to Southport? He hoped not. Solomon hated holidays. The first day or two he could sleep, perhaps, and pretend it was useful. But after that every day seemed such a waste of time, a profitless expenditure of hours away from the only thing that interested him.

He let the front door close behind him and heard the muted *Shhhh*! from behind the heavy door next to the stairs. They were expecting him to go in to them at once as he usually did. Tonight, instead, he walked upstairs with his heart beating faster than he liked. He needed to clear his head and prepare himself.

There were cream roses on the wallpaper. His wife's preference, of course; he'd never liked them. The framed pictures of rough seas were his choice. He understood the sea, and was glad to live in a city where it was a reality. But it wasn't a playmate, or something to visit and admire. No, it

13

was completely hostile to life. If you looked at it truly, you understood the whole intention of God which had nothing to do with them. Like the sea, seen from a boat on a long voyage, God was a wildness you could neither serve nor placate. Holidays by the sea were a kind of profanity of his sense of its hideous power. How could people enjoy running up and down the sandhills shrieking, in the sight of it? Irrelevantly, as he turned the stair, he remembered: not a single handful of his own family's earth had yet gone into the soil of this country. They were still visitors.

The light was on in his younger daughter's room, and he paused, looking in at her in her white muslin dress, tiny feet crossed, slender wrists holding a book, slender back bent with grace over it. Her fragility appalled him.

'What are you reading?' he growled from the doorway.

She looked up, startled, but her tender lips opened obediently, and her gentle brown eyes were truthful.

'*Jane Eyre.*'

He stared at her. She was wearing a simple gold locket, which he knew had his own picture in it. At fifteen her grace should have charmed him, but there was something in the way she held herself that Solomon disliked. Something in her goodness, something in her desire to please, angered him. She was the only child to offer him love; instinctively, like a flower offering scent. But he turned away from her without further comment.

Betty didn't interest him. Or what she read. Without another word to her, he turned away and walked up the remaining stairs to the bathroom. Or rather, if he thought about her at all, it was to imagine her delicately pouring tea from a silver kettle, tending the spirit lamp under it, smiling hopefully, as she played house. The hope in her face offended Solomon. It was unrealistic. But it didn't pain him. Born to marry a lout, he could see it. She had the temperament of a skivvy. Whoever he found for her, she'd make herself into a servant for him. And she was too *thin*. He'd seen her on the beach and he knew how boyish her thighs were. She wasn't built for childbirth. Men sense that, thought Solomon; even with her good-angel smile, and her tender, round eyes, it'll

14

scare them off. For one moment the memory of his own mother flashed into Solomon's mind like a lit face at the distant window.

Solomon had considerable respect for his eldest child, his daughter Dorothy. She had a tough, rangy quality, with red-gold hair, and eyelashes too faint to be seen. In Odessa, her dark green eyes and tawny colouring would have had jokers calling after her in the street: *Witch*, *Jewess*. But in Liverpool, it seemed, red hair was more likely to be Irish. The Jews who had lived there longest were dark-skinned and almond-eyed, not a red hair on their heads, not even the Dutch families. And Solomon shut out of his thoughts the image of those who'd come from Kovno or Kiev, and huddled now in the small houses of Bedford Street and Kirkdale Road. He knew exactly how they lived. Hadn't he lived his first ten years with chickens under his house, and the smell of singed birds and pulled entrails in his nose? But those Jews were a family he had left behind. And Dorothy could never have sprung from them. She was athletic, fresh-skinned, fearless. And she taunted him, 'Don't think to marry *me* off. I won't do it. I don't want to have a child every year.'

'That's not how a lady talks.'

'Mother says you can always tell a lady by her *gloves*! So there!'

She used her mother's words, but she did not want her world. For that, he was grateful. He knew he should be arranging a husband for her, but he was reluctant to do so. Why should she be plagued with the terrible duties of womanhood? He liked her toughness. *Survive, survive*, my girl, he wanted to say to her. There's nothing else to do on this vile planet. He admired her rude health. Where had she got it from? His wife had been sick after every child; it was hard now to recall if Elsa had looked altogether physically fit even on their wedding day. More than she guessed, he understood Elsa's hypochondria; which was more a fear of illness than a love of it, a fear of being unable to protect, of becoming instead a creature in need of protection.

*

The wood was bare on the landing, though he could well have afforded to carpet everywhere. He liked to preserve some austerity, not *brocade* his house like some he knew, who thought there was some kind of protection in it.

He found a clean collar. Detached the one he had worn all day from his shirt. Then he washed himself carefully. He had no need to tell his wife he was home. He was on time, and the meal would have been geared to that. In a moment the bell would sound, and he could go downstairs to the meal. He combed his hair.

Books.

On the whole, Solomon was against them, except in so far as the bones of a language could be learned from them.

He had no education whatsoever, but he had a good ear for languages, and he had taken pains to acquire the syntax of standard English. As a child in Odessa, he had learned Russian illicitly; but it had not gone deeply into him, and the long O's of native Russian speakers did not determine his accent.

In any event, he was a taciturn man, and he spoke English well enough; though he rarely wrote in it, unless to sign his own name. His lack of skill with a pen had never impeded him in business. People soon learned that Solomon Gordon's word was worth a great deal more than another man's piece of paper. He never went back on a promise, even when he had good cause to regret it. For *learning*, which had no function, Solomon had no respect, and some distrust. It went along in his mind with musty paper, old men bent over religious texts, and beards smelling of snuff. It was part of the heritage that led to shabby clothes, ill-housing and a reluctance to believe in cause and effect. English men in his position sent their boys neatly dressed to superior schools. But he was not convinced these schools fitted them for the world of commerce. He had also observed shrewdly that for all the airs Elsa's father gave himself, and for all the books he read, he'd been glad enough to have Solomon as a son-in-law. Solomon placed no great value on his own origin. He had seen clearly enough in Odessa that it could be a misfortune. He accepted so much, without resentment, with all the

16

bounds and limits it implied. Changing house changed nothing, nor would schools.

Elsa did not complain that Solomon was often morose and withdrawn. Her father, whom she adored, had sharply predicted as much and she had not chosen Solomon in the hope of being cherished. She had expected him to do well in the world, and so he had. She was satisfied. Without the least extravagance, she set up home and prepared to bear men children. For Elsa intended her sons to become English gentlemen.

About this Solomon was sceptical.

'Things change, my dear. You don't understand them. The Sassoons, the Montagues, the Samuels . . .'

'Money,' said Solomon brusquely.

'First perhaps,' said Elsa doggedly. 'Then a little learning. And good manners. That is the key to being acceptable in this country.'

Solomon had no wish to quarrel with his wife, and so he kept to himself what he thought of the value of learning. But she had accidentally hit upon an argument which carried conviction. He saw very well that men were judged by their manners, much as they were judged by their dress. And so he agreed to pay the fees for his son to attend a private school approved by Elsa's father. And Elsa's face grew broader and more cheerful as the first reports came in of his progress. Her son Francis appeared to be most remarkably gifted.

Solomon observed as much with satisfaction.

The Katz family lived by legends. Not all of them were lies. Abram liked to claim a grandfather from a wooden village with a watchtower in the Caucasus. The villagers' reputation for strength was supposed to be so far-reaching that no tsar's men ventured up the brown and purple slopes to bother them, even though their farms were rich and their soil health-giving. As to the facts: there had certainly been an uncle from Tbilisi, whose strength surprised even the Jews in Odessa's ghetto; but he was a small trader, and no farmer. The substance of the blessing they enjoyed, however, was indomitable health, which continued into old age. And there was nothing crabby

17

in them. They had no restraint, no belief in doing anything to make them sour. The other legends were more a question of what the Katz family expected from life.

To begin with, they depended on a regular flow of miracles.

No Katz ever brooded over bad times to come, or attempted to provide against them. It was a virtue to have rich food and sweet wine and presents for the children every Sabbath, whatever had to be borrowed. In part they were gambling on their willingness to work harder and longer than anyone else: get up before light, take a cart round the streets, keep going in all weathers.

But there was more to their confidence. The most important piece of the Katz legend centred on Abram's enjoyment of God's especial favour. Hadn't the Almighty given him the power to learn the whole text of the Bible by heart? So easily. In his youth, Abram had taken such a sensuous pleasure in the music of each line that every word sank into him without will or effort. Now, when he spoke them out of his memory, his voice brought ripples of joy to the scalps of all who listened, whether they could understand the ancient language or not. He had studied almost to the point of becoming a rabbi in the *yeshiva* at Odessa. He understood Rashi; he could quote from Akiba. And every Saturday afternoon fellow scholars gathered at his house after lunch to drink and argue on holy matters. Sometimes the children were alarmed by the violence of the voices then rising from the tiny front room, and the sound of fists banging the table. But by the end everyone was always singing and laughing, and Abram came out looking pink as a cherub, with blue eyes sparkling.

Abram's gifts were acknowledged without question in the family; and indeed they had to be, since no one else was ever given the time to ponder over books as he did. They were too busy working – brothers, sons, daughters alike – to keep the Katz enterprise going. And none of them ever suggested Abram should earn money by teaching Hebrew. They respected him too much.

Abram's entry into the wood trade had begun in the early days of his marriage, when the trade in timber first started to boom in the Pale, and he had learnt to bargain on the docks in Russian. Lumber was good business, except when there was not enough snow, and it was hard to haul the timber down to the rivers. There were laws against storing logs on land that belonged to the railroad, but Abram had no part in arranging such details. All his brothers dealt in wood, as carpenters and cabinetmakers, or carters of second-hand tables from house to house. Even after the move to England, Abram continued in it. It was something his bull strength fitted him for, much more than the traditional rag trade.

Abram, however, was not good with machinery. He found it difficult to keep his mind on its dangers. He put the dowelling up to the saw as he was told; and for a while he cut it with the instructions firmly on his lips. But in a matter of minutes he was dreaming.

The day he lost a finger he was dreaming of Palestine. It was a dream of great intensity. He and Rasil were standing at the harbour in Odessa. He remembered the pier across the Black Sea and the steamers that left for Constantinople. There were seabirds, white strong-necked creatures, over the boats; and he could see naval uniforms, and ladies with white parasols, and he and Rasil stood where the cattle were loaded. They were waiting happily to board a ship, and not just for Constantinople, either; among men with shaven heads, covered with sheepskin hats, Mohammedan Tartars making a pilgrimage to Mecca; among Chinese, Armenians, Africans. Yes, Abram and Rasil were not going north. There would be no more north, no more Europe. They were taking the children home. For in his dream, Abram already had a home. It was a white stone house with the sun on it, and Rasil was standing with her arms folded, looking angry as she did sometimes when she was very pleased and afraid someone was playing a trick on her. Her feet were straddled, and her head back. She wanted to be sure it was really theirs, this piece of God's country, a piece of God.

The circular saw took off the top joint of Abram's third finger on his right hand. He was taken, shocked, out of his dream of golden fruit and God's blessing straight to the Royal Hospital. And there, after giving him an enormous slug of

19

alcohol, they stitched him up as best they could. He was delirious for a day.

'My orange trees. My piece of God,' he called out.

They could only put cold cloths on his forehead to bring down the fever and keep him still on his bed, but there was no infection.

'He's tough for a Jew,' said one of the doctors, taking in the size of his shoulders. 'Must have done a man's work once.'

Abram's certainty that God would love and care for his family was not abated by adversity. But as 1914 opened trade had begun to go well. Abram had that very day been down to the riverside himself to buy extra supplies of Russian plywood. He had done so with the money that should have been paid to the grocer, but the Katz business was expanding. The grocer was his friend and would understand. Like the tobacco factories and corn mills and sugar refineries who were taking on more men, Abram was only responding to the change in pace brought on by rumours of war. And he had enjoyed his day, walking along the narrow shelves between dead water and warehouse walls. The soft groaning of ships at berth had stirred euphoric possibilities in him. He had looked across to the great dome of the dock board offices and felt its grandeur so personally that, when he looked back at the smoke-softened roofs of the city, everything looked flat and docile to him. In his thought, he was already a merchant trading between east and west; and if the slats of rain came down on him this grey evening, he nevertheless held himself like a man whom the king had already decided to honour. He felt no anxiety about his decision to expand the business. The family would survive. If he'd guessed wrong, they'd cope somehow. Somewhere else, perhaps. In some other town. Some other country? Yes, if it was necessary. They could pack, and move. They were used to it.

By then Abram had seven children.

They survived under his wife's eagle care.

Their two eldest sons had gone off to Canada to farm; and the two eldest daughters had married and moved to the south of England. They had been young to marry; but Rasil had been married young herself, and was satisfied to have them

20

follow their husbands.

The rest of the Katz family lived in a street off Brownlow Hill where everyone was Jewish, and every trade flourished. Those who had shops lived over them. It was a self-sufficient village of occupations: baker, tailor, fishmonger, butcher. The street was an island of animation and activity in Liverpool's greyest slum. To Abram, the other deprived and stricken people in that slum were chiefly remarkable for their gentleness.

When times were slow on the docks the men sat out on their doorsteps, and chatted sociably together until it was time to go to the tavern at the end of the street. Even the largest of the dockers had a kind of laziness in them. Their violence was largely domestic and individual; Abram had no fear of them surging into his own neighbourhood, like Ukrainians forcing their way into the ghetto to pillage and batter whosoever they found in their way.

The dirt and disorder Abram could see through the open doorways did not surprise him. He knew well how in each court there would be only a little dribbling pump for water. And it was a long way to the corporation wash-house; his own family had its problems getting there and back. It was the children Abram found disturbing: they were such mysteriously pitiable creatures, ragged, snotty and barefoot even in winter. And their eyes were closed, hostile and without hope. The voices that rose from the streets he walked through on the way home had Irish vowels corrupted by the Liverpool inflection, and Abram wondered uneasily about the world they would inherit. They didn't get enough to eat, he reasoned; their families spent too little on food, and some seemed to manage on bread and tea. Out of that, and the occasional piece of pork, the men found the vitality to unload the greatest ships in the world, and their women could take their turn in the tinworks for ten shillings a week. Their priests looked fat, as they always did. But who cared for the children?

Everywhere there was the smell of horses. Dray horses, delivering to the local pub, or carrying ice to the fishmonger at the corner of Eden Street. Just before Abram reached his turning there was a brothel. Heavily painted women sat out there in all weathers, waiting for custom. They were extraordinary, scraggy creatures. Abram always averted his eyes as he passed, not to avoid temptation but because he did not want to increase their humiliation.

As soon as Abram turned into Eden Street, he felt his spirits lift. The quality of noise and bustle changed absolutely. There were stalls everywhere still open. The dark street was a dazzle of wares lit by lanterns, or perhaps a candle on the edge of a wooden crate. The stall-keepers called out to one another: insults, gossip, financial suggestions. Most of them used Yiddish; but equally, most of them could speak either Polish or Russian as well. Even on this wet day, customers stopped to lift and examine the fruit, or take up a handful of sunflower seeds to nibble, while they decided what to buy. A youth in untidy ear-locks was selling prayer shawls and phylacteries, amulets and tin ornaments. Abram disapproved of him. Everywhere, the smells were of eastern Europe; rich, heavy and familiar.

Abram's was a terraced house at the far end of the street. His youngest daughter flung herself at him as soon as he opened the door, climbing into his arms, pulling his pockets down, wriggling to see what he had brought. He lifted Sarah without effort. She pulled his beard and demanded sweet cakes; but he set her down when his bowler fell on the floor. He could tell at once it was wash-day; but behind the odours of drying clothes came the deep smell of hot carrots and turnips.

'Where's my *Tsaddickle*?' Abram demanded.

At once Benjamin, the youngest of his sons, was there. At twelve he was already nearly shoulder-height to Abram. And whatever else he looked, it was not a little saint. He had large eyes of a greeny-grey colour, with changing flecks in them; and his eyebrows were thick as a brush, jet-black, and ran straight across his face. It was not clear why Abram so blatantly preferred him to his other children; but the child understood it was so well enough. Benjamin was not the cleverest child in the family. It was his older brother, Harry, who might have made a scholar like his father; and it was he

22

who won all the praise at school. But Benjamin was impudent and alert. And his father smiled on him.

'So how was school?'

Benjamin made a face, and grinned.

'Miss Biddle kept him in,' said Sarah importantly.

'Those old biddies!' demanded Abram comfortably. 'What do they know?'

And he put his hand in blessing into Benjy's thick black hair and planted a heavy kiss on his forehead, as though he were transmitting the favour of the Lord.

Rasil was in the kitchen, and when Abram tried to give her a hug she scolded him in a loud voice.

'Clumsy! You're too big to be in here! You'll knock all the clothes into the ash!'

But her face was warm and friendly, in spite of her words. Rasil had always been a fine woman. Even now, at thirty-six, there was not a wrinkle in her face, and her hair was black and thick and long. Abram loved it, and found argument after argument against her having to wear the wig most devout men of his generation thought necessary. In the day, she kept it pinned into a bun.

Rasil never thought much about God. Abram said that was all right for a woman.

Rasil thought about practically everything else. She kept chickens in the back yard, and fought off marauding cats with her bare hands. She couldn't read or write, but she could count; and no tradesman cheated her, because she could add up faster in her head than they could scribble. It would be a tough local man who would take her on, anyway, with her huge upper arms, muscled from swabbing floors and chopping wood. She was a handsome woman, and even with all her children pulling her about, and chastely dressed as she was, she couldn't disguise the heavy sexual health of her body under the folds.

Every morning Rasil washed in cold water, with coarse household soap. She liked to get up early, so that Abram should not see her on her knees. He liked to think of her always as a queen at the head of his Sabbath table; and he didn't want to feel guilty that he couldn't provide any helper

23

to do the heavy work for her. Rasil was contented enough. She cleaned out the grate and made up the fire until the kitchen was warm. And today she had done the washing. At the best of times, sheets were a problem. First, she had to lift them out of the gas-lit copper where they'd been boiling all night and carry them outside into a tub by the garden pump. There she gave them a last good thumping with her three-legged wooden dolly. And then she had to stand wringing them out with her own tough wrists, because even the heavy wooden mangle could not grapple with flannelette sheets when they were sopping wet. When the wet clothes could not hang outside, she had to put more coal on the fire and stretch them over the wooden maiden in the kitchen.

Now she bent over to close the oven door, and had the spirit to pretend anger.

'Do you want potato cakes for supper?' she demanded.

'Everything you make is good.'

'Then out with you,' she insisted.

'Listen, Rasil,' Abram pleaded. 'Today you can be proud of your old Abram. I made a bargain.'

At this news she paused in what she was doing, brushed down her petticoats, and looked at him shrewdly.

'You'll see how well things will go,' he promised her.

They were close enough for her to pat his cheek. Then she murmured, 'Today Becky came into the grocer's.'

'The grocer?' Abram stirred uneasily.

'Yes, with such a story. She said there's going to be a war. Bound to be. She read it in the papers. Their papers. What do you think, Abram?'

Abram shrugged. A deep, inimitable gesture of acceptance. The lunatics who ran the Gentile world were capable of any madness.

2

The Katz workshop smelt of sawdust and boiled glue; and Benjy was happy in it. But then he woke happy every morning. As he had none of the things the Gordon family associated with a good life, his more or less continuous good spirits would have seemed to them a kind of stupidity. A protection, perhaps, against knowing what the world had against him, and the limitations of his equipment to deal with it.

Benjy felt no sense of any such insufficiency.

The saw began to whine from six in the morning under the pressure of new orders; and when the motor cut out, it was Benjy who was called to see what had got into it. Benjy's fingers were surprisingly delicate in spite of their size and strength. So he spent more and more of the days he should have been at school alongside Abram and his uncles, and no one objected.

Things had taken a turn for the better, as Abram had always declared they would.

And so Abram had hired an Irish girl called Annie from the next street to come in and help Rasil clean the house. Rasil was not altogether pleased with her presence. She was pretty and cheerful enough, but far from strong; and it made Rasil restless to watch her bend over and scrub the clothes, as if it took all her strength. The girl was pale and bony, with untidy black hair and deep-set eyes. She had lived alone, except for her docker brother, most of her life. One day he enlisted in the army, and her eyes grew darker and larger, and she began to finger the cross on her flat, bony chest more and more and brood as she worked until Rasil was tempted to get down on the kitchen floor beside her. Instead she followed her about and chivvied. But for all her scolding, Rasil always pressed a

25

piece of cold boiled chicken, or perhaps a piece of fried fish, into the girl's hand as she left. The girl thanked her only woodenly; and the food made little difference to her scrawny, depleted body.

Benjy suggested she must be selling the food on the way home.

'If I had her in the house, I'd soon fatten her up,' Rasil threatened.

But Annie wouldn't hear of that. She had a horror of living in, or she might have had a job with a Christian family. And the Katz family were strange to her, though she'd lived round the corner from them all her life. She still thought of them as heathens and more than likely poisoners. And the rye bread and pink-herring smells did not reassure her. When Rasil lit Sabbath candles, and then closed her eyes while the yellow light filled the room, as if she were creating the first day itself, Annie shuddered with an ancient unease, and sometimes crossed herself.

Rasil didn't like that sign-making, even though she recognized it as an instinctive, childish gesture to ward off evil; she was sensitive herself because she thought she was pregnant again. She began to carry beads of amber about with her, because they had the reputation of magical powers of their own. And she wondered about the sign of the cross. But when she consulted Abram about it he gave her a learned discourse on the foolishness of superstition in all its forms.

Rasil badly missed her eldest daughters, married and in the south. She had several women friends but now Abram was talking of moving house to Upper Parliament Street, which would isolate her further. There was no point describing her feelings about the move, or a new baby, or indeed any anxiety to Abram. He would either shrug everything away, or rub his beard, trying to understand; but what he couldn't feel, he couldn't think about. All things worked together for good for those who loved the Lord, as far as he was concerned. So she didn't worry him about what was happening to Harry.

She knew Benjy was missing his schoolwork; and she knew he very rarely went along to the old man who was supposed to teach him Hebrew; she had some idea of where he went in the evenings with his older cousin, Len. But she didn't worry about Benjy.

Harry was another matter. He had a tender mouth, and serious brown eyes that looked out at the world with an eagerness that made Rasil's heart ache for him. And she knew something was making him unhappy.

'What *is* it, Harry?' she asked again and again.

She suspected he was taunted at school; perhaps bullied. But Benjy said he'd never seen any sign of it.

Most of March it rained heavily, and the full candles of the horse chestnuts were hardly out by the last week of the month. Sarah played indoors, and one afternoon she threw up a tin plate and broke off the gas mantle from the ceiling. Harry had just come in from school, and was setting down his satchel, when Rasil seized his arm and asked him to turn off the gas at the mains. But the tap wasn't in the cellar as Rasil thought, and Harry couldn't find it. So by the time Benjy got home he found them all sitting forlornly in the wet garden.

'You silly buggers,' he called out to them, divining quickly enough what had happened and locating the mains under the stairs with the meters without much trouble.

'Who you calling names?' Rasil demanded, rather less aggressively than usual because the gas had made her queasy. And when they came back in, she watched Harry's face uneasily, sensing a sullen shame in the boy, and understanding his sense of failure to do what his brother did so easily. She did not know how to help him.

At the end of term, when his report card came, she asked him, 'Aren't you proud?'

But she knew he could take no pleasure in it. Troubled, Rasil tried to prod Abram into showing some interest. Was he not a scholar himself? But Abram felt the learning of the Gentile world was at best an irrelevance.

Harry was not evading his mother purposely, but he could not explain what he did not understand himself. For what, after all, was there to make him feel any different from the rest of the family? He knew, of course. They expected to be happy and Harry couldn't. Or not often.

If only he was someone else, maybe, with a steady spirit

27

inside him, someone who didn't have to niggle and question everything. Someone who could cope with all the world's blackness that he sensed ahead of him. Or perhaps someone who lived inside a simpler set of expectations – some predictable world, where reward followed work sensibly, without intervening prayers. An ordinary, everyday world. Harry thought perhaps he could handle that.

Miss Biddle believed passionately that everything would look differently once he went to the Liverpool High School; but Harry wasn't sure he wanted that. A lot of kids from Eden Street went on to grammar school and Abram only shook his head over them.

'First they learn, and then they copy,' he said.

Did he want to be like them? To copy English ways, and move away from the family? To have Abram shake his head over him? I'll be lonely, he thought. Even lonelier. I wonder if I'm going to be lonely all my life?

'All you need is a trade in your hands,' said Abram.

Harry looked down at his own hands. They were bony and long-fingered; he supposed they must be good for something. But still he stared down at them angrily. He didn't really feel like relying on them. Where was it written that a man had to have brains in his hands? he wondered mutinously.

But he never questioned his father.

The trouble was, Harry couldn't be sure that any way he chose to follow would be the right way for him.

He could make no sense of any of it. His life. Anybody's life. He thought of poor fat Mrs Zussman, with her varicose legs and her heavy shopping bag, who'd died the week before. He could still remember what a good-looking woman she'd been before she got fat. Then her husband had gone off to Manchester to find work in the tailoring shops, and started gambling away his wages. Sometimes when Harry saw her crossing the road, he took her bags across for her, and she would smile and blink at him and say, 'There's a good boy.'

But one day she had a haemorrhage in her head, fell down, and it was all over. Everyone said what a good woman she'd been, what a good soul she had, how she'd always struggled on. But where was the sense in all that struggling? Harry wouldn't go to the funeral. No one in the family understood, and he didn't try to explain, but inside he felt it wasn't Mrs Zussman's death they should be mourning, but her life. The waste of all that struggling.

'She should have just given up,' he said to Benjy.

But Benjy shook his head over that. He couldn't imagine any point in giving up.

3

All that spring Elsa guessed she was ill; but she hid it from Solomon, and as far as possible from the children. Partly she was impatient at her own lethargy. When she tried to hurry she had the sensation of the roof of her head rising, almost as if she could float. A new clumsiness in her gestures also disturbed her. As she walked, the paving slabs rose under her feet, as if the earth were rocked by the sea; even sitting in her chair her balance was disordered.

All this she hid from Solomon instinctively; buying sweet-scented cachous to hide the metallic smell of her breath; and showing as few signs of fatigue in his presence as possible. Dorothy watched her narrowly these days; but she and Elsa were not close, and Elsa had a horror of her elder daughter's sympathy which she could explain as little as her need in some way to warn Francis. Unfortunately, Francis had become inexplicably remote.

There had been a time when he loved to do his homework in the breakfast room after tea, within earshot of her kitchen preparations; and she would feed him surreptitious pieces of crumbled cake, or allow him to eat the remains of the icing out of the whipping-bowl. He still sat downstairs, unless Dorothy was at home; but as he sat curled in a chair, she could see he was altogether part of his task. Her offered titbits were accepted with only perfunctory thanks; he barely raised his eyebrows from the printed word to do so. She felt wounded by this change in his attention, without being able to complain of any kind of snub. But she was bewildered by it, and felt it undignified to try and penetrate his withdrawn sufficiency. Only the strength of her need to talk to him overcame her desire for dignity as the weeks went by.

At last she abandoned all pretence, and came into the breakfast room herself to watch him: loving the soft golden hairs at the nape of his neck, and the curve of his chin when it was cupped by his hand.

And she tried to rouse him to her presence.

'Francis?'

He lifted eyes still focused on the print of his page.

'I want you to try to be more friendly to Da,' she began hesitantly.

Francis frowned at that, and his gaze blackened upon her, so that she flinched in the unfamiliar stare.

'Why?' he asked coldly.

'Dear, he wants the best for you, as far as he can, you know that.'

'I know he wants me in the business,' said Francis sharply. 'We've already discussed it.'

'Are you happy with that?'

'Mama, I can't think so far ahead.'

'Grandfather Groot says you have a talent for the law.' Elsa always referred to her father in that way.

'Then Da is right about one thing at least,' replied Francis coldly.

She did not want to press for his meaning, which was clearly critical of her father. Perhaps it was just the optimism in the opinion which he disliked. Solomon hated optimism, and Francis was like him in more things than he probably realized.

'I only want what is best for you, darling,' she said, with a catch in her voice which she absolutely could not prevent.

'Mama, I *do* know that,' he said, kindly enough, so that for all his elegant sprawl she was reminded again how young he was.

'The older boys are planning to enlist,' he said a little

wildly, as if to distract her, 'if it comes to a war.'

'How insane. Why? Surely they're too young?'

'Hard to resist, probably.'

He spoke as though he, too, were deceived into thinking it was a lark to go off like that. Elsa felt a little clutch of fear, but not for those unknown boys.

'You wouldn't do that? Would you?' she asked faintly.

Even the thought of it made the blood pound in her eyes. At the edges of her vision the air had gone as grainy as a poor photograph, and the ground under her seat ducked and flew sideways.

She did not hear his reply.

'Promise me,' she said urgently.

He was looking concerned now, at her face she supposed, and she felt for her handkerchief to dab the cool wetness from her forehead.

'Why are you so distant from me? *What* is it you hold against me?' she whispered.

'Nothing, Mama. Nothing has changed between us,' he assured her.

She nodded then. It was possible she had imagined their earlier closeness. Francis was not very close to anybody.

He was not an unpopular boy, but he made few close friends. Part of this sprang from a reluctance to bring them home to Solomon's beady eye; but there was another, deeper reticence of a grain not so different from Solomon's own. If Francis had to formulate what he felt about the world, it would not of course have been couched in Solomon's terms. There was nothing resigned in him, nothing he felt he could not reach for, nothing for which he felt he could not rightfully hope. The pinch in his soul took another form. Not so much an awareness of the bleak reality of things. More an impatient assessment: things like this are not good enough for *me*!

St Bede's had, as Grandfather Groot no doubt intended, introduced Francis into a world where children expected the world to yield them an entry into their chosen professions and a comfortable life thereafter. Somewhere, deep in Francis's spirit, was the conviction that there was more to life than that. But what was the *more*? What was it he was aspiring towards?

He could not formulate it accurately. He loved music, but he knew well enough that he had none of the talent to go along with his intense response to it. Elsa arranged piano lessons; but his performance was undistinguished, and he drew less pleasure from playing the instrument than from listening to others. It had once seemed to him that Elsa must know the answer, since she was surely the secret hand that planted the seed of this strange desire in him; now that he was older she must one day, like the godmother in a fairy tale, show him the way, yield him some golden key, or at the very least name the fortress he was surely appointed to storm.

This never happened. Yet as his eyes sharpened on the northern society around him, he understood that she had done so without noticing what she was doing, and that through her he escaped the terrible snobberies that would have otherwise held him pinioned.

There was of course a whole provincial world to which the Gordons would not be admitted: the dances of the gentry, their bridge parties and amateur theatricals, and some of their golf and tennis clubs would all be closed to him and the Groots as well because they were, after all, Jewish. In this as in other matters, the Gordons found themselves in an anomalous position. It was important to be acceptable among the finest Jewish families of the town. For this to be possible, there could be no hint of conversion, and not too much talk of religious unorthodoxy. And so, within the provincial world of north-west England, there was a clear line of social exclusion, which Francis would have borne impatiently, if it had not been for Elsa's unconscious teaching.

Elsa saw the horrors of provinciality. She made him feel the mean spirit of a bank manager and his querulous wife as essentially vulgar. They would surely be despised if they ever had to encounter the great houses of Europe, she suggested. She loved to hint at the Hungarian baron among her relatives, and speak of the great cosmopolitan virtues which made the social snobberies of Liverpool pettily meaningless. To have an aristocracy of mingled Jewish and Hungarian blood seemed to Francis a marvellous privilege. Through his sense of it, he developed an air of tolerant amusement towards the other boys in his class which gave him a kind of immunity from the treatment many other Jewish boys suffered.

He went into assembly with all the other children, and sang hymns alongside the only other boy he positively knew to be Jewish, without the faintest sense of conspiratorial irony. He had never been teased for anything other than his unyielding refusal to lie, which got other boys as well as himself into trouble, and which was derided as senseless piety. It was in fact a genuine obsession. Francis had drawn from his father only one certainty: that nothing based on self-deception could survive. That scruple led him to discipline himself into deceiving no one, whoever might be hurt.

Within the family, his insistence on the strict truth had gone down badly. His eldest sister, red-haired Dorothy, bullied him to admit he would draw a line somewhere.

'Surely to save Betty? Well then, Mama? What, not even if policemen were coming to drag her off unjustly to some horrible prison?'

'You see how you have to cheat,' he objected. 'If the prison was unjust I wouldn't have to lie, would I?'

'Wait! Yes. An *alibi*! That's it. Supposing you could save her with an *alibi*. What then? Wouldn't you? Wouldn't you *really?*'

'No,' said Francis, firmly.

'Then you're a disgusting little prig, that's all,' said Dorothy.

Elsa's bout of faintness had eased. She wondered if it had anything to do with the elastic gussets in her new corsetry. Nevertheless, she still had much to say to her son.

'When you are sixteen,' she began, 'there is some money for you that I have put aside. You may need it. To do whatever you want. It should be quite enough. Tonight I will give you the bank book, and you must lock it in your bureau and not speak of this to anyone.'

'Why tonight?' he asked, suddenly fascinated against his will by the intensity of her gaze.

'My dear,' she said pointedly. 'How can I tell you if you can't keep a secret?'

The day after the doctor called. Dorothy went in to sit on Betty's bed to talk about it.

'I wonder if mother is having another baby?' she asked.

Betty looked up uncomprehendingly from her book.

'Well, you must have seen how oddly she moves about. And men are such pigs.'

'But wouldn't she be fat again? I can remember how fat she was last time,' Betty asked breathlessly.

The idea excited her although Elsa had lost her last child. But on all medical matters concerning female welfare Dorothy had made herself expert.

'Not necessarily. Not yet,' said Dorothy, airily.

It was her father Dorothy questioned, not her mother.

Impudent piece, Solomon found her; but he reassured her neverthless.

'Well, that's something. Honestly! Who'd be a woman?' she challenged him.

'Well, that's how the world is,' said Solomon, more gently than he intended.

But she went on arranging her fine new hat in front of a mirror, and said persistently, 'It's a rotten life. I can't think why we flounce about like this. Do you know?'

'You keep us cheerful, my dear,' suggested Solomon.

'There. I'd like to do something more useful than help keep up one silly man's pride,' she retorted.

'But how *would* you dress? That's a pretty enough hat,' reasoned Solomon.

'But whatever is all this lace for? You're a sensible man, you'd never put up with all this on your head, would you?'

'That's how the world is,' he repeated.

But it warmed his heart for a moment that she'd called him *sensible*, so he was seduced into taking her seriously.

'Girls aren't built to live in a man's world. It's brutal and harsh. We dress you like this to show our respect.'

'Do you? If you respected me, you'd let me do what I want with my life,' she replied, too quickly.

And she had a long face when she turned to stare at him. He could see she might grow up quite plain and horsy, if she kept up that defiant expression. But the next minute she had shrugged it all off.

'Impossible, talking to men!'

'I saw no letter this morning,' remarked Solomon mildly.

Francis had been invited to spend August with Elsa's Austrian cousins. Rashly, Elsa had already told the child of the invitation, unable to silence her own euphoric memories of a house near the Hungarian border, with Persian carpets on oak floors and Biedermeyer furniture. There would be picnics, with wine and game pie, in the fields near the Danube, she told him. And every evening, music in the fine drawing room. And poetry.

She coloured a little. To conceal her embarrassment she continued to brush her hair with long, patient strokes, and gaze into her ill-lit pearwood mirror although Solomon had already lowered the jet of gas by the bedside table.

'But yesterday,' she hesitated, 'when I saw you were so tired when you came home, I didn't like to worry you.'

He had trapped her into a half-lie, and instantly she was ashamed. It was absurd. Unnecessary. And, perhaps as a result, his position had hardened. His smile, as she turned her face towards him hopefully, suggested that he had no difficulty following her thoughts.

'You waited three days,' he pursued her. 'To be exact. Why did you wait at all? If, as you say, it is a small matter and no expense?'

How could she explain?

Elsa was an affectionate woman, not a foolish one. Perhaps she had not married passionately; but she had married hopefully. Nothing in her own family had prepared her for Solomon's morose temperament. Even when she recognized the gloom in him, her instinct had been to comfort and to cure it. She had longed to warm him with her care, with a home, a young family; to turn him into a hearty, cheerful father. Instead, she herself had learned to be wary. For Solomon had no desire to soften. He despised the qualities she wished him to learn. But she was a brave woman, Elsa, even though her pulse might beat with apprehension under her solid flesh.

'The visit will widen his view of the world. Introduce him to

35

people of culture. Francis is such a sensitive child. Oh, I know Liverpool is a great city, but surely you see it is cut off from the great currents of our time? From Europe.'

'Exactly,' said Solomon drily.

It was his purpose in settling there.

He did not admire the cultured gentry of central Europe: febrile, extravagant, unreliable people. He knew well that many families had settled and prospered in that hospitable empire; but he suspected the grandeur of their fine houses, and the solidity of wealth. And worst of all their recklessness in his eyes was to allow their children to become writers, painters and musicians. That was stupider than luxury, which could be recouped. Art, he reckoned, was an enthusiasm which put men as much off-guard as love. In part, he had chosen England as a bastion against such folly. Let the English have their own artists. Their visitors would serve them as honest traders.

And so, in reply to Elsa's tremulous description of the enormous advantages offered his son, he replied briefly, 'No, Elsa.'

Elsa fell into cunning.

'He will learn another language. We trade with Germany? Languages are good for trade. You have often said so.'

'No,' he said simply.

'Why? Why? My cousins love Austria; it has been good to them. It is a rich, happy country.'

'Be glad you don't have their German name,' said Solomon. 'It will soon be no advantage in England, my dear, however grandly it rings in your ears now.'

'You are always so sure the worst will happen,' she flashed.

Solomon was not angered by her.

'It is my place to know these things,' he said matter-of-factly. 'You can't think. It's quite normal. You are a woman. No one expects it of you.'

And Solomon took off his slippers, heaved up the fine linen bedclothes, and without bothering to discuss his opinions further put the entire conversation from his calculations. No doubt the boy had already been told of the scheme, but what did a boy of fourteen know of what he wanted?

Elsa swallowed back her own thoughts, stilled the angry shiver in her own limbs, and lay beside him with no further word.

She was so still, Solomon wondered if her closed eyes were hiding tears. Not that she was a weeper, but something in her spirit tonight was unreadable, and he listened uneasily for a catch in her breath. She was not a noisy woman; whatever she felt there was not much show of it, generally. Certainly there was no moisture on her soft, clear cheeks. He could not detect any sign of passion agitating her breast. He was satisfied.

Beside him, Elsa accepted his familiar scrutiny with stolid endurance.

She thought: Very well. I will bow my head to this. I will accept your descriptions of me. I will do everything you tell me to do, and take you into my bed, and never ask if you love me. Very well. Very well. I will do this again and again. For all my children. But especially for Francis.

Francis was trying hard to sleep. Or, more exactly, to re-enter a broken dream. Impossible. There had been snow and a young girl in a fur hat. On skis she sailed away from him and, though he squeezed his eyes shut, he could not recall her, or even burrow down through the layers of his mind into that white world. Instead, he lay awake and his heart banged strangely, perhaps because his mother had been so very solemn about the letter and the opportunity it offered him. It wasn't so much what she had said about Austria and the forests that had so excited him, not even what she had said about the family. His uncle was a German poet, she'd said; and there was another brother who was a publisher. His aunt played a violin in a famous quartet. All these things were like fairy tales, and the dream too was like a fairy tale, with a promise of happiness. It was the only certainty that remained with him as his wakefulness sharpened: the dream had been filled with happiness, and it was that happiness he wished to regain. A magical sense of intense beauty; of being sweetly alive. Except no waking moment he recalled had been filled with that sense of life. Did anyone feel such joy, outside a dream or a book? He knew it was not the girl or her beauty that he wanted, but magic in the world itself, and that faded even as he tried to cling to it.

He stared up at the flat white ceiling of his comfortable room ungratefully. He thought of a golden-haired princess in his school book. She had a flat, pink face. No use to him, he knew it. Absurdly, it came to him that he did not want to marry a beautiful princess at all. Not any princess. He wanted someone who felt like he did. How could a princess understand? Better a sweet-faced crippled girl. Yes. He could bring her to a fine house, a girl with a stunted leg and tender eyes and a soul like his own. They would be happy together. And for him she would be beautiful because she had the same dreams.

The young girls of Liverpool did not dream of magical forests, as he well knew. Only yesterday, too stupidly excited by what his mother had told him, he had blurted out the news of his invitation even though he knew his father had not yet been consulted. It had not had the response he wanted. 'Boasting! Boasting!' they had gibed at him. And if the neat heads of the richer girls nodded over the description, they capped it with tales of beaches and French houses by the sea. And there was no dream in their eyes. Still thinking of that, resentfully, Francis saw that the night had almost gone.

That morning Solomon lay in bed next to his wife and thought about Francis's clear-eyed face, with its even features, good teeth and sandy hair. Yes, it was a small, tidy face, with nothing Asiatic or strange in it; and Solomon hoped that puberty would not lengthen the jowls or distort its happy regularity. It was an English face, he admitted to himself. An educated English face. Once again he thought about England and Germany.

'England is a fair country,' he muttered, sleepily.

His wife stirred.

He modified his opinion.

'A reasonably fair country, anyway.'

You couldn't expect miracles.

Solomon believed that decisions, once taken, should be conveyed as rapidly as possible, without any attempt at palliation or explanation. Accordingly, he sent for Francis himself just after teatime the following day to announce the disappointment. The boy received the news stolidly enough, standing before his father with his hands clasping one another behind his back, and meeting his father's eyes directly.

'I suppose your mother will already have given you some warning of this?' guessed Solomon.

'No,' said Francis.

Nor had she done so. If anything, teatime had been spiced with a celebration which to his mind prefigured the Austrian delights to come. Elsa had made honey cakes and almond pastries, and to crown the whole table a huge ice-cream pudding. It was true she had not spoken much; but there was such a bustle of festivity and setting things out on the white cloth as they should be, that he had paid little attention to her silence. Now he understood it perfectly. And the blankness of his expression showed not preparedness, but uncontrollable dismay at the extent he had already compromised himself in the eyes of the children in his class. He longed to fall on his knees and plead with his father to be released from the abyss of shame he now saw opening before him. Since he found lying difficult, it would not be possible to conceal his disappointment long. He was too proud to ask his father to give him any reason for his decision; and for his part, Solomon thought that a sense of the arbitrariness inherent in all authority was a good preparation for the world Francis would have to live in.

Matters were left there, and Francis never forgave his father for the humiliations that followed.

4

A teaching post at Eden Street Elementary School for Boys and Girls was not an altogether enviable appointment, and occasionally, before assembly, when the Gentile children filed into one classroom and the Jewish children into another, Miss

Biddle and the headmaster took together a cup of tea boiled on a boy-scout primus. This was not always, however, a companionable arrangement. And Miss Biddle sensed it was not to be so that morning. The matter of scholarship awards disturbed the headmaster greatly, and though all these matters were finally settled by open examination, the question of which children should be encouraged to compete was always a delicate one.

'You are too dedicated, Miss Biddle,' said the headmaster, at length.

Lettice Biddle was a young woman of twenty-nine with wispy hair and rimless glasses. She had a gentle, sensitive spirit, a little cowed by spinsterhood and some years spent nursing a widowed mother. When she read Tennyson aloud to the class, she often met two melancholy brown eyes that seemed to understand the sadness of the world as she did, and her own clouded in sympathy.

She did not doubt the headmaster's likely reaction to any account of such shared moments.

'Some of them show remarkable intelligence,' she repeated instead.

'We have to look for more than intelligence in human beings,' said the headmaster sternly. 'Morals are of equal importance. Mind, I do not blame the children. They can only be the product of their sad backgrounds.'

The headmaster leaned back in his chair, and motioned Miss Biddle to a seat. He enjoyed his role as mentor and guide.

Miss Biddle obediently settled her white skirts into the shabby button-back chair. As she was meagrely qualified for her post, and altogether dependent on her small stipend for survival, she lowered her eyes demurely to conceal how much the headmaster's red face and military back filled her with alarm.

In his turn, the headmaster addressed himself to her more passionately than he quite understood. There was nothing in his education that led him to analyse his own impulses.

'I blame Napoleon,' he said.

'How so?' asked Miss Biddle, startled.

'Western Europe was a community of Christians once,' said the headmaster darkly.

'I think he had little effect on the movement of these particular families to our shores,' said Miss Biddle bravely.

'No, indeed. There our own government was culpable. I agree. It was never our duty to accept these exhausted, broken creatures; dissolute as often as not. Pedlars, most of them.'

'They are not dull and torpid, at least,' ventured Miss Biddle.

'No, indeed. They push their way forward remarkably. In no time at all they are exploiting the rest of us.'

'I had no idea,' said Miss Biddle, 'that you were of such a socialist turn of mind. I had always thought you approved of entrepreneurial skills. It was only last week you explained to me how much you feared trade unions would prove our undoing.'

'And so I do,' said the headmaster energetically. 'No inconsistency there, Miss Biddle. But there is a greater danger and a more radical thinking than our own trade unions imagine yet. Why do you suppose these people were so hated in Russia, pray?'

'I understood it to be because they were all felt to be revolutionaries.'

'And how do we know they are not?' demanded the headmaster.

Miss Biddle was reluctant to allow the conversation to drift any further in this direction. For one thing, she could see very little in the present regime of the tsar that should recommend itself to any English spirit. And for another, when she thought of her own poor mother last year, near-sightedly picking away with her needle for the fine ladies who came to collect their mending, she was not sure that English society was much more worthy of protection. Nor did she have any vision of violence breaking out in the neighbouring terraces off Upper Parliament Street from which these children came.

'Don't you think that, as poor kinsfolk of our Lord, perhaps?' she began instead, therefore, a little disingenuously for she had lost her own faith some years earlier, and was only hoping to appeal to the headmaster's declared piety. She

41

went on, 'I have often thought their old and learned men do somewhat resemble the patriarchs of our childhood picture books.'

At this the headmaster exploded with indignation, and she saw that she had done more harm than good.

'Is it Christian to work fifteen hours a day?'

Miss Biddle could recall no biblical comment on the matter.

'Damnable cleverness, putting all that about,' muttered the headmaster. '*Coningsby. Tancred.* There's the damage. Pretending all the early Christians were Jews. Who killed Him, then, I'd like to know? Tell me that.'

With perfect candour, Miss Biddle admitted that she had read none of Disraeli's books, and could have no opinion on the matter.

The headmaster warmed to her again.

'Leave all that to those who know,' he agreed. 'And now let us come to names. As you see, there must be some kind of proportion. Where, Miss Biddle, *where* is a good Protestant name?'

'Seventy-five per cent of the school is made up of immigrants,' said Miss Biddle desperately. 'This is not a Protestant area.'

'Very well, very well. Let us go through slowly. Of the Russian names, at least, which so predominate, could we attempt some order of merit?'

Miss Biddle frowned, and tried to be fair. 'I suppose in that case the first name should be Harold Katz.'

The headmaster put down his pen and shook his head. 'Impossible. You mean that insolent, black-haired, unnaturally *large* child you sent in for me to deal with yesterday?'

'Oh, no!' Miss Biddle smiled, in spite of herself. 'There are two brothers in the class. The one you caned is Benjy – *Benjamin* Katz, not Harold.'

'A criminal face,' muttered the headmaster. 'Never cried. Grinned at me afterwards.'

'Harold,' repeated Miss Biddle. 'Not his brother.' She felt no confidence that the distinction was significant to the headmaster.

'Katz,' he repeated. 'I see. Now. Let us proceed down the list.'

Even Miss Biddle had to admit that the class which contained the Katz brothers – mainly other immigrant Jews from the neighbourhood – was exhausting to teach. There was too much spare energy in the air. If she asked a question, hands flew up all over the classroom, and if the class didn't agree with the answer it was difficult to stop them shouting out their disapproval.

Those who were silent were usually thinking about something else, and were best left alone. But sometimes she felt it was her duty to interest them. Who else could open a door for them on the outside world? Any of them could concentrate if they tried.

Which, especially today, Benjamin Katz was not. They were looking at an atlas, and normally geography was a subject Benjy liked. After all, it was at least about the world. It could come in handy to know where the border between Russia and civilization ran; he'd heard a hundred times how they crossed it at night. Borders were real. And rivers could be *uncrossable*. Then you might have to turn back and take the same risks twice over. You could pay a good deal for not knowing geography. Still, they were concerned not with borders today but with rock formations.

'Benjy Katz?' asked Miss Biddle.

Staring down at the pages of the open book, Benjy tried to make out the letters at the bottom of the page, but they skipped around. He couldn't make them into any word known to man.

'Ma . . . ' he began.

The class laughed. Benjy felt rage boiling up against this fair-haired girl in her white dress, who looked so fragile and could nevertheless reduce him to helplessness.

'Don't tell him the answer, Harry,' said Miss Biddle.

Too late, Benjy looked up hopefully in the direction of his brother. Failing to catch those useful eyes, now averted obediently, he turned his own upon Miss Biddle, and allowed the thick fringes of his lashes to droop over them sadly.

43

'I'm ill. My head is burning,' he said in a low voice, as if overcome by the pale February sun. And it came to him like the truth. As soon as he uttered the words, the room began to wave before him, and his skin became moist and salt. At once Miss Biddle relented, and transferred her question to Hymie Golding.

'Good boy. Quite correct.'

And Benjy was allowed to relax into his own dream.

He could be on the pier head with Cousin Len, he thought. Or over in New Brighton. Marvellous. Sand dunes and sharp grass and seabirds and brown slithery weeds to pop. And the dark winter sea rolling in.

'Your heart'll stop if you dive in that,' Len always said, looking blue and skinny with his clothes off.

'Not mine, it won't,' called Benjy, taking the dare, though the cold water made him catch his breath hard enough every time.

He didn't jeer at Len in spite of his puny ribcage and his thin legs. The open air wasn't Len's style. Benjy knew that. But then, Len had secrets. There was a lot Len knew about. He was all mockery. His eyebrows rose with it. And two small pads of flesh at each side of his narrow lips declared the same ironic relish. He was thin, but he was jaunty. And nothing worried him.

Only the other day they'd been walking together, he and Len, in an aimless kind of way – being truants – past the shop where Mr Krantz pickled the meat; and then into West Derby Street where the baker greeted them cheerily, because Benjy took the *cholent* into him every Friday. They were making for Kauffman's fish shop, in Brownlow Hill. Len had the pence, and Benjy hadn't questioned the invitation, because he understood Len had some kind of proposition. He was interested in that. Not that he trusted Len, altogether. Anyone could see he wasn't a decent Jewish boy, of the kind Abram wanted his sons to become. His pale face looked ten years older than a child's and he played solo whist every night in the week like an old man. But he wasn't scared. Benjy liked that. Len didn't even begin to keep the rules. Well, that was a common enough moan in Brownlow Hill. They were always shaking their heads over the young, and their English ways. But Len wasn't trying to fit in with the English world round him, either. He was a layabout, a no-good, Harry warned him. Had no respect. Didn't care. Maybe he was a crook? Whatever, Len wasn't *worried*. That was sure. And he wasn't worried, not because, like the Katz family, God's almighty hand held and protected him, but because he reckoned to live on his wits.

As Benjy greedily licked the salt, clean fish Len bought him, he got one thing clear. Whatever the proposition he had in mind, Len was in no need of anyone else's wits but his own.

Len motioned him away from the shop, laughing a little.

'Listen,' he said. 'Do you know why the Jews in Liverpool are so much stupider than anywhere else in Europe?'

'No,' said Benjy. For a moment he was angry, even though he expected a joke.

'It was like this. When they bought their tickets in Russia they bought them to New York. Right? But when their boat put in at Liverpool, the captain called out through some loud-hailer: America! This is America! See?'

Benjy began to laugh.

'You see? So those who believed him got off. And here we have them. The ones who believed him. The Jews of Liverpool. Believers all.'

Benjy said, 'That's a rotten joke, you bum. Maybe I'll punch you in the mouth.' His fists had formed already.

'I just bought you good fish,' protested Len, rather surprised.

'You make me angry, Len. I don't want to hurt you.'

'So please don't. Look. I got tin glasses. And I *need* you, Benjy. Listen. I want you to do a job for me.'

'What job?'

'Trip to London. See some people for me.'

'Why me?'

'Well, you're family. And you're honest.'

'And?'

'You're *big*, Benjy Katz.'

'Thanks, but no thanks,' said Benjy. 'I'm not that stupid.'

While Benjy thought of all this the lesson changed.

45

His brother Harry began to read a Keats ode most melodiously.

Too melodiously.

At the doorway appeared the formidable figure of the headmaster. He pointed an indignant hand at Benjy.

'That boy is asleep. He needs fresh air,' he announced proudly, as if he had made a medical diagnosis.

There was not much fresh air in the playground on dull February days, but Benjy made no complaint at being sent out into it.

At Eden Street, Jews and Gentiles played largely among their own groups. By being sent outside ahead of his class, Benjy found himself unexpectedly with five similar villains from another class who had also been sent outside for mis-behaviour. They studied him curiously.

Benjy was not afraid, even when they gathered round him, as he sat leaning against the school wall. He smiled in a comradely fashion. Did they not share the same enemy? Had not the headmaster picked on them all? But the other boys did not see it that way. There were five of them, and it made them bold. They tried out the words their parents used at home.

'Sheeny,' called one derisively.

'Von Jew.'

This last insult did not surprise Benjy. It was a common confusion among the people of Liverpool to take all Jews for Germans. Perhaps it was the language, perhaps the number of names with Germanic spellings.

'Go back home to Russia,' sneered the scrawniest of his opponents.

That last insult grated on Benjy as the others did not. For no one in Eden Street imagined there was a home in Russia for Jews. His childhood had been filled with the stories of what the real Russians had done to his own family. Those who still had relatives in Kiev read the papers anxiously every night. And it was only a week since a photograph of poor Mendel Beilis in his tin glasses and bowler had appeared even in the English press after his release from gaol. How could these boys know so little of the dark horrors that followed his arrest? And even his acquittal? Benjy sobered, as if his father's hand had soothed him. He blinked his large, greenish eyes. There were five of them, all his own age, and he did not intend to engage in argument. He didn't have to listen to the content of the words. He measured the situation as he sat, being fairly sure they would not jump him while he was sitting down.

He was going to have trouble.

The leader was thin as a sapling and, for all his gibing, no great menace. The others were dockers' sons, Irish and heavily built, and Benjy took in their broad-faced hostility with respect. Certainly he had to do something, for he couldn't stay sitting down until the bell went in ten minutes' time.

And so he leaned back against the iron bar of the school drainpipe and prepared for unequal battle, without much fear, but irritably; smiling as he usually did when adrenalin ran in his blood; and letting his body think for him.

So it was that the boys watched him lean back and bend the pipe away from the wall with a kind of awe. They watched the muscles stand out in his upper arms. They heard the pipe break away from the wall. And then, when he stood up slowly, took in that he was a foot taller than any of them, and backed off a little.

Their sneering leader backed away too, though his shrill voice went on, urging the others to attack. 'You're never going to let that stinking Yid get away with it, are you?'

But now, essentially, each boy was alone before Benjy and that lead pipe and felt himself to be so. They saw his heavy arms, and hesitated.

'You miserable buggers,' Benjy said with contempt.

He spoke impersonally, because it was not their people he despised, nor their religion he hated, but their mindless ganging together. He had split them now and they backed away, frightened.

'Benjamin Katz. Put that weapon down!'

Miss Biddle had at last looked out of the window.

His adversaries had spread out instinctively, so that it was difficult for Benjy to keep them all in view. And the half-brick, when it came, caught him from the left by surprise. The boys

47

cheered the blow as they might have applauded a good throw at cricket. It was meant to fell him; but although Benjy staggered, he did not fall. He could taste his own blood from the jagged tear in his lower lip, but he felt no pain. His head buzzed but he didn't fall. And it made them angry that he went on standing there, that his legs didn't buckle up as they expected, that he continued to shake his head to clear it, that he still looked dangerous, like a black bear surrounded by terriers.

And dangerous he was with that length of lead in his hand, even with the blood falling from his cut face. He could have killed any one of them before Miss Biddle bounded down the stone steps into the school yard, holding her skirts in one hand and securing her spectacles with the other.

Instead he just stood and looked at them, while the playground gradually filled with other children; and then he lowered the lead pipe altogether and walked unsteadily away.

He had to have five stitches in his lower lip, and one side of his face was so swollen that his left eye was entirely hidden in folds of black and puffy flesh. The jaw, however, had escaped injury.

Rasil put him upstairs to sleep, a candle alight by his bed, with one of the girls to call her if he began to bleed again. Then she came downstairs, stood in the centre of her kitchen, and stormed.

'I'll kill them. I'll go into that school tomorrow and find the ones who did it. I'll kill them.'

She looked as if she could do it easily, and on her own too, but Abram calmed her.

'Who? Who will you find?'

'I'll find,' she promised him.

'How will you talk to them?'

'God didn't give me a tongue?' she challenged.

Abram did not like taking action in the official outside world of the Gentiles. It was not his experience that good came of it; usually it was better to do nothing. But Benjy's injuries had upset him. Things were not supposed to go as badly as that.

On her way up to check that Benjy was still asleep, Rasil caught Abram off guard at his evening prayers shaking backwards and forwards without words.

'Nu. So what did I do wrong?' he asked out loud. 'That this should happen to Benjy.'

In the morning Rasil put on a black coat and a straw hat and walked off to see the headmaster. She recognized many of her neighbours' children on the way; in the playground were others from the terraces beyond. Some of them were only six or seven years old, fresh from infant school, with round, hopeful eyes. They watched her marching into the school with a kind of awe.

When the headmaster heard that Rasil Katz was outside in the corridor his heart sank with the immediate conviction that the child at the centre of yesterday's brawl was dead. It was a thought that made him tremble so much, he could hardly bear to confront the distraught and reproachful mother. Perhaps he also expected a pasty face and huge, grieving eyes. At any rate, he was quite unprepared for the bold, black-haired woman who entered his room and announced herself briskly.

'Rasil Katz.'

The headmaster stood up to greet her with caution, even though the healthy colour in Rasil's cheeks hardly suggested the hideous loss he had for one moment imagined. It did, however, cross his mind that Mrs Katz was an unusually powerful woman and might mistakenly hold him to blame.

'I am very, very sorry,' he therefore began.

But Rasil held up her hand and waved his words away. 'You have a difficult job,' she said simply.

The headmaster agreed with fervour.

'Maybe by now you have already punished the boy with the brick?'

The headmaster looked dubious. 'Not so easy,' he admitted. 'But we know some of the class involved. I'll see them all strapped, of course. But I wouldn't really advise your son – he's not too badly hurt, I take it? – to push, you know, to *push* the matter.'

Rasil leaned on the desk with one hand, and used the other

to help her in the description of Benjy's injury. 'Push?' she inquired, as if genuinely bewildered.

The headmaster hoped this great peasant of a woman was not threatening him. Rather nervously, he reached for the brass Victorian lady on his desk, who concealed a bell in her skirts, in the hope that Miss Biddle would release him from the situation. But Rasil's hand was fractionally ahead of him; she moved the bell out of the way, and went on smiling without rancour, as if still puzzled by a single word.

'*Push?*'

'Take it any further,' said the headmaster, weakly.

'Yes,' said Rasil. 'That's right.' And she put her own huge hand over the headmaster's bony one, as if to explain a problem to a very good friend. 'You see, not all the children here are strong like my Benjy,' she said apologetically. 'So that's why you take it further, so everyone understands. You want to punish a whole class? Madness! What is helped by such a thing? Who learns? No, you find out about the brick, headmaster. It's better.'

'Nevertheless . . . ' the headmaster sounded a little petulant, 'it may not be possible.'

'Oh yes, it is possible. Always possible,' Rasil reassured him.

The headmaster craned up his face to read the expression on the face above him.

'Take my advice. It's possible,' said Rasil. 'What is just is always possible.'

5

The last Sunday in July was a fine, hot morning, and Elsa was taking her children to visit her parents in Sefton Park. It was a visit she made formally by hired carriage, twice a month. Today, the girls were in white straw Watteau hats, silk hose and doeskin gloves; and Francis in a navy blazer. Elsa watched them proudly through the parlour window, even as she perfected the buttoning of her own coat. The sky was a flat, pale blue, as if it were hanging over sea, or marshland. The leaves of the maples stirred above the carriage like water, their delicate green picked up in the girls' carefully chosen taffeta waistbands. Elsa observed with a quiet satisfaction the demure bearing of the Gordon children settled in their carriage. They were a picture of cool tranquillity that confirmed her certainty she had been living her life according to the right rules.

Before leaving, she opened the door to Solomon's back room and called in to ask if he would change his mind and go with them. He refused, as he usually did, without offering any excuse. In spite of his discouraging brevity, she paused on the threshhold, and turned slightly to see if he would comment on her appearance in her new tiered dress, with its matching coat down to her ankles. He did not; but Elsa was undisturbed by this. Her own finery, quite as much as her children's, had been chosen with the delight of her father's eye in mind.

No one understood that better than Solomon.

For his part, Solomon watched his wife adjust her parasol on the steps outside the window – she was too superstitious to open it indoors – and felt sorry for her. Peace. All the frills and lace in the well-kept carriage spoke of peace. But the call for peace would have to be muffled now on the lips of those with foreign names, and those who were known to have cousins in other countries, even in other armies, as her own Groot family did. Quietly, quietly, begged the Jewish press. Don't give cause for alarm. Don't draw your money out of the bank. Don't speak with friendship of Austria or Hungary, even if they have befriended and honoured your family. You must silence your hatred of Russia. The Tsar is England's ally. Quietly, quietly, children of strangers. England is making ready for war, and there can be no neutrals.

Every time Elsa set out to her parents' house, she had the air of a girl expecting an idyll. And every time she returned he could read in the two red spots on her downy cheeks, and the tightened line of her mouth, that there had been difficulties.

What they were did not concern Solomon, since he did not believe in idylls and had no great interest in Elsa's family. But he suspected them of muddling her, and of being muddled themselves, with their great family abroad and their great pride in being English. In the name of pride Elsa brought up her children to bear themselves like English ladies and gentlemen. But it had been dreams of Europe that sweetened their childhood with fairy tales of a wide-flung romantic cousinhood, in castles with floors like shining water, glass like drops of fire.

There would be no idyll in the Groot household today.

'But who *believes* any of all that any more?'

The tranquillity of the three children poised in their well-kept carriage was already dispersing as Solomon's elder daughter, Dorothy, began to bait her brother and sister. Four years older than Francis, red-haired, green-eyed and handsome, Dorothy was Solomon's most formidable child. She had none of the delicate features of her sister Betty; her wrists were strong, and her shoulders square. It was usually Francis who took up her thrusting arguments with his own firm logic. But today he seemed reluctant to be drawn. It was Betty who tried to meet the challenge.

'What do you suppose Mama believes? Or the Groots?' she asked.

'Nothing,' said Dorothy, impatiently. 'Not the Groots.'

'Surely,' protested Betty, 'they wouldn't insist on us going to the synagogue, would they? If it didn't matter to them?'

'I suppose it is *something*,' said Dorothy, 'that we don't have sin and salvation dinned into us. As if there weren't enough horrors in the world. Imagine having to believe that killing a man or a god or a goat would save us. Our lot talk of piety, but at least it's only for form's sake.'

'It's not everyone who calls, Lord, Lord.' Francis entered the conversation, observing irritably, as he did so, how Dorothy's eye began to glint at once.

'Well, Mama believes it all. I know she does. In her kitchen, she keeps all the rules,' Betty continued.

'Well, of course,' said Dorothy. 'She thinks that's all part of being hygienic. When she looked at live lobsters with me once in the window of Frobisher's she almost swooned with horror. Imagine her eating such creatures! She couldn't.'

'Poor Mama,' said Francis.

'Exactly. What can she know of such things? Oh, I'm *never* getting married!' declared Dorothy with sudden savagery.

'Chance is a fine thing,' teased Francis.

'I shall have all the men I want to pick from,' said Dorothy.

And really she did look rather grand saying that, and tossing back her head as she did so.

Francis puzzled away at the first problem. 'When I was younger I could never see why, since the Groots care so little for Judaism, Grandfather was shocked if we treated it with the same indifference. But those four days a year Grandfather goes to Princes Road, he's a changed man. He looks in a book, and sounds all the words he can't understand, and for some reason demands the same patience of me. I don't say he doesn't follow the service. He does. He has the correct place most of the day and puts the book under my nose time and again for me to follow the passage. But as to any meaning, Betty – well, we yawn and doze through the day companionably, and that's all.'

'It's a social occasion,' said Dorothy.

'Don't you believe in *anything*, Dorothy?' asked Betty, troubled.

'No. And if I were a man I'd not addle my head with another thought on the matter,' said Dorothy vigorously.

'Oh? And what would you do?' inquired Francis, aware that this was the nub of the antagonism between them. 'You aren't going to turn into a suffragette like that poor lady in the Brighton Synagogue last month who asked God to forgive King George of England for the torture practised on his women subjects?'

'Well, and they *are* tormented. In prison and out of it. But if I were a man I suppose I could put all that out of my head easily enough. And then, well,' Dorothy looked mischievous, 'I'd go down to the docks and get a place on a merchant ship next week. And I'd see the whole world. China *and* India. That's what I'd do.'

53

Unexpectedly, Betty's thoughtful voice re-entered the conversation. 'I know what *Francis* is going to be. He told me.'

The other two Gordons looked at their sister with some indignation.

'How's that, Betty? *What* did he tell you?' asked Dorothy.

'I *know*. He's going to be a poet. He told me. He read me a poem.'

Francis had gone a very deep red. He had too much wit, however, to go on to the defensive under Dorothy's amused eye.

'It was a very fine poem,' he said loftily. 'But not mine. I should be proud to write one half as good.'

But Dorothy's green eyes were fixed on him with a kind of glee.

'Poetry is something you do in your spare time, isn't it? It isn't a trade or profession,' she said.

Francis swallowed his hopes and her words together, and they went down like a lump of cold lead into his soul and lay there with all the force of prediction.

'You could teach it, though, couldn't you?' asked Betty, reading some of that distress in his face.

Poor Betty. Already Francis thought of her in that way, as he thought of 'poor Mama'. It was only Dorothy he hated. Only Dorothy, and his knowledge of her strength, and the sense he had of being as powerless before it as he was on a tennis court before her hard forearm serve.

Only last night rain showers had entered his soul with the same hot, wet smell of the desolation he tasted now, facing her triumphant health and confidence.

'Poetry! You don't know anything about it,' he suddenly screamed aloud, as Elsa appeared unhearing, unabashed, smiling, and was courteously helped into the carriage beside them.

So it was the Gordons set off dutifully to Elsa's parents.

Two large portraits in oil of the Groot forebears who had first entered England in the early nineteenth century hung on the dining room walls facing one another. The man, dressed in a frock-coat, had a large, stern face; and this he turned fully upon his wife, a lady too mildly pretty to show any expression whatsoever. These two canvases dominated the oak board which bore the Groot Sunday lunch and by and large declared the situation below. On either side of this long table, with their faces all turned towards Grandfather Groot, sat the Groot offspring: sons, daughters-in-law, and grandchildren, including Elsa and her family, who all most solemnly ate what was put in front of them, and waited their turn to be questioned.

The uncles, as Francis thought of them, were narrow-faced men, already balding at the crowns of their heads, who dressed sprucely and always gave the impression of knowing far more than they spoke. Since they hardly spoke at all in the Groot household on family occasions, this could hardly fail to be the case. Perhaps they were fond of Elsa – they always kissed her soft cheek eagerly enough when they met – but they very rarely visited the Gordon family at home. On Uncle Leslie's last visit Elsa had brought him upstairs while Francis was working on the *Aeneid* in his room, and had watched eagerly while her brother looked over the Latin sentences which were the homework for that evening. His uncle had made no comment on the work itself; but he was very taken with Francis's handwriting, which was already an excellent copper-plate. For this he had what seemed to Francis a quite disproportionate admiration. When he risked saying as much, to his mother's alarm, his uncle had replied sagely, 'My dear Francis, when you enter the *real* world, you'll find that almost every step you need to take is by means of letters. And when you write to strangers, it is naturally your hand that they observe first. Why, it is the only knowledge they have of you.'

'Perhaps they might consider a little the words, too, that are chosen?' Francis ventured.

'Ah, but that is upon the second look, and by that time they are already predisposed to hear what you say by the way you have written it down. It is like dress upon the person.'

Francis nodded to this, politely; his mother looked pleased or perhaps relieved; and so Uncle Leslie went on his way, and sad Creusa's ghost re-entered the room and whispered her sad goodbyes to her husband in the ruins of Troy, and the young boy felt tears in his own eyes, though he could not have said why, or whether it was for Aeneas, or some other loss of his own he did not yet understand.

His uncles had married intelligently, as was to be expected of the Groots; Francis could find no fault in either the appearance or the manner of the wives they had chosen, though they roused no great affection either. When they were safely out of hearing, Dorothy often mocked them cruelly; but as far as Francis could judge they were simple, timid creatures, whose place at Grandfather Groot's board was as vulnerable as his own.

It was quite early in the meal that Grandfather Groot began to question Francis about his adjustment to St Bede's School. It was a school he had chosen himself with some pride; and although Francis, over the last term, had come to dislike it intensely, he was not so foolhardy as to bring this to his grandfather's attention. He was well aware, in any case, that his own objections would have seemed astonishing to a man who began his questioning with the following inquiry.

'Not becoming too much of a swot, I hope, Francis? Elsa showed me your report. You'll do well enough, well enough, in whatever profession you decide to find a niche, without stuffing your head with all that Greek and Latin they try and put into it.'

It was Francis's main complaint that there was very little love for any academic matters at St Bede's; more precisely, the masters had lost all personal enthusiasm for their subjects long ago, and were by now only concerned to process necessary texts through the heads of their pupils with as little emotion as possible. No literature of any other kind featured in the curriculum; and such poetry as Francis read eagerly on his own had recently been confiscated by an irate and ignorant master, who looked, now Francis came to think of it, not unlike Grandfather Groot himself, with the same highly coloured face and the same skinny neck.

'Well. And what is your favourite sport?'

Now Francis understood his relation to the sports field very exactly. It was never likely to be his destiny to excel there. At the same time, he was not averse to the charm of sporting occasions; and he had enough natural grace to acquit himself with *style* at the wicket, so he answered promptly enough.

'Cricket, Grandfather.'

'Splendid. Splendid game.'

For a moment it looked as though Groot might begin a blessed paragraph or two of personal reminiscence, but some other consideration suddenly focused his attention on Elsa.

'You have given some thought to Francis's future profession, I hope?'

Groot's sons had all opted for law, to which they had made their way through the portals of Liverpool University. Elsa was his only daughter.

Elsa hesitated.

She herself had every intention of seeing Francis develop in the same way; but she was too cautious to commit Solomon to a course of action he had not yet agreed.

'No, Father.'

'But the school suggested I might be entered for Oxford or Cambridge,' said Francis recklessly.

He knew exactly how rashly he had pronounced that possibility; his mother's face reflected it; but it was not a gamble. He had assessed the chances, clearly enough, of the same suggestion made in his own home, and it seemed to him that he could only improve them by throwing the thought into the general Groot pool. At once, Elsa's brothers shook their heads doubtfully. But Francis knew the internal disposition of power within the family well enough to recognize that it could well be a point in his favour. When one of their wives ventured to murmur that those universities were after all outside the mainstream of Jewish life, he could see that some headway had been gained.

For some time Groot devoted his entire attention to the carving of a great sirloin of beef, and let the conversation ripple along as if preoccupied with Francis's future. But when he lifted his head, Francis saw with disappointment that some remark had sent him off into another realm of conjecture altogether.

'It is a great pity that your husband did not see fit to join us today, Elsa,' he said abruptly.

Elsa looked a little flustered, as if she sensed some rebuke at hand, and Dorothy straightened a little and turned her wide, light eyes to the head of the table, as if preparing to defend her mother if it became necessary. But it was not.

'There were matters about which I had some need to consult him. Serious matters,' Groot added, surprisingly.

His sons now looked uneasy and, as much as they dared, indignant. Were they not in the distinguished ranks of the English bar, and were they now to be snubbed as advisers in favour of an upstart immigrant, who not so many years ago had to cycle the streets as a glazier, prepared to repair broken windows? Upon *what* serious matters could their advice be accounted less significant?

Elsa lowered her head with a certain quiet satisfaction, and Francis observed that his choice of a future career was no longer in question. But even as he felt the relief of having his grandfather's attention swing elsewhere to another grandchild, and a not dissimilar set of inquiries, a sharp question of his own formed in his mind. His father was oppressive, mostly unsociable and occasionally grim. Was there some wisdom in him that required understanding?

For Betty, the exciting hours were those that followed lunch. All the women withdrew to gossip cheerfully in the front parlour, and Grandfather Groot went off to rest behind a newspaper, while his sons smoked and told anecdotes. But the children were cast outside into sunshine and liberty. They could wander the whole length of the garden, which went far back beyond the green lawn with shrubs planted round it to a well-tended vegetable patch, with cucumbers under glass and rows of tomato plants. Further still, behind the asparagus beds, lay raspberry canes and gooseberry briars and trees of apples and Victoria plums. It was there the group of children usually hovered.

The enchantment for Betty, however, lay in the highly charged presence of one of her older cousins. A boy, much of Dorothy's age, with an angular body and an even-featured face, he had only one remarkable physical characteristic: dark green eyes which curved upwards like a cat's, and were altogether direct in their gaze. Those eyes rarely met Betty's, but when they did she had a sense of being assessed to the very depths of her being. She had probably never uttered more than a dozen words to him in her life; and those had been for the most part gruff monosyllables or muffled phrases writhed over in embarrassment afterwards. But the threat of being addressed directly only increased the excitement; and she had little need to worry about maintaining a conversation as long as Dorothy and Francis were part of the group. His presence charged the summer afternoon with magic. Whenever he wandered off, perhaps to find his younger sister and release her dress from thorns, or help her on to the old swing and hold her there for safety, Betty felt as if all the light had drained from the day.

His name was Alexander.

'One of Uncle Leslie's jokes,' Francis had explained it, laughing; he was a little envious of the ease with which the name could be shortened to Sandy, and the informality such a nickname produced. No one would ever do as much for Francis.

Alexander went away to school. On his way home, he had made a special journey through London to see an exhibition of Futurist art, and it was about this that Dorothy and Francis were questioning him eagerly.

Alexander's enthusiasms were altogether unselfconscious and he was undisturbed by Dorothy's mockery.

'It was marvellous. Absolutely marvellous,' he kept repeating, although he knew that every word of description was outraging his cousins, and had to hold his broad mouth in so as not to burst out laughing. And still he did laugh, against his will, and often, his lips spread generously over his even teeth, and his bony frame shaking with laughter.

'Well, from all you say it is certainly a *Jewish* art form, since it seems to resemble nothing in heaven above or the earth beneath! A Bomberg, and a Rosenberg, and a Gertler,' Dorothy declared at last scathingly.

'Why not?' said Francis thoughtfully.

The Gordon children took a particular pride in distancing themselves from any form of chauvinism in such matters. This

59

they had learned, without knowing it, from Elsa. So it was her Dutch forebears had learned how to live under the watchful eyes of a Grand Inquisition; and though the Groots might have chosen to forget that situation, they could not but pass on to their children a certain familiarity with protective clothing. To express themselves most daringly, to show themselves most independent of their own background, the children had only to adapt current habits of English thought for their need. And so they did. They spoke of H. G. Wells, whose recent comments after his visit to Russia had been so hostile to the constant Jewish complaints of persecution. Dorothy was disposed to forgive him anything because he had written *Ann Veronica*, and Francis was disposed to take most seriously Wells's description of how it felt to be in a truly believing Christian country for the first time.

Alexander was surprised to find that anyone took what a writer said seriously at all.

'You haven't read your Plato,' he insisted. 'You'd know what we have to do with poets then. Out with them.'

'Off with their heads,' agreed Dorothy.

But Francis refused to be drawn.

'I don't care about feuds in southern Russia, either,' he said loftily.

And from there they passed naturally enough to the administration of the Aliens Act, and whether its justice was impeccable, as Uncle Leslie had assured them over lunch, and whether it was their business if it was not.

'I suppose the great mistake is to think of the poor wretches coming in as people like ourselves,' said Francis. 'You just have to look at them, with their pathetic bundles and skullcaps and those long curls at the side of their heads, to see how remote . . . '

'Not their fault, of course, any of that,' agreed Dorothy. She had recently given a good deal of her time to Fabian tracts, and knew that the condition of any poor people was largely evidence against the society that oppressed them.

'They still mean *us*, though,' Betty suddenly blurted out, as much to her own surprise as theirs.

She didn't know why she had spoken her thoughts out loud.

It was so unlike her to do so that the blood rushed to her cheeks in embarrassment.

'*They?*' asked Dorothy frostily.

'She means the English,' said Alexander, rewarding Betty with a smile of such sweet understanding that it seemed to her she could live on it for a week.

'No, Betty,' said Francis, kindly enough, for he understood a generous objection when he heard it. 'It's a *pun*, that's all. The English don't at all mind people like *us* living here, whatever word we call ourselves. It's only lots of poor foreigners coming in who can't speak the language, and haven't enough money to feed and clothe themselves on. *That's* what they mind.'

Betty dared argue no further; and, now that Alexander's eyes had left her face, she leaned back against the squat apple tree and happily allowed Dorothy to take up the conversation as it grew more and more ferocious. She didn't remind them that Da had come from Odessa. Alexander's few words of understanding repeated themselves again and again in her blissful inner world. And she leaned back against the awkward, crabby bark of the apple tree to enjoy the sense of them and the July afternoon with all its warm, garden noises for as long as it could peacefully be prolonged.

6

The Katz back yard baked hot in the sun. The brief season of its flowering had passed, and only the neighbouring lilac tree dangled a few copper husks over the fence. The main sign of life was an enormous variety of insects: brown and grey and many-jointed. Benjy and Len inspected them all curiously and without malice as they talked.

They were also playing darts against a board which hung on the wooden door of the outside privy. It was Sunday, and the machines were quiet. Only Len was up to something. He had business. New business. He told Benjy about it as he threw.

'On a ship,' he said. 'A mate fixed it.'

'Get away!' Benjy's voice rose on the last two syllables with that lilt of total scepticism which was always part of Liverpool speech.

'Want to come?' asked Len, off-handedly.

'Need a bodyguard, do you?' jeered Benjy.

But he was curious. His face no longer showed any sign of injury except for a white scar on his mouth, which gave his grin an odd, crooked charm. Len pursed up his mouth, sucked in his cheeks, and let out a long and surprisingly accurate jet of saliva.

'Well, you get all sorts,' he admitted.

He was throwing for a tricky double. Just then, Harry came out of the kitchen door, wearing slippers and looking pale.

'Come on,' Harry said impatiently.

'Don't rush me,' said Len, his wrist poised.

'*I'm* in a rush,' said Harry.

'You're putting me off,' said Len.

'Let him through, Len,' Benjy insisted. 'Don't play silly beggars.'

Len shrugged, and turned away. He began to scuff his feet on the dried-up stalks of grass. He hated waiting for anything.

'By heck. How long's he going to be in there?'

'You've no patience,' said Benjy.

Len complained, 'I was on a winning streak till he trotted by. Tell you what. I'll give you a commission if you come,' he offered Benjy, thoughtfully.

'When?'

'Tonight.'

Benjy considered the matter.

'You don't need to bother about the money,' he said at last. 'You've got to think of your Mam.'

Len began to narrow his eyes and focus his dart. He knew very well how the rest of the Katz family thought of his Mam. Her widowing might not have been her fault, but her way of dealing with it certainly was. She had moved out of the acceptable Jewish streets into a cheaper neighbourhood, where she kept a scruffy house, and took to painting her eyelids and wearing too many cheap rings. But he wasn't going to discuss her frizzed hair and rouged face. Or her stall of dresses on the market.

'She's all right,' Len said ambiguously.

As he spoke the dart left his hand. And he certainly *had* lost the winning streak, because it sailed high above the board altogether and through the three-inch gap between the wooden door and the corrugated roof of the privy.

There was a sudden squawk of pain.

'That was a daft thing,' said Benjy angrily. 'Harry?'

'In my knee.' Harry was blubbering a little. 'It's stuck in my knee.'

'Open the door.'

'Doesn't sound like a major injury,' said Len.

Harry shuffled out with the dart in his hand and looked accusingly at Len, in no doubt from which hand the dart had flown.

'Could have blinded me,' he said.

'Didn't, though,' said Len quickly.

'You're bloody dangerous, you are,' said Harry. And he limped off, not without dignity, into the kitchen.

The other two boys laughed awkwardly, and there was a pause between them. Len broke it teasingly. 'Ever see a woman with her dress up?' he asked.

His words called up an alarming vision of some woman in a passageway lifting up layer after layer of skirts to show off a huge, ugly belly.

Benjy shook his head.

'Time you did,' said Len briskly. 'I'll be round tonight.'

'Might go to the Lyceum,' said Benjy, curious enough, but unwilling to be pushed.

'Nothing on tonight,' said Len triumphantly. 'That's fixed, then. And it won't cost you.'

It hadn't occurred to Benjy that this was a commercial transaction; but he nodded with a proper sense of favour. He was just old enough for his body to feel a rising excitement. Anyway, if Len could deal with growing into a man, so could he. But he'd have to slip out after supper without Rasil asking him what he was about.

Len nodded, as he said as much.

They took a tram down through Bootle, and then Len led the way into the dock area.

'Did you know one in seven of the world's ships come through here?' asked Len happily.

'Get away,' said Benjy.

But he was impressed. Huge cranes hung over the boats, outlined against the sky. The boys stared up at them. The smells on every side excited Benjy: some were sweet and sickly, like stored grain; others sharp. The whole area was a labyrinth of narrow shelves that Len beckoned him along confidently. Over the water, the gathering darkness was inhumanly quiet and wide, and the air was filled with the soft, moaning sound of huge ships at berth; their vast shadows leaned over them.

'That's the *Huskisson*,' Len pointed out. 'You always find the Cunarders there. Look. There. With the red and black funnels.'

'Where are you taking me? Do you know?' Benjy pretended to complain at the roundabout route they had come. But really he was delighted by the strangeness of it all. Delighted to be out of the small, tight world of the house and synagogue which clenched round his own family so protectively. Out. Yes. Len was somehow altogether *outside*. It was dangerous, and probably wicked, but that was why Benjy liked him.

Suddenly a not unfriendly Irish voice called out of the darkness. 'And what would you two boys be after, I'm wondering?'

Benjy would have turned at once towards the speaker; if not to answer his question, at least with his fists balled ready to fight. But Len's fingers gripped his shoulder urgently and made him stoop out of sight in silence. And then they were both running, bent. Over a bridge. To another granite island. Until they were both out of breath. Len seemed to know his way around like a wild cat.

'Here,' he said.

The white birds curved and dipped and called.

And Len helped him across a narrow plank aboard ship.

It was very surprising. Benjy had never imagined so many people could sleep so close together. It made the houses in Eden Street look like grand hotels. The men were all lying on bunks filled with nothing but straw, packed in one above the other. They welcomed Len cheerfully, especially a huge Swede whose big red face opened heartily to show perfectly white teeth when he laughed.

'So you come with us after all?' he asked, with heavy jocularity.

'Not me, mate,' said Len quickly. 'Me Mam wouldn't like it.'

'See the world,' said a big Negro, leaning down over his bunk and appraising Benjy's size and build. 'What about your friend?'

'Get off,' said Benjy, uneasily conscious of the narrow plank they had walked to take them on board ship, and the creaking of the timbers against the wharf; a moment could cut them adrift.

Yet Len seemed altogether comfortable. He had evidently bought and sold here many times; he was talking over a deal in whispers even now.

'How's your Mam for sugar?' he put out his head to inquire from Benjy briefly.

'Don't worry about us,' said Benjy firmly, impressed in spite of himself with the quick flurry of words, the exchanged notes, and his cousin's sharp-eyed coping.

'One thing you don't go short of with us, man,' said the Negro, and winked.

'Oh, aye,' said Benjy, squaring his shoulders. 'Do you get seasick?' he asked.

The big Negro laughed out loud. 'No more. But when I first came on, that was terrible. Because they make you work all the time. Don't matter how bad you feel.'

For some reason this made him laugh a long time, and then he held a bottle of some harsh-smelling liquor down to Benjy, who put it to his lips in a spirit of friendship and had to suppress a retch of horror.

'The sea. It makes a real man of you,' sighed the black man, taking back his bottle and drinking again.

Benjy could still taste the onions from the man's mouth. He began to feel queasy. But he was unwilling to disturb Len about his business. He set his teeth against betraying any discomfort. Lit a cigarette.

The oil lamp swayed a very little as the small boat rode the dead water.

He wasn't sorry to be back on firm land, even if he ended up humping a heavy sack because it was too much for Len.

And he hadn't forgotten Len's offer. But it was a long haul up the road to Bootle, and he'd gladly have let it lapse.

'Now comes the piece of resistance,' said Len after a while.

'What d'you mean?' said Benjy, feigning puzzlement.

'Except she don't resist. Suzie. I promised. Remember?'

Benjy said crossly, 'I'm tired carrying this sugar, Len. I want to clean up.'

'You can clean up at Suzie's,' said Len soothingly.

'A *shickser*, is she?'

'That's right,' said Len. 'I like them.'

Benjy shifted the sack from one shoulder to the other and thought about it. Abram's benevolent face came briefly to his mind; it did not seem particularly forbidding. Well, and there was a war coming. You could be taken off into the army any day and never a bit of sweet life to remember. So why not?

'Is she old?' he asked, cautiously.

Len said, 'I told you before, she's sixteen. Pretty girl, too.'

'Get away. What's she doing it for, then?'

Len laughed at him.

Benjy stopped under a gas light, slowly lowered the sack to the ground, and looked down hard at his cousin.

'We are dumping this first, anyways,' he said firmly.

'I told you, that's not necessary.'

'I am dumping this *first*,' repeated Benjy. 'So as I can wash. Where do you want it? Unless you want it left here.'

Len hesitated. Opened his mouth to argue, and decided against it.

Benjy had made up his mind, and when he looked stubborn like that even Len didn't fancy trying to change it.

66

7

The first September of the war was crisp and clear and blue, and the first of the High Holy Days, Rosh Hashonah, the New Year's Day which opens the Ten Days of Penitence, was particularly sunny. No one yet understood the enormity of what was happening in France, and both the Gordons and the Katz family went along to their very different synagogues to celebrate the festival in their customary way. Abram liked the small, homely synagogue on Shaw Street. It reminded him of how it had been in Russia as a child. On the High Holy Days it was noisy and packed with everyone's family down to the smallest baby. And the babble of conversation kept rising to the point where those who'd been called up to the *bimah* to read the Torah had to pause, and a loud *Shhhh* went out from the *shammus*. But it was not a scandalized hushing sound. That was right, Abram thought. Families were noisy, but they were what God liked to see. What did he care for shiny top hats and all the decorum of the bigger synagogues?

Upstairs in the women's gallery, Rasil looked magnificent. Abram knew that, without being able to catch her eye and smile. Never mind. Tonight they would love one another. God understood love. He wasn't against it. He was against nothing that made for life.

For a moment his thoughts moved to the war in Europe. *Meshugganah* wars. Always wars. For what? He could still remember the fear of conscription into the tsar's army which had haunted his own childhood. There it was a death sentence, he thought. Twenty-five years. They kidnapped young boys, starved them. Here, in England, he thought proudly, it is another matter. People love their country enough to volunteer to fight. They won't take young boys away from their mothers by force.

67

The sound of the ram's horn, blown well by Teichman, the *shochet*, brought him to attention. The man blows well, he thought. He has a strong throat, God bless him. It's a terrible job he has. Abram too had been trained for the ritual killing of animals, but he was too soft-hearted for it.

God was about his own business, mused Abram. Deciding who was to live and who was to die. It can't be easy for him, either. And his eye caught the text from Ezekiel: 'Whoever heareth the sound of the cornet and takes no warning, the sword will come and take him away.'

It wasn't a good New Year, he thought uneasily.

The story of Abraham and Isaac, to which the Hebrew kept returning, always oppressed him. Yes, it showed God's mercy; but the demand made Abram's heart fill with fear and a sense of unworthiness. Who could tell what the Lord would ask a man to bear? Mercy, Lord, he prayed. None of us knows what you want of us. And perhaps you are angry, because this generation is not very respectful to you. They know so little. The barmitzvah portion, perhaps, and the alphabet. And that was all. But then, they had to work so hard. And was it possible every man should be a scholar?

He became aware of Benjy and Len giggling in the pew to his left. He would have liked to lean over and cuff them as though they were still small children.

'*Yiskor*,' said Benjy.

He moved to get up. As a child with both parents living he was not supposed to hear the memorial service for the dead.

'And I want a fag,' said Len. 'I'll come out with you.'

There was always a crowd of children and adolescents outside in the street. The girls wore hats with wide feathers, and coats and skirts down to their ankles; some of them were neat in the waist and tightly buttoned at the ribs. The boys stood around in their formal suits and looked knowing and self-important. Most of the parental generation were inside, so it was a chance for a little flirtation. But Len wanted to go round the corner for a smoke. He seemed unusually pre-occupied.

'Did you see Mo Green?' he asked Benjy. 'Reckon he takes

any account of Kol Nidrei?'

Mo Green was a bookie who operated off Brownlow Hill. Benjy had seen Mo in the synagogue, rocking backwards and forwards, every Rosh Hashonah since he could remember. The rest of the year Mo never appeared. Solemn dress and a serious expression didn't suit him. His small pink eyes and slack lips were bemused by worship. He preferred to be out in the world, laughing with his friends, digging them in the ribs; the superstition which brought him back among the devout every year wasn't strong enough to hold his attention once inside the building.

Benjy looked at Len shrewdly. 'He ain't releasing any business of his own,' he remarked.

'Do you want a fag?' asked Len.

Benjy hesitated, as if Abram's eye was on him.

'Come on,' said Len, impatiently. 'You do it on Shabbos. I've seen you.'

'Feels worse on Rosh Hashonah,' said Benjy. 'I know it's not. But that's how it feels.'

His under-jaw jutted.

'Ten days,' mused Len. 'Not long, is it?'

'What have *you* been up to?' mocked Benjy.

'I've been a bit wild,' said Len sombrely, pulling on his cigarette. 'It's not just money, either. There's a girl, too. We shall see.'

Abram thought of his own dear dead parents, and the graves in Odessa he wouldn't see again, and the love and protection they had tried to give him, and his blue eyes were wet with tears. My Rasil, he thought. Without you I'd be lost altogether. And he dabbed his eyes without shame. English men don't cry, he knew. It was thought of as weakness. When he thought of that, Abram knew the meaning of exile among strangers. Why was it weak to feel pain for the loss of those you loved? Why were dry eyes manly? In the Bible, the greatest warriors wept. God wanted the heart. He had said as much. And so, as Abram spoke the great ancient prayer, he let his own feelings flow out of him until he was at peace.

*

Across the city, in Princes Road, Betty stared down from the women's gallery at the deep wooden boat of the synagogue. The red velvet curtains, embroidered in gold thread, were drawn back along their shining brass rails; the mahogany doors of the ark were opened, and the scrolls in their white Rosh Hashonah dress, with all their silver crowns and hanging adornments, were a blaze of light. The cantor had a light, mellifluous voice; he sang with precision. The harsh notes and ancient intervals were lost in the smoothness of his tones. It could be school prayers, thought Betty. But she was still too sore from the quarrel she had fallen into with Francis and Dorothy that morning to attend closely. She knew it was always a mistake to come between those two; they so rapidly turned upon her. And this morning they had turned on her with particular delight.

Elsa looked at the little watch on her wrist, and sighed.

Betty sighed, too; and for a moment Elsa turned towards her with a certain interest. The sigh was so like her own. She stood between her two daughters and felt the contrast between them.

Betty's sweetly oval face was so perfectly framed by the feathers in her hat; the new fashions clung so gracefully to her form. Whatever had brought that sigh from her lips, she stood gracefully and quietly; while Dorothy was jerky with impatience, and kept buttoning and unbuttoning her gloves. Betty stood demurely with her mother-of-pearl-backed prayer book in her hands.

Inside, Betty was raging.

She knew her intelligence and sensitivity equalled Francis's and was sharper than Dorothy's on literary questions because her sister had little time for anything but information. That morning, over tea and toast, Dorothy had said Hardy was unreadable. Francis had disagreed. And incautiously Betty had declared that *The Mayor of Casterbridge* was her favourite.

Unequal battle was then joined.

Betty's strength of love – one of the many ways in which she resembled her mother – came out in her passion for the characters in books, to whom she gave the kind of allegiance she would a friend. It was a passion that brought out the worst in Francis, who found it easy to bludgeon her down.

'It's not that I care about him selling his wife. Anyone might do that,' said Francis loftily.

'Really,' said Dorothy. 'Betty, how *can* you approve such a man?'

'Because it's not the point. What he did *then*,' said Betty.

'He got everything wrong. That's the point of the book, Dorothy,' said Francis. 'Henchard deserves all that happened to him.'

'Oh, no. Surely not?' Betty argued. 'He was such a *loving* man, he so wanted to be generous to everyone. You can't prefer that clever little Scot, can you?'

'Yes. Just because he had his head screwed on.'

'Don't you feel any pity for Henchard at all? Not even when he goes to all that trouble setting up a party? All those animals he wanted to roast. I could have cried for him when it rained.'

'But fancy not taking that into account,' said Dorothy contemptuously.

'I thought you said you couldn't read the book through,' said Betty, with a rare flash of rebellion.

'Not allowing for rain,' said Dorothy, who was never easy to put down. 'The man must have been a fool.'

'Maybe he wasn't calculating. But he was no fool. Look how he fought his way up,' said Betty.

'Any fool can make money,' said Francis.

'There's more to life than that,' said Betty. 'Don't you know that? Don't you believe that?'

Betty's exasperation with herself in these discussions was painful. She could not defend Henchard. She felt helpless. Of course, she could see he was a mess. How he couldn't cope. How he was bound to fail. But it was just the absence of calculation that attracted her.

Francis refused to continue the discussion.

Betty couldn't see how to put it better. It was like Antony choosing to fight by sea, she thought; that was foolish too. No one would have ever got Caesar to make such a mistake. Still, it was a noble mistake. A generous mistake. Henchard's mistakes were generous.

'What kind of rubbish is that?' said Francis disgustedly.

Betty saw her father's face on Octavius Caesar, and imagined his light form in the dancing Scot Farfrae. It was his code she was rejecting, and she believed in some deep, heartfelt way she was right to do so. If Dorothy failed to understand, it was only because everything, for her, was painted with a coarser brush.

Betty felt very lonely, standing there at the brass rail and looking down into the wooden pews below.

Alexander would understand at once; but she did not see him very often, and he had already enlisted in the army.

8

Benjy left school that term, more than a year before he should; Abram made no objection. He could see the business needed Benjy's particular type of acumen. For a long while all of them had come to rely gratefully on Benjy's knack of getting old machinery to work. Now the situation had changed. The government demand for wooden stakes had become insatiable. It wasn't a matter of kitchen cabinets any more, and someone with a head for such things had to set about buying new machines. The family were relieved to have Benjy to do it for them.

He had always taken the trouble to understand the inner workings of the machinery that his uncles used irritably. He enjoyed exploring any mechanism, to see where the stresses would fall; he enjoyed the elegance of anything well made; could feel how the bands ran between their cogs. He seemed to have an instinctive knowledge in his fingers. But really his knowledge came from bothering to understand. And because he bothered, he bought well and confidently.

'This is the Rolls-Royce,' he said, when his purchases were delivered to Islington, that street of Liverpool wood shops where the Katz family had their factory.

No one disputed his decision.

Harry heard he had won a county scholarship the same week that Benjy left school; he left on the same day. It wasn't exactly an act of imitation. He had felt forlorn from the moment he realized Abram wasn't going to insist on Benjy staying at school; it was as if the only advantage he enjoyed in the world were being rejected as unimportant in Abram's eyes. Didn't he *have* to have an education, then? Wasn't that the *only* way to get on? Evidently it wasn't Benjy's way.

When Harry left, Miss Biddle herself came round to the house to plead with Rasil to change her mind. But it was Harry's mind; and he was too sullen to listen.

No one pleaded to bring Benjy Katz back into the classroom.

And the business prospered.

Sometimes Rasil questioned Benjy, when he came home. 'All this money. We never *had* so much money. I can't help feeling somehow it's blood money. As if we were making it out of all those poor boys out there in the mud. Do you do a good *job*, Benjy?' she pleaded. 'You don't make things shoddy, do you?'

Benjy was touched by her sense of honour.

'No short cuts, Ma,' he promised. 'And the best wood. It's not my doing. That's what the uncles don't seem to understand. *Anyone* who's in business now is making money. It's the war.'

'But every week you read of some poor shop going bust.'

'Yes. Well, that's when the bread earner's taken off to fight. That's not right. Nor buying the shops up either, when they're going cheap,' said Benjy.

'I hope not too many of *us* get involved in that,' said Rasil apprehensively.

'Everyone with capital is doing it,' said Benjy soberly. 'They'll notice the Jews first, naturally.'

The first Katz to go into the army was Cousin Len. Everyone was astonished except for Benjy, and he kept his thoughts to himself. Mo Green and his racing world were far removed from Abram's.

'Don't worry, they won't get me farther than Aldershot,'

Len promised. But the next card came from France, and then, for several weeks, there was nothing at all.

Events in France were beginning to make themselves felt in the form of In Memoriam notices in the press. No one could imagine what was happening between Liège and Mons, or picture the landscape of the trenches, but everyone could understand death. And Benjy loved his cousin. Sometimes in the middle of all his exuberance he felt a clutch of fear for him. But Len's next letter was long and surprisingly perky.

They'd put him on a horse which kicked about all over the place, but he was skinny and he'd held on like a flea. He'd taught two Scots to play solo whist, and now he was in a place he wasn't allowed to name and couldn't spell, but the French women were marvellous.

Len had written that letter before marching off up the line, with cold, wet feet and a strap rubbing the skin off his shoulder, for the trench named Piccadilly.

'Keep in file. Close up and halt when the last man is in the trench,' yelled the sergeant, who was younger than Len.

All around were sodden fields, without any kind of hedging to break the wind or rain. And the trench smelt. Len could see litter and jagged tins in it. But down they all went and the men inside welcomed the newcomers. Len was given tea and a few scraps of bacon, and someone showed him how to wipe out his mess tin with straw.

The trench bulged inward, but the inner slats were firm, and they were told it was better than some. For one thing it was a back-up trench, even if the rattles and thuds of the front line were clearly audible. For another, there was a sump to take out the water that collected under the boards.

'Get *away*,' said Len, more impressed by such a sign of His Majesty's care than by their distance from danger.

'Got a match, Katz?' asked Jo.

Len liked Jo. He was another Scouse, and, together with the two Scots picked up at Aldershot, made up Len's solo game. Jo was young, with a high colour and a cough. The cold went through his thin frame right to the ribs. He coughed while he smoked. Len teased him. 'I don't know how a crock like

74

you got through the medical.'

'I faked it,' said Jo, deadpan. 'Told them there was TB in the family.'

Fifteen, thought Len, not more. Not even a wisp under his nose.

He put down his own mess tin, confusedly; lost the cover and laughed.

Some time during the day water got into the motor of the precious sump, and no one knew how to get it dry again.

Len thought of Benjy.

'I got a chum could fix that,' he said. 'In a minute.'

'Oh, aye,' grunted Jo sceptically.

They were building a sandbag rim to the edge of their trench when one of the younger officers came along and said, 'I shouldn't waste much time on that.'

'Why not?' asked Len.

'Because we aren't building in for a siege. That's not our style. There's going to be a big push any day now. These things – ' he gave a kick at the bags ' – they'll just be in the way. Stop you seeing what you're up to.'

'How about the wire, then?' asked Len, quickly.

The officer flushed a little. He could see the yellow balls of it rolled up and ready, and he wasn't sure where it should go.

'He'll pipe up in a sec, like a blooming *prefect*,' said Jo disgustedly.

'If *you* don't know, who bloody well does?' said another voice truculently.

'Whoever said that can take an extra turn on duty tonight,' said the officer, his voice rising a little in pitch.

'Gawd help us,' said some hoarse Cockney. 'We have to stop the buggers getting near enough to lob a grenade at us. Don't we?'

'Decisions of that kind are not your business,' said the young boy, shakily.

The men looked at one another.

'The wire should be close in. See to it right away.'

As it happened, a grenade was lobbed into Piccadilly the

same night, and one of Len's Scottish friends was hit in the chest by pieces of it. Len was part of the stretcher party that carried him back toward base, watching the Verey lights going up to the east, and wondering about the potholes.

A spoonful of rum, Len thought indignantly. They needed a bloody great jar of it. Each. His feet could hardly bite into the waterlogged mud. With one part of his mind, he knew that the rumbles and thuds all around them were shells; but most of him was still incredulous. Those sudden, ashen flashes were all someone's death. Crazy, random deaths. No hope of dodging, if they came your way. Much as anyone could do to keep stumbling on and not tip the Scot off into the mud.

'Mind the hole,' hissed a voice ahead.

Was that dark pit at his side made by a shell? Was that a hand moving in it? Or a dead branch? Or a rat?

'To the left.'

'Left be buggered.'

'Get down. All of you.'

Len heard the whistle of a shell close by.

'Why are we stopped?' he whispered.

'Hold on, chum.'

'We're going north,' Len muttered. 'Why?'

The slime was over his ankles. He'd almost forgotten what they were about.

At last they reached the firm road, and a voice ahead called out, 'All complete there?'

But the Scot had died on the way.

'I've made an error,' said Len. 'A miscalculation.'

He told Jo about Mo Green, and the other anxieties that had brought him to this zig-zagging underworld of Piccadilly North and South. Then they both had to lean against the hessian, weak with laughter.

Next morning, everyone ate breakfast standing up. Cheese this time, soggy bread, and a little jam. But daylight was better, and the landscape of the dead had a few unexpected visitors. French lads, not more than ten years old, squirmed out to Piccadilly with reminders of how close the soldiers still were to

76

an ordinary world. The boys brought tins of biscuits, English tobacco, and the *Daily Mail*.

They were cheered and tipped lavishly; and then Len was called on to read out the news. He did so with relish.

'We've had a grand victory,' he said at once.

'Which salient?' asked someone, seriously interested.

'This one, it says here. Didn't you notice? We pushed them back a hundred yards.'

'Does it say what it's like over here?' asked Jo.

Len said bleakly, 'Is that likely?'

'Come on you lot, start baling. There's a break in the boards,' the sergeant yelled at them.

On guard was worse.

Looking into blackness. What's that? In the tangled grass. Len huddled in his woollen comforter. He could hear himself shiver. Wet bloody through, thought Len. Catch me death.

His mind wandered.

He thought of dry wood. And shavings. He remembered being rubbed down by Aunt Rasil once, with embrocation, in front of a fire. How careful she'd always been airing sheets. He shuddered now in wet clothes that hadn't been changed for two days. Damp sheets? Auntie, you got to be joking.

It seemed a splendid piece of luck to Len and Jo.

They were being sent back to Edgware – a trench so far behind Piccadilly it was almost out of the war altogether. Ten of them. The lucky ones lurched into their packs cheerfully and marched off. The men sang lustily:

> 'Send out the boys of the Old Brigade
>   Who made Old England free,
> Send out my mother, my sister, and my brother,
>   But for Gawd's sake don't send me.'

Len liked the ordinary soldiers at his side. They were sceptical, unimpressed, life-loving as he was. Everyone was Tom or Jock now. No one's surnames mattered. He knew they respected a perky courage in him that was like their own.

And Edgware was everything they had hoped. It was dry and warm and in good repair. There was ordinary time there. Time to hold you hands over a little brazier. Time to get clothes off that had been caked in mud. Time to eat. There was even a random selection of goodies from home. Pickled pilchards. Gentleman's relish. Rumours had it, not far away you could get beer, eggs and chips for three francs.

There was even time for a little solo.

'Who's got the cards?' asked Jo.

They had just set up a wooden cartridge box as a table, and found a couple of chums who were willing to be taught the difference between clubs and spades, when the first shot launched on the new German trajectory sent its first sure projectile into the Edgware line.

It was one of the biggest bangs of the war, but Jo and Len never heard it land.

Len's letter to Benjy was followed by a silence that lasted more than two months. It was broken by a letter from south-east England which his mother brought round to the Katz household, distraught because she couldn't make it out. First Abram, then the rest of the Katz family put on their spectacles and peered at the scrawl. It looked as if it had been written with his left hand. Harry thought he made out 'Whist' and 'Whizz bang'. His mother wept inconsolably.

'Don't, Auntie. There are worse places to be than south-east England,' said Benjy sensibly.

The next day, a fellow from the same battalion wrote to say a shell had landed right on the four of them playing cards and Len had been lucky. But he wasn't so *very* lucky it turned out, because the next post brought a letter from the commanding officer, describing a wound in the thigh and giving the address of Len's hospital. It was Benjy who took money from the black box under Rasil's bed round to his aunt.

'You'll be wanting to visit,' he said simply.

'*Benjy*! That's a lot of money to be wasting on one poor old woman,' she said, too dazed to argue.

'It's only *money*,' said Benjy impatiently. 'Go on, take it, Auntie. Haven't you ever seen any before?'

'I've not seen so much all at once, and that's a fact,' she said.

'Well, pack up and get down to Lime Street with it,' said Benjy impatiently.

9

'Silly strutting men. I suppose you're a crazy patriot like all the rest of St Bede's?' asked Dorothy.

'I don't know what I am,' said Francis.

'We'll soon be able to put your heroic truth-telling to the test, then, won't we?' she prodded cruelly.

'I'm not really a conscientious objector. It's *this* war I don't want to fight. But I think I'd like least of all to be shut away in a prison or reviled as a traitor.'

'For goodness' sake, Dorothy,' said Elsa. 'His voice has only just broken. He's only a child.'

'I'm surprised *you* haven't seized the chance of doing something bold and manly,' said Francis, more angered by his mother's defence than his sister's gibing.

'And so I may. We'll see, won't we?'

Every week Elsa and Dorothy and Betty went with other ladies to a home nursing class run at a hotel in Sefton Park turned for the purpose into a Red Cross supply depot. The main purpose of this was to teach the women how to bandage wounds correctly. This Dorothy and Betty learned impatiently in the first hour. For the rest of the time well-dressed women, some in brand-new Red Cross uniforms, used the weekly occasion to chatter about their families.

'Doesn't it make you almost physically *ill*?' Dorothy glared round her without troubling to lower her voice.

Betty thought that perhaps the main use of it all was to take the women's minds off their sons at the front. She herself was much preoccupied with her cousin, who had already written to the Lancashire Regiment in the hope of obtaining a commission in it. She was ashamed of the hopeless love she felt for him which, even if she had been older – she was still only sixteen – could not possibly have been returned. Cousins did not marry, for one thing; and for another he had never treated her with anything more than gentleness. But it did not stop her fearing for him.

She looked round and sorrowed at the thought of smashed limbs and severed veins, while Dorothy fumed with hatred for the polite and elegant women around them.

Solomon knew the war was bad news, whatever the temporary improvement it brought to his account books. In the long run – and he wasn't so sure this was going to be a quick war – all wars were bad news. Europe would be left drained and sick and full of hate. England too. Solomon was not used to thinking of England as part of Europe.

He had no intention of expanding his business, even though Becker, an old rival whose son had gone off to the war, could have been bought out easily. It was not malice that led him to refuse. But he had not liked the way Becker ran his business, and he did not want to inherit the ill-will that would have come with it. Instead he continued to supply Becker with the plate glass he needed long after the rumour had gone round that Becker was about to go bankrupt.

There was some speculation about this perverse behaviour of Solomon's; and it probably helped to keep Becker in business another month or two, since no one could quite believe that Gordon had failed to assess his situation accurately. What these sceptics missed was that Solomon was simply keeping to his own standards of doing business. He was going to keep his word about Becker's plate glass, even though he was aware he couldn't hope for more than sixpence in the pound; and even though he could have enumerated all the creditors who would be before him in the queue as accurately as Becker himself. He was going to do so not out of any kind of commercial sense of the ordinary kind – he could hardly fail to be altogether out of pocket. There was no trick involved. He was delivering his glass to Becker because he had given his word to do so. And no one was ever going to be able to say that Gordon went back on his word. He knew that Becker would not understand, and would never have done the same himself. He even supposed that it would be resented by the man, thought of as spite, suspected.

But Gordon's word would continue to mean something.

In the satisfaction of that thought, Solomon walked home down the crisp January pavements of that first New Year of the war and reflected that, of all his family, only Francis would understand his motives. As usual, the sight of his own house lowered his spirits. Whatever Francis understood, or might understand, was irrelevant because the gulf between them had grown so enormous.

Solomon put the familiar pain away.

As soon as he entered the house, he knew there was something wrong. Something surprising. And for one hideous moment he thought: *Francis. He's enlisted.* But then he remembered the hurdle that would prevent it. There were many fifteen-year-olds in the army. But Francis wouldn't be able to lie about his age. Solomon went straight into the dining room without his usual ablutions. He could hear the silence from inside the room, aware of his arrival.

They were hushed, in their places round the table, except for his wife. For the first time, it seemed to him, her hair appeared grey at the sides. She had both hands together. The usual odours emanated from her well-tended body; yet there was another, too, and he detected it like an animal. It was the smell of fear. His wife said nothing.

'What is it?' he had to say at last, forced to question to the end, it seemed to him, as if no one could speak first.

'Dorothy's gone,' said his wife, almost inaudibly, twisting her hands together in pure terror.

'Gone?' Solomon was at first stupefied; then, as the silence around him continued, enraged by the economy of information. 'How gone? Where?'

He would have liked to shake his wife for her tears, and her ceaseless wringing of her hands. He turned his eyes to his other children, but they both dropped their gaze. Solomon found himself guessing wildly, the first worst mistake, in fantasy striking at the head of whoever had stolen her from

81

him, taking for granted it was a man.

'She's gone to be a nurse, Da. She left a note.'

'A note?' His eyes narrowed with the first scent of equivocation. 'You mean it surprised *you*? She didn't consult *you*? Didn't *mention* it? Not a word?'

His fury mounted in his throat at the obvious lie.

'It's a rotten life. She'll be back, Da,' said Betty's gentle voice.

Francis said nothing.

For the first time Solomon felt the family solidarity like a wall of misunderstanding. They imagined he grieved for *her*. For *Dorothy*. But no, it was because she had betrayed him, deceived him. Cheat! With a single slice of his will, he cut himself free of her. Dorothy! Dorothy! His spirit moaned for a moment, and that piece of himself too was dead.

'She'll be back,' repeated his wife.

Solomon's face looked up, ashen.

'No. She won't,' he said thickly.

And still he could tell they failed to understand him.

'She's never to be let in that door again. Do you understand? I won't even have a letter from her come in this house. I don't care if she starves.'

'Da, please!' The hurt voice of his remaining daughter rose almost against her will, to plead for her sister.

Solomon's attention was thus sharply attracted to Betty. She had never looked more purely oval-faced, sweet-lipped and vulnerable. Goodness lit her brown eyes; her hands lay open in her lap. Solomon's own gaze narrowed upon her with malevolence, and a momentary satisfaction stirred in his heart. This one's life at least lay under his hand, and he would shape it exactly as he wished.

10

The Gordon family would have been surprised to see Dorothy looking pale and exhausted but nevertheless triumphant at the end of her first day at the General. She had made them take her on. The matron had believed she was twenty! She had put out the trays stolidly, one after another. Cutlery. Biscuits. Cheese. Pears.

When she was allowed to go to her room she sat stirring coffee in a tin before the fire with an extraordinary feeling of exhilaration. Women weren't helpless at all. And the job wasn't easy. She had learned to balance two plates at a time on her arm, and carry them into the dining room. She had learned that only one light was kept on in that room, ever, for the sake of economy.

She liked the white clothes, the hidden hair, the stiff collar up to her chin; the rituals of drawing blinds and bedmaking – so precise and clinical. It aroused some residual Gordon instinct for *order* that the pillowcases had to be made to face the same way, so that Sister never had to look at an overlapping end, only a neat one. Certainly her legs ached all the way up scurrying to do all that was necessary; and so far she hadn't dealt with a single patient. There was a fishbowl in the centre of the ward, which had to be cleaned meticulously, water changed, and no gold slithery fish lost down the ward sink, every night. And she'd managed that. And there were fern pots in pink china, the sister's particular joy, which had to be brought out on to the landing at night; and it had been Dorothy's job to soak them under the tap. None of it very dramatic; but all of it took nerve in a way she hadn't expected.

Things came easily to her. And the sisters didn't frighten her, as they did the other probationers, who were often orphans. Their goodness, since they had come into the profession out of the sheerest necessity, was all the more remarkable. In many ways, she recognized, they were morally her superior. They had learned not to be squeamish. Neither vomit nor blood appalled them. And if the sisters frightened them, the big drunks coming in with a broken arm, ready to break in anyone's head who hurt them, for some reason didn't.

The fiercest sister of them all had a white face and rimless glasses, and something led her to admit to Dorothy she had a toothache. It was an unexpected confession, soon put down, but it threw a new light for Dorothy on the impatient way she'd be saying, 'Of course it hurts,' as if it were the most obvious thing in the world.

Does a good nurse learn not to understand other people's pain as real? Dorothy wondered.

Later in the next week, passing through the wards at night, she watched one of the badly wounded men trying to read by the light of an illicit candle. Amused, and reluctant, she paused at the foot of the bed and read, Katz, Leonard, born 1897, Liverpool, before he heard her arrival.

'Sorry,' she said, removing the candle firmly.

He handed over the candle mildly, watching as she read his notes at the bed-end. She wondered if he knew how ill he was. Tuesday, she read: Query amputation of right leg.

'I'm from Liverpool too,' she told him, smiling.

'Are you now?' He gave his voice the unmistakable lift. 'So don't let those notes get you down, love. I'm holding on to all my most important parts.'

She only hoped he was right.

'Of course. Goodnight.'

She took the book from him, and put it firmly on the table beside the bed. H. G. Wells, she noticed.

'Is it a good one?' she asked politely.

'Not really. I like his fairy tales best. Don't seem much like I'll get across to 1980, does it? And he's as likely to be right as anyone else.'

His thin, animated face intrigued her. She recognized

in it the unmistakable, inexplicable quality of natural courage.

'Well, 1980 would be pushing luck for both of us, wouldn't it?' she said quietly.

11

A good fire had been lit in the rarely used front parlour of the Gordon household at Elsa's express instructions. Domestic servants were now hard to find; and she had to chivvy the latest, undisciplined girl pretty severely about the dusting and polishing before the room was fit to receive Alexander and his officer friend. Alexander had privily warned them that this young man came from a brilliant Scots family. 'With a *Schloss* just north of Edinburgh,' as he put it quaintly, 'but no kind of *snob*.' That line in Alexander's letter had disposed both Betty and Francis to hate the newcomer on sight; but Elsa was delighted at the prospect of entertaining him, and had brought out her prettiest silver milk jug, and the best Rosenthal china.

'Are you sure that's *tactful*, mother?' Francis teased her. 'German heirlooms, and all that, when they're just off to fight the Hun?'

Elsa frowned. The European war could be no easy matter for her to contemplate. Only that morning she had received a disturbing letter from her Hungarian cousins. She read there was typhus in Prague; and that Jewish families in flight from the fighting were said to be carrying it. Shopkeepers were refusing everywhere to serve either them or the families who had put them up out of compassion. She guessed, through the censorship, how much the hardship of that whole branch of the family exceeded anything felt in England. The blackout and the food shortage and the fear of Zeppelins were within her grasp; but she found it hard to imagine the horror of lovely young men like Alexander taking up guns against uncles and cousins. We are Europe, she thought to herself. My family, and perhaps the whole Jewish people, riven and divided by this war like no one else. We *are* Europe, eating and destroying itself.

'My dear Elsa,' Solomon reproached her, 'since we have taken shelter in this country, it is our responsibility to support it. England must be our family now, and any other thought is sentimental.'

Was it? She could remember the crude shock of fear she had experienced looking at a cartoon captioned: 'Mrs Levy wearing her precious sugar lump.' Not that she felt it was directed at herself. She was not an ostentatious dresser, nor did she have any guilt about the common providence of laying in stores of food. She had stocked up, like a good housewife, in the first excitement. One of Solomon's vans had been commandeered and repainted as a mobile larder, and there was a run on food shops generally; she saw no reason to feel ashamed of it. What alarmed her about the cartoon was the implicit difference of regard in it not only for poor Russian immigrants, but English Jews as a whole.

Outside was a black, wet afternoon. Betty, who had helped her mother to bake almond macaroons, was now sitting with a book quite close to her eyes – their vague and tender brown had begun to show signs of short-sightedness. Francis looked impatiently at *The Times*, which described a heroic push twenty miles north of the Somme.

'What rhetoric, what unashamed gall they have. Am I supposed to behave as though I believe what is happening out there is rational or decent or admirable in any way? Will you tell me that?'

The dark October afternoon pressed in on them all. Elsa debated whether to switch on the electric light in the standard lamp at the corner of the room and draw the heavily backed curtains to hide the rain splashing against the glass. It made for more cosiness. At the same time it was not yet four o'clock; it was not their custom, and she did not want to provoke Francis's sharp tongue further.

'Will you put another log on the fire?' she asked instead.

Francis's mockery covered a bitterness of his own, which he had no intention of exposing to his family's inspection. At school the younger boys had begun to bait him for not enlisting in the army as so many of his form had already done. That he was not of age counted for nothing; and he did not make that excuse. Could none of them see the waste of the war, the stupidity of it? They could not. They were a generation of lemmings, he muttered to himself. What nobility was there in war decorations? Honour, they called it. And he'd quoted Falstaff to them on the subject, unwisely; and thus sealed his unpopularity. After that he found lacy cambric knickers in his school bag when he reached for his books; and periods set aside for private study no longer gave him any privacy.

'Cambridge. That's right. A good time to aim for it when your betters are dying,' they taunted him.

'Do *any* Jews fight?'

'Can they?'

Francis lifted his head from his books to answer patiently, 'My cousin Alexander has just received a commission, as it happens.'

'Rotten swot too, is he?'

Francis lowered his head. He was not going to justify Alexander to any of them. He didn't admire the commission, and was annoyed with himself for mentioning it; but he did admire his cousin.

'Is he?' they insisted.

'Alexander won a place to Cambridge and gave it up,' Francis replied reluctantly.

'A family of swots, then,' said his tormentors.

Not for the first time, Francis considered leaving school.

Elsa guessed none of this; but one day Solomon had observed shrewdly, 'You study most of the time on your own these days. You might as well do it at home.'

Francis, however, had drawn back from any step that would lead him into his father's business.

'Shouldn't you be at the office today, Betty?' he called over now.

Betty had left school the term before and did a little clerical

87

work for her father. She went in to the office only two days a week – Elsa could not spare her more than that – and, as Francis well knew, this was not one of them.

Betty did not answer at first; her own nerves were taut with a superstitious fear that Alexander would not appear at all. She had not seen him for six months, and then briefly. His last letter still echoed in her head. There was nothing in it more than cousinly affection, certainly; but he had taken time to write. He had thought of her. And now he was to appear she hardly dared imagine how he would be.

'How can you behave so *childishly*,' she cried out with unexpected vigour, 'when for all you know your cousin Alexander is off to France, and may lose an arm or a leg or never come back at all?'

'He isn't *going* abroad yet that I know,' said Francis pettishly.

'I hope not, indeed. Poor young man,' sighed Elsa.

Then the heavy old bell rang in the door, and Betty caught her breath.

Alexander's friend was a disarmingly shy and quiet young man, with eyelashes so fair as to be nearly invisible, and a vulnerable under-lip. He was introduced as Ian Mackenzie; thereafter it was Alexander who carried the conversation. His few months of officer's training had given him a new kind of assurance, and Betty hardly dared to raise her eyes to meet his.

Francis was assailed by a confusion of emotions; among them a kind of envy, which took the form of truculence. Even as Elsa delicately poured tea into the fine porcelain, he began to harangue his cousin, as if his fine bearing were in itself offensive. Alexander had begun by exchanging a word or two with his aunt, but the vehemence of Francis's attack turned him towards Francis in surprise.

'I had no idea you were so political,' he declared, with an air of amused tolerance which brought a dark flush to Francis's sallow cheeks.

Elsa was visibly dismayed at her son's behaviour.

'I read the other day that a skilled man in the docks here

gets no more than two pounds a week, and a private soldier's war widow five shillings a week. Five shillings! How do we have the nerve, the *gall*, to pretend these poor creatures have anything to fight for?'

Even Francis felt his indignation was a little shrill.

'What, not a good word for honour, duty, patriotism and the great white pinnacle of sacrifice?' teased Alexander.

'Bankers' words,' said Frances loftily.

'Not a bit. The last thing the banks want is Armageddon.'

'Of course. Nobody wants to *die*,' said Francis. 'They want to dress up as officers and give orders.'

'Well, you're young,' said Alexander, evidently somewhat annoyed by that last thrust.

'But, Francis, think of what happened at Whitby and Scarborough. Women and children killed at their breakfasts,' whispered Betty with a note of reproof in her voice, dismayed at Alexander's face, which had closed against them all.

'Well, I expect the Royal Navy has been firing into African villages for generations,' declared Francis, desperately.

With an odd, dream-like prescience he understood that all the words he was directing so ferociously across the room towards his cousin were really aimed at catching the attention of his silent young friend who was drinking his tea and watching them all politely. As soon as this thought became clear to him, Francis found it halted the flow of his voice altogether; and tea continued with admiration for Betty's skill at baking, and other harmless family inquiries.

It looked as though the brilliant Captain Mackenzie might well go away without uttering a single word. Francis's excitement subsided accordingly. He was embarrassed at his own display of emotion, and only longed for tea to be over.

As Francis looked down earnestly to his plate, Ian scrutinized Francis intently. The boy was just losing an early prettiness to a lengthening jawline, but he had alert, unfrightened eyes.

'What do you read?' Ian asked, expecting no great sophistication from the sixteen-year-old boy.

Francis looked up cautiously. 'Hardy, at the moment. He seems to have it about right.'

'The *mess* of it all, do you mean?' asked Ian.

Francis wrinkled his brows, puzzled in his turn. 'I wasn't thinking of the novels. I haven't looked at those for years. I meant the language of the poetry.'

Ian was immediately interested in an altogether new way. 'I'd say his diction was pretty high myself. But how interesting you should care.'

'I read novels too, of course,' said Francis, spectacularly encouraged.

'Kipling?' teased Alexander. 'Rider Haggard?'

'No. Conrad,' said Francis stiffly. He felt an unwanted edge to his cousin's remarks, which seemed designed to establish age difference and superiority. 'I prefer poetry,' Francis admitted.

It seemed that Ian had once met Rupert Brooke, briefly, through his brother at Trinity.

This stirred Betty to risk her own voice. 'Real poets exist, then, like ordinary people,' she exclaimed.

The boys laughed and teased her about the book in her hand.

'Don't you imagine Charlotte Brontë was an ordinary woman?'

'Oh, I don't think so,' she said decidedly. 'I have thought a great deal about it, and I can't believe so.'

Francis knew she was thinking of her sister Dorothy, and that the thought was painful.

'Well, hats off then. To those that are extraordinary,' cried Francis. 'For those that can, *shall*.'

It was his deepest conviction. There were many disabilities, of which being a woman was only one; and he had only begun to guess at the extent of his own in the last weeks of school. The thought of that put an unaccustomed edge on his voice, and Alexander looked at him sharply. Turning to Betty, he said, 'We shouldn't like to see so much aggression in *you*, should we?'

As Alexander wandered over to Betty, she flushed at his approach, and Francis saw she had become extraordinarily pretty since the arrival of the young man.

'What do *you* read, Betty?' Alexander inquired pointedly.

'Everything,' she smiled. 'I have no taste. I'm an enthusiast.'

'Bravo,' said Alexander.

'Except adventure stories; I can't, somehow.' She stopped, not liking to refer to everyone's anxiety.

'Quite right. All that's as male as cricket,' said Alexander.

He wandered restlessly about the room.

'And are *you* still writing poetry?' he asked Francis.

Francis felt the familiar curling and dying inside him, and he could not reply.

'No steeds and warriors and valorous strife, I hope?' mocked his cousin.

'Certainly none of that,' Francis said steadily.

'You know, this war is testing all the Gordon virtues really,' said Alexander. 'Obstinacy, inflexibility, self-righteousness, self-discipline.'

Francis smiled back at him, unwillingly taken by his cousin's self-mockery. And then, unexpectedly, Ian began to speak the verse of a poem.

> 'Honour has come back, as a king, to earth
>   And paid his subjects with a royal wage;
> And nobleness walks in our ways again;
>   And we have come into our heritage.'

Francis responded with an instant ripple of pleasure at the root of his neck. He had never been immune to rhetoric; now, against all reason, his whole mood was changed, as much by the poetry of the young, sweet voice as the words of the poem itself. From that moment, he knew himself not only willing but eager to set his life alongside theirs.

The three young men smiled at one another.

Solomon listened to his wife's extravagant praise of Alexander's new friend with mounting amusement.

'And why is the boy not with his own family on such a short leave?' asked Solomon shrewdly.

'They are all at the war,' said Elsa quickly.

She had not thought to ask the question herself, and Solomon knew it. Nevertheless, it seemed likely enough as an explanation. He had found the boy personable, himself; and Elsa's excitement was transparent to him.

'This war has one great and unlooked-for *goodness* to it,' Elsa said. 'That young men who would otherwise never meet, have the chance to do so as comrades and equals.'

Solomon understood that she had Francis's advantage in mind.

'And what if the young man in question is after Betty?' he asked, slyly.

It was not likely, to his mind; but he could not resist forcing her to recognize the path of her own logic.

Elsa was silenced. Unlike Solomon, as she believed, she knew her daughter's heart was set on her cousin Alexander.

But what *do* I feel about *marrying out*? she asked herself. Tacitly, she conceded to Solomon the certainty that she and Solomon could dispose of Betty's gentle and willing person as they decided. She had no ambitions for her daughter, but Elsa could not have forbidden her happiness. If it had been a boy, yes, then she would have minded. It would have meant sharing a son's love with another mother; and worse, being pointed out as *the Jewish grandmother*, to her own grandchildren. Betty she might let go. But not Francis. Never Francis.

12

Elsa would have been disappointed to see her first, long, admonitory letter to her runaway daughter tucked away with no more than a cursory glance into Dorothy's tin box. Dorothy's tenderness for her mother had not diminished; but the thick lilac sheets of paper spoke of a world she believed she had abandoned as decisively as stitched silk and embroidered underwear.

This was not altogether so.

She had learned a great deal, and the strangeness of what

she had learned was exhilarating. The loneliness of cold mornings and cold water were still an adventure. She was used now to stone floors, smelly kitchens and sink rooms. She was used to washing male bodies. What would Elsa have said to that? And how could she have imagined the rest of it? Scrubbing a bed mackintosh, for instance; or carrying away sputum cups and bed pans without disgust. Dorothy was very proud of the self-control that enabled her to face her duties in an acute surgical ward: to prepare dressing trays; and even support mutilated limbs for those whose skill was superior to dress. She could look without flinching now at limbs chopped like pieces of an animal on a butcher's slab; sometimes they were septic, slimy-green and swollen.

Over Bovril with her fellow nurses, in an exhausted half-hour before bed, she learned about another kingdom.

'There's nothing wrong with his *hands*,' said Mary Ellen, a young nurse from County Cork.

'He's a naughty man,' said another, affectionately.

They were talking of Len, whose thin-lipped impudence had made him a favourite.

'He's got good healing flesh.'

'It's a holy miracle he didn't have to be mutilated,' said Mary Ellen. 'I prayed for him to the Blessed Virgin.'

'Did you tell him that?' asked Dorothy curiously.

'Oh, he's a heathen,' said the other girl indulgently. 'There's no teaching *him*.'

'I could put me heart and soul into it, mind,' sighed Mary Ellen.

Dorothy saw no point in declaring her own religion, since she felt no allegiance to it. She could not understand how any of them could believe in a merciful God. In her first week she had watched a young man of barely seventeen carried in, with half-closed eyes and yellow flesh; and when his hands had stopped twitching, and his worn-out body had stopped moving altogether, she knew where she stood. If this is God, she told herself, then I am going to fight him. This is his world, and his work, and all I can do is oppose him. But I won't *care* too much for anyone, because those who do care become feeble and can't help anyone else. Because if you care, you

93

play God's game. And so her back grew stiffer and her head taller. While a great beauty shone from her face, as she walked through the wards.

'Have you got a lover in France?' the soldiers asked her, puzzled by her austerity.

'I'm not going to take a lover,' she answered them all.

'You're a daft thing,' said Mary Ellen.

One dark evening they were playing Harry Lauder on the gramophone, and Len watched Dorothy speculatively as she hurried along the ward, trying to place her on his Liverpool map.

'Are you a Scots lass?' he called after her.

She shook her head without pausing.

Sefton Park, he told himself. Sefton Park, or Princes Avenue. And what are you doing *here*, my lovely?

He asked her the same question.

'I'm looking after the likes of you,' she told him, severely, putting a thermometer in his mouth before his quick tongue could build on the confidence.

But she kept her hand on his thin wrist, counting the even pulse; and with his eyes and eyebrows he mimed paradise, until the colour rose under her fair skin.

Dorothy found herself liking Len; as much as anything else, because he had no sense of any disadvantage or shame in his Jewishness. It was a kind of joke that had been played on him, it seemed. And he was full of jokes.

'Well, do you know the story of the Frenchman, the Irishman and the Jew?' he asked as she set a tin of hot milk in his hand.

She smiled, although Francis had never cared for stories of that kind, and she'd heard few that took her fancy.

'Well, the doctor came to see them all and they were told: There's not a lot we can do, do you have any last wishes? So the Frenchman said, I want to see the most beautiful women in Liège; and the doctor said, so you shall. And the Irishman wanted a good bottle of whiskey from the best peat river in – '

'And the Jew?'

'He said: I'd like a second opinion.'

She laughed out loud, as much at the impudence in his face as the joke itself; and so, unexpectedly, did the Irishman in the next bed, who leaned across to Len as she moved off.

'One me old man liked, went this way ... Nurse, this'll disgust your tender ears.'

And she left them at it.

'So you don't believe in anything coming along after death?' asked Dorothy, amused.

'Never saw the evidence,' he said.

'Evidence? I never heard people needed evidence.' Dorothy lowered her voice.

'It's heaven here, in England,' said Len, as if he might say more.

'Nurse!' called a stern voice from the other end of the ward, and Dorothy hurried off.

Len was happy. It was golden September. From the window he could see red creepers, sun in the leaves, and the strange yellow brick. And he could watch ash trees moving softly against the pale sky.

'They say it will be over in a year. What will you do then? Go back home?' Len took the conversation up, as if unspoken words had run between them in the hurried, work-filled afternoon.

'Never,' she said.

'I'd look after you,' he offered.

'Don't be daft. How will you?'

'I'll always fiddle a living, don't worry.'

She thought about that. It wasn't how her father had ever talked of business, and she wasn't sure she approved of it.

'On a barrow, will you?'

'To begin. Why not?'

'There's a few think that,' she laughed.

Now Dorothy might have put Elsa's letter away in a tin, but she had not put away her precepts from her soul. The gentle friendship growing between Len and herself died the after-

95

noon Dorothy first set eyes on Len's mother. It had taken the woman some time to arrive. This was because, when she had received Benjy's money, she had spent nothing whatsoever on clothes, or the fare to London either. She had an Irish friend who had offered to take her south in his cart. Why waste? As a result of this trip, she had arrived at the hospital in the worst possible condition: at once a little scruffy, and painted-up for the occasion.

Len had always been tolerant of his mother's frizzed hair and ruffles, though he was too sharp not to know the effect they made. When the other mothers entered the ward, they looked ashen and red-eyed, and the nurses treated them with the reverence of martyrs. But his mother had rouged her cheeks, and her eyes flashed over the other soldiers speculatively before she sat at his bedside. And as Dorothy passed, and smiled, she caught the smell of peppermint and cigarettes in his mother's clothes and her nose wrinkled involuntarily at it.

Those slightly distended nostrils hurt Len. In defiance he made serious efforts to demonstrate his own loyalty. When his mother laughed, her voice was throaty with the tobacco of the poor. Len joined his own to it. When Dorothy heard that chuckle she drew back, as if from a whole landscape of hawkers and pedlars, jostling one another in her imagination of the ghetto. Len understood well enough what he was doing, though he could not have known how Elsa's watchful eye and mild disapproval continued to work in Dorothy's heart. He had guessed some Jewish blood. Now he wasn't sure, and didn't care; he only knew Dorothy had drawn away from him.

And he wanted her. For her quickness and her lively green eyes, and the fire in her. So different from Mary Ellen's. His mother cried a little when she saw him. And then nagged him about leaving home. Then, drifting off, as she always did from subject to subject, her eyes wandered restlessly over the ward.

'There's terrible things going on in Russia,' she said. 'Murders. Whole villages starved and pillaged.'

Her eyes glittered like stones, reporting it.

'Oh yes,' he said. He'd heard it too often.

'And back home they can't spend their money fast enough. It's disgraceful.'

Len said, 'May as well spend it, I reckon. We'll be dead soon enough.'

She nodded, approving that; and he warmed to her. Because she had a good-natured love of pleasure. She might be silly, and she might be slovenly, but she wasn't grudging. She might be greedy for sweetmeats, like a little girl, but she enjoyed life. And it wasn't her sort that sent men out to die; she left that to the moralists.

Some of the moralists might be golden-haired as angels, he thought resentfully.

'How's the family?' he asked.

'Now Benjy's a fine and handsome lad, but they say Harry's next to go.'

Len whistled softly. 'They'll not send *him* to France. He's too jumpy.'

'Did they test *you* for jumpiness? By heck, you should have jumped a bit,' she reproached him.

But Len wasn't interested in Harry; it was the thought of Benjy that brought lines of affectionate laughter to his face.

'The old horse. And his old man. Uncle Abram?'

She shrugged.

'When are *you* going to knit up and be well?' she demanded. 'When are they sending you home?'

'I'm in no hurry,' he told her.

And he wasn't. He wasn't ready for Liverpool. Or Scotland Road.

Later that day he called Dorothy to him for a cold drink, and she brought him a glass of water with a deliberate, cheerful remoteness.

'So you're like the others,' he said.

'What do you mean?'

'You don't like the smell of the ghetto.'

'I'm not a snob. Don't think it,' she said, stung.

He looked at her speculatively.

She bit her lip.

'I'll tell you who *I* despise,' he said, off-handedly.

'Did I talk of despising?' she interrupted hotly.

'People who have it both ways,' said Len. 'Shut their shops on the Day of Atonement because they're superstitious, and then put up a board to say "Stocktaking" on their door. Well, my Mam is straight, anyway. She's not a hider.'

Dorothy laughed. 'I'm not superstitious *at all*. Isn't that straight enough?'

'You're fine,' he said huskily.

He knew he had lost her interest. She had drawn back. And soon after that conversation she was sent off to another ward.

To be a Jew, she decided in her new and narrow bed, wasn't so much a religion as a misfortune. Then, in falling asleep, she remembered that it was Francis who had first said as much to her, and that it was a thought of Heine's.

A week later Len was sent home.

13

In some of the windows Benjy passed along London Road there were cards propped in front of the curtains which read: 'This house has sent a man to fight for King and country.'

Since these cards were printed (and there were discs too) it was impossible to miss the heavy government blackmail. Benjy, however, was not immune to the appeal. Have You A Reason Or Only an Excuse? he asked himself. But as he entered his aunt's house and caught the familiar whiff of peppermint and the snuff, he remembered Len's grey face on his last visit, and he found himself rephrasing the question.

'Why ever did you join up?'

'Well, I needed a change,' said Len.

Benjy laughed.

'I thought perhaps your sweetheart sent you off to answer the call,' said Benjy.

'There aren't many ladies, Benjy, giving out white feathers in Scotland Road,' said Len.

Benjy looked uncomfortably round the ill-furnished room. Two cheap decanters on a high mantelpiece were the only signs of pride or decoration. There was an oilcloth on the floor. He wondered what his aunt had done with the money he had given her the Friday before. Anyway, Rasil had bought five shillings' worth of fish and fried them up for 'the poor, wounded lad'. He hoped Len had eaten well for a few days at least.

Len coughed, and wiped his mouth. 'I like the English, Benjy. The ordinary blokes like me. There's nothing fancy about them. And they aren't daft either.'

Len had a crutch, and his injured leg looked skinnier than the other.

'Can you get about?' Benjy asked abruptly.

Len looked relieved. People who avoided the subject of his wound usually couldn't take their eyes off his body.

'It doesn't hurt much, I'm just clumsy,' he said. 'The doctor says I've got germs. I told him, funny thing, shouldn't be. There's enough alcohol about sterilizing the air.'

Len's laughter struck Benjy as bitter in a new way; and he guessed it was his mother's behaviour that was upsetting him. He tried to imagine how he would feel if his own mother spent half a crown a week on drunken tea parties. But he found it altogether impossible to imagine his mother drunk. Not that she didn't drink the sweet Passover wine with relish, but he couldn't imagine her swaying about without dignity.

He himself rather liked a drop of something harder than wine, so he didn't feel moral about it.

'Well, after the war *we'll* set up together. Shan't we, Len? We'll be rich. We're lucky. Don't you feel that?'

'After?' said Len slowly.

'It has to end some time. Someone has to win.'

He felt stubbornly that he knew more about fighting than Len. He clenched his fists at the thought of it. He liked it. Then he saw that Len was smiling at him as if he were a child, and he became angry.

'Even animals stop, don't they? When they can see who's

99

winning. One of them backs off.'

Len said, 'Benjy, Benjy. I don't want to talk about the war. What's happening here? What's new? Tell me the gossip.'

'There's a lot of women on the game,' said Benjy. 'New sort. Good-lookers. Cheerful.'

'You want to be careful, there,' said Len seriously.

'Girls walk around the streets now, Len. Noisy, healthy girls. I was in London. And I'll tell you something else. They like it as much as we do.'

Len burst out laughing. 'You don't have to go to London. Those girls hang around every army camp,' he explained patiently. 'It's biology probably. They want to get a child before all the men are killed.'

'They're great, healthy girls,' repeated Benjy.

'They'll be wanting husbands, then,' said Len. 'Won't they? You know what they say, better be married a minute than die an old maid.'

'I'm not *marrying*,' said Benjy, startled.

'And that's not the only risk,' warned Len. 'I've a friend or two who'll never be the same again after a bit of fun with someone in a fine dress.'

'Ma wants Harry to get married. Mind, he doesn't want to,' said Benjy.

'So they won't take him in the army,' shrugged Len. 'Well. Tell him there's no point getting the worst of all worlds.'

'You don't think they'll start taking married men, do you?'

'They'll have to,' said Len. He bit the side of his mouth, and jeered, 'Who does Auntie Rasil have in mind? Someone posh?'

'And why not?' Benjy was angered at the tone, which he could not altogether explain.

Len shifted his leg restlessly, with both hands holding his kneecap. He looked to be in pain.

'Don't get so mad, Benjy.'

'Listen. We're as good as anyone,' said Benjy proudly, his lower jaw jutting.

And he meant what he said, not because of the new

prosperity of the Katz enterprises, but because all Jews were one family to him. The only snobbery he had been taught was that which placed Abram's learning into the special favour of God. Who could have anything better than that?

'Benjy, Benjy,' sighed Len. 'You're an innocent.'

Benjy stared furiously.

'You want to avoid those uppity bitches from Sefton Park and Princes Avenue. All of them,' said Len. 'You don't understand. They are different. They're more different from us than the Irish on Scotland Road. Believe me. They got standards, Benjy.'

'So have we,' said Benjy, stung. 'They're just a bit better businessmen.'

'No,' said Len. Benjy felt his hands ball into fists. Was Len going to say anything against Ma?

'What else is it?'

'They've got English learning, right? *Not just manners*. They got an English diet. They look like the English themselves. And they're just as cold and grand.'

Len's face twisted.

'Benjy, they hate *us* more than anyone. We *frighten* them. *Remind* them. And they don't want to be reminded of us.'

Now Len could see Benjy understood, and disliked what he was saying.

'How is your sister?' he asked quickly. 'Does she go to tea dances? Or isn't she old enough for the Adelphi?'

'She's down at the shop all day. Has to be. We can't get the help otherwise. Sarah can cut a straight line with a circular saw a damn sight better than most men,' said Benjy proudly. He had never been taught that women were fragile creatures.

'What does Aunt Rasil think for her?'

'She's too busy, always,' said Benjy. 'Anyway, it's always Harry she worries about.'

Len hoisted himself off the couch, and pushed the crutch under his arm. 'I'm going to pee. I don't need any help,' he said.

Benjy listened to him clattering outside in the yard, miserably.

By the time Len came back Benjy had an idea.

101

'I know,' he said. 'I'll take you to the dogs.'

'How?' asked Len.

'You leave that to me.'

The next weekend Benjy came to collect Len in a hansom cab.

'Rank extravagance,' said Aunt Fanny, impressed.

It was a fine, autumnal day, and the cab set off along London Road at a brisk pace. Soon there were trees everywhere and you could taste the sea in the bright air. The gulls began swooping down in the leaves.

'Marvellous,' said Len.

'Soft going, mind,' said Benjy. He pushed something into Len's pocket.

'What's that?'

'You have to have something to *bet* with,' said Benjy, laughing off Len's embarrassment. 'Come on now.'

'Well. Look at this. Revolution. How do you fancy that? He likes soft going.' Benjy prodded his cousin to take part.

'Whatever you say.'

'No. *You've* got to choose,' insisted Benjy. 'And if you're quick about it, we can get a *double* for the next race. That means if you *win* . . . '

'*If.*'

'Like I said.'

'All right. Let's look.'

The fresh air and excitement had brought a little colour to the points of Len's cheekbones. It was as if the bustle in the crowd pressing round him, and their intense self-preoccupation, had freed him from his injury. Benjy noticed that he propped himself on the crutch almost as casually as if it were a railing, as he balanced the dog page of the newspaper.

'Pepper,' he said suddenly.

'Where's that? Hm, Track Six,' said Benjy dubiously. 'Well, OK.'

'It's great stuff, pepper,' said Len. 'Reaches through to you when nothing else will.'

Revolution was a graceful animal but it ran last, to Benjy's astonished disgust. Len couldn't help laughing at the way he tore up his ticket.

'You really expect to win?' he said incredulously. 'Don't you realize this whole tote is set up mathematically so nobody can?'

'I won last week,' said Benjy doggedly.

'All right, maybe Pepper will be lucky,' Len consoled him.

'It's no bloody good now about Pepper, you berk,' shouted Benjy. 'The second bet was tied in with the first!'

'All right, put *this* on Pepper,' said Len quickly.

Benjy looked down at the note in his cousin's hand.

'That's your army money,' said Benjy crossly. 'I'm not touching that.'

'Go on. For luck,' insisted Len.

Benjy frowned, and then saw there was no time to argue and agreed.

'It's like being kids again, isn't it?' he said happily.

'Benjy, you'll never be anything else,' said Len soberly.

14

'My dear Betty,' wrote Alexander:

I was very sorry to hear that your mother is unwell again, all the more since I guess how the responsibilities you carry will be made even heavier. Forgive me, I often think how much your sweet nature is put upon by the eagerness everyone feels to see Francis make the most of his talents. Still, I am sure whatever happens your soul will never become crabbed, or sour or angry.

I hope you will not be shocked if I say that I cannot master either your resignation or your composure. At least I have not yet behaved with notable cowardice; though I do not find it easy to stand up under fire, and I'm far more squeamish than I thought I should be. The men seem to me out of all reason courageous. They laugh and smoke and sing bawdy songs.

How kindly you write, and how good of you to let me write whatever I want in return. I must write to someone, you know, and you can imagine how impossible it would be to write home of what I see all round me. I don't think I'm a very good soldier, though so far at least I have done nothing really disgraceful. Yesterday I found two of my men – well, boys really, they can't be much older than Francis – lying dead in the bottom of a trench, and I don't even know what happened to them. I wanted to cry. One of them had a trickle of blood running out of his mouth, so it can't have happened long before I came on the scene. There are worse things than recently dead bodies, though, but I won't torment you with them. I wish I had never believed all that nonsense about war being glorious. There's nothing noble about it. In fact it's quite hard to hold on to ordinary civilian virtues. Dugouts get blown in. Barbed wire has to be mended.

Are you still gently reading poetry by the fire? I like to think of that. You mustn't get drawn away. Though when I think of your fine gaze, and how calm you are, I don't know why, I can't help feeling sad, as though I'm missing something, not understanding something about you. Why don't you write back to Ian? He was very taken with you, and I can't believe you share some stupid prejudice against him just because he's a Gentile. That would be unfair.

Betty stopped reading, and tears came to her eyes. Once again, just as it seemed that Alexander must be sharing her own emotions, here was proof that he was not.

Betty lifted her head to find her father standing over her.

'I think you had two letters this morning,' inquired Solomon drily.

'I did. One from Alexander. And,' she hesitated, 'a polite note from his friend.'

'I see.'

Solomon realized he had been wrong. He had imagined Betty was in touch with her sister, and that he had caught her at it. There was something, however, in the pallor of her face and the unusual intensity of her eyes which puzzled him.

'Let me see the letter from the young boy,' he asked her sharply.

The letter she had been holding up so closely to herself went away promptly into its envelope; and another altogether was obediently handed over to him. He read the neat pages slowly and carefully while Betty flushed and looked uncomfortable. Solomon lifted her delicate chin, and looked searchingly into her face.

'Perhaps you are attracted to this young Englishman?' he demanded.

'Not in the least,' said Betty, a little quickly perhaps, but firmly enough.

Solomon released his daughter moodily. So, then, it was only what he and Elsa already knew; she had set her heart on her cousin Alexander.

'Have you looked over what is happening in the kitchen, my dear, while you sit up here at your leisure? We cannot expect wartime staff to understand how things should be done.'

Betty stood up with apparent relief.

'I'll be about it,' she muttered.

For a moment Solomon was touched, by her very willingness, into a perverse rage.

'It was never too much trouble for your mother,' he insisted.

Betty lowered her gaze, gathered her skirts, and hurried out of his attention.

Passing Francis on the stairs she surprised in his face an expression rather like his father's; as if he too felt an impatient malevolence towards her. She could think of no way she could be said to have earned it. How she longed for their sister Dorothy's robust spirit.

'Is something wrong?' was all she managed, and she received no reply to her question.

'Stop scuttling about the place,' snapped her brother. 'You are a daughter of the family, not a servant. Try to carry yourself like one.'

Betty was offended and puzzled. She could not have guessed that what was gnawing away so viciously at Francis's heart was the knowledge that it was to Betty Ian Mackenzie had chosen to write, and not to himself.

15

'It's a miracle,' said Abram simply.

He was speaking of the Russian Revolution.

'God has rescued his people from their worst oppressor since Pharoah.'

In March 1917 no one from Brownlow Road to Upper Parliament Street wanted to talk about anything else but Russia. God's hand was plain. The long night of the Russian Jew was ending. That Grand Duke Nicholas who had carried out deportations of Jews in the war zone with such unspeakable cruelty was now himself arrested and deported.

'Who shall say now that wonders and miracles do not happen in our days?' demanded Abram.

Those who had turned to revolt in Petrograd spoke friendly words, not only of liberty but of equality. There was to be no more anti-semitism in Russia.

'You see how God looks after us,' demanded Abram. 'Supposing now Russia had been our enemy and not our friend. Then our loyalty to this new democratic state in Russia would have brought trouble on us here in England.'

'You don't get out much,' said Benjy.

It wasn't that he doubted the miraculous and prophetic truth of what Abram had said, but the mood about the Jewish area of Liverpool had blackened since the drowning of Lord Kitchener. It was not only *The National Review* that laid his death at the hands of the 'international Jews'. The choice that Russian-born Jews retained – to enlist in the British Army or be returned to Russia – had a bitter taste to it.

'Lenin,' said Abram seriously, 'is probably a Jew. He believes in peace. And his mother is a Goldberg.'

'Who knows that?' Len said impatiently. 'Uncle, who puts that about? Those who are already afraid the new government will take Russia out of the war and worse.'

'I'm altogether loyal to this country!' said Abram rather crossly. 'It's a decent country. A good country.'

'Like Sunlight soap,' Len teased him wickedly. 'Britain went to war with clean hands, I suppose.'

As the date of Harry's call-up approached, Rasil became tetchy with everyone. When Benjy and Len came in late one night and stole a leg of chicken from the pantry, she ran down the stairs with a mop ready to beat them black and blue; and although the boys held up their arms to defend themselves against her blows, enough reached through to them to have Benjy calling out.

'Give up, Ma. I'll get you another fowl tomorrow.'

'It's always tomorrow with you,' she muttered.

Sarah, who had to face Rasil's black-eyed fury every morning, was more resentful.

Harry's gingery moustache outlined his well-shaped mouth, and he had strong, even teeth. But there was something readily startled in his face. Something that perplexed Rasil whenever she watched his sensitive eyes flinch at unexpected criticism. He was the only one of Abram's sons who went regularly to the synagogue alongside his father: he read pleasantly and easily from the scrolls, and was often given a portion of the law to read on Saturdays.

Benjy kept the rules well enough when his father could see him; but he had none of his brother's new-found piety. And he couldn't understand why Harry took no interest in girls. It wasn't natural for a man to moon about his mother's house in the evenings. Rasil had stopped urging Harry towards early marriage, since the 1916 Act made married men as vulnerable as boys. All Harry could do was wait to be fetched, as he surely would be in September. And meanwhile Rasil liked to have him in the house in the evenings. If she could have fought the army, and its murderous claims, she would have boarded up the house and done so. It was because there was no hope of that, and nowhere to run, and no chance of defending him, that she had become so evil-tempered.

Even Abram felt the back of her hand when he tried to

press for his love at bedtime.

It was in June of the same year that Abram's eldest brother remarried suddenly, and decided to uproot himself from the family and go to live in Leeds. The Katz family accepted the decision. It was his new wife's doing, of course; everyone knew that she thought Benjy and Len had far too much say in the running of the business. She often muttered about it.

It was Abram who was most affected by the separation. He was still grateful to his older brothers for many years' shelter while they were still in Russia; he remembered how he had been put through his training at a *yeshiva* while this same man worked on the sawmills. So it saddened him.

And it was difficult to settle how much money the business could put together to help with the move.

'Let *her* family help,' said Rasil, with uncharacteristic sharpness.

Those who married into the Katz family usually learned where they stood at times of difficulty; it was generally agreed that the new in-laws were less helpful than they should be. But at length Benjy saw his uncle well provided for.

No one was surprised to hear, however, only a fortnight after his arrival in Leeds, that the effort to find premises had gone badly. His uncle's wife's family needed most of what Benjy had given him. And there wasn't enough left over to buy tools, still less to set up in the rag trade as his wife had planned.

'What can you expect?' said Abram, simply.

It was always so with those who chose not to stick with the Katz family ark, he implied; and men said Leeds was a difficult town. Equally, there was nothing the Katz family could do but respond to the cry for help. The only question was how to send it. Harry wasn't used to travelling about the country as his brother was, still less to carrying rolls of money; but Benjy couldn't be spared that week, and Harry was willing to go.

'Is that wise, Abram?' demanded Rasil.

'If a man is old enough to go into the army,' shrugged Abram.

And he put on his *tefillin* and would discuss the matter no

108

further. He was angry, because he knew she was worried about Harry's coming call-up; and was still punishing him for it.

It was a hot, sweating journey, and a long one. When Harry arrived in the town he went into a pub for a drink, and was at once aware that something unusual was happening. A number of other men were sitting about with red flags draped and propped everywhere.

"Who are *they*?' Harry asked the man behind the bar, who had a small, rat face and a pronounced (Harry suspected artificial) limp. The man looked nervous and lowered his voice.

'ILP,' he said.

'What?'

'Independent Labour Party,' muttered the bartender.

He could see the bartender taking in his own dark eyes, and placing him.

'Russkie, are you?' he asked.

Harry couldn't understand his jumpiness.

'Not me, mate!' he said. 'Anyway, you don't have to worry about revolution here.'

'And why not?' asked a large, evidently Clydeside, worker from Harry's side of the bar.

Harry smiled nervously, and raised his beer in salutation. 'You got a meeting here, I see,' he said. 'Supporting Petrograd workers, right? Well, I'm all for that.'

'I'm a union man, and I'm here to speak for *our* problems. What we want to know is who's going to compensate the families of my members, if the Germans aren't made to pay for this bloody war.'

'I see,' said Harry.

'Well?'

'The British shipowners?' suggested Harry tentatively.

At that the Clydesider clapped him on the shoulder companionably.

'Scouse, are you?' he asked. 'Right! That's bloody right. But only if we *make* 'em, eh? What you drinking?'

Harry accepted the beer thoughtfully.

109

'What we need is a British Soviet,' said his new-found friend. 'Here. And today is going to take us one step in that direction.'

A number of other representatives or flagbearers had by now joined Harry at the bar. They all agreed with this noisily. Harry decided that most of them had passed over the crucial line between euphoric enthusiasm and coherence some time earlier, but he bought his new-found friend a drink in return all the same.

'See you at the meeting,' he called on leaving, with no intention of keeping any such rendezvous.

But as he walked the streets, guided by a note of his uncle's address, he began to see it would be difficult to avoid it. There were policemen everywhere, some on horseback. Elsewhere bands of men were marching confidently towards the square under banners such as 'Gas Fitters' or 'Dockers'. There were also, he saw, large numbers of the young Jewish population of Leeds, much of his own age, also marching towards the meeting.

Harry found his uncle, in his one-up one-down terrace, as alarmed in his own way as the bartender.

'Aren't you pleased by what's happening in Russia, then?' asked Harry, perplexed.

His uncle said gloomily, 'Russia is Russia. I believe in the British constitution.'

Harry found his uncle's new situation an awkward one. He gathered that business in Leeds was not good; in Leeds you had to be in textiles, and his uncle was generally downcast at the prospect. Meanwhile his uncle's wife had made a great deal of food which Harry ate in a preoccupied fashion; and his uncle spoke of other unhappiness.

'When a wife dies, Harry,' he sighed, 'you can't imagine. Only you shouldn't even know how it feels. However good my Becky is.'

And Becky did indeed seem to be good, clucking over the food Harry didn't eat, and dealing kindly with her husband's misery.

'So you can't find any help here?' said Harry at last.

'It's natural, when I'm no help to anyone,' said his uncle.

At that moment there was the unmistakable sound of shattering glass.

Both Harry's uncle and his new aunt went pale. Harry said quickly, 'Get back from the windows. Get in the kitchen. I'll see how many people are in the street.'

Then he rushed up the stairs himself.

An astonishing sight met his eyes. The piece of waste land he had walked over earlier was filled with about a thousand youths. None of them looked like the huge gas fitters or dockers he had seen earlier. They were younger and paler, and carried no banners. And they were solemnly smashing in one shop window after another along the row of pre-dominantly Jewish shops. Whoever they might be for, it was absolutely clear who they felt they were *against*.

His uncle joined him at the window, shaking with terror. 'Listen to that.'

Glass shattered in a baker's shop facing them. The chanting became audible.

'Russian Jews don't fight. Jews eat and don't fight.'

Tears began to run down his uncle's face, and he sat down.

'Look,' he said. 'Mrs Hirschel. Her son was killed last week. There's a card in the window.'

'The bastards.'

To Harry's terror a small rosy-cheeked woman, a little overweight, had come out to reason with the mob. She was not immediately attacked but Harry knew with absolute certainty she would be. He looked on with amazement. There were lots of people simply walking about their own business, not interfering; ordinary Leeds citizens. Would they protect her? Harry rather thought not.

His mother's face came vividly before him, superimposed upon the brave, lone woman below him, bringing an unwanted, weakening moisture to his eyes. Was he to be feeble for ever? And yet he knew he could not try to force his way through the crowd. With sudden resolution he deter-mined to find his own way round the cut at the back, and stand at her side.

It was dark, and his hands were wet as he climbed over a garden shed. His nerves were twitching and his limbs trembling; the cries of the hostile crowd, the heavy June air, and his own fear, brought the sweat to his face and body. And just as he came out in front of the mob, one of the ringleaders lifted a heavy stick and felled Mrs Hirschel with a blow.

Harry cried out in sick horror, 'What are you doing? Is this the worker's Soviet? Or *what* is it? Is this going to help the people of Leeds. Beating women?'

Benjy would have punched the man, thought Harry miserably, as at last a few policemen came on the scene. And indeed the crowd, hearing the horses and seeing the blue uniforms, had begun to scatter and to regroup at the far side of the waste land.

Harry saw the man who had struck Mrs Hirschel was also moving off, and the injustice of it suddenly made him seize the man by the arm.

'Here,' he said to the policeman. 'This is the man. I saw everything.'

'Did you now,' said the policeman, taking in his age and his sensitive eyes, and not much impressed with either.

Harry felt humiliated. He could feel the laughter rise around him more strongly than his own danger. For almost the first time in his life he wasn't afraid at all. He was angry.

'I saw it all.'

'You? Who's going to believe you? Scouse git. And a Yid too, I should think,' taunted his victim. Harry still had him by the arms.

'Will you take him into custody?' he asked. 'There are hundreds of witnesses.'

'Not unbiased, though,' said the policeman glancing, in a not altogether friendly manner, at the group of ageing Jews who had begun to come out of their houses.

Harry was incredulous. 'This man hit a woman old enough to be his mother, and you tell me you aren't going to take him *in*?'

'The ringleaders, that's what we want,' said the policeman. 'The Bolsheviks.'

And he began to move off. Which was when another member of the mob, who had slipped round the back to free his friend, gave Harry a blow on the back of the head.

The policeman watched him fall indifferently, and made no move to arrest the man Harry had been holding. The whole crowd buzzed for a moment; but no one interfered.

That night neither the police nor the uncommitted citizens of Leeds had the courage to do anything against the looters who took everything they could reach out of the broken windows.

And Rasil didn't have to worry about the dangers of the Western Front for Harry, that year or any year. He spent the rest of 1917 in hospital with a fractured skull.

Even Abram did not dare claim it as God's mercy.

16

Groot had come to take a meal with the Gordon family, because he was worried about his daughter's health. But quite soon he and Solomon were discussing politics.

'They'll take Russia out of the war, of course,' said Solomon.

He was holding a glass of brandy in cupped hands, savouring its warm breath. An unusual luxury, to mark an unusual visit.

'Red flags, red ties,' grumbled the other, whose face had got slightly purpler over the war years. 'What do you think of that vicar of Altrincham, chairing a big meeting in Manchester to welcome the Revolution? Do you think that is how pulpits should be used?'

'Nothing wrong with peace,' said Solomon. 'If that's the result.'

'You're thinking of Francis, I know, I know. These are cruel times. But *if* Russia goes out of the war,' began Groot.

'Exactly,' said Solomon. 'It'll take more than Clara Butt singing "Give Us Peace in Our Time" at the Albert Hall.'

'How do you feel yourself? How does Francis feel? He's a young man with sense.'

'Well, his cousin Alexander and one or two officer friends on leave went to the big open-air demonstration in Liverpool. Both of them call themselves Socialists, and this young man Ian Mackenzie is quite a fanatic, I believe.'

'You don't mean that rich young man Elsa was describing to *me*? I do believe they are the very worst,' declared Groot.

'Francis tells me it is an honourable tradition. Science, Cambridge and Socialism,' said Solomon mildly. 'The whole family share the belief.'

'It's a very great pity that the German Peace Note in 1916 was couched so aggressively. We might all be out of it by now. With some dignity.'

'Are you afraid then of some kind of Petrograd here?' asked Solomon.

'Is it impossible?'

'I think it unlikely,' said Solomon.

'Remember Leeds,' insisted Groot. 'These people have as little respect for the British constitution as Russians had for the Romanovs.'

'Do you think the Russian-born will now be anxious to return home?'

'Perhaps.'

'I should not be tempted,' said Solomon. 'I have very little faith in the forms of government. The Russians will remain Russians, and the English have calmer temperaments.'

'You are not always right, you know, dear son-in-law,' said Groot.

'I may not be right about the English,' said Solomon. 'But I would not put a *kopeck*, let alone the future of anyone I loved, in the hands of Russians.'

'We have to do something, or the island will starve to death.'

'I should say there were more people starving in England before the war than there are now,' said Solomon drily. 'I'm not so dismayed as you are to go short of white bread.'

In another room the Gordon children were discussing

114

Francis's decision to enter for a Cambridge scholarship with Alexander, who teased even while he encouraged him.

He said, 'You are wondering if they'll let you in, really. Otherwise you'd not even hesitate.'

'Of course,' said Francis coolly. '*You* only want to be part of the glorious pro-le-tariat.'

But even as he smiled, he couldn't help taking in, with a certain envy, his cousin's physical ease. It was such a truly English asset. He was an upright, woolly-sweatered sportsman. He had a healthy no-nonsense tan, and an outdoor face.

Whereas I, thought Francis crossly, am a *night* person. Sports bored him. The only physical accomplishment he had was itself a little *foreign* and suspicious. Alone among his age-group he could dance well, and not just *well*, but inventively. Ian's sister liked dancing, he said. But then she was a woman, and none of Ian's other friends did it. They stumbled around and giggled most of the time, and Ian had once said the tango was for Italians.

My goodness, it would have done him more good to have less sway in his hips and a better golfing stance, thought Francis. And he didn't really like animals.

'What about poetry?' he asked loftily. 'Do the proletariat have any time for that?'

'They do in Russia,' said Alexander.

Solomon came in just in time to catch the last remark, and raised his eyebrows. He could hardly recognize the country his nephew described with such enthusiasm as the peasant Russia he had known all his childhood.

Abram had begun to suspect that God's hand might be less involved in Russian affairs than he had hoped. Where then should his people look for help? As the weeks rolled on after Harry's injury, he became more and more convinced that the answer was quite simply Palestine.

And by August he was saying, 'We were misled. They told us that the Russian Jews are free and will need no place of refuge. It isn't true.'

'But Palestine,' argued Len. 'It's bare rock and sand, Uncle.'

'I have been a farmer,' argued Abram.

'Oh yes, a fine farmer you were,' shouted Rasil from the kitchen. 'I remember. You yoked a young horse with an old one once and broke the plough.'

'I have worked on the land. Land is good,' said Abram with dignity. 'Even harsh land. And our own land.'

Benjy said, 'We don't yet *have* land of our own.'

'Wait,' nodded Abram.

'If it lies in the hands of English Jews, we shall never get it,' said Len.

There was a pause while Abram thought about what Len had said.

'Assimilated *mamserim*,' he nodded.

'They're looking after themselves, that's all. Edwin Montague wants to stay in the Cabinet,' said Len.

Benjy frowned in concentration.

'But what are they *against*?' he asked abruptly.

'Look, they're *nationalized*, *naturalized* or whatever. Aren't they? They don't want to be bloody foreigners again.'

For once, Len's pessimism was confounded. Against all rational expectation the British government declared itself in favour of a homeland for the Jewish people. And the November declaration brought tears to Abram's eyes; the rest of the neighbourhood were out on the streets singing and blessing the name of Balfour. Everyone felt the elation. It was as if three murderous years were, for a day at least, redeemed with a sense of purpose.

'So why are you crying, Abram?' asked Rasil.

'To be alive in such times,' he murmured. 'To see the dawn of such hopes.'

Meanwhile the war looked as if it would continue for ever.

'I'd better hit you over the head, too, Benjy,' suggested Len. 'They'll be fetching you next.'

'Be quiet, loud-mouth,' said Rasil.

Winter came, and heavy fog hung over the city from the docks to Lime Street Station, a deep yellow fog which made it impossible to make out the lively young girls on Bold Street, or find your way home from the Rialto. No New Year had ever found the Katz family in worse heart; and though Abram barely acknowledged the English change of year, he shook his head over the opening of 1918.

A list of decorations was published in the January newspapers.

'A buggered kneecap,' said Len, 'comes out about the same as having a few soldiers out to tea. No, I'm daft. Your country *expects* you to die for Ypres. But the rest is beyond the call, isn't it?'

The Katz family were not very interested in the lists, but Len followed them eagerly.

'Working late on HMSO accounts,' he noted when the second one was published. 'There's a good one. And supplying iodine capsules. I like that.'

He began to hum:

> 'She said "Dear me" and "Oh I see",
> And she (thank God) is an OBE.'

'Only don't use the holy name,' remonstrated Abram. 'You are alive. Be grateful.'

'And who will my daughter look to for a husband?' demanded Rasil, not for the first time.

'Sarah is young,' said Abram hopefully.

'Not so young. At her age I already had two children.'

'They were different days, Ma,' said Benjy.

She looked at him sullenly.

There was queuing outside the butcher's, and even Rasil couldn't bully the grocer into giving her the flour and margarine she needed.

'Try the Adelphi,' suggested Len, wickedly.

Hotels still added whipped cream to their soup and had no problems with bread. Meanwhile, there were queues in the snow for horseflesh; and people who hoarded food were fined. Rasil's store of sugar and rice had been used up long ago. In that winter the Katz family would have managed badly without Len, who always knew where to collect a good supply of tinned food.

117

'Found it on the seashore, Auntie,' he always said.

He would take no money for it.

'Maybe it is even true?' Abram wondered.

If the U-boats were sinking English ships, it seemed natural enough for the goods to be cast up on the sands eventually. And certainly the tins had all the appearance of sea-corruption. The labels had been washed off; and no one could tell what was in a tin until it was open. Abram declared fruit, baked beans and tinned anchovies were kosher; and argued for a long time about pink fish with a visible backbone which might not be salmon.

There was general agreement among the citizens of Liverpool that rust was safe enough, but squeaks of air from the tins were dangerous.

The year wore on, and no one expected the war to be won, any more.

Or even end.

As it suddenly did in November.

17

'You're a very good sister, Miss Gordon,' said Matron. 'And what are you planning to do now this terrible war is over?'

The matron's face had a habitual severity of appearance which sprang not so much from her nature as from a dryness in her skin that had brought premature wrinkles to her pursed lips. Her eyes were kindly bent upon Dorothy, however.

Dorothy was pleased but not flattered, since she had always understood exactly what made her advancement from nurse to sister so rapid. It was not a question of intelligence so much as a habit of *bothering*, a precision which came from her training and not from a warmth of heart. Four years of war had left little ordinary warmth in her; and she had only an incredulous admiration for the Mary Ellens and Rosies, so often in trouble for small mistakes, who went on nevertheless with the help of their good, caring hearts. But Dorothy knew it wasn't a good, caring heart that Matron was praising either; any more than she would have wanted to see such a soft and vulnerable organ lying uselessly and untidily about in the ward. It was blind, steadfast organization that made Dorothy invaluable, and she knew that. What she didn't yet know was how to make the same quality useful in a civilian world.

Matron had taken the decision to expect nothing more than a lifetime's discipline of service a long time ago. She did not recognize it in Dorothy's fresh cheeks and glowing hair. And her fine eyebrows shot up in surprise when Dorothy replied, 'I can tell you what I *want* to do. I want to train as a doctor.'

'But my dear.'

'I know it will be a great expense,' said Dorothy.

'But surely there will be some young man?' The matron had no wish to probe. She supposed that, like so many others, Dorothy must have lost the man she loved in the great slaughter that had now ended. Yet Dorothy was not defeated in appearance; and Matron was sure there would be other opportunities.

Dorothy understood her mistake, and allowed it to continue. It was easier than trying to explain how deeply she herself rejected all those possibilities. She felt as though she had already channelled all of her female energy into a single, narrow course. Though she knew the problems; and she could see that to be as dependable as steel would have less value in a world rapidly getting back to normal.

'I have no intention of marrying now,' she said abruptly.

The matron nodded, her tight lips relaxing a little in some kind of remembered tenderness.

'If I were your mother,' she said gently, 'I would want you home again now. You're very young.'

Dorothy felt a twinge of pain rising, as if from the same source, as if the unexpected softness in the matron's voice could call up her memory of Elsa's last letter.

Her mother had written:

Francis is already in uniform, so you can imagine with what rejoicing all of us thank God for the end of this terrible war. And surely now you will come home and we will all be a family again? Sometimes I am so horribly afraid that I really have lost you for ever, my darling girl.

I hope and pray if you come back now your father will put all his awkward ways on one side, and everything could be as it was. But you know how stubborn he can be. And I don't want to blackmail you with my own health, but I don't need to tell you that all this year I have been weaker than I like.

Please, Dorothy, don't leave it too long.

Elsa's soft, pleading voice mingled with the unexpected warmth and friendship in the matron, and came close to weakening Dorothy's resolve, so that she spoke more pertly than she intended.

'My brother Francis is to go up to Cambridge now. I see no reason why I may not hope to have ambitions, simply because I am a girl.'

'But there must be children,' said the matron, humbly enough. 'Children, after so much dying.'

'I shall help them to be born, then,' said Dorothy quickly.

Children. And that was another thing she'd learned. From Mary Ellen who'd leant once too often against the wall with a lovely lieutenant and found herself three months gone and no idea what to do about it.

'Is it ever worth it, Dorrie?' she groaned. 'And what will I ever tell me Mam?'

'Are you going to have it?' said Dorothy, rather surprised.

'Is there anything else I can do? Dorrie. Can you help?'

Dorothy said, 'I've never had the experience.'

But she was to know more, and soon; because of course Mary Ellen went elsewhere for help. And the help made her so ill that Dorothy came off duty one night and found her lying in a pool of blood on the carpet in her bedroom.

'Christ,' Dorothy said.

'I'm dying, Dorothy.'

'No, you're not,' said Dorothy energetically. 'What foolish things have you done to yourself and how?'

But she knew, really, that the baby was gone. And Mary Ellen began to snivel and panic; and Dorothy cursed all men and the silliness of all women.

'I'll pack your womb,' she said quickly. 'Listen. That'll be right. Lie still. Gauze, I need. Stay quiet, you idiot. It'll stop if we pack you tight.'

'God won't let me live. I'm a murderer,' said Mary Ellen. 'Will you give me the cross from my bag. I'm dying.'

'No, I won't. And you're not,' said Dorothy. 'Open your legs. Now for God's *sake* breathe on this, or I'll never get a finger into you. Have you no *sense* at all of what has to be done?'

The ether over Mary Ellen's mouth stopped her thrashing around but it didn't stop her voice, or her dreams, or her praying.

Systematically and coldly Dorothy tamped the womb. She would live, all right. The danger was infection, of course; but Mary Ellen would be used to that.

The morality of it all was bewildering.

'You soft thing,' she muttered when the job was done, and Mary Ellen was moaning safely on the carpet.

Dorothy put a pillow under the girl's head, and covered her with all her own bedclothes. Then she put the only remaining coal on the fire, and sat up shivering in her coat.

However could Mary Ellen imagine that one little death mattered to God? What? After all those young boys dying. In the cold hours of the morning she said viciously, 'Why ever didn't you have it, then?'

She also felt there was something horribly wrong with the destruction of life inside your own body. 'I would have had it, blast her.'

But then, she was free to do what she liked. She had no chances to ruin.

Now she said stubbornly to the matron, 'I don't want to have children of my own.'

It was only half the story. Children, yes, she did want children. But she wanted no man to go along with them, bossing her around.

'My dear, you don't *have* to be a doctor to help other women to have children,' Matron said wanly.

She had altogether misunderstood Dorothy's thoughts, and imagined she was afraid of childbirth.

'It's what I want,' said Dorothy doggedly.

She had written back to Elsa's tender letter with a most careful piece of pleading. There was a Groot dowry. She was sure of it. And it wasn't going to be necessary for Dorothy, since she was determined not to marry. Surely it was only equitable that the trust should be opened for medical training, even if Solomon was adamantly turned against her. Surely it was only right that she should have what Elsa's family had intended for her?

The week of waiting after that eager missive had gone off brought an unexpected answer; a curt little note from Solomon explaining that her mother was ill in bed. With a nasty clutch of fear round the muscles of her heart, Dorothy decided that Elsa must be ill indeed for Solomon to be writing even so much to his errant daughter. He did not ask her to come home. He did not mention her proposal about the trust fund. The whole issue had become of secondary importance. Her mother must be very ill, thought Dorothy, if she could no longer prevent post falling into Solomon's hands. She could not imagine her large-breasted, hopeful mother no longer caring what happened to her children.

But Dorothy did not go back home, as Solomon expected. Instead, early in 1919 she applied for a post as sister in a maternity hospital in the south of France.

October 1920

18

In late October 1920 Francis was surprised by his cousin Alexander and Ian Mackenzie in Ogden's bookshop in Bridge Street.

'Secretive little sod,' shouted his cousin, delightedly.

'You've been hiding,' said Ian.

'Not exactly hiding,' said Francis.

But certainly he was not yet ready to see them.

He felt like a mole, trying to understand an environment he perhaps would never learn to see in sharply, still blinking in Cambridge and its autumnal radiance. He was bemused by the glow of the browning hops that framed his lodging-house window, and the dried leaves in the grass of Jesus Green. Even the barest branches of the willows were golden. The air itself was yellow, he thought; there was nothing harsh in it; and its benevolent, milky warmth had altogether transmuted the phlegm of his ordinary responses.

As a result, his supervisor had been a little testy with him that morning; it was not thought precise to read poems with such woozy pleasure.

I shall have to fight it all off, thought Francis, if I am to come to terms with this city. This is a Victorian city, built on reason. A rational town, dedicated to the conquest of vagueness in all its forms. He was not here to enjoy the magic of words, but to subdue them into critical harness, just as he had learned to control every feeling. He must learn to write as cleanly as if he, too, were part of that Department of Natural Sciences which already understood its primacy here. All the gods had gone from the city, for all the spires, and all the radiance; and now it belonged to the powers of human thought. And Francis envied his cousin Alexander and Ian Mackenzie for their understanding of that world of experi-

125

ment and analysis.

Nothing in his winter tour of Europe's museums had prepared him for this golden light. The streets of Vienna had been flooded with rain; and Paris had been still sullen with war. It had all been too soon. But worst of all was the way the trip had riven a new line between him and the other two.

The other two had been in the war in any case, and he had not. They had both been accepted by King's College, and Francis had only just slipped into Jesus, on a last-minute telegram. But that wasn't the most serious part of it.

'What have you got there?' asked Ian, looking at the cover of the book Francis had been turning over.

Francis found himself flushing. It was a copy of White-head's *Science in the Modern World*; and some part of his shyness focused itself at once on the pages under his hand.

Alexander laughed. 'Might have guessed.'

'Bernal says,' began Ian.

And in no time at all they were off in a discussion of men he did not know, and ideas to which he had no access. I am living, he thought, in the heroic age of physics and chemistry.

'Come to tea, Francis,' said Alexander suddenly.

Francis hesitated for one moment before he could take himself firmly in hand.

'Of course,' he said then. 'I'll make a note of your address.'

When Francis appeared on the following Sunday, he found Alexander and his friends had just returned from cycling to Ely, and were lying about the room in attitudes of mock exhaustion. By the gas fire someone was toasting muffins. The room was buzzing with noise.

Francis felt isolated in a number of ways; for one thing, he guessed that most of the undergraduates in the room were older, and had been in the war. Their ease came from long acquaintance, he sensed, from which he was excluded.

'It's Cousin Francis,' cried Alexander suddenly, levering himself off the floor with a comic groan.

Alexander's eyes were still green and cat-shaped, and his even mouth still ready to break into laughter easily; but his voice had a new carelessness which Francis took to be studied.

'There was going to be champagne,' said Alexander. 'And

smoked salmon in neat brown rolls from the kitchens. But they talked me out of it. They're all Marxist, this lot.'

A burst of laughter greeted this sally; and Alexander took a green handkerchief from his pocket and sneezed once or twice.

Francis looked around the young men on the floor, and thought they might be Marxist, but they didn't look very opposed to personal extravagance. Winchester, Eton, and Oundle, he'd have said; and rather nervous they made him. There had been stories of young rugger toughs breaking into the rooms of those they disliked as swots, and throwing them into the Cam. The casual clothes and easy, sprawling limbs of these young men made Francis conscious of the formality of his own dress.

He made a mental note to correct it.

'Oh dear,' said Alexander, laughing, and tucking his handkerchief away. 'All this exercise is supposed to make you healthy, but I don't know.'

He looked well enough, Francis thought.

The man at the gas fire looked across at them, and smiled at Alexander. 'Aren't you going to give me a hand buttering these damn muffins?'

Francis saw the speaker was a weary-looking thirty-year-old, with a fair, Slav face and sandy colouring. There were laughter wrinkles round his eyes.

As Alexander turned towards the voice at once the thought crossed Francis's mind that there was something unusually close in their relationship. Nothing erotic, perhaps; but an enviable closeness. Francis endured a pang of loneliness before he found a cushion, and there he sat primly, eating the muffin so that no butter dribbled down his shirt front. Outside the window, the light was almost gone from the sky.

He was joined on the floor almost at once, to his surprise and relief, by Ian Mackenzie, who pointed to the man at the gas fire and said, 'You know who that is, of course?'

'No,' admitted Francis.

'Most brilliant mind of his generation,' said Ian, telling him. 'Don't you admire his work?'

'I never mastered the maths,' admitted Francis.

'But the concepts. Don't you find them exciting?'

127

'How can I tell when I don't understand his diagrams? Do you?'

'Francis, *don't* be unkind,' said Ian.

Francis absorbed the possibility of shyness other than his own, and was almost at once cured of his own unease. Looking around the room, he now saw variations in what had seemed a homogeneous group. Youngsters with pink cheeks; some silent, some giggly. Francis's belief in his own worth hardened.

"It's awful here, isn't it?' said Ian. 'I just feel battered. If you say a rough word, I'll collapse like a Roman ruin.'

'Do you feel old age approaching so fast, then?' asked Francis.

'Well, I'm twenty-two,' said Ian. 'It's a serious age.'

Francis laughed at him.

'We're just growing up,' said Francis.

'But I shan't grow up like Alexander, will I?' said Ian.

'Do you want to?'

'Well, he has some kind of *place* here.'

The thought astonished Francis.

'For myself, I don't know,' continued Ian. 'I do bits and pieces. I'm not sure I have the discipline to put in ten years' hard slog at anything. Which is what you need in our game. To do anything important, I mean. Alexander knows how. You all do, probably.'

'*All?*' Francis wondered what group he was being placed among.

'Your family. The Gordons.'

'I see.'

'That's Haldane,' said Ian, pointing to another figure.

Francis let him explain. He was a family friend, it appeared.

'I'm afraid we don't really have that kind of glamour in the Modern Languages faculty yet,' said Francis.

He watched his cousin with a new interest. What he had always seen as malice on his face he now recognized as suppressed energy; his face was alight with it. Francis thought: He's like a motor finally engaging as it should.

*

Francis stayed longer than he intended at the tea party; so late that he missed Hall, and found himself writing his weekly essay well into the night. It was the first time he had done so; but once he had subdued his initial shame at getting behind, he found himself intoxicated with an unexpected sense of power. He read his thoughts out with more confidence than usual in the morning, and his tutor praised him.

To celebrate, Francis bought himself some tangerines and nuts from a market stall; and determined to go to Rivers' lecture on psychology. There had to be something afoot in his own world that compared to the excitement he had glimpsed at his cousin's party.

That evening, however, he had an unexpected visitor. It was Ian, who had cycled round in great agitation because Alexander had begun to do more than sneeze, and had been taken off to the College sick bay.

'Supposing it's influenza?' demanded Ian. 'What can we do?'

Influenza was the last of God's four horses of destruction, and there was nothing anyone could do about it; the very word brought prickles of dread to Francis's neck.

'The worst of the epidemic is over,' he pointed out.

'Francis, he's very sick.'

'I'm sorry,' said Matron impatiently to Ian. 'We aren't letting anyone see him.'

'He's family,' insisted Ian.

She looked at Francis dubiously.

'Cousins,' said Francis.

'His fever is too high. He won't recognize you.'

'Can't we just see him?'

'He looks awful,' she said, with brutal honesty.

It was no more than the truth. Alexander's face seemed to have swollen up; he thrashed about as if he were in pain and he cried out words that no one could understand, ones of horror certainly.

'He's in the trenches,' said Ian.

129

His face was ashen.

'Oh God,' said Francis.

Ian's face was pale and inscrutable as they left the sick room together, and then he said abruptly, 'Let's walk.'

Francis had been intending to spend the rest of the afternoon in the University Library, but the plan suddenly looked callous in the light of Alexander's condition. At the same time, Francis recognized that he would have had no hesitation in working on, callous or not, if it hadn't been for the presence of this fair young man at his side.

'All right,' he agreed.

With unusual passivity he let Ian choose the direction of their steps and the pace of their conversation. Indeed, they walked in silence down Silver Street towards Newnham, as if neither of them had any thoughts to share. The weir by Foster's Mill had a desolate sound, and the light was going. The Backs opened to their left in shadowy blackness, only faintly lit by gas.

'*Hell*,' said Ian, pausing.

'Do you think he's dangerously ill?' risked Francis.

'Of course he is,' said Ian impatiently.

Francis's face lengthened appropriately, though he could not help feeling that Ian was too much touched with the melodrama of the situation; that he was allowing himself to enjoy the horror. He was almost tempted to say as much, when Ian suddenly burst out, 'I can't get used to it.'

'What?'

'The stupidity of it all.'

Francis was ready to agree to that. They turned away from the Backs and began to walk towards the mill pond and the Darwins' house. A baker's cart came clopping slowly by in the deepening gloom, and at last Francis began to feel he was entitled to ask, 'Where are we walking?'

'The fen. I want to see a few cows. Get out of this town light. Helps me think,' said Ian.

Francis was too astonished to reply, and they began to cross Lammas Land, which was muddy and ruined Francis's shoes. Ian seemed indifferent to what was happening to his clothes. The river could just be heard now as a low murmur.

'No, really,' said·Francis, pausing. 'He'll be all right, Ian. I'm sure he will. That matron said nothing to suggest he's going to *die*, or anything. Did she?'

The word hung between them.

Ian went on walking as if he had heard nothing; and after checking a moment more, Francis followed him.

'You must write and tell Betty,' Ian said presently.

'Why?' asked Francis.

He was a little puffed because Ian's strides were wider than his own, or he would not have spoken so sharply.

'If you really don't know, I will,' said Ian.

He seemed preoccupied.

Francis saw they were now walking along among black, stolid cows. A few horses grazing freely on the commonland lifted their heads as they approached. Somewhat to his relief Ian was too deeply turned inward to witness Francis's mild anxiety; but he was glad when he reached the towpath.

'There,' said Ian.

The walk seemed to have helped him. At any rate, he held out his hand and said to Francis, 'I'll see you tomorrow, then.'

'Well, tomorrow,' said Francis confusedly.

Was it really necessary, he wondered, to devote his entire energies to a bedside vigil? For how long? It was all right for Ian Mackenzie, he thought crossly. He could *slide* through his course, take a degree, and no one would ever, ever ask what class it was. Probably he didn't even need a degree; he had so many friends in laboratories already. Whereas for Francis this chance was the only one he was likely to get.

Ian misunderstood.

'If anything happens in the night, I've arranged to be told,' he said firmly.

For a moment Francis felt a genuine clutch of fear. But it wore off as he turned back again up King's Parade. It might have something to do with the war, he decided. The whole generation was infected with the same hunger for disaster. It was like the ripple of excitement as people took in the news from Russia. Famine, war, and death. Always death. It was inexcusable in a sober man like Ian.

The next day he looked into the College sick bay just the

same. He heard that Alexander's temperature was down a point, and that his limbs were more tranquil. There, Francis told himself; and went off to a lecture on Greek prosody, which was not even part of his tripos.

He gave hospital visiting a miss for the next couple of days, and worked at Early French.

Alexander was unconscious for a week, in which the weather changed from autumn to winter. All the October gold vanished. Bare, black boughs stood out all over Cambridge; and on Friday snow began to swirl down over Jesus Green in ferocious whirlpools, sticking in the crotched branches of the crabby cherry trees, and turning the landscape into an etching. Across the new whiteness, men walked like black matchsticks. Francis looked out over the frozen soil and thought how strangely unimportant everyone looked; and how each had only one life, to which he was passionately attached. It didn't seem fair that the whole of the human spirit and even the strongest aspiration should depend on nothing solider than four black sticks. He said something along those lines to Ian when he reached the College sick bay.

Ian shook his head; but whether in denial, or amazement at Francis's innocence, was not clear.

Alexander had died that afternoon.

Betty looked at Ian's handwriting with some surprise. What could he want? She felt a peculiar reluctance to open the letter, which she could not explain. And from the far end of the table, where Elsa was reading a letter from Francis, came a little cry.

Betty looked up, short-sightedly. She could not make out the expression on her mother's face. Really, my eyesight is getting to be impossible, she thought, inserting a knife blade into her own envelope, before setting her spectacles delicately on her nose.

At first she could not make out a word of it.

Someone was dead, and Ian was incoherent with grief, and so was Francis, so it couldn't be him.

Then Betty understood everything, and it seemed as if her own life came to an end.

She did not faint.

She did not take off her spectacles.

She felt as if she would never bother to take off her spectacles for daily wear again.

19

Francis wished he could identify any of the other visitors to Castle Glen. All Ian had said was, 'Don't worry, Jimmy will bring you up here in the car.' But how to identify Jimmy? There was also the question of how Jimmy would recognize him. Had he been told, for instance, to look out for a thin, slightly too well-dressed young friend of mine, decent enough? Surely no one spoke like that to servants, Francis thought nervously. At the same time, he wondered how he could have been so *mindlessly* careless, not even to ask what kind of things to wear.

In the event the problem solved itself, because, as he was letting a porter help him off with his heavy leather case, he caught sight of someone else from Jesus who at once said, 'Isn't Ian an idiot. How on earth are we supposed to find his man?'

'I expect we'll just stand about,' said Francis, his spirits rising abruptly at the discovery that his problem was both impersonal and reasonable.

And it was easy. Jimmy spotted them and quite soon they were piled into a warm, heavily upholstered Daimler and covered with thick blankets.

'It's about an hour,' said Jimmy, and went round to the front.

Francis peered out at Scotland, but could see very little except for rain and mist.

*

Francis's heart began to bang as they drove up the long drive, across a bridged river in spate, to face the full grandeur of Spurling's Castle. This could not have been built as long ago as Francis had imagined. The stones were yellow, and only a little weathered, and there was nothing gaunt or alarming about it. There were windows everywhere, filled with light. It looked more a fairytale palace, set in a hollow of many smoothly rounded purplish hills. The car took them to the main entrance, and for one irreverent moment, seeing the Latin inscription over the door, Francis was reminded of a College. Then a round, homely woman welcomed them in; commiserating over the mist, explaining that all the others were already toasting themselves in front of a great fire in the drawing room.

So it was that Francis had his first understanding of the difference between being rich as his father understood the word and the splendour of the world that Ian Mackenzie inhabited.

'Will you have a drop of the malt?' suggested Ian to the two late arrivals in a mock Scots voice. His companion, as Francis could see, was more visibly impressed than he was. That, Francis reflected ruefully, was simply a matter of Gordon training. As Solomon had often advised, you should never look eager in the sight of something you want.

And as he looked round the group of people at the fire, Francis knew he was looking at everything he wanted. He also knew it was unlikely to be his. It wasn't only a question of money. Ian had once admitted to the nineteenth-century origin of his family's fortune. But when he looked at Ian's lovely sister Vivien, dressed in a green of exquisite absurdity, he knew that generations of opulence marked her more deeply than Mackenzie. For his own part, he had no doubt that his own origins were known to them all.

Out of this despair grew a kind of boldness, and he began to clown, and mime, always with one eye on Vivien's lips for approval, to hide the measure of his awe. A Gainsborough hung over the marble mantel, and the casual log fire.

His nervousness led him to drink far more than usual, and he was glad to be allowed quite early to take himself off to

134

bed. To do this, a servant guided him up the main stairs with an oil lamp, and then he had to take another turn around a landing, to find himself in his own room, with a huge four-poster bed, and many windows. Ian had said, 'Draw the curtains. Take a good look out of the windows in the morning,' and Francis resolved to do so. His training led him, in spite of his fatigue, to think first of putting away his clothes. But when he opened his case he found nothing inside. He experienced a moment of panic. Was it some practical joke? And how could he meet the days to come without evening clothes? Then he realized, with a shock of incredulous delight, that someone had simply taken all his clothes out of the suitcase and hung them up. The same invisible hand had put a hot-water bottle in his bed and tucked his nightclothes close to it. In those, accordingly, he rolled himself, and was soon most cheerfully asleep, dreaming of Vivien Mackenzie.

Francis's sexual experience was entirely literary, though in so far as he had been aroused by books he had been quite shamelessly pleased rather than guilty. This was simply because his father had no sense of this potential area of corruption; sex had never seemed much of a passion to him, so he had not bothered to discourage his children from it. Francis had once long ago seen his sister Dorothy naked; but she had been quite unalarmed, and he had felt nothing whatsoever, except for a momentary admiration for the healthy firmness of her body. It would have worried him more to see Betty undress; but he could not quite say why – perhaps because he did not like to associate her virginal little face with sex in any way.

The thought of Vivien Mackenzie, however, put him into a state of such almost permanent excitement that he felt constrained by the physical pressure of blood to his groin.

The next morning he washed and dressed carefully before coming downstairs, and found he had timed his descent pretty well. He had been prepared for the splendours of an English breakfast, but nevertheless the hooded, silver dishes of bacon and scrambled egg, kipper, porridge, and kidneys, indeed the beauty of so much silver stretched out on the mahogany top itself, was hard to approach nonchalantly. Francis rarely ate breakfast at home, and the kidneys, sausages – and could it be sweetbread? – filled him with a certain squeamishness that mixed strangely with his delight. A faint moisture came to his palms as he prepared to help himself. With delight, he found what looked to be some particularly succulent mushrooms; and with these, and a little scrambled egg and toast, he joined the others at the table.

Everyone was reading the newspapers. It was very restful. Elsa had never allowed him to read at the table at home; it was thought the depths of rudeness. Yet Francis could not imagine anything more delightfully considerate and civilized, in an early hour, to be permitted simply to sit at a table, and as it were, *recover*. There was nothing friendly in the silence; but nor was it inhibiting like the silence of a library. Ian, who had noticed Francis's momentary reluctance in opening the silver dishes, remarked sympathetically, 'Hangover? My head's a bit like that.'

The light did, indeed, hurt his eyes. The splendour of this style of architecture, Francis reflected, was the amount of glass it permitted to be set into the walls. Back home the breakfast room, for all its finery, had only one bay window which let in light, and it faced north; so that frequently breakfasts were coloured almost as yellow as suppers in winter. Here the whiteness of the linen, and the walls, and the rush of white sunshine from the cold day outside, were almost blinding.

Peacefully he read the news of the day; taking in, with his usual pleasure enhanced, the balance of the sentences in the leader, and feeling a full acceptance of the world he had been so privileged to enter.

'Boots on,' called Ian.

'Boots?' asked Francis with a certain hollowness in his voice.

Francis was not an athlete, and he had rather hoped that the languid behaviour of his Cambridge friends would continue into the day. He had brought woollen sweaters just in case. But no boots.

With a kind of awe Francis looked round the huge acres of

hills on either side, which ran above purple slopes to a white snowline, and thought how strange it must feel to be the heir of such an expectancy.

But now everyone was assembled in the hall. No one had brought boots. Wellingtons were there for walks; as indeed the whole house existed to maintain the life around it.

Francis found himself wishing he had some of poor Alexander's striding slimness. He feared he might cut something of a comic figure. Vivien, who was coming on the walk too, miraculously did not. Wrapped in warm clothes, she looked exactly like Natasha in *War and Peace*, thought Francis. Pleased with himself, he moved across to tell her exactly that.

'God, I hate those long Russian novels,' said her companion, and Francis had a momentary clutch of anxiety at his heart. What if this lovely girl, too, had a soul so dead that neither Chekov nor Tolstoy moved her?

'You *can't* say that,' Vivien flushed. 'Oh, Natasha is my favourite person, Francis. The most beautiful young girl in the whole of fiction. Better than anyone. Only I can't bear it, really, that she gets so dowdy at the end.'

'Don't you like Pierre?' Francis asked. He was relieved to find that outside, striding determinedly up the slope of dead-brown bracken, towards a snowline which was endlessly much farther ahead than he thought, the sexuality of his feeling for this girl had at last reduced to the point where he could utter complete sentences.

'He's too *good*!' She made a little pout.

'Ah,' said Francis, who had thought about this, and argued it already with his Cambridge tutor. 'But that's Tolstoy's genius. He's all the things bores are *supposed* to be.'

'And a freemason,' she teased.

'Well' – Francis was momentarily stopped, with a faint doubt that he was being mocked. But then he continued, as her green eyes widened, and waited for him to do so. 'I mean, we ought to think of him as a victim and a cuckold and hopelessly unsuitable for love. And yet he has the greatest soul of them all. Hasn't he?'

Vivien said, 'So you believe in the soul?'

Francis felt a little uncomfortable. He had wanted to be gay and witty and dissolute; not *pious*, for God's sake. What error had brought him to Tolstoy?

'Not exactly. Not in the sense of anything that lives on, you know,' he said judiciously.

'Good. I'm an atheist,' she said firmly.

For a moment he wondered whether she might not actually be rather silly. Then she said, 'Do you read poetry much? Ian says you're brilliantly clever.'

Francis scrambled up through the bracken, panting a little.

'I *write* poetry,' she said.

Francis was appalled.

'What kind of poetry do you write?' he asked politely. 'Or perhaps I should ask who are your favourite authors, as Ian did when we first met.'

'Eliot,' she said readily. She stopped for a moment.

He was astonished. He had only just read Prufrock, a little uncertainly, himself.

'How *fashionable*,' he said, not wishing to be outdone in sophistication.

And then he slipped on the frozen brown leaves, abruptly; so that he caught his coccyx a painful blow on the ice, and for a moment he feared his spine had cracked.

She let out a cry which even at the first note had a kind of pleasure mingled with horror; and then as he struggled to his feet, red-faced and carefully brushing off the snow from his coat, with shafts of pain still running in his back, she began to laugh. He was furious, or would have been, if Vivien laughing had not been the most enchanting vision. Her very red lips, so thin, parted to show the smallest and whitest teeth he had ever seen – except, it occurred to him irrelevantly, in the mouth of his sister Betty. But Betty could not have laughed so unkindly.

'I think I may have damaged my backbone,' he said with as much dignity as he could muster.

'Oh Francis, I'm sorry. Disasters have this terrible effect on me. I'm not wicked, it's a kind of nervousness. People only have to tell me about ski accidents, and I giggle. Do you want to go back to the house?'

But Frances didn't want to leave her. Vicious as she

seemed, or even sick, he realized with a pain that he didn't want to leave her then; or preferably, ever. With a sinking of his heart and an unpleasant transmutation of his earlier localized sensations of pure lust, he groaned. Not with pain, but with the recognition of a longing he could feel almost no hope of appeasing.

He was still limping slightly along under the white columns of the great entrance hall, and had just paused to examine what was actually a particularly fine portrait by Sir Joshua Reynolds (wondering again why it *was* that Blake had so disliked him), when the voices of Ian and Vivien came out of the library with sudden clarity. It was what Vivien said that froze him.

'Tell me about your Jew friend,' she said casually.

A cold hand clutched at Francis round his bronchi, as if he were going to have an asthmatic spasm. He had never heard the word Jew used like that. It came to him now that writers like Buchan might use it so; but he could never recall hearing it in conversation. That she had said she liked or quite liked him was totally irrelevant. It was as if she had remarked on the good qualities of someone's horse or dog; so alien a creature did the remark make him feel. He was indignant. What could it mean? He'd always thought it was only the nasty-minded lower classes whose own insecurities made them speak so. This was evidently not so. But for God's sake what did it mean? He wasn't foreign. His English was as flawless as theirs, and on paper decidedly sharper than Ian's. He was at Cambridge. How did she know he was a Jew? Not his name. And not his face, though it was long and thin; it was not swarthy, and his lips were not grossly thick.

He realized that he ought to move; that otherwise there was a real risk he would be discovered, thought of as an eavesdropper, what else not. But he couldn't move. He was afraid his tread would be overhead; though the pile of the carpet would probably have prevented that. So it was he heard Ian say, 'Yes, he's clever, isn't he? But be sensible, if you can possibly be, Vivien, this time. I'm sure he's horribly susceptible. Don't imagine he's used to pretty women.'

'What are his family like?'

No, positively, no. He must move. He forced himself to walk away. He could not bear to hear Ian characterize anyone else.

He flung himself blindly on the four-poster bed that had seemed so grand and lay on it for more than an hour, his mind blank, and his eyes tearless and hot. A cold purpose formed in him, however. Even as he lay there in torment something was at work in his mind. He would find out about this Vivien in a rather different spirit. There was something odd about her, he knew that now, and she had something in her that was familiarly anxious. He placed it. She was older than usual to be unmarried. He teased his brain to be sure of it; but then it came to him, with sudden clarity. Ian had told him she had been engaged before, and the engagement had been broken. There was something unstable about her, perhaps more than that. He was sure suddenly that she too was vulnerable.

After dinner he asked her, quite coolly, if he could look at her poems.

She said, 'We're going to dance, I want to teach you the charleston.'

Francis was quite firm. 'We can do both, can't we?'

Vivien's surprise at his change of tone gave him a new pleasure. Over this odd, extravagantly beautiful creature he now felt he had a certain power.

'I might publish them,' he said off-handedly. 'If they're any good. Did I tell you, I'm putting an anthology together this term.'

The poems, however, astonished him, and for a moment he had some trouble re-establishing any kind of authority.

'Rather a heavy influence of Eliot,' he muttered, to cover himself in case they actually *were* copied from a book of Eliot's he had never read. But for some reason her gift as a poet only contributed the more to his sense of power over her. Poetry was his country; at least in one sense: he could, he knew, recognize it always and at first sight. At the same time nothing he had yet written himself, or perhaps ever would write, was as good as these poems of Vivien's. In his present mood, that was irrelevant, for one thing he knew with absolute certainty. If she had been a trivial poet she would not have the same trouble with the young men around her. If she had painted watercolours, it would have been the same. But a real talent for poetry was different. Poetry, unlike novels, was a spinsterly art. Novels were jollier altogether; everyone could enjoy them. He knew now that it was her gift that made her a stranger to her family. And that strangeness related her to him as another alien, more strongly than it related her to them.

He let her try to teach him to dance without embarrassment; delighting in her skill. And she had the most marvellous ankles. Francis found he learned the steps with a certain ease. The new dances put off the English as a rule. They preferred the old rhythms. But Francis liked them. And while he learned the slow, erotic postures of the tango, to the noise of a gramophone that had to be wound up continually by an old lady in a grey dress, Francis made his mind up.

It might take a bit of manoeuvring, but he was going to marry Vivien.

20

'Where does it say Rasil Katz has to feed the whole street?' demanded Abram.

Now that her own children were grown up there was usually a strange child or two at the Katz table these days, eager to drink her hot, golden soup.

Rasil's black eyes snapped, and she bustled the dishes away, because she didn't know what should be done either. Times were hard. Not everyone had three strong men to work every hour God sent; and there were lots of hungry children as the new decade began.

'It's like the Ukraine,' she said heavily. 'God help us all.

Poor men sitting in the streets, with their tins and blind eyes. The children have nothing on their feet and nothing in their bellies. There's a terrible time coming, Abram. I feel it.'

'Can we help what is coming?' asked Abram.

He, too, felt disappointment everywhere. Disappointment, and sourness, and rising hatred. The men had come back from war and found themselves betrayed. There was no work, no trade. Even the healthy, and those who worked together as a family as the Katz brothers had always done, could hardly scrape a living.

Merseyside had grown grey and angry in the poverty that had come in the aftermath of war.

Earlier that year, the Katz family had to move out of Upper Parliament Street, back to Islington; the street of *stollers*, where Abram had first set up when he arrived in Liverpool. It was a question of living over the wood shop again. Rasil didn't weep over the move. You don't weep for furniture or bricks and mortar. She came from generations of tough women who had learned to move house without grumbling; she put on her pinny, and packed up the boxes of daily china, and the china for Pesach, and the bone spoons her mother had given her long ago. And she watched Benjy load up the handcart to take it round to Islington without complaint.

Abram's brothers had already concluded that the family business couldn't carry so many families, and some of them had moved off: to Leeds, Manchester, Leicester. There were too many cabinetmakers trying to scrape a living; and no one wanted kitchen cabinets.

It was left to Benjy and Len to decide what to do.

Benjy had grown into a handsome young man; white-skinned, black-haired and powerfully built. His dark eyes looked the world full in the face. He wasn't afraid of it. And the young girls hung out of the windows to watch him pass. He didn't flirt with Jewish girls; it was too dangerous. Times might be changing everywhere else, but you kissed and cuddled on Bedford Street only if you wanted to get married.

'Don't want to marry anyone. Not me. One family is enough to support,' said Benjy.

142

He was sitting in the living quarters above Wolfie's newspaper shop with Len, considering their future.

'I can't think what's got *into* it,' said Benjy despondently. 'Or what else to do.'

'Pack it in,' advised Len.

'And do what?'

'I got a plan. Listen,' said Len.

'I go out in the morning with the cabinets, and you can't give the stuff away. Not even for cost,' muttered Benjy.

'Hard work won't do it,' said Len.

'Now what exactly do you recommend?' jeered Benjy. He was tired and his good nature had frayed.

'Thinking,' said Len. 'Now. Why *don't* people want to spend money any more?'

'Any fool knows that,' said Benjy. 'Can't spend what you haven't got, can you?'

'*Listen*,' insisted Len. 'They can only furnish a bit at a time. But there's still money about if you have the right goods. Look at this catalogue.'

'Who are the Islington Furnishing Company Ltd?' asked Benjy unbelievingly.

Len said, 'I am. Listen. It doesn't cost so much. Seven quid. To be a limited company. And it's got advantages. Everyone should be a company.'

'I know what it *means*,' growled Benjy. 'I don't like it. It means if you haven't got enough money, they can't get you.'

'Yes. Can't take your house. Your goods.'

'Like I said.'

'It's an advantage,' said Len.

'Not to me,' said Benjy. 'People round here know us. So if we owe them, they know they'll get their money, don't they? You start putting Co. after your name, they'll think twice about credit.'

'Think bigger,' said Len. 'Look, Benjy. Three-piece suites, Chesterfield with drop ends, upholstered in silk damask and stuffed with fibre. Thirty-four guineas.'

'Who's buying that? And we don't upholster.'

'From me,' said Len. 'Four pounds down, and thirty weeks at twenty-five shillings.'

'And who collects?' asked Benjy shrewdly.

'Leave that to me,' said Len. 'I'll keep my ear to the ground. How about this, Benjy? Elegant burr walnut bedroom suite with four-foot-six kidney-shaped dressing-table. Can you make that?'

'Not where we are I can't,' said Benjy, considering the matter. 'You need space to do work like that. Look at all the turning it needs.'

'I'll find you space,' said Len. 'If you'll take a risk.'

'Where?'

'The property isn't too good. But it's cheap. On two floors. I don't know if the top floor will take machines.'

'Where?'

'Old warehouse, really.'

'Derelict, you mean.'

Benjy considered the matter. You had to be careful. Men would work anywhere these days; they put themselves in danger of their lives for shillings a week. You could always get a work force. But Benjy didn't fancy it.

'Come to supper tonight,' he told his cousin. 'I'll think about it.'

'If you can make that I can sell it,' said Len. 'Have you any other propositions?'

'I said I'll think about it, didn't I? We're not bosses, Len. I work the machines myself.'

Len shrugged, and didn't argue any further. Benjy would make up his mind when he was ready, and there was no point trying to push him.

It was Friday night; and the brass Sabbath candlesticks stood on a white cloth, along with a bottle of Palwin wine, and two plaited loaves under a beige lace cap. Abram was waiting on his feet for the two boys to come in, and poverty had not diminished his dignity.

'Straight from the street to the table? And this on Shabbos?' he demanded.

'We'll just wash, gov'nor,' said Benjy hastily. 'Sorry, Ma.'

Abram nodded, and waited for the boys to wash their hands. The clothes he wore were much the same as they had

144

always been; a heavy brown cardigan hung slackly at the back, and an embroidered black *yarmulka* sat on the back of his head. His beard had whitened, but the hair on his head was still thick and wiry.

And when the boys were standing in their places, he began to intone the ancient prayer from his heart, because Friday was the most blessed evening in the week. Even Benjy made sure to be home for it, and wore a skullcap, though it was usually invisible in his thick black hair. And for the length of the prayer Abram felt there was order, as there should be order: not some dead structure of laws, but order as in the creation of the world, when God commanded the earth to rise, and the creatures of the earth rose out of the dust at his word. The holy words made Abram's scalp prickle. He passed the silver cup of sweet wine to his wife, and motioned her to send it round the table; then he blessed the bread, tore off a piece, and sent that, too, ritually on its way. The day of rest was part of God's order, and to enter it gave Abram peace.

But as soon as the wine and bread had passed round, Rasil leaped to her feet, and shouted at Sarah to get plates of soup from the kitchen. And Abram sighed; he understood her vehemence, and the new burdens that had come on her; and the energy in her that made her long to get things moving. In Rasil's childhood it was not unusual for a Jewish wife to earn the living while her husband studied; her mother had travelled to market among drunken peasants every week. And Rasil was cast in her mould. It was hardest of all for her to be passive. So she did everything fast and fiercely that lay under her hand. And at the moment she was trying to marry off her children.

As they reached the lockshen pudding, and Abram was just enjoying the hot explosion of sweet raisins that she filled it with so liberally, she began again about that.

'Forbidden? Who has forbidden it? A *Zionist* dance, Abram.' Rasil's eyes blazed.

'Dancing,' said Abram, shaking his head. 'The Adelphi.'

'And to find a husband for my youngest daughter? Isn't that a *mitzvah* too?'

145

'Times change,' said Benjy.

Abram glared and said, 'They always changed. We don't change.'

'You don't want grandchildren,' threatened Rasil.

'Why not? How did my other daughters get married? Did they go to the Adelphi with their skirts caught up to their knees like whores? Aren't they married?'

'That was before the war,' said Rasil.

'Before, before.' Abram was honestly puzzled. 'Before, I think, was better.'

'And what about my Harry?' Rasil demanded.

At these words Benjy rose, and asked if he could leave the table. The situation of the family as a whole was difficult enough without facing daily the question of what to do with Harry.

Rasil did not readily accept Harry's condition. She got up every morning of her life before six and swept out of bed to wash; when she was coiffed and neat she appeared at Harry's bedside.

'Time for breakfast, Harry.'

'I'm not hungry.'

'How can you expect to get better if you don't eat?'

'I don't expect to get better,' he'd say.

And what's more, he didn't. He couldn't see how his situation could possibly improve. In the whole of his life, things had never so far been any good at all. At school they said he had imagination and a talent for words. It hadn't impressed his father, who took him out of school anyway. But he had none of the *feeling* for the world that Len and Benjy had. He had no natural talent whatsoever with his hands. He was a big, handsome but timid lad; and he didn't know what to do with his life. His sister Sarah found a wood shop natural enough; she enjoyed the smells of plywood and glue; and she could do quick mental arithmetic, no problem. She was as strong as his mother, with her sloping dowager bosom. Even though the business was in trouble and the family was fighting, he could see no point in joining his puny efforts to hers.

146

So Harry stayed in bed. He liked it. He got his head down under the blankets and dozed all day long. He wasn't ill. It was nothing to do with his fractured skull. He knew very well what was going on in the world below and outside, and he didn't want any part of it. He wanted to sink down, out of sight; to be under the bedclothes and invulnerable.

'Might as well be *dead*,' Benjy said once, looking down at his motionless form.

But Harry knew that wasn't true. Being *asleep* wasn't being dead. He was warm, not dead; comfortable, too. There was no comfort under the soil. He was lying warm and safe; and could think what he chose. When you were dead, you went into the cold, wet ground, and soon there was no more left of your flesh than if you were a herring. In bed his thoughts could fly anywhere. When he was younger, and still believed as his father did, he had sometimes taken down the holy books of the Cabala from their place and looked into them for magical words, so that angels might burst through the ceilings of Brownlow Hill. Now he could summon them into his dreams without sin. He could travel through the markets of Palestine, and with one shout open the gate in the wall of Jerusalem through which the dead must enter into Paradise. Whole villages lost under the heel of pogroms rose again; mothers and sons and flocks of geese flew south into the sunshine of the Holy City and put their lips to the golden walls of Solomon's temple.

The doctor said, 'I'm afraid he has a depressive temperament. Give him these. And these. And perhaps these.'

So Rasil frowned over her son.

Outside the comfortable warmth in which he swam, the air blew cold. You had to turn up your coat collar, and bend your neck muscles to put yourself into the wind, when it came in harshly from the sea.

Why would anyone rise? Did they know what for? To work? Harry had no work. To read? The books he brought home earned him frowns. For what, then? To please?

Why should he please, or seek to please, since his whole life was so altogether a failure?

Downstairs were problems.

Adding up money and finding you were short. Electricity bills. Rent. Angry creditors.

Downstairs was one trouble after another, and Harry knew he could avoid them all by putting his head down under the sheets. So he did.

The doctor said, 'These ailments usually cure themselves in time. Maybe a few months. Maybe weeks. Have patience.'

Nothing else appeared to be curing itself, however. As fast as Benjy found the money for one debt, another appeared. He got up as early as the old rag-men, and loaded cabinets on to a cart. By evening, few of them had been sold. Occasionally he took a meeting hall, and set up his wares for auction. Sometimes Len stood in the audience and made fake bids, and they got rid of some of the goods that way. But Benjy had set his face against Len's old warehouse. No one else had taken it on either, he pointed out. The floors were rotten through, and the windows didn't open.

Then one day he came home late, and the house was in confusion.

Abram was sitting at the table and staring down into his soup. He was crying shamelessly. Benjy's heart was squeezed so painfully at the sight he thought his lungs would die for lack of oxygen. His strong father. Like an ox. With his red hair and his blue eyes. Weeping. What could have happened? And to whom?

Then his sister Sarah came in and told him sharply to get his filthy shoes off. Big bold Sarah.

'Sarah, what is it?'

'Ma. She's all right now.'

Benjy looked at his father, still crying. Something didn't make sense.

'I said, she's all right. She lost a lot of blood, but she's all right. Look at you, big baby,' she scolded Abram.

'We should have got a doctor. I wanted to get a doctor. You think you're so clever,' he cried.

'It wouldn't have made any difference. What do they know, these doctors?'

'Take this soup away,' he said crossly.

He didn't believe in doctors either. But he was ashamed.

Times are bad, thought Benjy. There's no money. And even Ma gets sick.

So he took the derelict warehouse.

It was hard work setting things up. Len borrowed the money. Benjy saw to the rotten floorboards first, then bought in second-hand sanders and saws, found the wood, hired the men.

'If this doesn't come off,' said Benjy, 'we'll have to do a moonlight flit. No question. Did you ever count up how much we owe?'

'No,' said Len. 'I don't believe in it.'

'It's lucky you can talk the hind leg off a donkey,' said Benjy.

Len was a natural salesman.

And luckily business began, slowly, to pick up again that year. Nothing glamorous, but enough money came in for even Harry to come downstairs and face the world. Benjy found his brother something to do. He could write invoices. Benjy gave him a room on the second floor where they couldn't put anything heavy, and Harry sat there writing out the bills and receipts in a neat hand, and keeping the books. It seemed to make him happy. He came in smoking and whistling, and ground his cigarette out on the workshop floor with something like confidence before stepping upstairs to his den.

Benjy always stepped on the butt afterwards thoughtfully; and sometimes growled up the stairs. 'Be a bit careful, can't you? We're not fireproof.'

Benjy sat nowhere. He had no office. He was always up and down the shop. He'd introduced piecework because the men wanted it, but it made them take crazy chances. They took the guards off the machines to make the work go faster as soon as his back was turned. He had to go round and yell at them to put them on again. And, as he paced up and down, the place screamed and whined. The air was filled with dust and shavings and the ubiquitous, sweetish smell of glue.

One day in November was particularly cold. The sky looked heavy with snow through the cracked windows. The only heat in the shop came from brazier fires at each end of

the room. Even the keenest men were taking breaks to warm
their hands. By late afternoon, the dark outside was oppressive; and it was hard to see by the light of the few bare bulbs.
Benjy was binding the hand of one man who had narrowly
avoided more serious injury, when a curious hush fell on the
room. An ill-lit, unnatural silence. The power had given out.
The machines had stopped. Then came the first unmistakable
smell of smoke.

'Out. Out,' yelled Benjy. 'Any way you can.'

It was difficult to see where the smoke was coming from.
Benjy held up an oil lamp at the entrance to the ground-floor
room. And the men pushed past him in a kind of primeval
terror.

'Fire! Fire!' Benjy yelled up the stairs.

The fire began to catch on the wood shavings and take hold.
The flames reached the ceiling now, and would be licking
through the planks of the first floor. Three or four men from
upstairs rushed past Benjy; he could see their terrified faces
clearly by the yellow light of the flames.

'Harry. Where's Harry?' he tried to ask them.

But they only wanted to find their way out into the air.

'Harry?' Benjy yelled up the stairs.

The office was at the other end of the warehouse. If Harry
was still there he would have to be reached from outside.

Once outside, Benjy saw how badly the first floor was
blazing already. There were flames coming out of the windows. And the street was packed with screaming people.

'Len. Have you seen Harry? Is he *out*?' Benjy asked
urgently.

Len shook his head. He had nothing to say.

By now a hose had arrived, and was being trained on the
flames.

As Len and Benjy watched, a figure appeared at a window
of the first floor in a gust of flames and prepared to jump.

'Wait!' A yell went up from the crowd.

But the heat was intense, and the figure could not wait for
the safety net. He jumped into the arms of the people below. A
groan went up from them as he landed.

'Twenty feet,' muttered Benjy.

He could not wait himself. Harry might well be stunned, suffocated, dead. But he was in there. What was needed was a ladder. He snatched up one of the firemen's steel ladders and propped it against the wall near to Harry's office. Even as he did so, a piece of the building crashed into the narrow street, and the crowd moved away, reminded of its own danger.

Benjy took out a handkerchief and tied it over his mouth and nose. It wouldn't help much, but the acrid smoke belching out of the broken windows was already burning his lungs. He climbed the ladder, coughing, unable to call out, leaden with fear that he would find Harry already burning like meat.

He was level with the office window, but he could see nothing through the dirty windows. And the sash would not yield. Impatiently, Benjy knocked the glass through with his arm. He felt the glass splinter and bite into his flesh.

Then he could see more clearly than he expected, because the office had not filled with smoke. The door to the work benches had been shut. Harry was lying across the desk. A beam from the roof had felled him as he sat.

Benjy tried to decide what to do. The smoke was already coming up between the cracks of the floorboards, and he needed help to lift the beam. But there was not time to wait for help. The whole floor might give any moment, he could hear the roar from the crowd below. Then water splashed in after him. Though it was meant helpfully, Benjy saw that it only increased his danger, as it weakened the wood of the floor.

He put all his strength under the ceiling beam.

Harry stirred.

'Push up, Harry,' Benjy urged desperately. 'I can't shift her alone. I can't.'

But he had. With a final shove, the cindery wood yielded.

And Benjy lifted his brother over his shoulders as if he were still a child, and stepped out over the sill into the arms of firemen.

No one blamed Len for the fire. There were debts now, and no insurance had covered the machines. But Len carried his share of the trouble. Harry was still in hospital. No one had died, though a man who had jumped from the second floor had broken his back. A few people muttered about the man who rented out the warehouse. But, after all. Two floors high. They'd been lucky.

Len knew his old friend Mo Green had moved to Leicester. He was a fat, bald man now; with greyish-pink flesh, and almost invisible eyes. He had opened a pub on the Humberstone Road, near the Clock Tower. It was popular with sportsmen. Fighters. Fight promoters.

'No one's making any money,' said Mo.

He meant no one else.

Mo wasn't the only friend to move to Leicester. One or two from Len's old racing days had sized up the situation and made the same decision. They hadn't all got Mo's capital, either. Or his connections. They set up stalls in the big market. Took small shops and sold anything from pressing irons to pencils. Leicester wasn't flat broke like the north.

'Things are still moving there,' said Len. 'Listen, Benjy.'

Benjy glared.

'I'm putting an oak floor in a new house for a mate of mine. I've got enough on,' he said.

The Katz family had now moved down into the basement, and the upstairs rooms were filled with strangers. These were the days of bread and margarine, and chicken *schmaltz* when they were lucky. Len's face grew drawn and grey with thinking of ways to make a living.

'When men are out of *work* there's one thing they have got, and that's time. So. They'd like to do something useful, wouldn't they? I'm going to help them.'

'How?'

'Let them make their own cabinets. I'll sell them the wood. Like radios, for instance. How about that? Everyone wants radios.'

'Go round the streets with wood?' asked Benjy dubiously.

'In Leicester you don't have to go round the streets,' said Len. 'I've looked into it.'

'I don't fancy it,' said Benjy. 'I'm not getting behind the counter like some bloody shopkeeper, saying Yes sir, no sir, not for anyone.'

'Please yourself,' said Len. 'I'm pissed off with this city, myself.'

'You remember what happened to the uncles?' asked Benjy heavily.

'I'm not worried,' said Len. 'I'll look after myself. Always did.'

'Sod you, then,' said Benjy. He was bitterly miserable in a way he couldn't altogether name. 'We always said we'd stay together after the war,' he muttered.

Len knew his cousin felt cheated and unhappy, and he was sorry. 'Look,' he began.

'No, sod off,' said Benjy, annoyed at feeling so much unexplained emotion. 'I don't need you. Anyway, doing it yourself? There'll be no money in that. Stands to reason.'

By April Len was restless; and one day, he declared, 'I'm going on Thursday.'

Benjy stared.

'You can't.'

'Why can't I?'

'It's Pesach.'

'So?'

'Where will you have a Seder night?'

'Go on. You don't still believe all that? Do you? Miracles and promised land and all.'

'Ma works so hard getting it ready.' Benjy shook his head. 'It wouldn't feel right. Ignoring it.'

'I've seen *you*, Saturdays,' said Len.

'Saturdays are one thing. If I didn't work Saturdays we'd starve. There is no call telling anyone about *that*, mind,' warned Benjy.

'Oh, give up.'

'Wait another day,' urged Benjy.

Len was touched. 'You really care about people, don't you, old lad? All right. Next week, then.'

'It's worth it for the meal,' Benjy teased him. 'Don't look so noble.'

21

In Provence Dorothy's puritanism began to soften.

In the early spring of 1923 she was appointed sister in a maternity hospital set in the hills just behind Cassis. And nothing in her life had prepared her for the pleasure she began to take in the surrounding countryside. Everything seemed alive in it. There were lizards in the grass, and a hint of more dangerous creatures in the bramble and brushwood. March in Liverpool had tasted of the brown sea; but here it was aromatic with scents she had to learn to give a name. The stone buildings were white, rather than grey: instead of Lancashire hill towns based on mill and mine. The Provençal villagers worked outdoors on terraces of vines. Asparagus and thyme grew wild, and olive trees crouched everywhere. By the time the sun had begun to show its power, and she could feel the heat underfoot in the white powdery soil, Dorothy bought a parasol. Her delicate skin did not tan in sunlight. And she began to feel treacherous stirrings of other interests.

None of the doctors in her wartime hospital had attracted her in the least, and she had parried their advances without difficulty. In Provence she perceived that she was an object of interest to several young French men; and, a little to her annoyance, she was not all averse to the idea.

Not marriage, she thought.

But she knew enough now to realize there were many alternatives.

Down on the coast, the bright young rich of all over Europe had thrown off the shackles of the grey world Dorothy remembered; northern Europe was gone and all the scruples of her adolescence. Now there were new dances; girls showed all their legs on the beaches; and the young spent their nights drinking and gambling. Dorothy thought they were idle, feckless creatures; she had no envy for them. But quietly, imperceptibly, their fearlessness reinforced her own desires.

She did not meet Gérard Bernac in the hospital, but sitting in a café, set where the fountains splashed together in the centre of Aix. She had come there on her own on her day off; a little petulantly, because the other English nurse in her ward was 'so tired, Dorrie' she couldn't face the walk from the coast road.

Dorothy was tired too; but marvellously. The air about her was warm and pine-scented; and when the light went altogether, the Roman statuary looked like natural rock outlined against a sky that was as blue as ink. The lights from the café made a magical pool of gold around the chairs on the pavement.

She had ordered a glass of Pastis, and added water to it as the waiter told her; and even though she hated the liquorice flavour, the few sips of unaccustomed alcohol together with the fatigue of the day induced a light-headed trance.

'May I join you?' asked a fair young man, in barely accented English.

Dorothy looked up, startled, and her back straightened. She was not wearing her nurse's uniform, she remembered; and no doubt the young man took her for one of the usual band of English tourists, and thought she was eager for company. But before she could reply, he continued.

'Miss Gordon, don't be angry. I am not a wicked foreigner trying to slip into your friendship. We work in the same hospital.'

And then she recognized him as a doctor; and moreover the son of the director of the hospital itself. Dorothy was annoyed, however, at the ease with which he confidently took the chair next to her even so. He was behaving as if he and his family owned the town.

'I love your English hair,' he said at once. 'And your skin. But I don't think that is how I am supposed to talk, is it?'

'Your English is excellent,' said Dorothy crisply. She could hardly snub him, as the son of the director. Or not altogether. But she had no intention of becoming one more pretty English nurse to fall under his spell.

155

'But you think I am a Don Juan,' he said, crestfallen. 'Not true. I am very respectful. Respectable. Which is right?'

'For you? Neither, I should think,' Dorothy laughed.

The English abroad had a reputation for being loose-living and eager for sexual experience. Dorothy did not blame him for assuming she would be the same.

'I am not *fast*,' she said.

He did not know the slang and looked puzzled.

'Would you like another drink? You don't seem to be enjoying your Pastis,' he suggested.

'I don't drink much. I'm very puritanical,' she warned him.

Then she looked at him closely, and something in the silhouette of forehead and nose affected her strangely. He was a very beautiful young man, she admitted to herself. An unaccustomed and disconcerting sweetness began to run in her blood, and the sensation confused her, although it was pleasurable.

He urged her to try a sweet Armagnac.

In her confusion she agreed, and while they waited for it to appear she studied him carefully, liking what she saw, especially the coat-hanger neatness of his blue suit, his narrow figure and his good, straight features.

He owned an Italian sports car, which looked like one of the cards she had collected as a young nurse from packs of cigarettes, and she did not resist his offer of a lift back to the hospital. On the contrary, she felt intensely happy to be sitting at his side, as his car took the curves in the road.

'Too fast?' he asked her.

And she shook her head.

I suppose this is a pick-up, she thought, and I'm enjoying it.

But when they arrived at the hospital Gérard only put out his hand, very tentatively, to the nape of her neck, and the hand fitted gently, just under the short hair. It was oddly comforting. For a moment they sat in silence. Then he kissed her. It was a short kiss, with a hot, open mouth.

Nothing more.

Dorothy began to feel an unfamiliar excitement impeding her breath. Unlike almost every other man she had sat in the

156

dark with before, Gérard did not try to touch her further, and she felt her own desire racing far ahead of his. He did not reach for her again, but got out of the car to help her from the low seat politely.

'I'd better go in before Matron spots us,' she said uncertainly.

'Yes. Goodnight, Dorothy.'

She lay awake until it was nearly time to get up, wondering if Gérard had any intention of seeing her again.

They did not meet for another three days; and then only by chance in a corridor. But he asked her to drive out into the hills with him on her day off. She agreed without coquetry. He looked relieved, as if he had feared a rebuff.

'What would you like to see? The Cloisters in Arles? The marshes? *Le vieux port* at Marseille?'

'I should like to see everything,' said Dorothy.

He laughed.

That Sunday they drove downhill towards the sea, which could be seen as a single creek of blue between white slabs of stone. The air had a chill brightness.

'First I am going to feed you,' declared Gérard.

Dorothy protested. She had a distrust of foreign food; she was not used to thinking of meals as a form of pleasure.

'You haven't eaten *bouillabaisse*?' He was horrified.

Dorothy wondered whether she had some residual fear of the shellfish that had been prohibited throughout her childhood.

'I've always been afraid of it,' she admitted.

He was delighted. She could have said nothing that pleased him more. It was part of her Englishness, and apparently it was her Englishness he loved.

'In a good *bouillabaisse*,' he explained, 'you need many fishes.'

'Fish.'

'Fish, then. Eels, perch, mullet, crab, *cigales de mer*.'

'*Cigales*?' She shuddered at the thought of grasshoppers in her food.

He ignored her shudder. Or enjoyed it.

'And of course onions, peppers, fennel, bayleaves.'

They ate looking at the fishing boats afloat on the narrow, still-water port of Cassis. They laughed all through the meal. And while they were drinking coffee, he said, 'It is never my good luck to fall in love with a Catholic. It is because I like English ankles. But perhaps you don't have strong religious principles?'

'Oh but I do,' she said. 'I hate the Church.'

She watched him flinch.

'No popes,' he nodded, as if he had heard as much before.

'Not only popes. No priests either. No Church. It's all one long plundering and blundering as far as I can see.' She didn't feel apologetic. 'And you're trained as a scientist. How can you believe all that nonsense?'

'So, if I am a doctor. Can I cure what I want? Can I give new limbs?'

'Look, I understand what we *can't* do,' she said patiently. 'But how does some poor body nailed up on a cross help?'

He put her hand gently over her mouth.

'Don't. You are too lovely to be frivolous.'

'Don't be daft,' she said angrily.

He was uncertain about the meaning of the word 'daft', but he backed away from her anger.

'Maybe it is better you are not a fanatic Protestant,' he said.

This time Gérard did not drive her straight home, and he was altogether less polite. For some reason, Dorothy was infuriated. It was as if she had given him some kind of signal without intending to, and she resented the rapid change in his behaviour. It was not that the gestures offended her. On the contrary. That unfamiliar sweetness that had touched her on the first evening she now felt concentrated precisely in her breasts and between her legs: only some residual obstinacy made her push away his hands, because she felt she had been misunderstood.

'No,' she said. 'No.'

When he tried to put his hands on her breasts, she felt herself shivering uncontrollably.

'Damn you. No.'

So he stopped, looking penitent and bewildered.

'I'm sorry.'

'Why do you think all English girls are whores?'

'Because they have no religion,' he answered readily.

She was astonished at the simplicity of his viewpoint.

'What about French men. Have *they* no religion?'

'Good Catholics understand the flesh is a sin.'

'The flesh? God, you are young.' She looked at him in astonishment. 'You must have been in medical school and missed the war. The flesh. Oh, Gérard.'

He hadn't followed her; but she could tell he was not altogether displeased by her anger.

And as she struggled to open the car door, he nodded.

'You are good. I am sorry,' he said formally.

She thought that was probably that. But instead, he asked her to his home the following week for Sunday lunch. Dorothy was amused at the formality of his tone; and his evident anxiety about what she would wear.

'Don't worry. I won't wear a skirt round my knickers. Or my nurse's uniform. Or bright scarlet.'

'Don't mock me. I very much want them to like you.'

He called for her a little before noon, which involved her asking for an hour off. He must, she thought, have fixed that for her; because the request went through smoothly. Even so, she found him waiting impatiently.

'Are you ready?' His eyes went over her neat beige coat and dress with approval.

'Toot sweet,' she teased him.

'Dorothy, your French is terrible. Really terribly,' he sighed. 'Only an English girl could get away with it. But surely you can speak a little?'

'Only to shop.'

'You will learn,' he ordered her. 'I will arrange lessons.'

'No, thank you. I have no time for lessons. Or if I did, I would learn something *more useful* than that. I would attach myself to the Faculty of Natural Science here,' she flashed.

He laughed at her vehemence.

It was an interesting break in tradition, she thought. It had been said of her family that they could be dropped anywhere, and in one generation speak the language like natives. But the English had another set of rules; and she had learned them without knowing it. How could he understand what an inheritance she was denying? Perhaps they were Solomon's rules, for certainly his sardonic eyes flicked into her mind. She had to blink them away. 'You don't need Russian,' he had always told the children. 'Or German. Just learn the sound of the talk around you.'

'The French,' said Gérard, almost as if he had heard her thought, 'want people to speak *their* language. And my mother speaks no English.'

Dorothy had guessed uneasily that Gérard's house would be alien territory, but she had not imagined its grandeur. And as they turned in towards the fine house at the end of a column of poplars Gérard must have guessed her thought, for he said quickly, 'The house has been in the family since my grandmother.'

22

Francis was given a room in College in his last year. He lay back on the comfortable pillows with his eyes shut. And Ian leaned over him and said, 'I can tell you are dreaming of sensuous foreign girls.'

Francis flushed. 'Nothing was further from my thoughts.'

If there was anything he did *not* want, it was dark, rich flesh. What he was after, what he needed, was a certain wildness in the spirit. The flesh in itself had no power to move him.

'My appetites are a little different,' he admitted. He did not like to explain to Ian how very precisely by now they had focused on his sister Vivien; how indeed he only had to close his eyes in order to see that peculiar fresh white skin, and admire the narrow, perfect mouth, with its total absence of sensuality. The very spite in her gave a glitter to her eyes that no other woman seemed to have. At that very moment, he was not so much fantasizing about her, but scheming for her and how to have her.

His mother was ill. He knew that; but the pain was remote. Last time he had seen her he had the ugly, unfeeling certainty of impending death. He had seen her fall back on the pillows wearily, had been waved away, had known, even as he went, that some buried part of his brain was saying shamelessly: So you're finished then.

Quite coldly it spoke. He thought: I will have a little capital, but hardly enough.

'Shall you stay on and become a Fellow?' asked Ian lazily.

The thought this time chimed ironically with Francis's own.

'I shall go into the business for a few years,' he said.

Ian stirred with surprise.

'I have no intention,' said Francis crisply, 'of being a poor and honourable scholar, however much *trade* may be despised by your lot.'

'But Francis. You'll find it boring. You're teasing me.'

'Boredom doesn't come into it,' said Francis, in a matter-of-fact voice.

I want a house in a Georgian square, he told himself. I want good furniture of my own, and wine and good clothes. They are necessary things; you can't love poetry without them. They are the blood of poetry; all the garret stuff is nothing. You need comfort, a fire, beauty. And, by god, he needed Vivien.

She won't marry a glass merchant, he knew that. Supposing she married someone else in the meanwhile? Before he had become *himself*. As he meant to be. He had no illusion about the strength of her attachment. She had given him no cause to feel any. But the war was on his side, he reflected. She was part of the lost generation as surely as the men who had fallen in those sodden trenches. Her hopes had been cut down there, too.

'Not even if you get a first?' pleaded Ian.

'Oh, I'll *have* to get a first,' said Francis. 'Everything depends on that.'

161

23

Dorothy found Sunday lunches with Gérard's family increasingly oppressive as the months wore on. Even the first day had been something of a warning to her as a newcomer. His mother had failed to come downstairs at all to receive her, and could be heard pacing about on the floor above.

'Like Rochester's wife,' Dorothy whispered nervously.

'Migraine,' Gérard had explained, perhaps fortunately failing to understand the reference.

There was a very large family; most sons and daughters apparently continued to come to Sunday lunch with Mother and Father after they had married and set up home, even if they lived miles away. No one, as far as Dorothy could judge, had ever got farther away than that.

The food was rich and exotic, and a great deal of wine was drunk with each course. As a result, by the end of the meal all attempt at sustaining conversation in English was abandoned, and Dorothy was left to fend for herself in French as best she could.

Driving back to the hospital, even that first time, she had said irritably, 'I don't think I can bear all that.'

But if Gérard heard there was no sign of it, and he kissed her with such sweet intensity that she pushed all reservations about his background far from her mind.

By June the soil had turned to white powder on the hillside below the hospital, and Dorothy began to find the heat oppressive. One afternoon there was a fire in the dried-up trees, and for days afterwards the air dried the membranes of her nose so that she woke one night with blood running into her pillow from her nostrils.

'The south doesn't suit me,' she said to Gérard.

'I love you. Just for that. You are pure. As the north.'

On the terrace of Gérard's family house, on Sundays, Dorothy learned to drink Pastis with ice, quietly, while the others talked. It made her restless. When the wind rose, and the dust blew between the dead grass from the fields around the house, she thought her nerves would snap; and one day, knowing that she was not allowed any such initiative, she got up without explanation to find shade under the withered trees. It was a rudeness she could not help. It was no good. She had no desire to be acceptable to this family. She had not left Solomon's house to have a new kind of docility imposed on her. It would have to end.

But when Gérard came to find her, he was apologetic.

'Politics,' he groaned. 'I *know* it's boring for a woman. Forgive us.'

She had not listened enough to gather what he meant, but she was surprised. They had not seemed a political family.

'We talk about Italy,' said Gérard.

Dorothy found his penitence disarming, and they went into lunch together. It was a very charming interior, she reluctantly admitted to herself. Red tiles underfoot, and a trestle table set with highly coloured dishes; a spicy tang of black olives and anchovies rose from the wooden bowls.

As if to placate her, Gérard's father spoke in English.

And Dorothy listened more carefully than usual to what he was saying. He turned to her more often of his own accord, to make sure she understood what he was saying.

'My own few *hectares*,' he said modestly, 'they go back to my grandfather. We are country people, Dorothy. You must agree with us. In every country it is the peasantry you trust, isn't that so?'

'We don't really have peasants in England,' said Dorothy boldly. 'And cities are useful, too.'

'Cities are corrupt,' said Gérard's father.

Dorothy thought of the generations of city people behind her, but said no more for the moment.

'Apéritifs, tobacco dens,' said the director. 'That's what you find in cities. Here we have good food and a good life. Which means discipline and order.'

163

She understood he was now once again thinking of Italy. That he was approving of Mussolini.

'Order is a virtue everywhere,' she said with as much steadfastness as she could muster.

'Ha. Only those of good family understand order.'

'And peasants,' said Dorothy slyly.

For a moment the eyes on her face were beady and cold.

'Exactly. There has always been a bond between the peasantry and those who own land. We understand what we have in common. Round here,' he said humorously, 'it is not such marvellous land. We can grow olives maybe. But not vines.'

In the car, driving back to the hospital, she said, 'It's no use, Gérard. I just can't.'

'I don't understand. Is it something father said? Surely you aren't going to mind about *opinions*. Everyone has opinions.'

'Why don't you see how it is? I don't care about any of that. But I can't be a wife, Gérard. Probably I can't be *anyone's* wife. They have to *please*. And I hate it.'

He was shocked.

'But I have not asked you to please. Not pushed you to change. Never suggested a visit to a priest, or anything that could offend your susceptibilities.'

'I'm not offended,' said Dorothy wearily. 'But the role of good woman doesn't suit me. That's all. I feel pinned in. Stifled. Ill, really.'

'But you told me you *were*. That you had *never*.'

'That's true,' she said, amused.

'I have behaved as I thought you deserved,' he said formally.

'I know.'

Looking at his dark, perfect profile, she put out a hand to his arm.

'I do love you, Gérard,' she said, like a confession.

He pulled off the road so that he could stare at her.

'I could be your mistress, happily, Gérard,' she said steadily.

He laughed, shortly.

'A mistress? That is not the word people will use round

here. And they will all use those words, you know. There are no secrets for long. And once such a thing is known, it will be impossible for me to marry you, don't you see that?'

'Of course.'

'Even if you are pregnant.'

'I won't get pregnant.'

'You are a completely wicked woman, then,' he groaned.

'Don't be such a child,' she said impatiently. 'It would never have worked. Why don't you *know* that? Now if you want me, I'm here. For a while. But don't imagine I'm going to sit about like patience on a monument.'

He did not know the expression, but he understood her face, and its determination.

And, after all, he wanted her.

She was never invited to his home again. Gérard was a good lover, she found, and not an inexperienced one. She knew that he confessed his sins every week; and that she had become one of them. Nevertheless, she was happy enough, though not with that peculiar winter-sun radiance at the opening of their relationship. Gérard spoke more casually to her; but more variously too.

One evening, he began to fulminate angrily about another doctor at the hospital. Dorothy was surprised to find the man had aroused such animosity. He was spectacled, decent and sallow-skinned; he rarely interfered with the nursing staff; and she herself had been impressed with his intelligence.

'I think he would rather have been some kind of chemist than a surgeon,' she said to Gérard, as he began to explain there was some kind of quarrel between the doctor and Gérard's father.

'Exactly. He's *too* clever,' muttered Gérard.

'But sensible. Not pretentious. Where is he from?' she asked thoughtlessly.

'Aha. So even you can tell. He isn't French. That is part of his trouble. He is *Métèque.*'

'I don't know the word.'

'And I don't know the English,' said Gérard, puzzling for a moment.

'But the country. You must know the name of the country he comes from.'

'Algeria. He comes from Algeria.'

'An Arab?' Dorothy was surprised. She knew few Arabs, but they had all been somewhat swarthier. Well, perhaps she was unwittingly prejudiced.

'Not *Arab*,' said Gérard. 'Not anything. He's mixed-up. Like a dog.'

And now she understood.

'Half-breed,' she said.

She was angry.

Really she should have broken with Gérard there and then. But she still wanted him. She wanted the sweetness of his neatly formed mouth, and his body pushing into hers. And she said no more, even though she guessed the days of their love were already numbered.

24

How could he bear it?

Betty watched her uncle drink tea and eat a piece of lemon and coconut sponge exactly as if Alexander were not dead. With his habitual care he took sugar in Elsa's silver tongs. He congratulated Betty on her culinary flair. Asked after Elsa's health. Inquired into Solomon's trade.

'So. Life must go on,' he said, almost as if guessing his niece's thoughts.

And with his eyes on Solomon he asked, 'Do you have any plans for Betty?'

His niece looked up, startled.

Solomon said, 'She has enough to occupy her.'

'Is that so, my dear?' her uncle inquired.

Betty was not used to questions about her own wishes. It seemed to her that her place in life was settled.

'I like office work well enough,' she said, steadily.

Indeed her days out of the house, though they were fewer now that Solomon had as much help as he needed, were the happiest of the week.

'My dear, I was not thinking of finding you a career. I am not so modern,' cried her uncle. 'I was thinking of finding you a husband.'

At this Betty protested defiantly, 'Please do not trouble to do any such thing on my account.' The declaration angered her. Her face went pink with indignation and astonishment. How could I forget your son so quickly? Have you altogether forgotten him? But she saw he understood well enough, for he lowered his eyes quickly.

'Very well. Very well,' he said kindly. 'Then why not come and work for me? Solomon tells me you have a remarkably clear head for long words and don't get flummoxed by documents. Well now, a law office needs secretaries with a bit of a brain. Why not have a change?'

'She can only spare two days a week,' said Solomon.

Betty saw that her father's mouth had closed into its tightest line. Generally, when he looked at her in that way, her heart began to jump uneasily. She was afraid of him; or more exactly, of displeasing him.

'I am sure your father will not be selfish about it,' said her uncle pointedly.

It was almost as if she could see Alexander in her uncle's face, and she was emboldened to say, 'Well, I think I should like that very much. Thank you.'

Her reply astonished Solomon, and his eyebrows rose in surprise. For one moment, Betty expected him to intervene and forbid her making any such decision. But evidently he decided his original reservation was sufficient.

'Two days, then. And she's not to be employed on any special terms.'

No special terms were necessary. Betty found the job pleasantly easy. And it was not only that her uncle was pleased with her; she enjoyed sharing the office with a group of lively young girls, all uncowed, and friendly, who lived in an

167

altogether new world of adventure; of dances, boyfriends, phone calls, and meeting people under the big clock at Lime Street.

They teased her, and took her glasses off, and made a kind of pet out of her. Nicknamed her Goldie. Betty had never had a nickname before.

'Why don't you come along to the Adelphi tonight?' Margo asked one morning.

'Da wouldn't like it.'

'Oh, go on. It's a Zionist dance. Why not?'

Margo, like several of the girls, was Jewish.

'Well, I can't really dance,' said Betty.

'You've just the build for it. I don't know how you stay so slim,' marvelled the plumpest of the other girls. 'I'll bring a gramophone in. Tomorrow, after tea. Give you lessons, I will.'

'But I mustn't be home late,' began Betty.

At that, the girls all burst out laughing. They belonged, Betty saw, to another generation. They were the girls who had inherited the world after the war; and they were tougher, bolder, and braver.

Betty was tempted.

'Just for half an hour, then,' she agreed. 'Uncle is taking me back.'

And no one wanted to be in trouble with Mr Groot.

'Isn't she good?'

'Light as a feather.'

'She can follow *anything*,' said Margo triumphantly.

Betty let herself be swung in a long spin from one foot to the other, round and round, until she was dizzy; but she lost neither her footing nor her balance. She knew they were right. She had found something she did well. Her natural grace was finer than theirs. Her feet learned the most complex hops and locks of foxtrot and quickstep as if they had always known them. And she carried her head proudly on her shoulders as she followed Margo's embracing arm into a chassis or a glide.

'*Really* good,' said Margo.

'Shall we see you on Saturday, then?'

'Oh, I don't know,' said Betty.

168

'She's frightened of her Da,' they teased her. But their teasing had no malice in it. For the first time Betty asked herself whether it was reasonable to be afraid of her father. And she was grateful to Uncle Groot; because if he hadn't taken her into his office, she would never have asked herself the question.

After all, what was the worst he could do to her?

'He doesn't lock you up, does he?' asked Margo, intrigued at the possibility.

'No,' said Betty. 'Nothing like that.'

'Well, what then?' they cried.

Betty wondered what he could do. Hit her, she supposed. He had as a child. But she wasn't afraid of that. Cast her off? He *might*. He'd always loved Dorothy, after all, and never seemed to mind not seeing her. Was that the worst? In an odd, steely way, Betty sensed she could cope in the unprotected world fairly well, even so. That wasn't the source of her fear.

No. The worst would be Elsa's loneliness. *That was it*. Betty couldn't bear to think of Elsa alone, with no children to love. Alone with her husband. For Betty knew her mother was lonely now that both Francis and Dorothy were away from home; Elsa needed someone to save, or to serve; and even if Betty could not see herself in either role, she could not leave her to Solomon's mercies. I'm not selfish enough, thought Betty. That's what it is. Mother needs someone with a very determined self to love properly.

As she hesitated, and gathered her breath, she sensed from the sudden hush in the other girls that her uncle had come into the room.

Uncle Leslie had a fine new Bentley car which he had recently learnt to drive himself, and on Thursdays he usually took Betty home in it with a certain ceremony. When she saw him standing in the doorway, Betty wondered how long he had been there; whether he had heard the music; whether he had seen her spinning from toe to toe like an abandoned creature in Margo's arms.

If he had witnessed any of this, no sign of it disturbed his Groot features.

169

'Come along, Betty,' he called.

And helped her into her heavy camel coat.

As he looked sideways at his niece in the car, she observed once again something in his face that recalled Alexander.

'You do a good job, Betty,' he said. 'I'm exploiting you, aren't I?'

'Good heavens, no,' she exclaimed.

'Alexander would have said so,' he said. 'You are worth more than I pay. And more than I ask of you.'

Alexander's name lay heavily between them, but her uncle shifted his weight in the driving seat and continued his own line of thought.

'You are too gentle,' he said. 'Like your mother. How is she, by the way?'

'Better,' said Betty.

'I suppose she must miss Francis. Since he moved south. Still, she must be very proud of him?'

Betty thought so.

'Yes. Knew what he wanted, Francis. Always did. A first essential,' said her uncle. 'Do you?'

'Well, I *don't* want. Don't *need*.' Betty stopped.

It wasn't true.

Why should she pretend she had no interest in happiness? She had come to put it to one side, certainly. Somehow she had put it from her, as if she could manage without it.

'I think life could be a bit *jollier*,' she said uncertainly, remembering the bright, intoxicating music, the twirling feet, and all the gaiety the girls in the office took for granted. Her uncle laughed.

'What about Dorothy?' he asked. 'Do you hear from her often?'

Betty bit her lip, and wasn't sure what to answer. Her mother heard less often from her sister these days; but letters still arrived at the house, and Solomon was not supposed to know of them. She could not know whether Elsa confided in her brother.

'Mother often speaks of her,' she answered ambiguously.

'She was a lively lass, that one,' said her uncle, and added

170

again, 'Knew what she wanted, you see.'

The repetition seemed to Betty to contain a reproach, and she would have made an irritable reply if they had not been nearly home. Her uncle had something else he wanted to say to her.

'You remember that young boy, Ian Mackenzie?' he said, at length. 'Nice lad, for all his politics.'

'Yes, of course.'

'Well. He's passing through this weekend. Courtesy call, I suppose. Would you care to come round and take tea with us on Sunday?'

Betty hesitated.

'I'll come in and speak to your father about it if you like,' her uncle offered.

'No. That's not it. But it's all wrong for me to see him,' said Betty, agitated in several ways.

'Nonsense,' he said. 'It'll liven you up. Why not? Part of the family, nearly. Why not?'

'All right,' said Betty, queerly.

She felt dizzy, as if she were still spinning round and round again between the heavy desks of the office. Ian Mackenzie had once written her a love letter; but there was no reason to imagine him now as anything but a friend of Francis. No reason at all for her heart to bang.

Her uncle and aunt had lived since Grandpa Groot's death in the old, familiar house in Sefton Park. And to visit that house had once been a pleasure that altogether overwhelmed Betty's natural shyness; some of the excitement persisted against all rational expectation as she set out in the car her Uncle Groot had sent for her. For there would be no Alexander inside the familiar oak doors; and Betty had no great affection for her other cousins. She had always been rather afraid of her aunt.

And then, how they loved *things*! She remembered as she looked round the glass cases of the heavily furnished room. In comparison, the Gordon house was bare, even puritanical, declaring her father's tastes. Betty's eyes wandered over the dainty, impudent Meissen figures which were her aunt's, she

171

guessed. Her mother had porcelain on her dressing-table, of course, and in the cupboards for use. But there were few pieces on open display.

As she entered the room, her uncle rose with a young man so altogether a stranger that Betty did not recognize in him at all the young, pale-haired officer whom she had been imagining all these years as Ian Mackenzie. He had thickened, and his hair had darkened, though his eyelashes remained the same almost invisible blur.

He came towards her and took her hand at once, with an assurance that made Betty flush. He was behaving as though they met frequently. As if he were in some way part of the family, she thought. Why? Of course, he had loved Alexander, and was honouring his memory by this visit on his journey north. Nevertheless, it disturbed her as Ian's eyes searched her face intently.

'You haven't changed much,' he said.

That word *much* struck to Betty's heart, and she drew her head away quickly.

The girls in the office had made her forget, she thought. She was nearly twenty-four; nearly an old maid, that is, however red her lips and however fine her complexion. And of course the years had made themselves visible in her as they did in him. Ian was now a confident, successful man, and for all his earnest scrutiny there was a glint of worldliness in him. A habit of mockery, which she had not remembered.

'We are all *sadder*, I suppose,' she said, subdued by her own thoughts.

Ian flushed, and she saw that he took the words for a rebuke. Unintentionally she had called up Alexander like a ghost and a reproach. It was too late to correct his impression, and she moved away, with nothing more than a formal nod, towards her aunt in the window seat.

Never apologize, never explain, as Francis had once advised her.

But it was a mistake to seek out her aunt. Elsa herself was often a little uneasy before this particular sister-in-law. Something in the pearly teeth and formidable bust declared an unshakable complacence that came out in her first inquiry about Elsa's health.

'How is your poor mother?'

'Very well,' said Betty, lying instinctively and protectively, as though in doing so she could deflect the comment in her aunt's eyes. Her aunt was clearly always healthy herself.

'Your uncle tells me you are bookish. Could be a lawyer, he claims, but I hope you cannot be so foolish as to consider any such thing. You are far too pretty.'

'I enjoy my work,' said Betty, a little angered by her aunt's certainty.

'Work is all very well, as long as you don't forget to get married,' said her aunt.

And immediately Betty felt like a Meissen figure herself. On sale. Up for auction. From the other side of the room, she could hear that Ian and her uncle were discussing miners, and jobs and the fate of the country.

'Poor Dorothy,' began her aunt.

'I am sure Dorothy is *not* to be pitied,' burst out Betty, indignantly, and rather more loudly than she intended.

Her aunt only shook her head, wisely, and rang the bell for tea.

'If Elsa were stronger I am sure she would say what I do.'

After tea, she and Ian walked out into the garden. It was February; sunny but still cold, with a few buds breaking through the wood of the forsythia, and none of the luxuriance Betty remembered from the days of Grandpa Groot.

'Are you still pious?' Ian asked her humorously.

'Well, I believe there has to be some sense to so many people suffering,' she said softly.

Ian laughed at her. 'But perhaps there's no need for the suffering?' he suggested.

'Of course. You are a Socialist. I remember Francis telling me so.' Betty shook her head. 'So, when the revolution comes, will everyone be happy?'

'At least they might have enough to eat,' he said sharply. 'Have you ever wondered how it is your family and mine are so well-placed? Other people's children aren't so lucky.'

Betty did not reply. Sometimes her heart burned with all

the things she wasn't brave enough to say. Some of Elsa's relations in Austria were far from comfortable, or even safe.

They turned at the garden end, and he sighed.

'I might have gone into politics once,' he admitted.

'I suppose science must be very pure in contrast,' said Betty, thoughtfully.

He stared.

'You worry me,' he said. 'I don't know why. But you always *did*, you know. Do you remember my letter?'

Betty lowered her eyes.

'Please don't,' she muttered awkwardly. 'I can't talk about it.'

'I don't mean to talk about the war,' said Ian impatiently. 'But what I never understood is why you let something I don't believe in *matter* so much.'

For a moment she saw the vulnerable eyes of a young boy stare out of the confident face of the man.

'I'm here for a few days,' he began. Betty quickened her pace towards the windows under their curving iron arch, with last year's honeysuckle over it. 'I thought I might drive into Cumberland. See Wordsworth's house. And the Lakes. Perhaps – '

'I'm sorry,' said Betty.

She was more tempted than he might have guessed.

That evening she took Elsa up her supper on a tray, and was rewarded with an approving smile.

'Francis may be coming home the weekend after next,' she said. 'I must try to be a bit livelier by then.'

Elsa looked into her daughter's face carefully, even anxiously. There was something in her expression which recalled her own girlhood before she had married Solomon; something tentative and hopeful and new.

'Are you content, Betty?' she asked her daughter, putting out a gentle hand to her hair.

'Of course I am,' said Betty steadily.

And that night she lay in bed and thought of her mother's soft hand and her kindness and she determined: Oh, I *will* not. I will *never* do anything to hurt you, mother. Never leave you. Never disappoint you. Never do anything you wouldn't like.

Francis did not return the following weekend. Instead, a letter came announcing his forthcoming marriage to Vivien.

Solomon and Elsa read his letter over breakfast, and for a while said nothing to one another. At last Elsa sighed. 'Well, I'm not surprised. Of course. And yet, I don't know if I will go to the wedding.'

'Why not? Surely you will be able to enjoy a most remarkable sense of privilege. Or do you feel the Mackenzies are not quite as grand as your Hungarian forebears?'

'As you must know, they will hate us,' said Elsa. 'We should be there on sufferance.'

'Not so. They are all most anxious to form links with the lower classes. The most ardent Socialists. Francis explained all that in his last letter. No, the family have made no trouble at all. I thought you might approve.'

'I don't know,' said Elsa. 'I feel we've lost him altogether somehow.'

'We lost him long ago,' said Solomon.

Elsa denied that sharply.

'His letters were warmer once,' she insisted.

'Not that I recall. Or not to me,' said Solomon drily. 'Mind you, I'm sorry too.'

Elsa was surprised to find they shared an emotion.

'I suppose the girl must have her reasons,' said Solomon dourly.

25

Possibly Dorothy would never have left Gérard if it had not been for Mme Mansour.

Mme Mansour was brought in by ambulance late one

175

evening near Christmas. She was a woman who had lived all her life in Marseilles, but her husband was an Egyptian; a good class of Egyptian, as Gérard put it, while observing snidely that his wife might be shy and pretty, but had clearly come from somewhere round *le vieux port*. She was certain to have a difficult confinement, since her blood count was low, and the baby awkwardly placed.

Dorothy had come to feel, as many of the nurses did, that the maternity ward was their domain. The doctors generally were content to leave matters to them. And Dorothy found Mme Mansour's pathetic attempts to outface snobbery around her especially moving. Something in the slight bones of her face, and her narrow body, reminded Dorothy of her sister Betty; and brought out a fierce protective instinct.

Her concern irritated Gérard; and as Christmas approached, and the child in Mme Mansour's womb failed to put down its head as it should, he began to press Dorothy more and more cruelly to take her leave a week early so they could have some time together before the days of family festivity were upon him.

Dorothy refused.

She wanted to be close by to help this woman through her confinement. It was something in the way the woman put her hand out so trustingly to her. But something, too, in Gérard's questions and insistence made her more stubborn. And so Christmas approached.

Everywhere except in the labour ward hung the tinsel of Christmas decoration. Patients recovering from childbirth were surrounded with branches of holly; and the cradles were decorated with the reverence due not only to a new life, but to the season of its holiness. This year, the scent of seasonal Christianity around her was very hard for Dorothy to stomach. She observed how the priests came round more assiduously than usual; and the nuns, too, came sick-visiting and bearing gifts. And one cry rose up from the whole hospital.

'It is all God's will, my children. God's will.'

'Why do we bother at all in that case?' Dorothy demanded of one Irish sister from County Cork, without much hope of being understood.

'But that is God's will, too,' she said serenely.

Dorothy was on night duty when the news came that Mme Mansour's waters had broken, and that she was already shaved and bathed and lying in the labour ward. Dorothy hurried to see how she was getting on. As she expected, she was sitting up dully; the pains had stopped; and she was listening with fear to the moans that rose from the curtained-off booths on either side.

Dorothy smiled encouragement, and felt for the baby's head, which had still failed to engage.

'Keep still,' she advised her. '*Restez tranquille. N'est-ce pas?*'

And she bent over to listen to the child's heart.

'Have you given her any dope?' Dorothy asked the nurse on duty, another English import, as she described herself.

'No, I was told *not*. The child's not in a good way,' said the girl.

'Is there a doctor about?'

The other girl shrugged, as if to say that this was no matter for doctors.

'Good. This one will be slow. Don't rush her,' said Dorothy.

Halfway through the next day, Mme Mansour's pains were coming faster; but they came irregularly and they were not powerful.

'Her cervix will never open that way, will it?' said another nurse, not unkindly.

'And the baby?'

'Not so good.'

She crossed herself. 'Christmas children are supposed to have God with them, but I never saw any sign of it.'

Said Dorothy crisply, 'Shouldn't we be trying to ease the baby round? The poor woman will never live through a breech.'

The other nurse looked at her shrewdly.

'It is the director's son on duty,' she said.

Dorothy guessed at her meaning.

'Where is he?'

The nurse shrugged. For the first time, it came through to Dorothy very clearly that the staff did not have a high opinion of Gérard's efficiency. Just for one moment, her main concern was eased to one side.

'You think he couldn't cope?' she asked.

'I wouldn't send him in if I could help it,' said the other incautiously. And coloured.

Dorothy understood then that her relationship with Gérard was common knowledge; but she was more interested in Mme Mansour's danger.

'But someone has to try and turn the child,' cried Dorothy.

'I have already,' said the other wearily. 'There's nothing else we can do. And when the pains really begin we can't give her anything for them. Mind you tell *all* the nurses that. They're soft.'

'And if it's still a breech? How long can we wait?'

The nurse could be drawn no further.

Dorothy spent her day off trying to rest, but it was impossible. All the nurses were disturbed by Mme Mansour's long-drawn-out howls of animal pain. She had been cleared into a side ward. Her eyes were unseeing, as the pains came too fast for her to catch her breath between them. Her face was wet and grey. Dorothy sat at her side for a time; and then put up her practised fingers to test the widening of the cervix. As she feared, the long hours of agony had exhausted Mme Mansour without doing much to open a passage for the child.

Gérard was in a corridor outside the ward, talking in the tones of a man of the world to M. Mansour.

'Well? Well? What can be done?' The poor man was pleading.

Dorothy heard Gérard's bland voice of male reassurance without understanding the words. Then she called Gérard towards her, urgently.

'I don't know if the child will live the night,' said Gérard gloomily, before she could speak.

'Mme Mansour too is *very* weak,' Dorothy added warningly.

To her surprise her words angered Gérard. 'Do I make you so nervous?' he demanded.

178

Dorothy hesitated. For a moment she thought he had been drinking.

'No one in this hospital thinks I can do anything. They think I was given this job because of my father. But I'm as competent as anyone else here.'

His voice rose. Mercifully, the Egyptian did not understand English. Dorothy shuddered.

'And nurses are the worst. You think you know everything,' said Gérard. 'I can't think why I should listen to you. I've had Matron breathing at me like a dragon. But it's *my* decision.'

'So you'll go in,' said Dorothy, with a little chill at the nape of her neck.

'Miss Gordon, Matron wants you in the theatre,' called the nurse from Mme Mansour's ward.

'I'll be there right away.'

And so Dorothy was there.

She had worked with other doctors in the theatre, and she was moved with horror as she watched Gérard. He was a blunderer. And he panicked. She watched as the child was drawn out bruised and bleeding. There were forceps marks deep in his tender skull. Instantly, the merciful ether was wrapped about Mme Mansour's mouth so that she should not despair at the sight of her dead child. In a moment, the placenta was delivered peacefully. Then Dorothy met Gérard's eyes for one moment over his white mask; and read in them a confusion of indignation and self-pity.

The next day she received a letter from Francis, with news of his impending marriage.

They had not been much in touch, she and her brother, but she sensed in his letter some need for encouragement or blessing. Dourly, she knew she could offer neither. She felt tired and indifferent at the thought of anyone's marriage. He wanted her to go to the wedding. She thought she might manage that. It had at any rate one enormous advantage.

The journey would take her away from Cassis and Gérard.

*

On the train north, as the weather grew uglier and the blue frost in the hillside stubble turned to the deep snows of the central plateau, a kind of freedom began to fill her spirit.

North. Yes. She wanted to go north. Even in England she would go somewhere stern, where there would be neither comfort nor corruption.

Newcastle, perhaps.

On the train home she drafted a letter for the position of assistant matron in a maternity hospital near Consett steelworks. She also wrote a letter of resignation. She wrote nothing to Gérard.

There was really nothing she wanted to say.

The crossing was very rough. Dorothy wrapped up warmly, and stood on deck to avoid the passengers being sick. Snow fell on her hair, and caught in the ropes and all the wooden corners, and only vanished in the brown sea. With the engine in her ears, she thought about the changes in the Gordon family.

She knew Solomon and Francis had sold up the warehouse. It was a planned decision, and left both of them comfortably placed. Solomon had been buying property since before the war; in Seaforth, Liverpool and Bootle itself, and could live well enough from the rents. But Francis had evidently bought himself shares in a publishing firm. Dorothy wondered how he had persuaded Solomon to that. If there was one thing people could do without in hard times, it was surely books. It was a gentleman's job, of course; and that would please her mother. But hardly Solomon. Dorothy smiled, thinking curiously about the girl Francis was marrying. She looked a minx in the photographs.

She wondered what her brother Francis was turning into.

26

The whole tenor of Francis's life in the year following his marriage went exactly as he had planned. His home in west London was furnished with chic by one of Vivien's friends, and Francis allowed his wife a certain controlled extravagance for which she was surprisingly grateful.

Francis had always thought his father a mean man, and disliked his parsimony; not for its selfishness so much, as the way his nature denied any importance to pleasure. Francis was unashamed of his own sybaritic nature. He was inclined to understand it as a consequence of other disappointments; though he let no one into his own knowledge of those.

Now that he had what he wanted, was he happy? Francis had not often asked himself such a question; but now he thought of it the answer was almost certainly *Yes*. It gave him a deep, healing pride to take Vivien into dinner at Ciro's; to know the waiters, and see friends from the theatre and music worlds as well as his own. Vivien sometimes teased him about his pleasure in being made welcome.

'All those theatrical queens are so bogus, how *can* you put up with them? Honestly, you just sit there like a fat tom cat.'

But Francis enjoyed her sharp tongue.

'All that flash,' she always said as they left.

'You just don't see the point of homosexuals,' said Francis, who had become aware of the voracity of Vivien's sexual appetites.

'No use to me, are they?' she agreed.

At home, they were still passionately happy in bed; but there were some areas of potential disagreement.

Vivien was surprisingly, even grossly, untidy.

Francis, who had always imagined that order was a natural

part of aristocracy, had not allowed for the effect of having people pick up clothes for you all through your childhood. There was a maid, of course; and someone to do the housework. Vivien could have afforded as much even if Francis had not been as successful as he was. It was her *style* of behaviour, a kind of careless *messiness*, which began as she flung off her clothes to get into bed, that irritated him first.

He described it as a grand refusal and tried to see it as a lovable eccentricity.

Her attitude to post, however, brought them to their first quarrel.

For Francis, letters were important.

Vivien enjoyed them, too, rather as a child might; picking out the personal ones from her friends, and throwing all bills, and typed envelopes for Francis, and anything that looked boring on to the breakfast table. One evening, Francis came upon a clutch of unopened letters in the dustbin.

The bills were all reminders, which angered him even more. Like his father, Francis was scrupulous about paying all tradesmen at once. It was a matter of honesty not to use other people's money unfairly.

'What a fuss,' Vivien said petulantly, when he put this to her. 'They don't *expect* to be paid at once. Good heavens, it would make them quite suspicious. I don't know *anyone* who pays their bills like that. You mustn't be such a fanatic, darling.'

Francis tried to explain that he had to be; that his credit did not rest on the broad acres of Scotland.

She didn't really listen.

'And there's a letter from Mother,' he said, hotly.

Truly, it had been hurtful to see that neat, violet hand lying untended in the dustbin.

'Surely you admit to an ordinary interest in wanting to read one's own post. From one's mother?'

'As you know, I can't imagine what it would be like to have a mother,' said Vivien.

Her face had gone dull and sullen. She was not used to reproach; and Francis found it difficult to win her back to her usual animation. She seemed to have passed into a strangely remote state; and looking at her for a moment he was almost afraid. Of her and for her. As if he had accidentally pushed her over one of the downhill slopes of the mind it was easier to slip down than to struggle up again.

'Vivien,' he cried urgently.

She turned her large green eyes on him. She wasn't angry; just miserable, he could see that. But when he put out a gentle hand to try and stroke her, she started away from him like a wild creature, and his mood changed to bewilderment.

He was so appalled by her behaviour that he stuffed the letter from Elsa unread into his pocket.

A few days later he suggested putting two letter boxes in the door, with a small cage round his own.

'Put a lock on, while you're at it,' Vivien jeered.

She had recovered from her deep sulk, and was trying to make him feel petty. Francis himself could see the absurdity of a front door with two apertures. It might become a good joke, on Vivien's acid tongue.

He abandoned the idea. The first post, after all, presented no problem; and he arranged for all his bills to be directed to his office.

Francis had chosen his own way of life carefully, confident of his ability to judge the exact publishing worth of a book. And there he had not been mistaken. His fellow directors, who had let him buy into the firm largely because it was in financial trouble, were now altogether in awe of his knack of making the right decision.

They had given him his head because their own collapse was so imminent. But Francis had bought carefully, and well, and there had never been a time when it was easier to find good writers. 'Money is made in slumps,' he'd said, unconsciously quoting his father.

The first successes had brought a mixed fame, but Francis was careful to remain very much part of the gentlemanly club world of London publishing. He had no desire to be pointed out as the outsider, cleaning up while established imprints foundered. One part of him felt that he was entitled to avoid that smear, if only because right from the beginning he published a good list of poetry.

Francis was no longer writing poetry himself. It was almost as if he had burnt out all the joy he had once taken in words, during those last, rigorously scheduled months before he took his first in the tripos. He had deliberately streamlined his thought then; cleared and ordered all his responses; it was at least possible that in doing so he had permanently impaired his emotions. For whatever reason, he only received the old joy now through the words of other people. He could not find his own.

He was not without feelings; could still experience both elation and clutches of anxiety.

'What's wrong with anxiety?' Vivien teased him. '*Excellent* source of contemporary verse, that.'

And Vivien continued to take pleasure in finding words. He included her poems on his list with mixed feelings. Some of them were good enough for him to feel a twinge of envy. But not all. And that was a problem he tried to handle tactfully. He let her choose the cover of the book first, and then the type, before raising the question of the poems that fell below standard.

She was sullen for days.

'I can't *push* the book if you don't take them out,' he tried to explain. 'They offer such an easy target. Their debts are too obvious, don't you see?'

Vivien greeted his difficulties loftily.

'Good heavens, I don't expect you to go around touting my book. What a horrid suggestion. Good poems look after themselves! I don't want you grovelling about for *me*, thank you.'

'No,' he shook his head. 'That's never true in the short term about *any* book looking after itself. And the short term might easily include our own lifetime. Books have to be presented and marketed like anything else.'

'Nonsense. You aren't selling cheese or toothpaste.'

'I know what I'm selling,' he cried, exasperatedly. 'Don't you want to be sold?'

Her sweet red lips turned into a furious thin line.

'When I want to tart, I'll do it for myself. I shan't need

you as a pimp.'

There was a bad week after that, only alleviated by an unexpected invitation from her brother Ian to come and spend a weekend in Cambridge.

To Francis's astonishment, since he had never appeared to be working at all, Ian had taken a first himself, and was afterwards given a Fellowship at Trinity.

Vivien was enormously proud of him, loved Cambridge, and was instantly transformed at the prospect.

'Maybe if we get out of this stinking city we'll feel better,' she suggested.

Francis was too relieved by the change in her mood to disagree about London. And he stifled his sense of mild claustrophobia at the thought of returning to Cambridge. It was enough that her fury might be abating. His sexual need for her, which had not yet slackened, led him to say at once 'Marvellous, darling. And by the way, I've arranged a party to launch your book.'

Her little face lit up, and he realized she had been much more anxious about that volume than he'd realized.

For one moment he considered raising again the question of her early lyrics. Then he bit his lip and dismissed it.

It was a failure of nerve he was to regret.

Ian's rooms in Trinity were grander than either of them had expected; but he had booked them a room at the Blue Boar. For the proprieties, he announced. And then described a recent College scandal, which included a pair of silk stockings being discovered hanging from a Fellow's window.

As they crossed the cobbles of Great Court, they could hear a choir rehearsing the *Messiah*. Ian and Francis groaned simultaneously. Francis's own spirits rose; and he began to look forward to the party with a livelier affection.

It was a very good party, though Vivien drank too much, and in the outcome it seemed more sensible to sleep in Ian's spare bed than stagger drunkenly past the porter at 3 a.m.

'Illicitly,' said Vivien, enjoying the thought.

'We'd better be up early,' said Francis, who did not.

Vivien took a long while to settle.

185

'What a lovely lot of bachelors there are in Cambridge,' she said at last, taking off her knickers and looking for a chair to hang her stockings on.

Francis groaned.

'Handsome,' she said. 'And rich.'

'It's easy to be rich if you're a bachelor,' said Francis.

He had never put it to himself quite in that form before, and it was a thought of such unpleasant vigour that his brain doused his consciousness instantly and he was asleep before Vivien got in beside him.

Soon after that weekend Vivien took to playing the gramophone to herself alone in her room with the volume turned up very loud. When Francis brought work home in the evening, he could hear it through the walls. At first there was a great deal of ragtime. He imagined her dancing about cheerfully to it. Making fun. Miming in front of a mirror. The thought pleased him.

Then the mood of the music changed.

She began to play one movement of a Beethoven septet again and again. The same movement. Pam-*pam*. Pam-*pam*. It was an insistent tune. Francis found it extremely difficult to ignore.

One evening he strode into her room to ask her why she kept playing the same side. Over and over again.

She looked up dully.

'It helps me.'

'Helps what?'

'It lifts me. You know. It's like a shot of coke.'

'Why should you need drugs?' he asked bewilderedly. 'Aren't you happy?'

She laughed at him.

He repeated his question with growing anger. It seemed to him that if he was happy, she ought to be happy too. Why not, anyway?

The question infuriated her.

'God damn you, what did you think I wanted to do with my life?' she shouted. 'I didn't mean to sit looking at these green walls every night.'

'My dear, if you want to go out more . . . ' He was penitent at once.

'Don't you think if I knew where I wanted to go, I would go?' She was not mollified by his change of tone.

He sat down heavily. He knew it was true.

'If it's your poems . . .' he began.

She turned away from him, at once, towards the gramophone.

'If you put that blasted thing on again, I'll break it,' he said angrily.

'Francis,' she cooed. 'It's like chemistry. Why can't you feel it? Listen. Everything comes all right again with the first notes. Listen.'

He seized her arm. He had simply wanted to prevent her putting the record on the machine again. But the gesture changed her mood. With a white face she snatched the record, and banged it on the table so that the bakelite shattered.

He was nonplussed. Stood there. He had no idea there was so much violence in her. And yet he was not, as he ought to have been, afraid of it. She was so slender, so pretty, so well-groomed in spite of the gesture, that he almost laughed at her, almost spoke as if to a child.

'Now look, what a silly thing to do,' he said humorously, as if the breakage had been an accident.

She was infuriated. She used a shard of the broken record quite calmly to gouge a long, deep cut in the back of his hand.

'What have you done?' he said stupidly.

He was bleeding quite fast.

Vivien gave an odd laugh. Francis watched his blood falling over the thick white carpet, and rang the bell for his capable housekeeper to take charge of the peculiar situation.

Francis began to travel on his own. It was necessary to quarrel with Vivien before that was possible, and Francis still hated to hurt her.

'I'm going to Paris for the weekend,' he would begin. And Vivien would look up eagerly.

'Shall I come?' A wave of optimism lit her face at the thought.

'No,' said Francis without looking round. 'I can't see the point. I'll be in meetings all day.'

'Very kind of you,' she said furiously. 'Why did you mention it, then? Just to tease me?'

'To explain.' Francis pretended to be puzzled by her intense reaction.

But he really was sorry for her, and guilty, too; because he hated to see himself mirrored in her eyes as a brute. It was unjust. There was nothing brutal in him. He had meant to be offering her love and protection. What else? He knew she would be alone and lonely abroad, and what was the point in that? And lately she'd been white and faint.

'I have friends in Paris,' she cried out.

'Who?'

She thought for a moment. There was a kind of wildness in her face; her fine eyebrows rose above her shallow eyes, and sometimes the perfectly chiselled lips furiously filled with lust around a hot red mouth in her white face.

He turned away from her.

'Why do you have to nag and chivvy away like that?' she muttered angrily.

'I have to know you'll be OK. It's called planning,' he said. 'Intelligent appraisal. I realize it doesn't go along with euphoria, and you have no stage between euphoria and depression, but that's how it is.'

She stared at him as if he had come at her with a meat cleaver, and then a single tear came to one perfectly round eye, and ran down the white cheek.

The weekend in Paris came just a week before the publication of Vivien's book, in early March 1925. On balance, Francis decided, the trip was necessary, if only as a useful lift to face what looked like a bad week to come.

She was pathetically grateful to be taken; but the trip was not a success.

The reason for her pallor, and her lack of interest in food and wine, only became clear to Francis when they had returned to their hotel room on the first evening.

Vivien was sick into the bidet.

'Dear God,' said Francis in disgust.

'Can't you help me? Don't you see what it is? I can't go through with it, Francis.'

And at last he did see, with a kind of bewilderment, what was wrong.

'Why not?' he said at last.

'It's not my style,' she said sullenly. 'And I'm afraid.'

'Women go through the same thing all over the world.'

'So do animals. I don't want to. I don't want to be a mother, Francis. Have you thought about it? I'll lose my shape, you won't want to make love to me any more. Oh, it's horrid.'

Francis didn't want to make love to her now. But he conceded that her swelling body was even less attractive in prospect. Did he want a son, though? He rather thought he did.

'That's nonsense,' he said, generally.

'Really?' Her face brightened. 'You'll take me away with you more? Even so? And we'll be gay together and dance like we used to?'

'If you feel up to it.'

Her clown's face changed instantly to despair. 'You see.'

He seized her by her fragile shoulders, and made her look at him.

'Vivien, I forbid you to try to get rid of that child. It is *our* child.'

'Oh, Gawd,' she mocked him.

'The child of our love,' he said desperately.

She began to giggle.

'All right,' she said. 'If it reduces you to rubbish like that, I suppose you really must want the little bugger.'

'Do you promise?' he said urgently.

'I promise. To do nothing whatsoever one way or the other. Mind that,' she warned. 'I don't intend to go to bed one hour earlier, or drink milk, or suck iron jelloids, or anything horribly sensible.'

'You'll be all right,' said Francis.

'I'll go riding if I feel like it.'

'You hate riding.'

189

'*If*, I said.'

'All right, I take the point. The child must look out for itself. Fine.'

'But I won't get rid of it,' she said. 'Oh Francis. Perhaps after all you really do care for me?'

She put one long, rather spiky arm round his neck and dragged him down towards the bed, smelling of very expensive perfume and sour gin at the same time. He let himself be drawn, half hypnotized by her, half repelled.

'And when I want to make love, I shall,' she said drowsily.

Francis made love to her as firmly as he could. At the end he was drenched in sweat and exhausted, and it was necessary to go and change his pyjamas. Vivien had fallen asleep. Looking down at her, Francis saw that the beginnings of a line at each side of her mouth were even deeper. She had begun to look drab. Out of condition. And as she slept she breathed through her mouth.

For one moment the regret at the new bond that would be linking them was stronger than any amount of family feeling. When he had washed and dressed it was in his mind to wake her up and tell her that he had changed his mind.

Ian, he remembered, had always warned him she was unstable. Supposing the child was unstable? Whatever did he want with a difficult son?

'Where did you go today?'

Francis bent over his wife's body. He knew she wasn't asleep. And he could smell the warm, clean perfume rising from her flesh. Short hair framed her face vividly, with black eyebrows and red mouth clearly marked.

Her eyes opened.

'Shopping,' she said drowsily.

'Where?'

'To choose material for the new curtains.'

'That's not a long job.'

'Did I say it was?'

'What then? When did you come home?'

There was a little hesitation. Francis caught it as a heron might a fish.

190

'You should have been back at five. Were you?'

' I had one or two other calls.'

'Purchases?'

'No, darling.'

'Where, then?'

She closed her eyes as though her longing for sleep would stir compassion in him. Instead her fatigue angered him further. He was as tired as she. He'd had an appalling day. Sales figures. Costings. Decisions. And he knew she'd been to his office. And not called on him.

'You wanted to talk to the new poetry man, didn't you?' he asked flatly.

Her lips tightened.

'I called as I was passing. As I happened to be.'

'Along which road did you happen? In EC4,' he jeered. 'I've told you not to go there.'

'I wanted to know.'

'For goodness' sake, do you think he knows something I don't?'

'He likes the book, darling. Talks about it. Cares about poetry.'

'Don't you think I care?'

She didn't answer.

'Have you been to the hospital?'

'No.'

'Now that's silly.' Francis was white with anger now. He could feel his heart pounding with it. My God, he might actually burst.

'You're silly,' he said helplessly. 'A silly girl.'

'Hate hospitals.'

'What do you think they're going to do to you?'

'Shut me in,' she said.

Francis sighed. He lay on the bed covers.

'The doctor said,' he began.

'Horrid old doctor. Foreigner. Why can't I have an English doctor?'

'He's the best there is.'

'I don't want a Viennese with a *Cherman* accent,' she mimicked beautifully.

191

'I'm not sentimental about it,' said Francis, after a pause. 'I didn't choose him because he's some kind of refugee. I thought he was rather *wiser* than the others.'

'Good with neurotic wives, you mean? Because everyone is neurotic in Vienna.'

'Well, perhaps that's true,' agreed Francis.

He felt a new, sleepy affection, and bent over to kiss her neck. When she flinched away from him he was deeply offended.

27

Dorothy needed a corset to flatten her bosom for the interview. She wore a small straw hat with a soft roll-up brim, and a two-piece suit with a long waist and box pleats. She smoked without asking permission from a packet of Craven 'A' she kept drawing from her handbag. Her smartness rather intimidated the other four candidates.

She knew it was an impudence to be asking for a job as assistant matron so young; but looking about her at the weary faces of the other women she could not see why her freshness should be held against her. Their sadness seemed to her inappropriate. It was a sign that they had not chosen the shape of their lives; that they had only drifted into their present situation.

And as Dorothy had walked around the corridors of the red brick country hospital that morning and talked with the soft-spoken English cleaners at work on the red floors, marvelled at the tennis courts in the garden, and the raspberry canes and fruit trees everywhere, she was determined to have the job.

The matron, however, relaxed her stern face to smile when she saw Dorothy.

'Well,' she said. 'Do you like the hospital? I'm told you've been walking all round it this morning.'

'I love it,' said Dorothy.

'We are a country hospital,' said the matron. 'That means we have women brought in every day in severe difficulties. It is a grimmer job than it looks. I'm not sure that your experience in a private hospital in the south of France will be a very good preparation.'

Dorothy nodded, because it was a question she had been expecting. 'I have worked in the theatre,' she said. 'Things go badly sometimes anywhere. I am used to keeping cool.'

'You served in the war,' agreed the matron, sizing her up.

'May I ask you a question?' asked Dorothy.

The matron looked surprised.

'Do you find yourself training young doctors in the hospital?'

'Certainly not. Both are old and experienced men.'

Some flash of an unreadable emotion crossed the matron's face. She hesitated. 'Let me tell you what worries me, Miss Gordon. About you.'

'If it is my age,' said Dorothy.

'Not entirely,' said the matron, briskly.

Then she took two notes from the file. They were clearly references from her hospital at Cassis. A dull anger ran through Dorothy's nervous system, but she kept her face as blank as she could. There was no point leaping to defend herself until she knew what had been said against her.

'One of these is from the director.'

'Yes.'

'And one is from the head of the nursing staff. A nun, it seems.'

'Yes.'

'They don't agree,' said the matron. 'Which is unusual, since these things are more often than not concocted by consensus, as it were.'

Dorothy waited, then shook her head. 'I'm afraid I can't help you decide between them.'

'Let me leave to one side the sexual immorality ascribed to you, though I must tell you I am very old-fashioned in these matters,' said the matron.

'Does the director say anything against my diligence?' asked Dorothy stiffly.

'Not precisely.'

'What *do* you want to know from me?' cried Dorothy, flustered now.

'I want to know why you left the hospital with such haste.'

It was Dorothy's turn to hesitate. 'All right, I'll tell you,' she said at last.

The matron made the odd note as Dorothy told her story. And Dorothy spoke without flinching, and without hiding her relationship with Gérard.

'I have to explain these things to my board of governors,' the matron said at length, looking up at the end of the history. 'Thank you for being so honest with me.'

Dorothy left with the miserable certainty that she had not, after all, been appointed. A thin, grey-haired woman, in a shabby grey costume, went into the room after her.

The garden was cold, and lit with a wintry sun. There were lilac trees everywhere, but their husks were no more than bunches of copper wire. Even the Virginia creeper, which covered one whole side of the building, was nothing more than a sinewy web of grey wood from which a few brown leaves still hung from last year's autumn. Dorothy walked round and round the paths; there was frost in the air now, and the path crunched under her feet.

She had never wanted anything so much in her life, she thought. Was it *always* a mistake, then, to want things? She wasted no time on the basic injustice of her situation; nor did she bother overmuch with the fear that the same reference would now pursue her everywhere. What troubled her was that she *wanted* to be here. Through the long windows she could watch mothers with their newly delivered babies at their breasts; some of the women still bulbous in pink candlewick dressing-gowns; steelworkers wives, Dorothy guessed, with broad, cheerful faces. Dorothy felt she understood them. Respected them. Damn it, she preferred them and their problems. Wanted to help them.

'Miss Gordon! Miss Gordon!'

A voice called from the door she had just left, and Dorothy turned towards it. No doubt she would be given tea civilly, with the others, and then the unsuccessful candidates would learn of the appointment together.

But it was Matron herself who was standing in the doorway; and it was Dorothy who had been given the job.

Two years later Dorothy had a letter from Francis, telling her briefly about the birth of a daughter. He did not sound particularly pleased about it, though the child, he emphasized, was perfectly sound. He was off to Budapest the following Monday, and would stay in touch, he concluded. Dorothy imagined Francis impatient with the ordinary tedium of domestic life, and put the letter aside with a flash of irritation.

There she was unjust.

28

The last months of Vivien's pregnancy had been harrowing enough, but her condition after the birth of the child was another matter. Francis was reluctantly forced to question exactly how he was going to cope with the situation. At first he was eager to listen to the reassurances of the St Mary's staff, who explained how common such disorders were. A Caesarian section was always difficult. She was still in pain. Sedated. Post-natal this and that. He wanted to believe them. But as her stay in hospital necessarily prolonged itself, a new and icy certainty filled his veins.

'Thank you. You sat there all the time,' Vivien said to the chair, while Francis stood on the opposite side of the bed, watching a nurse arrange the flowers for her.

'It's only the morphine,' whispered the nurse. 'She'll be

off it tomorrow night. Why don't you come back then?'

Then the next night she greeted him as if he were a total stranger.

'Good heavens, how remarkable to see you! Aren't you an old friend of Ian's? In the war, was it, we met, or just after?'

'She's pretending,' he exploded to Ian in the corridor. 'Punishing me.'

'For making her have the baby?'

'So she told you?'

'Well.'

'Perhaps for that.'

'Mother died of it, you know. We can't imagine how frightening it is for them.'

'Like war.'

'Worse.'

'Was your mother . . . ?' Francis simply could not frame the question.

'Mother was always perfectly sane,' said Ian calmly.

At last Francis let himself admit the terror he felt. 'And Vivien? Vivien?' he asked urgently.

But he knew the answer. He had always known the answer.

'I thought you would protect her, you see?' said Ian, conversationally.

'I did try,' said Francis.

A childhood memory flicked into his mind. A girl on a ski slope, was it, or some far-off princess in a childhood book? He had wanted to protect and guard someone once. Even now the word reached some buried piece of him.

'Did you?'

'I let her do whatever she wanted.'

'I always felt you quelled her, somehow.'

Francis was astonished.

'I thought you loved her. And the poetry in her.'

'I did.'

Now Francis was ashamed. It was an old guilt. He knew it was what she needed.

'Well, you know how it is,' said Francis awkwardly. 'It isn't always possible. To give people what they want.'

Of course he had failed to nourish that piece of her. How could he have done anything else when he had extinguished it so firmly in himself? You couldn't split yourself in two so thoroughly. Ian was lucky not to understand how it was.

'Science is very straightforward,' Francis said.

Ian looked at him queerly.

It wasn't fair, he wanted to shout. Other people were disappointed, as Vivien had been; and they bore up under it. And he couldn't have protected the book against being ignored. Lots of good poets were ignored. Vivien was unstable. Always had been.

Hadn't he always known that? It was how he had won her.

'Let's go and look at the child,' said Ian.

The girl had very little hair, and the wisps were red. The two men looked down at it uncertainly.

Ian laughed. 'I suppose it is yours, is it? There's no one red on our side.'

'Oh well, yes.' Francis looked at the severe, rumpled face, pushed into the pillow. The resemblance was quite strong for a moment. 'Looks like my sister Dorothy,' he said. 'Not on a good day, though,' he confessed.

'Pity.'

Francis knew Ian was thinking of Betty, and hastily changed the subject. He supposed if you were going to have a daughter, Betty's simple, pretty features would have been more of an advantage.

For the first time, looking down at the child, he asked himself: Now what the hell am I going to do?

29

In 1929 only Len made any money.

He had set up his first Leicester shop on Frog Island; it did so well, in six months he had another in Granby Street.

On dark afternoons he could see its shop front, lit with full electric light, for about two hundred yards. He sold cheap plywood, dowelling, and screws in both shops. And they were always full. He had to take on men to help him cut the wood; but he was never far away himself. His sharp eyes watched everyone who came into the shop.

If he hadn't still enjoyed gambling he'd have been a rich man. Even so, he was happy.

One December afternoon he arrived back in Islington wearing a huge fur coat, and bearing a box of fat cigars for Abram, two bottles of Avocaat, and liqueur chocolates stamped 'Kosher for Pesach' with the mark of the Beth Din. Outside in the road stood a Wolseley car with a smart white running board.

'Brand new,' marvelled Benjy.

'Our Len's not daft,' said Sarah slyly.

Rasil fingered his coat wonderingly. 'Such expense! Sarah, take it next door and hang it where it won't be ruined.'

'Just throw it down anywhere,' said Len, his eyes wandering around the room and absorbing the unmistakable shabbiness of the furniture. The piano had gone; and it was a long while since anyone had changed the wallpaper. The unfamiliarity of the household smells made him acutely conscious of the damp.

'So,' Abram beamed, nevertheless. 'My Rasil has a plate of soup for you. Come. It's suppertime.'

Len had expected as much, and followed obediently.

'How are things?' he asked Benjy.

'You can see.'

Abram shushed his son. And Benjy shrugged.

Rasil set out bowls of chicken soup so hot and rich that it had to be scooped from the side, to avoid the layer of burning fat. As he ate, Len began to explain the success of his shops, and his theories about expansion.

'What about it, Benjy?'

Benjy looked sullen about his lower lip.

'I'll set you both up, you and Harry,' offered Len.

'Not *me*, you won't,' growled Benjy.

'Why so quickly?' Abram temporized. 'Listen first.'

'This is the proposition,' began Len.

'Leave me out. It's not my nature,' shouted Benjy. 'I'm not a shopkeeper. I make things. That's what I can do.'

'It's not needed today,' said Len.

'What do you want, all the *stollers* in Islington should throw themselves in the Mersey?'

Harry had been eating silently. This was his usual manner, and his quiet voice surprised the table. 'You can help me, if you want, Len.'

Len stared at him.

'Ma and Sarah have to eat, don't they? We can't go on like this.'

For a moment Len frowned. He had been prepared to take Harry in as part of what he hoped his enterprise might carry. Then his face cleared, and he agreed.

'You sly bastard,' said Benjy slowly. 'You think that'll *make* me go in, don't you? Once we're open.'

Len smiled his old impish grin.

'You won't let the family go under, will you?'

Abram laughed.

'A Talmud *chochom* you'd have made,' he said with approval.

And so it was, that at a time when few families in Islington could scrape a living, the Katz family found itself in 1930 with three prosperous wood shops. The immediate stress of financial ruin retreated, and Rasil began to address herself again to the problem of finding suitable marriage partners for her children. Unlike most mothers, she did not begin with her remaining daughter. She was plump and red-cheeked and still young. It was Harry that worried her, as he always had.

'It's time,' she threatened him.

But Harry was not interested. He marvelled at the energy his mother put into meeting and cajoling her friends to find young girls, pretty girls and rich girls who were eager to meet him. Sometimes he went and sat in the front parlours of Hope Street and Brownlow Hill, simply to keep her happy.

But nothing came of these meetings.

'Now Harry,' she said, one day. 'Listen to me. For once. *This* time you must try harder. Say a few words. *Look* at the girl, at least.'

'What's so special about this one?' asked Benjy, amused.

'Solomon Gordon's daughter,' said Rasil, with a certain triumph in her eyes.

'Gordon? The old landlord? The one they call the monkey?'

'I never heard that. Yes, he owns houses. Is that wrong by you, Abram?'

'Someone has to own houses,' shrugged Abram.

'Well. His wife is a sweet, gentle woman,' said Rasil firmly. 'And her daugher too. I met them at Princes Road Synagogue.'

'You walked all the way to Princes Road?'

'Why can't I walk?'

'This girl,' said Benjy. 'Is she ugly or sick or what? There must be some reason Gordon wants to marry her off.'

'She's a sweet, shy creature,' said his mother. 'I've met her. Would I try to marry my son to a cripple? What ideas you have. See her, Harry. For me,' pleaded Rasil. 'I won't be here for ever.'

'Ma. You aren't old,' cried Harry, horrified.

And her hair was indeed as black as it always had been; and still wrapped round into a bun. And she stood as straight and proud as ever she had.

'But you *need* a wife, Harry. I want to see you married.'

Harry agreed lamely to do as she wished.

Meanwhile, Solomon looked into his wife's pale face, framed as it was by ashen hair, and listened to her description of her encounter with Rasil Katz.

'Yes, yes,' he interrupted after a time. 'The old man is a *frummer* from Russia. I remember. He rented from me for years. Sometimes he was behind.'

'This boy has three shops now.'

'Elsa,' Solomon reproved her, and then stopped.

His wife was ill, and wanted to see her daughter married. Did he care so much what happened to Betty? It was true she had been useful when Francis was home, and there had been a problem finding servants; but there was no such problem now. And it had to be admitted that more equal matches proposed for her by father-in-law Groot had come to nothing. It was what he had always feared.

'But the Katz family?' he wondered, uneasily.

'I know. They are not well-educated as perhaps I should once have liked. But they are ordinary, respectable people. He is a handsome boy.'

Gordon looked at the photograph of Harry, which Elsa produced for him.

'A weak mouth,' he said at last. 'But well, to see him hurts nothing. What does Betty say?'

'Nothing,' said Elsa, a little troubled. 'She takes no interest.'

It was Benjy, however, and not Harry who arrived the following Thursday in Len's fine car, because at the last moment Harry had been overcome with terror at the whole proceedings.

'So cancel it. Cancel,' said Abram, almost as agitated as his wife.

'How can I cancel? I should be there in an hour.'

'A telephone. Phone them. Let Benjy phone them.'

Rasil wept. 'So what could he say?'

'Anything,' cried Benjy, losing his temper. 'Bugger it. I'll go. What do they care which Katz son arrives? The Gordon family don't scare me.'

Abram said, 'Good.'

Now Elsa had chosen Harry Katz for only one reason; the broad, gentle features in some small way reminded her of Alexander. She had hoped her daughter, too, might have seen some resemblance in them to the cousin she had lost. Perhaps she had; but if so, she showed no sign of it as she sat at the fire with a book, listlessly waiting for her suitor to arrive.

It was something of a shock to Elsa when Benjy Katz answered the door. His dark face, bold eyes and confident manner seemed to Elsa decidedly alarming. Even as she ushered him over to greet her daughter, her own thoughts formed themselves round the conclusion: she had made a mistake.

Benjy took in the extraordinary splendour of the Gordon

201

room; and adopted something of a swagger to cope with it. The girl at the fire, he saw at once, was a pretty enough creature, though not his own type; he had never found fragility attractive.

'Nice place you have here,' he said, sitting at Betty's side.

Elsa flinched, and Betty looked up, startled. The noise of the voice was a surprise to her. It was deeper, and more strongly accented than the voices that usually found their way into this room.

'You don't look in the least like your photograph,' she said involuntarily.

Benjy was used to women. As he looked at her, she reached up her hands to remove her reading glasses. If he'd been on his own territory he'd have known, there and then, it was all right to reach across and pat her knee.

She looked at him very seriously.

'Will you have some tea?' suggested Elsa, with a tone of alarm in her voice.

Not only was the boy larger, physically, than she had expected; he was not in the least cowed by his surroundings, as she had somehow imagined from peering down at the photo of Harry's face in the synagogue.

'You wouldn't rather come for a spin?' he suggested. 'I've got my car outside.'

'Your own car?' asked Solomon, a shade quickly.

'The family car,' said Benjy, not in the least fazed.

He looked at the older man, and a flash of dislike ran between them.

It was probably decisive.

Up to that moment, Benjy had been concerned only to keep the family end up, so to speak. Now he confronted active hostility and he looked back at Betty with different eyes.

'What does Betty think?' he prodded gently.

'Well, what I think . . . ' She stopped.

'Would you like to come for a drive? We can go to New Brighton and have tea in a hotel. Just tea, of course.'

She saw, with a kind of astonishment, that he moved in a world where her father's power had no evident relevance. He wasn't afraid of him. He wasn't even especially impressed by him. It's just ignorance, I suppose, she thought sadly.

'I'm not sure it would be proper,' began Elsa.

'Then you must come too,' said Benjy.

And he smiled his openest, freest smile.

Three shops, thought Elsa, overcoming her initial unease with difficulty. Betty said, 'Oh yes, Mother, do let's go.'

Solomon's eyebrows rose almost to his hairline.

'Very well,' said Elsa firmly.

And Betty smiled.

Betty's smile was the most touching feature of her face; it lit her brown eyes, and brought life to her cheeks. Quite suddenly, against all his intentions, Benjy felt enormously protective towards her.

The wedding was arranged in a matter of weeks, and it would be hard to say which family was more astonished. Of Betty's wondering joy there could be no doubt; but Elsa could not help questioning her closely.

'He doesn't *read*, does he? I can't make you out. Your father has no opinion of him as a businessman, either.'

'So he told me.'

'Perhaps he'll be good-natured. Still. You were so cold with the other boys. What do you see in him, Betty?'

'Mother, you won't understand this, but I don't feel ashamed with him.'

Elsa was genuinely bewildered.

'All those others. I could never have. You know, the first time we drove alone down to the hotel, I wanted to go to the ladies room. And I'd never have *dared* ask. Not even the Groot children. But I didn't feel shy with him. So I knew then right away.'

'Good heavens!' Elsa looked quite perturbed. And she remembered her daughter was nearly thirty-one.

To Solomon she said, 'He's just an animal, I suppose.'

'His physical constitution,' said Solomon dryly, 'is likely to be the most reliable thing about him.'

'You look quite romantic,' Len commented to Benjy as he straightened his tie in the mirror over the fireplace.

Benjy threw a half-hearted punch in his direction, and then looked at his own face. At twenty-nine it was lineless; his full lower lip looked tender and vulnerable. His big eyes looked oddly peaceful under the thick black eyebrows that still ran straight across his face.

'Makes you happy, does she, Benjy? Won't you miss the other girls?'

'She's good. Loyal.' Benjy shrugged; he wasn't used to analysing his emotions.

'You'll have children,' Rasil said, and dabbed at her eyes. 'What does he want with girls? He's had enough girls. I know.'

The wedding was enormous, and as part of Betty's dowry Solomon Gordon gave the young couple a house in Princes Road and all the furniture in it.

30

Rasil's youngest daughter, Sarah, married a boy from Manchester shortly afterwards. But Harry remained at home with Abram and Rasil. He was now over thirty.

'He must be married,' Rasil jogged Abram awake at night to mutter. Abram agreed. To be married, to have children: this was the good life that God had ordained for his people. The rabbis had no praise for the celibate. Even for a bachelor son whose work helped to keep the household solvent.

'But what can I do?' he asked, and left the problem with God.

Harry was not particularly unhappy, however. Rasil looked after his clothes, and fed him when he came in from the wood shop. And until he met Josie he had no real sense of what else a man could need from a wife.

Josie was the daughter of an Irish sailor, and she worked behind the counter at Fischer's newsagents. Harry always collected the newspapers for Abram coming back from the wood shop, and sometimes bought himself a twist of tobacco at the same time.

Josie had blue eyes, curly brown hair, and a broad, pleasant smile. Harry thought of her as a child, because she stood little more than five feet tall and had soft, fat hands.

One spring day, however, looking down at her smiling face as usual, he found himself noticing how plump and tender her breasts had become, and the thought so confused him that he turned away from her without waiting for his change. She had to run after him and call him back.

'Harry. Your seven pennies.'

'How do you know my name?' he demanded from her, turning nevertheless and taking the coins from her. As their hands touched, she blushed.

'Well, I asked about you, of course,' she replied with a touch of impudence.

Harry stood and looked down at her in astonishment, as her broad white teeth came out to bite her lower lip in sudden shyness.

She was flirting with him, he realized.

Harry went home with his head in a whirl of unfamiliar thoughts; and Rasil watched him suspiciously as he ate his supper.

'Are you sick, Harry?'

'No, Ma,' Harry insisted.

But his dreams had raced so far ahead of his actions that he could hardly find the words to ask for the newspapers the next time he went into the shop. It was Josie who asked him boldly, 'Do you like going to the pictures?'

'Yes, I do,' he replied, more confident now.

'So do I.'

That evening they sat in the dark together, and Josie's fat hand lay in his. Harry dared do nothing to discover if her soft, baby cheeks and fresh lips were as sweet as he had imagined.

It was an innocent episode in itself and might have developed no further if a friend of his mother, still annoyed by Harry's disinterest in her own marriageable daughter, had not brought round a report that Harry had been seen with a *shickser*.

Rasil didn't believe a word of it.

'Harry? Someone else you must have seen,' she told her friend.

But Abram wasn't so sure.

'Don't jump down his throat, Rasil,' he begged his wife. 'Give him a chance.'

But Rasil was waiting to tax her son with his behaviour when he came in.

He admitted it at once.

'You saw no harm?' she shouted. 'No *harm*?'

Harry had never before resisted his mother in anything, and he did not intend to take her on openly now.

'All right, Ma,' he agreed meekly. 'If you say it's wrong.'

After that he was much more careful about where he and Josie met, and since she was often alone in her own rooms in the evening their relationship developed much more quickly than he could ever have expected. They were probably the happiest months of Harry's life since he had left the school in Eden Street where he had once been coaxed and encouraged.

Even so, he was ridden with guilt. Because he knew he would never have the courage to marry her. And although he had explained as much to Josie he felt their love was unfair to her.

When he spoke of it, she put her sweet fat fingers over his mouth and said, 'I know. But it's all a sin. All the pleasures of the world.'

And Harry sighed at the impossibility of understanding her beliefs any more than she could understand his.

'Will you tell me what's evil in a strip of bacon, for the Lord's sake?' she demanded once, when he turned away from her offer of high tea.

'The smell,' said Harry.

And then he thought about it. He had altogether stopped asking questions like that which had once piqued him. Certainly, he had long ago stopped asking why the Jews should keep themselves as a separate people. He no longer imagined the Gentile world had a place for any of them.

One evening, he came in later than usual, found Rasil waiting up with a stormy face, and guessed she had heard what was going on.

'Of all my children, *you*, Harry! Why? And what's become of your life? You were the brightest of all my children and you've thrown everything away.'

'Nothing to throw away, Ma.'

'Harry. Harry. You'll not marry that Irish slut?'

'She knows I can't, Ma.'

Rasil sighed. 'Then maybe there's no great wrong.'

But there was, and Harry knew there was. It was the wrong done to Josie, and his own power to love innocently.

Soon afterwards Rasil found him a young girl with a friendly face who was the daughter of Grossmann, a local tailor. To everyone's relief Harry agreed to marry her, without making any fuss at all.

31

As a wife, Betty found herself enjoying approval and praise for the first time in her life. Betty was five years older than she had admitted to Benjy. He never cared about her age. She was a source of amazement and delight. Her quiet, orderly way of living in a house was so different from Rasil's energetic bustle. She troubled in ways that were new to him. Icing cakes, for instance; or using lace on their everyday table.

'It's all dainty,' he marvelled. 'And it's all done when I don't see it.'

Betty had never before felt that anything she did was either special or clever, and she blossomed and grew with a new sense of her own worth.

Nothing she had feared turned out as she expected. She had naturally feared the bedroom. Not for what he would do to her, but in case she should be ungainly. But he had found no problems. He said, 'I'm going to educate you.' And laughed, as if he were pleased to find one area of life he understood better than she did.

The whole Katz family, who had terrified her on their first meetings by the pitch of their voices and the energy with which they criticized one another, all accepted her readily.

'She's too bloody good for you,' said Harry.

'Keep him in order. Start as you mean to go on,' Rasil advised her new daughter-in-law.

Betty couldn't imagine what they meant. She could see her husband was a proud man; but it was an innocent male pride in his physical strength, that had no call to subdue her. He liked to take his coat off to load the heavy tables on to a lorry himself. And when he came home, he cared for his body fastidiously; not, she saw, as a Gordon might; not only to clean it from the day's effort, but with a kind of reverence. When he had brushed his black hair back, with his unguent of Old Spice, he stared into the mirror and asked her if she found him handsome.

And truly she did; and thought him sweet-natured as a child for asking. When she moved through the streets of Liverpool at his side, she saw the glances of other ladies confirm it; though it was more his style and physical confidence than his lop-sided face that brought those inquisitive glances.

He brought her gifts daily. Sweet-smelling flowers, chocolates, fruit.

'It's like a continuous *birthday*,' she said, bewildered. 'Can we really afford all this?'

'It's on the slate,' he said.

It was not an expression with which Betty was yet familiar.

Their first financial problems, however, did not spring from Benjy's extravagance.

When Abram was left alone with his older brothers and Harry to carry on as best he could, times were hard; and Len took himself back down to Leicester where the situation was better. Abram wouldn't follow.

'There aren't any Jews in Leicester,' he said. 'What'll I

do there?'

'You'll work and you'll eat,' said Len. 'Up here, the firm can't carry so many mouths. Listen to me, Uncle Abram.'

'Benjy will look after me,' said Abram comfortably.

'Benjy is married now, and he has a wife of his own to think of.'

'If I need help, he won't turn me away,' said Abram.

And so he stayed in the north, and continued to bend over his books, while Harry and his wife stood in the shops and served the customers; until, that autumn, it became very clear that one at least of the shops in Seaforth would have to go. And by the time Abram came to call on Benjy there was really no Katz business to save.

He could hardly have come at a worse time.

'I haven't got it, Dad,' Benjy said, helplessly.

Abram looked round the room of elegant furniture, and picked up the silver cake knife which Benjy had given him to eat his strudel. He put his cigar down on a pewter ashtray; and drew a handkerchief stained yellow with snuff out of his pocket. He blew his nose, and shook his head.

'This is poverty? Come and see how *we* live.'

'None of this is mine,' said Benjy abruptly.

'Not yours? And the house. Is that yours?'

'Don't you understand? I can't touch it.'

'What use is a dowry if you can't touch it? Do you mean even if your own business needed money your wife wouldn't help? *Meshugganah*!'

'Dad, don't pressure me. We've only been married a year. I can't start selling off wedding presents.'

'What good are pieces of silver you can't sell?'

'Dad, I just can't do it. She'd lose faith in me. Please.'

Benjy was embarrassed. Any moment Betty would return from shopping, and might hear the conversation.

'So. Are you telling me to go? This is my son. Are you sending me back to your mother empty-handed? Is that it?'

'Dad, this is the week's wages, take it,' said Benjy, in an agony of shame. 'I don't know how I'll manage, but I'll think of something. Only you must remember I'm a married man

209

now. I can't keep everybody.'

Abram stood up with great dignity. 'Thank you. Where is my coat?'

'Dad, you *have* to understand. I've always tried.'

'The family has always stuck together,' said Abram. 'That's how we've survived.'

Benjy bowed his head. When the door closed on his father, he heard it clang shut like a gaol. It was not the wage packet he had lost that so alarmed him. It was the certainty that Abram would be back for more. And he wasn't sure he had the strength to refuse him.

And what shall I do? When Betty has children, he thought.

That evening Betty sat ordering her needlework box, and he wondered if he dared ask how much money Solomon Gordon had put into her private account. Money wasn't like presents. It was for using. Surely she could see that? You needed it, or spent it, or invested it.

She felt his eyes on her, and raised her puzzled and trusting face to meet them. And he groaned inwardly. He surely couldn't ask her. It would confirm everything her father thought of him. He could not ask.

The next morning Betty sat in the window seat and looked over the garden. The leaves had gone from the high boughs, she saw. There were dry piles of yellow leaves under the oak. The sky was powdered blue with clouds. There was something wrong, she could tell that. Something to do with money, she guessed. And Benjy was too proud to admit it to her. He would *never* admit it. Her heart was squeezed with love for him, because of that pride.

She felt differently the following month when he abruptly proposed they should take out a mortgage on the house. Gordons did not *have* mortgages on their houses. She had learned the principles of mortgages well enough, when she worked in her father's office. It was a method of acquiring houses to rent; and the rent covered the mortgage.

'Who will pay for it?' she said.

Benjy explained patiently, 'We will invest the money in the business. I need to expand. These days, you either expand or go under.'

'I don't think it's a good idea,' she said calmly. 'There must be other ways of doing it.'

Her firmness astonished him; and he knew he was powerless, since the house had been put into her name.

'You mean however badly I needed the money?'

'Do you?' she asked steadily.

He hesitated. 'I'm closing down one of the shops,' he said abruptly.

She knew then what was coming; but it was well into the spring of the following year before they had to close both shops. By then it was a question of selling up the house in Princes Road, rather than taking out a mortgage on it.

As Betty watched the furniture leaving her wedding house, she had a moment's disloyal memory.

'He's a bad choice, my dear. If you want him, have him. Only don't come back to me and beg for him, will you?'

'There'll be no need for that,' she'd said in a flash of righteous indignation.

Now she wondered.

Fortunately Benjy never asked her to go to her father; if he had, she would have turned against him for ever. They used what was left of her dowry and the proceeds from the sale of the house to set up in a small terrace off Crown Street.

'A Katz is never down altogether,' said Benjy when the move was completed.

'How are your father and mother coping?' Betty asked.

'They are all right for the time,' said Benjy.

She was astonished to see that he was not only his usual cheerful self; but even elated.

'Someone has lent you some money?' she guessed.

'Sharp,' he said, amused. 'Well. The day I can't raise money, I'll be really finished. But it's better than that. I've found a little place I can work in. On my own. Using *these*.'

He held up his hands.

'And I'll leave the bloody shopkeeping to Len. He understands it. What I know about is machines. So you'll see. We'll not starve.'

The cheap place was in a road off Islington. And Betty stared round the new workshop incredulously. Every wall was rotten back to the plaster; and the floor was piled up with wood shavings and old newspapers. There were broken bottles, and opened tins of food.

'The wiring is a bit ropey,' admitted Benjy, watching her face. 'The floor's OK, though. It'll hold a sander.'

'How can you work here?' she asked doubtfully. 'It smells as if there might be rats.'

'Rats don't worry me,' said Benjy. 'The place needs cleaning out, I know. It's no place for a lady, but it doesn't worry me. It'll take machinery.'

'Who will work the machines?' exclaimed Betty.

Benjy held up his two huge hands, chuckling. 'I've made a living with these, Betty, since I was twelve years old. So don't worry. We'll be all right.'

She looked at him. 'I'm having a child,' she said dully.

She had intended the news to be a surprise to him. Now, in this dingy lair, smelling of creosote, she felt nothing. The doctor had said thirty-three was a little old for a first child. She suspected as much.

Now this strange disorder released her forebodings.

Benjy was all concern at once, as if she were a precious creature. He put everything aside to protect her.

'Well. How bad is it?' Solomon asked his daughter when he came to call on her one afternoon at her new house off Crown Street.

'No one has ever treated me so well,' she told her father defiantly.

Solomon sat in one of the few comfortable chairs they had rescued from Princes Road. He clasped his bony hands and stared hard at Betty.

'That doesn't answer my question.'

'Nothing is bad,' she cried loyally.

'Well, he's still in business. That much I hear. Did you hand over the lot?'

'What do you want, to see my bank statement?'

'It's not my business,' said Solomon. 'That's all I want to be clear about. I've other children. I want you to understand.'

212

For a moment he looked like an old man as he crouched in the chair like a thin, bony bird, with blue veins in his neck, and dry wrinkled skin.

'We know that. We're happy with that,' said Betty.

Solomon frowned. 'To bring you here, from Princes Road. To leave you without so much as a maid,' he said.

'Luckily we don't need your money,' cried Betty.

'That's as well,' said Solomon. 'I don't believe in throwing good after bad.'

'It's a bad time all over England,' said Betty. 'You are being unfair.'

The idea of a 'bad time' she had picked up from Benjy.

'It's always bad for the stupid,' said Solomon.

'Well.'

'Your mother would like to see you. Especially now she hears . . . ' Solomon stopped.

'Is she ashamed to be seen in this neighbourhood?' asked Betty.

'She's ill, you know,' said Solomon apologetically.

'What is the news of Francis?'

'He is prospering. Naturally,' said Solomon. 'If you have a son, you'd better hope he takes after our side of the family. Either way don't expect anything from my will.'

'I'd have thought you needed someone to give it to,' said Betty, flushing a deep and furious brown. 'You've already cut Dorothy out. And Francis, I hear, is going in for politics.'

'Hothead,' said Solomon tolerantly. 'What's the difference what he calls himself? Let him be Labour, Socialist or Communist if he likes. He won't go short.'

Betty bit her lip. 'I think you'd better go now.'

'I'll tell your mother you don't look too bad,' said Solomon, considering her.

'We're very happy, you see,' said Betty.

It was no more than the truth, though after her father had left the house, she cried a little at his harsh words: 'Remember what I said. I don't throw good money after bad.'

Betty's pregnancy was not easy, and many days Rasil had to be called in to help out.

'She's not strong,' Benjy said.

It wasn't a reproach. It was a cry of bewilderment.

'Let her keep still,' said Rasil, who had assessed both her age and her health with a practised eye. 'She'll be all right through labour; she's brave enough. But she might lose the child before then. I've seen that often.'

'Will you be near her, Ma? I've got to work every hour God sends.'

'I know it.'

'But things are turning,' said Benjy. 'Things are getting better.'

'Are they, son?'

It wasn't the way the newspapers saw it.

March 1934

32

Francis sat in one of the many large leather armchairs in his club waiting for Ian Mackenzie. Well, Ian had introduced him into the club some ten years earlier. Francis had been grateful. It must, he now knew, have taken a bit of steering through, for all Ian's assurances to the contrary. People looked very closely into origins these days. Foreigners weren't liked. Not any kind. And those without a good Church background least of any. Besides, he was rich. That was never popular. People never like to feel bought. Francis understood that. Then he thought again about Ian, and how uncomfortable he had sounded on the phone.

Jumpy. Perhaps he was in trouble. Needed something.

Francis thought about the nature of friendship, and what you could expect from it.

He also thought about love.

He didn't seem able to love anyone as he had Vivien.

Vivien would have seen the joke of that, he acknowledged ruefully. Her theory had always been that he loved no one and could love no one. Well, whatever it was he had felt for her, and however briefly, it had been sweet and intense and it had never come his way again. Sometimes, there was a little, mean flicker of desire; for beauty or fragility or grace. The girl he lived with now was prettier than Vivien had ever been. But it was Vivien's face that dragged upon his thought. Vivien's loss that made it impossible for him to befriend his own daughter.

Vivien.

Francis looked at himself in one of the heavy baroque mirrors which were so much a part of the furnishing. He was still a slightly built man, though his cheeks were heavier and redder than they had once been.

Why do I feel uneasy today? wondered Francis.

Something nagged in his brain. What was it about 6 March? He had asked his secretary to tell him everything he had down; but even as she reeled off his appointments, he knew that none of them was anything to do with the sensation. I've forgotten *something*, he muttered to himself, and checked his watch. Ian was late. Without moving from his seat, Francis looked out over the square. There were no leaves yet on the beeches there, and a few lilac trees, with their coppery husks, looked particularly sad. It was a late spring.

Abruptly, memory returned: 6 March. How could he have forgotten it? His mother's birthday. Francis felt like a selfish schoolboy. It was the first year he had not noted it in his diary. She would understand, of course. It had been a busy year. The year before he had sent her flowers and chocolates. A perfunctory gesture, perhaps; but he knew she had been pleased.

It wouldn't be enough, he thought, to do the same thing again. He must go down to the silversmith after lunch and buy some pretty piece especially for her.

Even as he thought these things, he saw that Ian had arrived. He had paused and was talking to another friend; then Francis watched him come across at his familiar athletic pace. The two men shook hands formally, and examined one another's faces. Ian did not look well, Francis thought. His smile, engaging as ever, had begun to cut deep lines in his cheeks

Ian looked closely at Francis too, but made no comment on what he saw.

'Will you have something to drink before lunch?' Francis suggested. 'Whisky?'

'Thanks.'

Francis signalled for the drinks to be brought, and watched Ian slump into another chair.

'How is your work going?'

'Well enough,' said Ian, without much enthusiasm.

'Have you joined the Party yet?' Francis was only half-joking. 'They tell me it's all the rage at Cambridge these days.'

'Not yet,' said Ian quietly.

Francis pursed his lips.

'Shall we go in and eat?' he asked practically.

'Yes, If you like.' Ian looked round at a group of men talking over by the windows, and grimaced. 'Look at them. Honestly, Francis, how can you bear it here? Don't you know *who* that is?'

'Of course.'

'But he supports Mosley.'

'I read the papers,' Francis pointed out.

'Do you know the kind of thing they are doing in the East End? His thugs?'

Francis knew very well. Moreover, that particular group were not inactive in the club, either.

'Nothing would make them happier, Ian, than to hear of my resignation,' he remarked by way of explanation.

'They blackballed one of your writers.'

'Yes.'

'Well, you know what they say. Let one in, and they'll keep the rest out,' said Ian brutally.

Francis flinched. 'Was that what you wanted to talk to me about?'

'Of course not.' Ian looked white. 'I'm sorry. I just don't understand how you can allow yourself to be in the same room.'

Francis shrugged.

It wasn't until they had begun to eat the soup that Ian said, 'I'm worried about Vivien. Have you seen her recently?'

The name stabbed home under Francis's ribs, and made it impossible to swallow another mouthful.

'In spring. I'm going in spring,' he muttered.

And then he saw the torment in Ian's face, and knew that something had changed.

Francis stayed overnight at the Hotel Euler in Basel, and ate in its excellent restaurant, on his own. He had friends in the university, and also in the local theatre which was that week staging a play by one of Francis's authors. But he could not face anyone. In the morning, he would have to visit Vivien.

The thought oppressed him. Always, he looked forward to

seeing her with a crisis of memory and longing, though exactly what he hoped to find was uncertain, as he admitted grimly to himself. She retained a potent hold on his feelings; and yet he would have been afraid to welcome her back into his life. When Ian had spoken to him recently, distressed by a visit, Francis knew his own would be even more harrowing.

And so he stirred his Vichyssoise moodily. Ordered snails, because he fancied the pungency of the garlic butter. And then ate none of them. At the next table, he could hear a group of people speaking in very strong *Schwyzertütsch* about Hitler. It was hard to catch all the words without being seen to lean forward; but they did not sound disapproving.

Francis felt his spirits fall even further.

The train pulled across the Rhine, still brown after rain. It was hot, thundery weather now, and the sky was piled up heavily with dark clouds. Francis hoped the weather was cleaner and sharper in the mountains.

The hospital was glass and steel, so that the leafless trees and the wild white peaks themselves came into every room. Francis wondered if this was conducive to emotional calm. Still, as he sat in Dr Grossman's waiting room he found his spirits clearing in the thin air. For a moment he allowed himself to look across the encounter ahead to the week following: theatre outings, dinner with friends, work to be done. Yes. It would soon be over. He would be able to return to normal life in all its variety. And yet some part of him groaned with a sense of irreparable loss.

Dr Grossman appeared to take him along to Vivien's room in person.

'Her brother tells me she seems much better,' Francis questioned as they walked the corridor.

It wasn't quite what Ian had said, but he wanted to hear Grossman's opinion.

'*Seems*,' said Dr Grossman firmly. 'Please remember that your wife has good days. Today, for instance.'

'And your diagnosis?'

'The same. The same. She is schizophrenic. Classic case.'

'And can nothing be done?'

'Not in the present state of medicine,' said the doctor. He paused. 'You are the publisher, aren't you? I saw some of your books on sale in a bookstall in Marktplatz when I was last in Basel.'

Francis waved the fact away impatiently.

'That German writer you're so fond of. Did you know he's been in *gaol*?' asked Dr Grossman accusingly.

Francis felt a ripple of horror. Many kinds of madness, he reminded himself. The sane may yet be the ones we ought to lock up.

'He's in exile now,' he said. 'In England he is not considered a criminal.'

'So much the worse for England,' said the doctor.

Not for the first time, Francis considered changing Vivien's clinic. Last time Vivien had been puffy-faced, and her eyes had lacked lustre. Today she was sitting in the glare of the window, and Francis felt as he glimpsed her as though some brutal hand had taken hold of his heart and squeezed it until it was bloodless. She had lost ten years. She looked exactly now as she had when he had first seen her at her family house in Scotland. No lines. No powder. And those long and narrow lips, whose flesh he could still remember, were parted in a teasing smile.

'My dear Vivien,' he said shakily. I will take you home, he promised, inside himself. Oh, yes, I will take you away from this bleak and terrifying place. It has all been a terrible mistake.

'You look marvellous,' he said.

'Come a bit closer.'

He came and sat at her side. 'What a marvellous view.'

'Except I *hate* mountains,' she said. 'Look at them. Great inhuman crags. When did we start feeling reverent toward them? With the Romantics, wasn't it?'

'Probably.' Francis couldn't take his eyes off her animated face.

'Ian says you are very successful.'

'Does he? Vivien, you are looking so beautiful.'

'Have you come to collect me?'

Francis hesitated. 'Are you bored here?' he temporized.

221

'Is there anything you need?'

She laughed at him. 'Yes, of course. I need *life*, Francis. I need a bit of fun. The other patients really aren't much of a party, you know.'

Francis seized her hands. 'If you're sane. You *do* seem perfectly sane.'

She groaned. 'Oh, seems. I know not seems.'

'I'll talk to them,' he said eagerly. 'Of course. It's the most cruel thing in the world.'

A crafty look crossed her face. 'Do you pay to keep me here, Francis?'

'Only to have you attended. Not locked *up*,' he insisted.

'So you can take me out?'

'More or less.'

Francis tried to control himself.

Vivien nodded.

'He is a Nazi, you know,' she said. 'He wants to keep me here because I am a Jew.'

Francis felt the first trickle of fear at such a surprising delusion about herself. She was still smiling. Her tone was still conversational.

'But Vivien.'

'It will soon be the same everywhere.'

'Someone must be mistaken,' said Francis, hopelessly.

'And last night I saw what they were doing, he and his nurses. It was filthy. *Filthy*. Shall I tell you?'

Francis said woodenly, 'No. No. Let me talk to him first. I believe you. Of course. Let me try and arrange something. I will come back in a few moments.'

'You won't,' she said with amusement. 'They have corrupted you too, I suppose. Well, I'm used to that. Ian was the same.'

Francis hated the smooth Swiss face of the doctor who watched him with pity as he went through the files.

'So you see. And last week she attacked a nurse with a pair of nail scissors.'

'Trying to escape?'

'No. The nurse tried to stop her defacing a photograph. I believe it was of a small child. Perhaps herself. Perhaps you

222

would like to see the pieces.'

'It's irrelevant,'

Francis didn't need to see any more. He already knew why Ian had broken down; and yet he felt treacherous. He was convinced. And yet he hated this man and his illiberal opinions, and couldn't bear to think of him having Vivien under his power.

'Listen,' he said hoarsely. 'I believe you. Naturally. So I cannot take her home with me. All right. But I *am* going to transfer her to another hospital.'

The doctor raised his eyebrows. 'So many moves?' he queried blandly.

'Yes. I'm sorry. She has never liked mountains,' said Francis hurriedly. 'Well, I will decide where she should be taken. Perhaps out of Switzerland altogether. France. Yes. Somewhere in the south of France. It will be more congenial.'

The doctor frowned, and Francis felt absurdly afraid that he might object. Try to prevent it, even. But, of course, he was only going to mention money. The matter of notice.

'Of course,' Francis agreed with relief. 'But if you don't see any reason why not, I should like to move her next week. Yes, perhaps it is extravagant, but if it is a question of peace of mind?'

He knew it was his own peace of mind he intended to preserve. And Vivien was quite right. No more than Ian could he bear to go back and tell her what he had done.

May 1935 found Francis for the first time in Budapest. And Budapest surprised him. It was warmer than Paris, less cloying than Vienna; and, for all the political unease, the people were ebullient.

He and his cousin Milos sat at a table outside Gerbo's café at Vorosmarty Ter. Milos was small, neat, fair-haired and brown-eyed. He carried himself in a faintly military manner; but there was nothing austere about his taste for cakes, which were subtler, nuttier and more complex in texture than anything Francis had enjoyed in Austria. The horse chestnuts had just come out, and the smell of spring in the air aroused Francis's blood. The girls seemed to him extraordinarily elegant, and prettier than they had been in Vienna. Their shoes were smarter, and the colour of the leather matched their handbags. And their faces were solidly built, and open. They smiled readily. Francis felt a dubious kind of kinship to them all.

'Well,' said Milos. 'It is said Budapest is a city of Jews. I don't know the percentage. But in the arts. In music. Drama. Publishing and so on.'

He shrugged.

'Is the Grand Hotel comfortable?'

'Yes,' said Francis.

'I have always preferred the Gellert. If you had asked my advice. Well. Tonight you will eat with us.'

'You are very kind.'

'Look, that is Ilyes,' pointed his cousin. 'Our best poet.'

'Do people read much poetry here?'

'Enormous. Everyone,' said Milos.

'I shall walk you round the castle area,' said Milos. 'And then I must be back at the opera for rehearsal. At five.'

'I don't want to be a nuisance,' began Francis formally.

'What nuisance?'

From the castle, the Danube looked quiet. Francis looked down in the sunshine at the Chain Bridge, built by an Englishman; and the green dome of the Parliament building. It was a fine city, he thought. Milos showed him Matthias church, which was tiled like many a Swiss münster in green and gold, so that outside, you might have been in some cobbly piece of Basel. But once inside, the painted column of gold and green and the keyhole arches were there to remind the least curious visitor that the Turks had once taken Budapest, and left their mark upon it.

'But everyone takes Budapest. We survive,' explained Milos. 'That is the character of Hungary. Every movement of the arts, too.'

Francis decided not to raise the question of political movements.

Milos's house, he was told, had a tram stop by the door; but

Francis took a cab instead. He had expected something modest, for his cousin had begun with an apology. Hard times had forced them to close down their house on the Danube bend. Now they lived in the suburbs, without fuss or ostentation, he said.

But not only was their town house high in the Buda hills; their terrace commanded a view of the Danube between the Elizabeth Bridge and the castle. Inside, it was hung with the treasures of many generations.

'Too crowded,' said Milos, 'with furniture from the country house. And you can't give it away these days. Do you like these chairs? All Biedermeyer? Just look. This painting is one of my aunt, and that little girl might *just* be your mother. Well, it is an English cousin. I'm not sure.'

Francis wandered curiously around the eighteenth-century glass cabinets, which were crowded, too, with rich objects in a profusion which recalled the Pitt-Rivers Museum. A piece of carved jade. A horn of Chinese ivory.

'My uncle brought those back. He was a great wanderer,' said Milos. Then, seeing a young woman in the doorway, he added, 'This is my wife, Julia. Forgive her, she doesn't speak English. Only German. But she has one great virtue: she plays the violin exquisitely.'

She was also remarkably beautiful, noted Francis with a twinge of envy.

It turned out she was an excellent cook in addition, and had herself prepared the most elaborate dishes in Francis's honour: stuffed mushrooms, cream cheese wrapped in spinach leaves, sour cakes. What care, thought Francis, what endless *bothering* such preparation implied; what faith in life and pleasure. He was filled with admiration for her. As the conversation moved inexorably towards politics, Francis began to find his cousin's dapper confidence irritating.

'I am tired of hearing about Versailles,' Francis exclaimed at length. 'How is that relevant to Horthy allying you now to a monster?'

'Transylvania,' said Milos. 'If we don't have someone strong to protect us, all of it will be swallowed by Romania.'

'Is that a comparable evil? To *Hitler*?'

'Hitler is on our border anyway. You could argue he is less dangerous as an ally.'

Milos's shrug annoyed Francis.

'Will Horthy protect *you* against *him*? You have two small children. A beautiful wife.'

'Tell me. Do you think you are bringing me some kind of *news*? About this monster?' demanded Milos. 'He's not the first, he won't be the last, Hitler. When my father was still alive, just after I came out of the army, we had a revolution. OK. I was not unsympathetic. Things were not easy, though. Then we had a counter-revolution. That was worse. And the White Terror? Now that, my English cousin, *was* a bad time. Bad. Well, this year, things are difficult economically. For everyone. But it is peaceful. You know, it's not Poland here. We are assimilated. Hungarians. Go to the Opera House, look around you.'

'For God's sake, Milos, what is so marvellous about central Europe? said Francis. 'Apart, that is, from the food.' He nodded across to Milos's wife.

Milos translated the compliment; and his wife smiled. Really, Francis wanted to add: *And the women*. The extraordinary beauty of the women, and their sensitive faces. Perhaps if he could hear her speak, this gentle creature, he could dispel his dreamy illusion of the intelligent feeling behind her loveliness? He had seen the same features so often in the last two days; not all of them could surely be so worthy of love.

'Germany is one country, Hungary is another. And Budapest is a third.'

'I don't understand.'

'Here we are understood. It's our city. I love every stone of it.'

'London has many beautiful squares,' began Francis.

'But *people*. The *people*,' said Milos impatiently. 'Don't you feel the difference? Music *matters* here. It's life to us. Poetry, too.'

'The Germans love music,' said Francis.

He felt gloomily that it was not his place to be telling them what was happening in Germany. But already it was clear that neither talent nor scholarship were going to be a defence against it. He had been afraid in Berlin, even with his Scottish name and his British passport. He would not go readily again, he thought.

'There will be a war,' he said instead.

'No. I was in Paris,' said Milos. 'The French won't fight. If England fights, it's another matter.'

Francis thought of the bitter country he had left.

'Why should anyone go to war again?' demanded Milos, filling Francis's glass. 'If you want to help someone, I know someone who needs it. And without fighting.'

'Family,' said Francis briefly. 'I can only help family.'

'There is a girl who has no family,' began Milos.

'Before you go on, I can't *marry* anyone,' said Francis, with a brutal directness which rose from his last week in Berlin, where he had heard the same opening many times. 'I probably can't help her. I *am* married. Unless something happens to the law, I always *will* be married, because my wife is incurably insane. So in that area I am useless.'

'Well,' said Milos. 'That is another tragedy.'

In the drawing room there was an oil painting of Mahler.

'A relative?' asked Francis dubiously. He had never been sure how much Elsa exaggerated.

'Of my wife,' nodded Milos.

Thoughtfully, he went over to the piano, sat at the stool and began to play. First Beethoven. And then Bartok. Then he stopped abruptly.

'Ach,' he said suddenly. 'Let's have a little brandy. Have you tried our plum brandy?'

Francis accepted the offer.

The door bell went about a quarter of an hour before midnight. Francis looked startled, but Milos did not. He returned from the door with a girl of about twenty. She had the same fine features that had been following Francis around the streets; and in addition a transparent skin that looked as if a light shone from within it.

'Agnes,' said Milos.

Francis found he needed to revise his decision about the extent of help he could offer.

33

Len still drank in Mo Green's pub, even though Mo himself
wasn't there often these days. He liked a bet now and then,
even though times were getting grimmer in Leicester. He liked
the customers, too; preferred them, really, to all the respectable Jewish family men he could have met at the little
synagogue in Tichbourne Street. Len played cards, dominoes,
darts. And talked. Leicester wasn't a blackshirt town; or not a
stronghold, anyway. And he liked to speak his mind freely to
whoever showed up.

One of his London friends from the market warned him
against it.

'Don't cross the buggers, Len,' he warned him. 'They're
rough. There'll be a real set-to, one day. You'll need a few
tough blokes like me to put them down.'

'I'm not afraid of them,' said Len.

'I'm telling you what, Len. You *should* be. They'd beat your
teeth in if they catch you on your own.'

Len was often on his own. So by and large he took his
friend's advice. Once, though, he teased a blackshirt in
uniform with an old joke.

'It's all the fault of these new-fangled cyclists. They're
ruining the country.'

'Why the cyclists?' asked the man, puzzled.

'Why the Jews?' asked Len.

He tried to make a run for it. But two of them trapped his
gammy leg and held him down, and gave him a few kicks in
the gut before they were pulled off him.

He didn't make the same mistake again. But he made
others. And one of them was marrying Sophie Brenner.

When Len met Sophie Brenner money was getting tight.
Worse, he had fallen behind with the business and Mo Green

at the same time, and Mo was not a patient man. He met her at the Starfish Club on London Road, where he was eating with a couple of billiard-hall friends. 'A good meal, might as well,' Len told them.

Mo owned the Starfish Club, and it was a rash place to be eating.

'Give us that song again, love,' he called over to the singer. 'It's my last supper.'

When she came over to join them at the table, Len looked at the blonde hair piled high on her head.

'What colour was it to start with?' he asked.

And she said pertly, 'If you want to look you'll have to take off my wig. I don't do that in public.'

'You're from Liverpool,' he said, awed.

'So are you, from the sound of you.'

'What brought you down to this?'

'Down?'

'Geography,' he explained.

'I wanted to be an actress, didn't I? But not the kind they want down here.' She nudged him.

And suddenly he recognized her. She was a kid from Crown Street. His old Mam had been a friend of her mother's.

'A nice Jewish girl like you,' he said, only half-mocking.

'Now then.' She looked round, a bit scared.

One of his friends kicked him under the table. Len guessed correctly that Mo Green had come into the room, and the time had come to settle the bill and leave. He ignored their signals.

'How do I find you if I want to look under your wig?' he asked instead.

'You can come back if you want. After the show.'

'I have to see your boss,' said Len. He hadn't consciously made any such decision.

'Len,' his friends protested.

'I want to work for him,' said Len. 'It's just come to me.'

They watched her go back to her station at the piano. In a moment she was launched into a full-throated performance of 'Some of These Days'.

'She has a kind of *directness*,' said Len, appraisingly. 'She's quite good.'

'Len,' protested the others. 'Sophie Brenner wasn't *good* by the time she was twelve. And what are you *playing* at? Work for Mo Green?'

'If you can't beat them, join them,' said Len. 'Bookies *win*, don't they? I can't afford to be on the wrong side of this business all the time.'

'But what can you put up?'

'Listen. You go,' said Len. 'I can *talk*, can't I?'

'Let's just hope Mo sticks at talking.'

'Anyway, where am I supposed to run?' asked Len. 'From Mo. Tell me that. And tonight I feel lucky.'

His friends left before Sophie joined him again, and when she did she was curious about him in a new way.

'You're a rash little man, aren't you?' she said, not without a certain respect. 'I've talked to Mo. He says why don't you leave. He likes you.'

'Because I want a chat,' said Len, tilting his chair backwards.

Then big Mo was standing over the table, looking down in a puzzled way and frowning.

'What use are you to me, Len? You're straight. Times are hard, but they'll turn. What are you after?'

'He's from Liverpool,' said Sophie.

Mo looked at her blankly.

'Listen to Mae West,' said Mo. 'The queen of logic herself. Do you play cards?' he asked Len suddenly.

'A little.'

Mo laughed. 'Let's cut for your stake,' he said. 'You haven't anything to begin, have you? Let's see if you're lucky.'

'Of course I'm lucky. I have to be lucky,' said Len.

And he kept his eyes on Sophie all through the game.

She's a good girl all right, he thought.

Which was how he came to work for Mo Green. Almost as an afterthought he married Sophie.

She said, 'If you ever make any money, will you see me on the stage? I mean the *real* stage?'

Len said he would do what he could; but in daylight he could see it wasn't going to be easy.

34

It was Solomon who decided to summon Dorothy home.
Everyone knew this could only mean that Elsa was dying.

Dorothy took the telephone call from her Uncle Leslie in the
matron's office. She had spoken to him very little over the
intervening years, and seen him not at all. But as soon as she
heard his voice, she knew. Not only who he was, but the news
he had to give her. She spoke with pain in her throat.

'I'll drive across,' she said. 'Over the Pennines. It's best.'

Her uncle evidently could not imagine a woman in sole
control of a car, and hinted that it would be better not to come
alone if possible.

'I'm *always* alone when I travel,' said Dorothy, with a trace
of her normal strength returning to her voice.

Luckily it was June, and there was neither mist nor ice to
fear, because Dorothy drove more carelessly than usually. Not
only because the roads were quiet, but because her mind was
buzzing with thoughts she had not let herself think, feelings
she had not even known she had buried.

Mother, she thought, forgive me. I could have seen you.
Any time I wanted to. You must have known that. I wasn't
afraid of *him*. What could he do to me, the old man? I'm taller,
stronger, younger. And if I'd faced him out, don't I know
underneath he too would have been glad to see me?

So why did I keep away all those years, and leave you to
wonder what was happening to me, to give me up, keep me as
a secret? Why?

The winding road was always a difficulty. Today the turns
and the hot sun together made Dorothy feel sick. At times she
had to stop at the roadside and vomit into the grass. Nerves,
she told herself, angrily; I wish I'd brought some kind of

231

sedative. But she knew that the dizziness came from some part of herself that was out of reach of alkaline comfort.

I was as mulish as he was, she admitted. I punished *her*, in showing him that I didn't care. I left her to him. How could she forgive me that? All those years?

She wondered what had become of Francis. At his wedding she had seen he was no longer a mother's boy. But was he prematurely old, as she felt herself to be? Prematurely wise with the burden of other people's sorrow, safely with none of his own, as she had thought herself to be. More than fifteen years. I must be a stone, she thought, to have left it so long. And had to pull into the kerb again.

Would she be in time? In her imagination she gathered her mother lovingly into her arms and held her close many times before she found the road that signposted Liverpool. But when at last she drew up outside the old, familiar house, she knew it was already too late.

The sadness, thought Dorothy, of spending the last years of your life waiting for people who never came. For Francis would have returned home rarely, she knew him well enough for that; even though he would have been welcome. Now he stood there alone, looking a little balder than she had expected and faintly paunchy, though his structure would always be narrow. All the Gordons were narrow men.

Dorothy looked around for her father. Where was Solomon?

She hardly recognized him for one moment after he came in the room, so much had he aged. He had no hair, his moustache was grey, and his shoulders were stooped. Then she recognized the same sharp eyes, the narrow face, and the watchfulness in him.

'Well, Dorothy,' he said. 'I got it wrong. She knew you were coming, and she was happy all morning. Then . . . '

He stopped.

'I'm sorry,' he said queerly.

Dorothy wished she could put out a hand to him, or to any of them. Instead, she felt a new dizziness overcome her, and she sat on the edge of a chair.

'You sit down too, Da,' said Betty quietly. 'I'll get some tea.'

'Someone had better do the arranging,' said an unfamiliar voice.

Dorothy looked across at the unfamiliar giant sitting in the dark corner of the room, and supposed the voice must come from Betty's husband. She had not been to that wedding; it was too much a family affair; Solomon's occasion; even Betty understood the impossibility. Even through her grief, Benjy's size and physical presence struck Dorothy as alien.

'I've seen to all that,' said Francis with a touch of irritation in his voice. As if any matter of organization could be overlooked by a Gordon.

On the way to the cemetery Francis and Dorothy sat side by side in silence. At length Dorothy roused herself to examine her brother closely. He looked far older than his early thirties. It wasn't just the silver hair at his temples – which suited him – or the red cheeks of the *bon viveur*.

'How's your wife?' she asked abruptly.

She had to repeat the question.

'Vivien, I suppose you mean. She's in Geneva.'

'Of course I mean Vivien. Do you have more than one wife?'

'She's in a clinic,' said Francis. 'We are more or less separated.'

Dorothy knew she was supposed to leave the matter there.

'What kind of clinic?' she continued, nevertheless.

Francis's urbanity cracked. 'You were always a nosey bitch,' he remarked.

'Well?'

'She's deranged,' said Francis coldly. 'Hopelessly, out of reach of all treatment. *Mad*. Do you understand that? I don't.'

'It's uncommon. What have they used?'

'Everything. Shock. Electricity. Drugs. She doesn't say anything now. Just sits. In one position. Dorothy, you can't imagine the nightmare.'

'Schizophrenia.'

'Yes.'

'You mustn't blame yourself.'

233

'I wasn't thinking of it,' said Francis.

Dorothy sat silent.

'Look at the world,' said Francis. 'How can you bring children into it? Any children. To be hated, or sent to die. Dropped out of windows in Poland. Slashed with cutlasses in Odessa. Starved in Romania. It's not a world to bring children into.'

'It's always been that kind of world. When was it better?'

'There's another war coming,' said Francis. 'You may not feel that up in Newcastle.'

'Durham.'

'If you travelled round central Europe you could smell it. The excitement and the fear.'

'When was it better?' repeated Dorothy. 'Hope. Children are hope, Francis. I've seen miners' wives who'll be back on their knees scrubbing as soon as they get back home, whatever I tell them. And they can smile. They know how to love.'

'They're too stupid to know anything else. They're lucky. Like animals. It's more than war I'm afraid of.'

He was still shaken by his last visit to Berlin.

'Do you know what's happening in Germany?' he asked.

Dorothy shrugged and said, 'I take what I read in the newspapers with a pinch of salt. Remember those Belgian atrocities?'

'This time it's all true,' said Francis. 'Old men standing in the snow for hours with placards round their necks. Young men looting and raping.'

'And your daughter?' asked Dorothy, after a pause.

'As far as I can tell, perfectly normal.'

'I mean, who is looking after her,' said Dorothy patiently, 'if you're away so much?'

'Nannies. Bloody expense, they are.'

Dorothy examined her brother closely.

'You can't really be as cold a fish as you seem.'

'I hope I'm neither cold nor hot.'

'Aren't they the ones Christ spewed out of his mouth?' cried Dorothy.

'Probably. Not like you to go in for quotation, though.'

'I can't bear what's happened to you,' cried his sister. 'You

234

were always the one she loved best; she'd have so hated to see it.'

For a moment they were both silent.

Then Francis said, a little gruffly, 'Well, she never did see it.'

'She saw what there was,' said Dorothy.

'You know, I wonder if men ever feel her kind of love? For children. I thought I would. I wanted a child. And then . . .'

'I want your child,' said Dorothy. 'I'll look after her.'

She hadn't known she was going to say it, and it left her breathless.

Kaddish. A strange prayer, mused Francis. No word of consolation for loss, no hint of where the spirit had gone, only praise. Praise for God at least. But what of the flesh gone into the sweet-smelling earth?

He could not follow the Hebrew as the service continued. His eyes flicked over to the opposite page to follow the English: 'As for man, his days are as grass; as the flower of the field so he flourisheth. For the wind passeth over it, and it is gone; and the place thereof shall know it no more.'

Francis's heart felt cold and heavy. He hadn't seen Elsa all year; he'd been too busy expanding the business in Europe, too busy enjoying his London club life and his literary friends. Too *busy*, altogether. Doing what? He couldn't be sure. The year went hazy in his memory as he tried to remember it. The wind, he thought, the wind. It passed over and through me.

I'm afraid, he thought. That's what it is. I'm thinking of my own death. That's why I'm shivering. He watched his father's face. Woodenly, the small, neat mouth was repeating the worn phrases as if from somewhere in his childhood. He was grieving, thought Francis, more than he expected to. Well. And Dorothy? Her eyes were unashamedly red.

Who will mourn me? wondered Francis.

And then gave himself a shake. It was no way to live, that, thinking of death. A man had to live as if he was immortal.

'If a man live a year or a thousand years, what profiteth him?' the rabbi intoned.

A good deal, thought Francis grimly.

And a friend of his had said exactly that, the other day: I want to live for ever and ever, he'd said. Anyway, that's what I'm going to pretend.

But *he* meant a life's work, thought Francis, with his spirits falling. Even the hope of fame had a certain corrupt joy attached to it. What am I working for? Money? He had enough. A good publishing list? Well, I thought I was building a life's work once, he thought; but it makes no odds. Everything vanishes together.

'A woman of worth . . .'

His eyes caught on the familiar words.

Stop, prayed Francis. Oh, stop. This is terrifying. I don't want to feel this. I don't want to feel *any* of this. I don't *want* to remember. I don't want to think of her, bending over me, scented with lavender, stroking my hair back.

'Francis.'

All right, thought Francis dourly. She was a good woman. So what kind of a life did she have? Had she ever been able to lift up her head as she should? She'd been cowed all her life by a man half her size, who never *knew* her worth while she lived. And even now. He looked across at Solomon suspiciously; but the face remained impenetrable. Habits formed over sixty years are not broken easily.

Then Francis noticed himself standing with his hands clasped across his waistcoat in the very same attitude as his father. My God, thought Francis.

Am I turning into him?

Mother, he tried to explain. I had to push for something. Had to. What else should I have done with my life? That *was* what you wanted for me. Wasn't it?

The coffin stood on a small wheelbarrow, ready to be pushed outside on to the burial ground. They all followed it. Francis thought: She's in there. Inside that box. If I lifted the lid I could see her.

They were standing on the planks round the grave. More prayers. More sonorous Hebrew. And then, to Francis's surprise, Betty's husband thrust a shovel into his hand.

'Go *on*,' he said quite gently, as if talking to a child.

And Francis, as the only son, followed his father. Together they shovelled the first black soil on to the wooden box in which she lay.

Solomon had arranged to sit *shiva* as formally as if he had lived all his life a devout Jew. All the mirrors in the house were covered and low stools were brought from Fountain Road Synagogue. Solomon sat on one of them with Francis and Elsa's surviving brother beside him. He had provided all of them with skullcaps. Before the prayers began, mourners filed by to shake hands and wish all them long life.

There were several men from the Katz family. Abram had said, 'You know, they might have trouble finding a *minyan*.'

Among them was Len. He had thickened in recent years; he wore a trilby now, which he slanted over his forehead, and a well-cut dark suit. He recognized Dorothy at once and easily – he had seen her photograph on Betty's sideboard – and he watched her for any flicker of recognition with a bleak, masochistic sense of his own ageing.

Dorothy felt his eyes on her, and their curiosity aroused her own. Men did not look her over so often these days. Her hair was darkening at the roots, and her dry skin had lined early round the eyes. Today, she knew, there were pouches under them. There was no trace of memory. As she looked at him covertly, she saw only a middle-aged man with a sallow face. In her northern village there were few Jews; and she had not visited London for years. Len's heavy features, and his way of standing in a kind of slouch, were altogether alien.

Afterwards, as they were eating hard-boiled eggs and chopped herring, she went over to him and said abruptly, 'I know you, don't I?'

'Do you?' he asked.

The voice rose mockingly; and suddenly Dorothy wondered. It brought back memories of a young boy, a torn leg, and an impudent grin. And yet the face remained unfamiliar.

'From the war?' she asked uncertainly.

Her mind had been jumping in and out of childhood squabbles and forgotten conversations all day.

Len was pleased, and nodded.

'What on earth are you doing here?' she asked.

'You weren't at Betty's wedding, or you'd know.'

He nodded across at his cousin.

Horrors, thought Dorothy. Poor Betty. And her mouth tightened with her distrust of the whole Katz family. Len saw as much, and was angered.

'You won't find a boy with a better heart anywhere,' he said abruptly.

'He's not too bright, though, is he? Da says.'

'He's stubborn,' said Len slowly. 'And there's a kind of sense that has nothing to do with being bright.'

'Is there? Well, I wouldn't bet on it,' said Dorothy.

'I'm a betting man,' said Len. 'It's my trade. I'll give you long odds.'

'What do you mean? You're a *bookie*?'

'Anything. Cards. Dogs. Roulette. I was in Le Touquet last weekend.'

'And you make money at that?'

'I live on my wits,' he said. 'It's up and down.'

Her eyes took in the neatly tooled cigarette case he opened for her. She nodded thoughtfully.

'Doesn't it worry you?' she asked thoughtfully. 'That you're just the kind of Jew the blackshirts have in their minds?'

Len laughed at this until he coughed. 'An international *banker*,' he mocked her. '*Really*?'

'No. But you cut corners. You aren't straight. That's what people say about us. Isn't it?'

'Us?' he jeered. 'Exactly. They say that whatever. Always have. They say it about tailors laid off from work three years. *And* their kids. I wouldn't think you know so much about that. It's some conspiracy we're running, the poor Jews in Whitechapel Road. International money? They can't pay the gas.'

Dorothy lit her cigarette impatiently.

'*Money* isn't honest,' said Len. 'That's the truth of it.'

'Miners earn honest money,' argued Dorothy.

'They earn a slice of bread and dripping for their kids, maybe. Only don't talk to me about mines now. I remember when they lost their fight in the twenties. We all knew what was coming. My lot had nothing to do with it.'

'In this country you can still get a job if you don't mind work,' insisted Dorothy.

'Tell that to the cutters and pressers in Stepney. And *they're* the ones whose kids get their heads banged on the paving stones by the blackshirts. Since you mention the buggers. Tell you one thing. If those swine ever do get to any kind of power in this country, I know who I want standing by my kids,' said Len. 'If there's real trouble. Benjy Katz. Not your sodding brother.'

Dorothy looked across at Francis, who was delicately patting the herring from his lips.

She laughed.

'All right.' Then she hesitated. 'You're married, then?'

Len took her left hand and looked down at her ringless fingers. 'Aye. Well, it's not been so marvellous,' he admitted. 'No point grieving, though.'

35

Francis's daughter Katharine had small features, a round and dimpled face, and golden-brown curls. She stood in the hall of her father's flat, ready and packed to go away with Dorothy. And her docility, obedience, and ceaseless *smiling* struck Dorothy to the heart. She knew very well that all those things were signs of terror; ways to ingratiate the stranger; to placate the new and dangerous holder of power. Katherine was about ten, and Dorothy wondered how many nannies the girl had faced with the same repertoire of charms.

'I am your aunt. But you may call me Dorothy,' she said hopefully.

'Are we going by *train*?' asked the girl.

'Car,' said Dorothy. 'Why?'

The girl seemed relieved; and Dorothy judged that Francis

had usually explained precious little about her destinations on other occasions.

'Let me tell you *where* we're going. We're looking for a road called the A1. Then we're going to drive straight north. Up the Edgware Road. All the way up England to where I live.'

'Up?'

'North,' said Dorothy. 'When we get home I'll show you on a map. But it's a long, long drive. Maybe five hours.'

'Oh.'

'So you'd better snuggle down under those blankets on the back seat, and go to sleep. When it's time for tea I'll wake you up. What do you like for tea?'

The girl had already arranged herself under the blankets on the back seat, and didn't answer the question. Rather surprised. Dorothy repeated it.

'I don't know,' said Katherine.

'Everyone knows what they *like*,' said Dorothy impatiently. 'Hot chocolate? Fudgecake? Crumpets? Anchovy toast?'

'Ugh,' said the girl.

'*Which* is ugh?'

'Anchovy toast,' said the girl. 'Had that lots.'

Dorothy was rather surprised to hear it. Francis must have employed a very high-class type of nanny, she decided. Probably had tea at Fortnum and Mason's each afternoon, and ordered what she liked herself on Francis's bill.

'Well, we shan't have any of it, today,' she declared. 'Don't care for it myself much. *Toast* is all right though, isn't it?'

'Buttery toast,' whispered the girl.

'Lovely. Now go to sleep.'

Dorothy knew there was bound to be some stir of excitement at the unannounced arrival of a dependent child; and she wouldn't have been surprised at a little unkind speculation about their exact relationship among the nursing staff. She had been appointed Matron a year ago; and she knew she could deal with it. What she *hadn't* expected was a problem with the girl herself. Dorothy was very matter-of-fact about the hospital; the child was rapidly installed in the spare room

240

of the matron's flat; and she made arrangements for her to attend the local school. At least during termtime, when Dorothy was always available before supper, she expected the child to find it easy to feel her situation was a normal one.

But it took a long time to gain the child's confidence. Francis phoned once a week; and whenever the child took the phone to speak to him, her face fell into the same falsely ingratiating expression she had worn to greet Dorothy on the first day.

'Yes, Father. *Very* happy. Am I going to be staying up here all term?' she asked politely.

Dorothy could not help but wonder what went on in her silky golden head; and what she was being told at the other end of the telephone.

She had never had much time for fiction. Now she found children's stories to read to the child before she went to sleep. Children were not like babies, she discovered. They needed more than warmth, food, and cuddling. They had another need: *entertainment*. A basic human need, too, Dorothy reflected. So she read the child story books with skills of an actress she had never known she possessed. And she used the name for Katharine the nurses used: Kitty. It seemed to please the child.

There was always a large Christmas tree at the hospital. Parcels for Kitty from all the nurses were hung on it weeks in advance. The child was fascinated by it. At the same time, there was something she seemed to dread. Dorothy guessed she was expecting to be removed by her father before she had a chance to open the parcels, so she rang Francis.

'Have you any plans for Christmas?' she asked.

There was a silence at the other end of the line.

'Hello?'

'My God, Dorothy, have you any idea what is happening in Europe? Do you know what is happening in Prague? In Vienna? All over Germany? Christmas. My God, I thought you at least had more sense.'

'You aren't coming up here, then,' said Dorothy.

The relief that flooded her was like alcohol.

'Must I? I can arrange something, I suppose. If it's necessary.'

'Francis, I'm only trying to be sensible,' she said. 'Of course not. I only need to know.'

'I'm sorry if I was irritable.'

'Will you be alone?' she asked, with sudden curiosity. She did not know why.

'No,' he said, after a pause. 'I have a young Hungarian refugee with me.'

Jubilantly, Dorothy guessed at months and months of secure mothering ahead.

She explained as much to the child gravely.

The reaction surprised her. Kitty burst into tears. Dorothy put out her arms unthinkingly, and the child rushed into them, and sobbed bitterly while Dorothy tried to imagine what to do for the best. It was difficult to explain a father to his daughter.

But it seemed she had the diagnosis entirely wrong. When the child had wiped her nose and her eyes, and was sitting on Dorothy's lap, she did not speak of her father. She said, 'Aunt Dorothy, I wish it was true what the nurses say.'

'What's that?'

'That I'm *your* baby.'

Dorothy held her close.

'Do they? Foulmouths,' she said.

'Then I could stay here,' said Kitty.

Dorothy was moved. 'Kitty, you can stay here as long as you want.'

'But you'd have to keep me yourself, wouldn't you? If Daddy didn't pay you a lot.'

At this, Dorothy felt herself going red with anger. 'Nobody pays me,' she said.

'You mean you just keep me for *nothing*?' asked the child incredulously.

Dorothy nodded. For love, she thought.

After that, she felt the child belonged to her for ever.

36

The name of Betty's daughter had always been a source of controversy. She should have been named after someone dead; and the Katz family had a host of suggested names of dead relatives who could be invited into the baby's soul.

'No,' Betty had said stubbornly to them all. 'Not Leah, not Becky, not Deborah. I'll know the name when I find it.'

When she did find it, everyone was bewildered.

'What kind of name is that? A real *yokkische* name.'

'You can't call a child after a heathen goddess.'

'It's not in the Torah,' said Abram finally.

Benjy was perplexed.

She had had a difficult time giving birth; and though Benjy would have liked a son, he was pleased enough with the bright-eyed miracle of flesh that was his daughter.

'Listen. What *we* call her, what *we* put on the birth certificate. Abram doesn't care about that. Call her Becky Diana. He'll use one name, we'll use the other. Why do you *like* this name so much, anyway?'

'It sounds so clean. So strong,' said Betty.

She thought of her sister up north, of seabirds, of wild and lonely creatures. But she stroked Benjy's enormous hand and said none of that. She had learned there were many things he did not understand, and she did not want it to become a source of estrangement.

When his wife was a little stronger Benjy arranged to take her on a weekend to Southport.

'Can we afford it?' she asked, troubled.

'Let me worry about that.'

But she knew he didn't worry; that he never would. And the memory of her own childhood rose up to bewilder her. Solomon had always thought of holidays as *wasteful*, and some

243

part of that training remained. The kosher guest house in which they stayed was more expensive than anything Solomon would have chosen. Her nostrils widened with disapproval when she saw the rooms, and she was glad to think of her daughter safely back home in Rasil's care. Was the food *clean*? she wondered apprehensively. And such a price.

But the sands were white and shining under the spring sun. Betty had never learned to swim; Benjy threatened to teach her. But the sharp salt wind on their cheeks made him hesitate.

'I'll just have a dip, first,' he said.

He threw off his trousers and in he went in his trunks, his arms breaking the surface of the waves strongly as she watched.

The piled sand sheltered her from the wind as soon as she sat down, and the sun began to burn her face. When he came bounding out and threw himself into the sand beside her she made no protest, even though the wet sand went all over her new coat.

'Lovely,' she agreed.

'Just what the doctor ordered,' he said approvingly.

'What are you thinking of?' she asked.

'I was remembering,' he said drowsily. 'When I was little. Ma once threw hot boiled syrup on to the snow. And it turned into toffee. Delicious. Come on.' He jumped up. 'Let's run.'

She looked uncertain.

'Take your shoes off. You aren't an old lady yet.'

He has taken my years away, she marvelled. He has given me back my girlhood. He took her hand, and snatched her to her feet, and they ran together with salt on her lips and the seaweed smell in her mouth, until her heart began to bang and her lungs ached.

'Stop,' she called out.

And he did so at once, obediently, even anxiously.

'There. That's brought a bit of colour to your cheeks,' he said.

'I'll never have red cheeks like your sister,' said Betty ruefully.

37

As a small child in a small bed, in Arundel Avenue, Diana loved her parents with a fierce possessiveness. She watched the pear tree shadows on her bedroom curtains, and liked to think of her parents near at hand.

'Mum,' she often called first.

And then, if there was no reply, in a rising voice, with fear beginning to send the blood racing round her body, 'Daddy. Daddy. Where are you?'

She would call again then on a shriller note; but no one came. Neither mother nor father. What *could* have happened to make them abandon her?

Sometimes, as she began to sob piteously, she heard shuffling, slippered steps coming upstairs, and she remembered. And then she knew her grandfather was staying with them. That knowledge did not soothe her, because it didn't explain what had happened to the only people she cared about. And Grandfather himself was always a little strange to her, especially in his nightwear; and she couldn't always understand what he said.

Nevertheless, he took her firmly out of her bed and sat her on his knee like a pet, so that her fine skin was up against his white, scratchy beard.

'Nu, little *mädel*? What is it? What hurts so much?'

But as Diana went on crying he added softly, 'Can't they even go to a cinema alone?'

'But why aren't they *home* yet?' She understood quickly enough, and her screams of alarm dwindled to sobs.

'What's so terrible? It's not even late.'

Her face was cherubic and pink, and his blue eyes twinkled; he was jolly and well-meaning enough. But it was no help to her, his good nature. What if they *never* came back? What *then*?

The terror of it swept over her. She would be left in the small box room with this white-bearded stranger for ever.

'What do you want, my little *mädel*? Chocolate? A hot drink?'

'*No. No. No.* I want *them* to come home. That's all I want.'

'Don't they have a life? Can't they have a little time away from you?'

'Supposing they leave me behind for ever, go off on their own and leave me?'

She'd never imagined anything so horrible; but suddenly it seemed possible. And he made the mistake of trying to tease her out of it.

'What then? Wouldn't *I* do? I'd look after you.'

She screamed in horror at that. For he wouldn't do at all. She wanted her father's familiar, deep, strong voice and reassuring arms. And her mother's nod making everything right.

At last the puzzled old man and the child together heard the key in the lock downstairs, and even before a chuckle confirmed her father's presence, relief swept through the child's body like a chemical in the bloodstream. Safe. She was safe.

Her grandfather went to the stairs and looked down at them.

'Has she been difficult?' she heard her mother ask dubiously.

And her grandfather admitted, 'I'm sorry. She wouldn't have anything to do with me.'

Her mother restrained her father.

'Now *don't* go straight up and disturb her. If she isn't crying out, she must be fine. Do you know, the other day he was driving her round the block all night in the car? He's a mad father,' she said without anger.

Diana loved her father best in the whole world; but she loved Grandpa Katz too, because he told her stories that were better than fairy tales.

'Once,' he said casually, 'when we were slaves in Egypt . . .'

246

And Diana had broken in, 'When? When? When was that?'

But Abram's world was one continual present tense.

He told the story of Pharaoh as though it had happened to him and his own family. Diana thought it had, until Betty rather crossly corrected her.

It was Betty always who gave her a precocious sense of reality.

Once, sitting on Abram's knee, she asked, 'Are you *very* old?'

And he thought for a moment before answering with absolute precision, 'Sixty-three.'

'That *is* old.' Diana was impressed. 'You must know you're going to die soon,' she said thoughtfully.

Abram wasn't angry. 'Everyone has to die,' he agreed.

Diana thought about dying, and of disappearing into a black *nothing*. 'Aren't you *frightened*?' she asked.

Abram too thought about it, and looked into her serious child's face. It's easier as you get older, he thought; but it was hard to explain that to a child. And yet. In the end, all he could do was shrug.

Life was sweet, of course, nobody wanted to give it up. But what could you do?

'That's how it is,' he said simply.

And yet for all Grandpa Katz's gentle presence, Diana found the Katz family household alarming. At her own home, everything was quiet and peaceful. There was always time to read. With her father's family, everyone seemed altogether too strongly and physically present. There was no let-up; no chance to switch off and daydream. No possibility of privacy. The Katz aunts – and although they had married, Benjy's sisters still thought of themselves as part of the Katz family – had huge, bold faces, and enormous limbs. Giants, they seemed to the child. Handsome, laughing giants, who all spoke at the top of their voices in Rasil's small kitchen. The child felt as if to enter it with so many large creatures moving about was to risk some hot pan of soup being poured over her.

They were tireless. When there were guests they cooked huge meals for them, even though they had been standing all day in their wood shops next to their men. There was always too much food: too many *kneidlach*, too many *blintzes*, too much rich fat brisket. Diana couldn't cope with the excess.

'The child doesn't eat!' cried one shocked voice.

'Come on. You can manage more than that,' shrieked another.

And Diana ate obediently. But she was always defeated. Everyone was defeated. It was the intention. Rasil wanted to shake her head over how much was left. Sometimes Betty disputed the necessity for so much forced feeding, but she was overruled.

'Her arms need filling out,' said Rasil.

'She's perfectly healthy,' Betty insisted.

But the only voice that could rescue Diana was Uncle Len, and he'd say, 'Don't be daft. She's a lovely shape for four.'

Uncle Len was Diana's favourite.

It was already clear Diana was going to be clever. By the time she was four Betty taught her to read, and she wrote a letter to her brother Francis, asking his advice: was it worth sending a girl to a private school? The letter that came back promptly was polite but indifferent: 'It's not a question of *sex*,' Francis wrote. 'Probably most money spent on education is wasted. If there is any talent it always comes out.'

It made Betty frown with anger, remembering how much Elsa had struggled for Francis.

Betty, too, was determined. What she wanted for her child was nothing less than the certainty of independence. Not that she envied her sister; she knew herself to be happy in a way that Dorothy would never understand. But just *because* her child was a girl, she might have to *wait*. Wait on men's whims. Wait to be asked. Perhaps just *wait* all her life long, for a joy that would never come her way. Unless she could stand alone, on her own two feet.

Betty set herself the task of saving money every week out of the housekeeping and putting it into her private account. She did all her own baking; and she played fair. But the money accumulated all the same. It was easy, she found, to save money. You simply spent less than you were given.

But all the while she planned for her daughter, the child's eyes were turned towards her father.

Diana loved him, first of all, because he was so marvellously *large*. He lifted her so easily; always carried her on his shoulders in a crowd so she could see. Wherever she went with him, even when they talked to men with huge forearms scarred with blue anchors and painted red ladies, his presence made her feel safe. And she was proud of him. She was Benjy Katz's daughter. She felt as if she was the daughter of a king.

Betty saw this worship without jealousy. She wanted Benjy to know the love of children. And this so far was the only child Betty had carried successfully to full term. She had been pregnant again more than once; but she was beginning to doubt if she would ever bear another child. It wasn't just her age.

About six months after Diana was born, Betty had become pregnant again.

Benjy was delighted.

Her doctor was not.

'Didn't you understand my advice?' he demanded. 'Your body needs a chance to recover.'

'But I am perfectly well now,' said Betty demurely.

'Let us hope you will be sensible and rest as much as you can.'

Betty dutifully rested; but she miscarried after three months, nevertheless. And the doctor returned once again to the delicate question of contraception.

'No doubt to a lady of gentle breeding . . . ' he began.

'Doctor, truly, I understood exactly how to use all the equipment. It is not a matter of any embarrassment to me. But I want another child.'

Her firmness disconcerted the old Scot, who looked in her notes again, before asking gruffly, 'There is no religious objection?'

'None whatever.'

'Then I must tell you how very foolish I think you are being. And I should like a word with your husband, if I may.'

'I absolutely forbid you to do any such thing!' cried Betty. She rose to her feet indignantly. 'I shall change my doctor *at once* if there is any such possibility. It would be a complete breach of trust.'

'Well, I wouldn't say . . . ' began the doctor.

'I am asking for your word you will do no such thing.'

The doctor sighed.

'I think you are a remarkably stubborn woman,' he said irritably.

Betty carried her next child into the seventh month; but when she gave birth, the child was dead. A boy, the sister told her quietly. And in the privacy of her own bed, Betty wept over the loss of a perfectly formed male child. How perilous, to have a whole future life in so frail a form. And she thought fiercely: If I could only have had him safely out in the world, I could have nursed him to safety. I would never have *let* him die. Her own nearness to death did not preoccupy her. She had lost a great deal of blood, and had to remain in hospital for several weeks. Rasil looked after Benjy and Diana.

There were no more children for Betty. There was something in her blood which was inimical to further children. She had rhesus factor blood, they said. Dorothy knew about it, and could not promise any cure.

So, as she saw the love growing between Benjy and his child, Betty was happy to stand aside and serve them both, effacing her own importance. But it was Betty who arranged for the child to take an examination to a good school; she who produced the fees, when Benjy hesitated; Betty, finally, who persuaded him that girls were worth educating.

'Do you want her to work in a wood shop like your sister?' demanded Betty.

'There are worse things. She's happy. Married now,' grumbled Benjy.

But really he didn't want any such thing. And she knew that. He wanted his daughter to be a princess. And when he saw her at seven in her neat navy tunic and huge velour hat, with the school crest on it which almost obscured the big dark eyes staring up at him, he was filled with pride, and astonishment.

'You're a little marvel,' he told the child.

'Now don't spoil her altogether,' warned Betty.

It was 1938.

*

Diana was precious, loved, miraculous.

Except for the frequent outings to the beach at Southport. There the Katz women seemed to belong to another species. Their rounded limbs were immune to the cold. They ran, with her father, full tilt into the waves of the cold sea.

'By! That's good,' they shouted to one another.

And they tried to drag Diana in, too. She resisted, screaming. She was slender like her mother, and felt the cold badly. But also she was afraid of the grey, bitter sea; the salt burnt her mouth. Grandma Rasil carried her in and shouted to the child, 'Let go! Let go!' but she couldn't. Her hands clutched to Rasil's woollen costume desperately.

'Don't you want to learn to swim?' her father asked her.

She did. It was what she dreamed of. Night after night. But she couldn't. She could not let go and commit herself to that bitter water.

'She's too skinny,' said Len's wife. 'You want to fatten her up.'

Betty flushed indignantly at the idea that anyone should want to be such a huge unfashionable shape as Sophie.

'She eats perfectly well,' she said, huffily. 'She's healthy enough.'

Diana felt her father's presence assured her of safety. It wasn't safety that her mother taught her, though.

'You learn to stand on your own feet, my girl,' she said from the day Diana learned to walk at all.

And she heard the same words whenever she met Grandpa Gordon.

To visit Grandpa Gordon was a formidable undertaking. Diana put her lips to his leathery old skin with great reluctance. Usually, they shook hands; and she found even his hands alarming; their skin was so dry, and there was so little flesh over the knobbly bones. At the same time, his eyes were sharp and critical. He made her aware of her hair and her clothes. He didn't make her feel loved. He made her feel judged.

Her mother's brother and sister were not frequent visitors. Diana had been very impressed when her mother showed her

251

Uncle Francis's name on the spine of several books. When she discovered that he had not written the books himself, it was a great disappointment; but the shadow of his presence was everywhere in Grandpa Gordon's house, and her mother always spoke of him with a reverence she expected Diana to share, even if she never met him.

Aunt Dorothy always brought the child gifts, usually gloves or a pretty purse; never anything to play with. Somehow, in her presence, Diana never felt physically comfortable either, though Aunt Dorothy had a kind voice, and laughed easily. But Aunt Dorothy always brought Diana's cousin Kitty with her.

Diana knew there was something interesting and odd about her cousin; but her mother only folded her lips close when she was questioned, and Diana never got to the bottom of it.

And so, while Betty and Dorothy talked to one another, the two girls played in the rough patch of land behind the garden. Diana knew it best, and took the lead; for Kitty's extra years had made her gawky, and Diana had stronger arms anyway. She found ways up the pear tree which Kitty could not risk; meanwhile her cousin sat cheerfully on the lowest branch, eating the redcurrants they had picked for jelly, and not talking much.

At teatime, Kitty never took her eyes off Aunt Dorothy.

Diana began school and did not understand what was wanted from her. She put her hand up with the answer every time, until she was rebuked. And after that she fell into a mutinous silence. She felt different from the other children, without knowing why.

'She's the only Jewish child in the class,' she overheard her father say irascibly after the first speech day.

'Does that matter?'

'Aye. It matters,' said Benjy. 'For the child.'

In the first half term, Diana was given a sense of what her father meant. She was sitting on her own among the wet mackintoshes in the school cloakroom, when a girl with a very red face and no eyebrows hissed at her: '*Dirty Jew.*'

She still didn't understand the insult, but the venom in the voice made her cry; and she cried again, telling her father about it as he was driving her home, looking at the reassuring width of his shoulders and his powerful neck.

And he was silent for a moment.

'The bastards,' he said then, helplessly, 'the little bastards.'

Benjy was in the habit of collecting his daughter from school at lunchtime. He liked to go home for his lunch; and he didn't approve of school meals. The child usually waited for him on a seat in the railings. Her legs were not quite long enough to touch the ground as she sat there. He was never late; and she liked watching the snub V-nose of his second-hand Armstrong-Siddeley as it came up behind the trams and cycles.

In some way, the car had the quality of the man. All leather and wood. A heavy, reliable car. Solid, well-built and durable.

At teatime, her mother usually collected her, though it meant a long tram ride to do so. But as her parents' world began to darken, her father began to collect her in the afternoon as well.

38

Harry's shop stood in a hinterland between Islington and London Road. Benjy hadn't liked the site when he saw it, though he could offer no reason why. It didn't *feel* right. Didn't feel *lucky*, was all he could explain.

What he was picking up was the changing quality of the street, which soon grew clear enough. By then most of the shops had been boarded up, but a few Jewish families remained, living over locked doors. Most houses were tenanted by the unemployed from the docks, the shut-down sugar refineries, and Liverpool's other collapsed industries. Young men ran along the street calling blackshirt slogans, and some scrawled up on the wooden boards across broken windows Jews Out and No Jews or Pigs.

It was unsurprising that Katz Do-It-Yourself was not flourishing.

'You should get out of here,' Benjy said, every time he looked in.

'I can't afford it,' said Harry.

'At least move your wife out,' suggested Benjy. 'And the kids.'

Harry's recent marriage had already produced two children.

'I'm not making that kind of money,' said Harry.

'For God's sake. They beat in the glass down the road, at Cohen's delicatessen,' said Benjy. 'And someone put paraffin in the letter box. Maybe they meant to burn them down; maybe not. It didn't catch. The Cohens aren't waiting to see.'

'How will it be better if they herd us all into a ghetto round Bedford Street?' asked Harry.

'*In* or *out* is safer,' said Benjy shrewdly. 'They aren't having much trouble round Sefton Park yet. And *we* can spot the sods a mile off coming into our area. They've got more sense than to take us on. We'd bloody murder 'em.'

'I'll think about it,' said Harry.

One cold, rainy evening, a little after this, Abram was minding the shop for Harry, while his son took his wife and children across to their in-laws in Crown Street. Abram was in his middle sixties by now, his hair and beard white, and sitting behind the till with his glasses on, reading his Hebrew newspaper, he must have looked a pushover to the two boys who put their shoulders to the door of the shop and set the bell ringing.

'Move over, Grandad,' said the tallest.

Abram looked up a little hazily. He had been reading an article about the British Fascist meeting at Olympia, and what happened there to young men who had tried to ask Oswald Mosley a question. Thugs, it seemed, were everywhere. These two were thin and white-faced, and for all their ugly gestures they looked scared and hungry. Both were wretchedly dressed; but the more emphatic of the two wore a blackshirt armband.

'What do you want?'

'Stop mucking about. Let's have your takings,' he said. 'You lousy Yid.'

Abram was glad he was alone and didn't have to be careful. He could hear the edge of nervousness in the boy's voice. That was dangerous. It meant he was likely to be violent, whatever happened.

'Never mind the politics,' said the other, thicker-set youngster. 'While you're talking someone else'll be in. There's the cash register.'

Abram said, 'Nothing in it. Look.'

They looked, and flung it from them.

'He's a Yid, isn't he? There's got to be money somewhere,' said the blackshirt.

Abram had been sitting in the shop all afternoon and not yet taken five shillings. He told them so, quietly.

'Don't give me that. Where is it? The gold, the money.'

The voice became more urgent, as the thinner, narrower-faced boy approached the counter.

'Where would I have money?' asked Abram reasonably.

'He's right. Where would he? Look at this pissing hole.'

'Don't you believe him,' said the thin one, his eyes narrowing to slits. 'They're just bleeding mean, Yids. Like to live like this, see. Don't know any better. Never mind your head how they're making their money. They do. All of them. Even this one. So. Where is it?' he demanded.

The other boy began to walk irritably about the room, and spilled a few trays of nuts and bolts and a tin of picture hooks on the floor. The noise rattled his friend.

'There isn't any other money,' said Abram.

He stood up, because he could see he was in trouble. But he was still well-built and he reckoned he could have given either one a substantial fight. Both the young men observed as much.

'Look, we don't *want* to do you over,' said the calmer of the two.

'Why not, fat arse?' The blackshirt could not contain his impatience. 'They're what's killing the country, aren't they? Living off us. Feeding their gut. It'd give me great *pleasure* to do him over.'

So Abram said to himself: God, faithful King, this could easily be a very stupid thing to do. And he brought out the broom handle he had been clenching behind his back and banged it down as hard as he could on the boy who was wearing the armband. As he judged, the boy went down easily enough. But of course he was barely stunned. Not seriously hurt, and the other, thicker-set, youngster was more of a threat. The whole thing turned on whether there was any great loyalty between them.

'Gawd,' said the stocky boy, looking down at his fallen friend.

And he just stood there. But the other boy began to stir on the floor again and Abram could see that he would have to contend with both of them. On an impulse, he picked up a hammer. It was a weapon with which he had absolutely no chance, since it required a close short swing; and he couldn't risk getting that near. But it felt good in his hand.

I'm sorry, Rasil, Abram said inwardly, as the young man on the floor began to rub the back of his head, and his friend helped him to his feet. I'm a stubborn old man. If I'd had any money they could have had it. But they'd have beaten me up anyway. I had to try something.

The blackshirt looked at the blood on his hand with bewilderment.

Then the two boys both turned towards the old man; and the one he had hit first punched him in the eye. His glasses shattered on the floor. As he fell over backwards, Abram heard the crash of his own skull on a metal shelf. Then a ring, like a doorbell, before he lost consciousness.

Luckily the bell *was* real. And Benjy Katz stood in the doorway; over six foot, heavily built and powerful as a young bull. He'd come to give Abram a lift home.

Rasil scolded both her husband and her son equally while she bathed Abram's eye. 'You encourage him,' she yelled at Benjy. 'He could have been killed. And how do you know they didn't have guns? Don't you know even Benjy Katz can be killed with a gun? *Meshugganah* men,' she moaned.

'The day they start coming at us with guns we'll be in trouble, right enough,' said Benjy soberly.

'Don't you read the papers?' cried Rasil. 'It's already happening in Germany.'

'Ma, what should we do? Do you want us to pack up and move again?'

'I'll pack,' cried Rasil. 'I'll move.'

'Listen, Rasil,' reasoned Abram. 'Liverpool isn't the Ukraine. There are police here, not troops. Mosley isn't Prime Minister.'

'All right. All right.' Rasil was mollified. 'All the same, I've my own thoughts.'

She thought, by the time Mosley is Prime Minister it'll be too late. And where were the police last week in Stepney?

39

Every morning Benjy looked into the *News Chronicle* and sighed.

'The world's gone mad.'

And Betty's face grew thinner and wearier as the year turned onwards.

She knew that Francis was sending his own child to America. He sounded gloomy when she spoke to him on the telephone.

'The war,' she guessed.

'Not only. That of course. But I've quarrelled with Dorothy,' he admitted. 'She'll get over it, I suppose. She doesn't see I'm doing what's best for the child.'

She's heartbroken, thought Betty, imagining it. But she was not close enough to Francis to risk saying so.

Betty thought about what would be best for her own child, but as she mentioned what Francis had said Benjy exploded in fury.

'No. I won't *have* it. No,' he shouted, in altogether uncharacteristic rage.

'I'll ask the old man for the money,' said Betty.

'No. You won't. If I thought it was right to send the kid to America, I'd find the money without him,' said Benjy. 'Bugger the money. But we have to stay together. Don't we? The three of us.'

'All the Groots are sure there's going to be a war,' said Betty.

She didn't often argue with her husband.

'If they don't let the bastards walk in,' said Benjy. 'If there is a war there'll be U-boats like last time. Who knows if those bastards aren't waiting already? Sod them,' said Benjy. 'This is where I *live*. I've never been pushed out of anywhere in my life.'

'Is it the house?'

'No,' he growled. 'I could leave it *tomorrow*, don't you know that?'

'In Vienna, Francis told me people hated leaving their furniture.'

'In Vienna they thought they were important. Indispensable. Arrogant lot.'

'Don't say that,' she flinched.

'I know. I know. I can read the papers. That's not the point. Why should we go running away? Why? I've worked hard all my life. I've never cheated anyone. I don't understand it. Why? I won't bloody *move*. And I won't send my child away either.'

Benjy paused and looked at his wife.

'Are you all right? Why are you clutching that hot water bottle? I'll make the fire up if you're cold.'

'It's nothing.'

'You've a pain again,' accused Benjy.

'Nothing.'

'So damn brave,' complained Benjy. 'I'm not used to it. You know where you are with my family. If they hurt, they cry.

258

People know.'

For a moment he looked hopeful.

'Perhaps,' he began.

'No, Benjy. That's not likely. You know what the doctor said.'

40

Just after the Munich crisis Francis went to visit his father. He had not attended his mother's stone-setting, and he got out of the train at Lime Street knowing it was really for her he had come. The pointlessness of the gesture hurt him, as the house declared her absence. It smelled differently. The sweet polishes had been changed. The hall was colder, damper, older, shabbier. Unnecessarily shabby, thought Francis angrily. Silly to let it run down. The old man should have more sense. Solomon no longer cared, Francis supposed. Not for the house, nor for his own comfort, nor for what anyone thought. And yet he seemed alert enough. Well, he'd never been an especially *feeling* man, thought Francis.

'How do you manage on your own?' he asked.

'Well enough. The same char comes in, and I cook a bit myself.'

'You should have a housekeeper, Da,' said Francis irritably.

'Oh, I don't want anyone about the place,' said the old man. 'Fussing.'

He was a natural bachelor, thought Francis. Tidy, pernickety, and mean. And yet he had gone to some trouble to mark Francis's visit. He had lit a fire in the dining room; set the table silver; put out decanters on the sideboard.

No mistaking it, thought Francis. The old man is glad to see me.

Over a whisky Francis found himself talking about his own

259

inexorable gloom.

'Oh aye, there'll be a war,' nodded Solomon, adding with wry amusement, 'I've blacked me windows.'

Francis observed as much.

'Dorothy is lecturing to the villagers on ARP,' he said.

'She's become another optimist, then,' said Solomon.

'I wouldn't say that,' said Francis heavily.

A lonely old man, thought Francis. Spry, bony, unloved, and largely unforgiven by his family. But disciplined. A shrewd man, Francis admitted to himself.

'You are as cruel as Da,' Dorothy had said to him coldly only the week before. 'You thought to be so damn different, but who else would take a child away like that? A reasonable man. *Well*.'

She'd stopped there, not needing to add anything about his wife; not daring perhaps in the face of his black-eyed fury.

'I'd have thought you had enough on your hands,' he said. 'And if you loved the child you'd want her to be safe.'

'There's more to life than being safe,' she said. 'She'll be safe and lonely again. Unloved maybe. How could you send her away like that? Anyway, bugger off. You've taken her now. I've nothing more to say to you. And I'm busy.'

He'd heard her feet, clopping off down the red-tiled hospital corridor. Could still hear them.

'How are the family?' he asked.

Solomon shrugged. 'Betty looks pale and thin. Does your friend still think Russia will come in and save us all?'

'Probably,' said Francis sombrely.

He had not seen Ian for months, and last time they had quarrelled violently. Over politics, perhaps; but unquestionably Ian also held him responsible for his sister's illness. Perhaps he even resented other things.

'I was gonged in the last honours list, did you read that?' he told his father abruptly. Of course, it was the kind of news to have altogether delighted his mother. Too late, now, he thought, wondering why he had mentioned it.

Solomon smiled and Francis saw that he had already heard the news, and was not unimpressed.

A friend at one of the ministries was asking Francis to join the intelligence service; he was useful, evidently, because of his knowledge of central Europe.

'Well? And your culture, I hope,' Solomon mocked him. 'Is it helping them out, your mother's relations, their music and poetry?'

Francis conceded miserably that it was not, that cousins in the universities had lost their jobs, that worse things had happened.

'It's all true,' he said hopelessly. 'But at least the Nazis are still letting people out with their lives. Once that stops, they will settle down to organized murder. And, God help me, no one cares.'

'You have learned nothing if that surprises you,' said Solomon with sudden vigour. 'Most Jews are weak, poor and helpless. In that situation, who has friends?'

Francis said, 'That's a bleak vision.'

Solomon looked coldly at his son. He said, 'There is some soup on the hot plate. Shall we eat?'

'All right.'

'There'll be war, anyway,' said Solomon, abruptly. 'You must know that. It's not a question of caring. It must come.'

'Yes.'

'England won't go under so easily,' said Solomon.

'Everyone here is bumbling,' cried Francis. 'So slow, so improvident. By the time they understand it will be too late.'

'The mistake is to be weak,' said Solomon.

They ate the rest of the meal in silence.

When Solomon suggested brandy, Francis found himself saying abruptly, 'We're *all* weak, Da.'

It wasn't often the two men spoke of anything deeply felt, and Solomon didn't reply for a moment. Then he nodded, and waited. Francis took the brandy gratefully and cupped the glass in his hands, holding it under his nose to savour the reassuring warmth that rose from the liquid.

'Something happened to me. In Berlin.'

'When?'

'On my last trip.'

Francis had described his experience in Berlin to no one.

The memory was painful and he wasn't sure why he now wanted to discuss it with his father, of all people. Yet he knew it was strongly connected with the part of himself he had taken from the old man. He had learned the limits of that wiry strength, he thought. He knew now that no one could make themselves free or safe; that anything could be done to anybody; that a shrewd eye and a clear brain were no defence. The knowledge often woke him in the night.

Perhaps he wanted to exorcize it.

'I was walking down Feuerbachstrasse,' he began. 'I was looking for a friend of the Mackenzies, my wife's family, you remember. Well. I don't pretend to be very brave. As soon as I got to the entrance of their block of flats I could see Gestapo men were everywhere. Perhaps it was just coincidence, but I hesitated about going in. The Mackenzies, you know, are all left-wing; probably their friends also. So I hesitated.'

Solomon grunted.

'Of course, with a British passport I should not have worried, but I had seen such terrible things, Da. I don't mean broken shop windows, looted stores. But all those yellow stars. Whole families being taken off God knows where. And *nothing* counted. Age. Iron crosses. Distinction. I saw an old professor from Heidelberg among them. They lifted a whip to him, when he stumbled, like everyone else.'

'What happened to you?' his father asked directly.

'While I was hesitating at the doorway, I felt in my jacket for my passport. It was an instinctive gesture; I wasn't exactly checking. I never dared move a step without it. So when I couldn't find it, I didn't understand at first. The explanation didn't occur to me. Then two officers stopped me and asked me why I was loitering. I blurted out something in German. Perhaps it was speaking in German that was the mistake.'

Solomon looked shrewdly at his son. 'Age brings out family resemblances,' he said. 'Perhaps they thought you looked Jewish?'

Francis returned his look with a certain hostility. 'It was a put-up job, of course. They *knew* who I was. They knew I had published German writers in exile. Socialists, that kind of thing. They had stolen my passport while I was in the restaurant. They were just pretending not to believe I was British.'

Francis lapsed into silence, as he relived the horror of that. The helplessness. The questioning. And of course Solomon was right. They had known he was Jewish. A man had asked him to pull down his trousers. He had refused. Insisted on calling the British consul.

'They locked me in a cell,' he said at last. 'I was frightened, naturally. They intended me to be frightened. I could hear yells of pain all night. Women sobbing.'

And the cell was cold, he remembered. There was not so much as a bench; nowhere to relieve himself. And when the guard brought a bowl of soup in the morning, he had called Francis 'Jew-scum'.

They had called him back in for questioning and refused to listen to him. No, he could not wash. No need for that. Jews didn't wash. And one of the brutes had held his arms while another man pulled down his trousers, both of them laughing at what they found. They must have known as well as Francis that the circumcision meant nothing. His passport was already in their hands, in any case. They were simply enjoying his fear.

Francis told his father some of this.

'They roughed me up a bit. Then someone came with my passport. Apologies all round. And didn't I agree it was all an unfortunate mistake?'

Francis paused.

'Did you find yourself arguing with them?' Solomon asked.

'No. That would have been stupid, wouldn't it? I could see how it was by then. Documentation no longer meant anything. The only really sensible thing was to get out of the country.'

'It was humiliating?'

'Yes.'

It was more than that, thought Francis. Not that he had behaved so badly, not that he had betrayed anyone or done anything for which he ought to feel ashamed. But he was ashamed. He had been made to feel ashamed. He didn't know why.

'Your generation has been fortunate not to learn that lesson earlier,' said Solomon.

Francis missed the force of that as he continued to puzzle at the discovery of his own vulnerability. Then he pulled himself together, and felt in his pocket for a rare cigarette. What a strange idea that his father could have any relevant thoughts on the matter. A foolish hope.

Solomon let out a bark of dry laughter. 'I knew all that in Odessa when I was twelve,' he said. 'I've lived with it all my life.'

41

Benjy bought an Anderson shelter for £7, and set about putting it into the garden where the cucumber frames usually went. Betty watched from a couch inside the house; and Diana sat on the tussocks of the overgrown rockery under the pear trees and watched her father. It was cold weather, and she had swathed herself in a patchwork velvet rug which usually covered the Put-U-Up in the front room. Benjy worked all day to dig a hole more than seven feet by six, into which the curved steel sheets could be fitted and bolted together.

The child hugged her knees as she watched him. There was a circle of sweat under each of his arms, and presently he took the shirt off altogether. The structure he was building grew into a small, dark, tin shed.

'Can I go in?' she asked.

'It's going to be wet,' Benjy muttered. 'Wet and cold and dark.'

'Is there *really* going to be a war?' she asked. The prospect excited her.

'Go in to your mother,' he said wearily, and he wasn't angry with her, though he could read her thoughts. 'Help her get tea. We've visitors.'

Abram and Rasil were talking to Betty in hushed whispers.

'Shhhh. The child,' said Rasil as the girl opened the French windows.

'Children are very tough,' said Betty. 'And we're taking in a refugee from Breslau. Someone her own age. Diana's bound to hear the stories.'

'Zaide,' the little girl asked Abram clearly. 'Why is God letting all these things happen to the Jews? Is it because they don't keep his laws? About meat and milk and kosher food?'

Abram lifted her on to his knees thoughtfully. 'You know, Hitler isn't the first. And he won't be the last. God always looks after us,' he said.

'Have you got a gas mask?' said Diana.

She enjoyed the funny, rubbery smell of the masks, and the noise she could make when she blew out hard through them. Betty had taken lessons at the WVS and knew how to use them properly. At school, all the children carried them importantly about in square cardboard boxes. Recently, they had been advised to carry a small khaki sack containing, among other vital safety aids, a torch and a packet of Sun-Pat chocolate-covered raisins. Since no one was allowed to eat these the chocolate went stale, and if you opened the packet there was a smell of cardboard and musty chocolate.

Abram pulled the child's head under his beard, and said something to his wife in Yiddish.

Betty said, with relief, 'Here comes Benjy now.'

'My *Tsaddickle*,' said Abram proudly. 'I always said he was my best son.'

The child hopped up out of his grasp. Against all the dangers of the outside world her father seemed to offer an absolute protection, his strength an unbreakable defence. She relied on him completely.

But Merseyside was going to be in danger if there was a war. They were going to evacuate the schools. They were told Diana would have to go with the rest of her school to Wales.

Benjy couldn't believe it. He wouldn't have it. How could they take little children, label them like parcels, and post them off to this village and that? It wasn't human.

'I'll not let them do it to her. We'll all move to Wales, if we have to.'

He thought about his house and garden; the shelter under the turf, the cucumber frames, the tobacco smell of the ripe tomatoes under glass.

None of it mattered. But Wales? That felt wrong.

'We'll go to Leicester. Len'll see us right. I'll talk to him.'

'But what will we do there?' Betty thought of the sweet-smelling linen in the chest upstairs; of the many kinds of china; the whole weight of putting order into confusion.

'We'll be together,' said Benjy firmly. 'It doesn't matter what we do. I'll see to it. Don't worry.'

He didn't want to tire his wife with the problem, and he knew he'd manage somehow.

So it was that Diana came to spend her war in Leicester. In Len's town. With Len's family. Part of Len's world.

Len was part of the wartime licence Diana was allowed. Part of the world of smutty shows at the Palace she and her cousins went to as a family on Saturday nights. The world of Max Miller and old men dressed as women and her cousins, all with the same bewildered faces, too early old. Her mother didn't like any of it. But no one liked to leave children at home alone, either. The theatres weren't safer. But the important thing was being together. The dread was always of going back home and finding the house gone, and whoever was in it lost for ever. So Diana went along to the poker school that met three times a week and played into the morning. The haggard, war-tired children sleepily imitated the game in the next room. Part of an underworld that knew where to find sweets and stockings.

Betty disapproved of the black market. But Benjy shrugged off the description.

'Where's the harm? A few sweets.'

He wanted to sweeten Diana's life while he could; to make sure she had some kind of life. Just in case. Leicester didn't have much bombing, of course, but sometimes the bombers lost their way to Coventry, or junked their bombs before making off for home.

Her mother wanted her to be happy, too. In another way. But she was fighting a losing battle against the racy world of her father and Uncle Len. Diana was unimpressed with all the cold houses on leafy roads in the south of the city to which her mother tried to introduce her. When her mother tried to take her round to meet 'nice young people' Diana hated it. She had to wear a stiff, formal suit and doeskin gloves; and her hair had to be dressed for the occasion in tight little curls; not fluffy, as she saw people wearing it in American films.

'What is so marvellous about these people?' she demanded.

'They're a *good* family,' Betty pleaded. 'I want you to have nice friends.'

But Diana thought them all comic. Like the girls at school, who didn't listen to AFN and couldn't dance at the end of an American arm.

'Pearls and twinsets,' she giggled afterwards, and made her mother really angry.

At the same time, she was aware there were areas of life where her mother was more at ease than her father. On parents' days at her new school, for instance, it was always her mother who came, neatly dressed, with good leather court shoes, and calm as could be wished. Diana was always a little nervous of her new headmistress, a fine-featured, grey-haired woman, whose smile seemed always about to freeze into disapproval. Her presence made Diana feel shaky. Even if she only had to go and collect a form medal or a prize, she had trouble getting her words out clearly. Yet in that formidable presence her mother seemed altogether at ease. Diana could not understand it; but she knew her father shared something of her own uncertainty, and that was why he never went along to school events.

Not that Benjy admitted to any such emotion; on the contrary he always scoffed at the headmistress. He had no respect for educated women, he said.

Her mother said, more thoughtfully, 'It's part of her job, Diana. To seem severe.'

By the last years of the war Diana was leading two quite different lives. A daytime life, at school, in which she took no care of how she looked and sat on the school radiators slouched, sullen and indifferent. And her evening life – her true life, as she thought it – where she played at painting her lips with a dark lipstick; prinked her hair; and pancaked her face to make herself look older.

Her mother fretted over this, but could not reach her. 'Diana, you're too *young*,' she kept saying.

But Diana didn't want to be young. She didn't wear the lipstick because it suited her, but because the harsh edges it gave her mouth made her look ready for sex. And she wanted to join in that particular game; to be part of the generation which, as far as she could see, was having all the fun.

She had no sexual urges of her own. At eleven, when the American soldiers arrived, her breasts were barely developing; she had to hoist them up viciously to make them point out through her sweater as she wanted. She had not even begun to bleed every month, though she bought sanitary towels and looked eagerly and often in her knickers for the first sign of it.

At parties when they played kissing games she closed her eyes, and was disappointed because she felt so little. Once, in a dream, she had felt a sharp, whirring moment of pleasure that she guessed must be the joy they were all singing and writing and giggling about.

Diana was trying to grow up as far away from her Gordon self as she could.

Her father was still at home. He had been too old to be taken off with the first call-up, though he wouldn't have minded having a bash at the Germans himself, as he put it to Len. His cousin shook his head at his innocence.

'You never get near enough to give anyone a bash. Couldn't, even all those years ago. Not often.'

'Might, though,' said Benjy with a certain relish. Physically, he felt himself in his prime; and he didn't like to be thought too old.

'Oh, it's all tanks now,' said Len. 'Bombs and tanks. A shrimp's as good as a giant in this war.'

Len watched his own sons sombrely when they were playing at soldiers. There were several Katz cousins in uniform already. 'At least this war is *about* something,' reasoned Benjy.

'Oh, aye,' said Len. 'It makes more sense than the last bundle. But if you're killed in it, you're just as dead.'

'They can have me if they want me,' said Benjy.

But by the time the army got around to thinking of Benjy's age-group the war was nearly over, and his factory was making too many useful things for them to let him leave it.

42

Abram and Rasil stayed in Liverpool. They moved in with Sarah and her young babies – her husband had gone into the army – partly to keep her company and partly because her house had a deep cellar, with electric light and water piped in from the mains.

All through September 1940 the whole of Sarah's family and Abram and Rasil with them went obediently down into that cellar whenever the siren went.

But as the winter drew on it was cold in the cellar, even with the bar of the electric fire running all night long. Very soon, Rasil was refusing to go down with the rest of the family.

'No lavatory,' she insisted mutinously. 'That bucket may be all right for children, but not me.'

Abram agreed about the bucket. And the cellar was cramped and cold. But the truth of it was that he felt, as he always had, that their lives were arranged by God, and could not be preserved or damaged against His will, so he did not very much resist her wishes.

And the decision was made for both of them when Rasil fell ill in November with a 'cold on her chest', as she called it. Sarah quietly explained to Abram that she had contracted pneumonia. Clearly, the damp in the cellar was more dangerous to her in that condition than German bombs.

All one night Abram sat up with his wife, listening to her painful breathing, and watching through a chink in the blackout curtains how the fires blazed in the docks, and every moment released a sputter of explosions among the houses nearby. Watching, with his forehead against the glass, Abram had a terrifying vision of the enormity of God's responsibility. There was even one desperate moment when his faith in the power of God deciding between one terraced house and the next faltered and almost failed.

Rasil wheezed and fought for breath, while Abram quietly refreshed the cold cloths she held against her forehead. In her delirium she was a young girl again tending geese. Every so often, she smacked them away from her. Then, just before the first grey light of morning, an explosion shattered all the windows on the first floor, and splinters of glass showered all over the floor. The cold blew the curtains away from the window, and Rasil called, 'Abram. Hold me. The cold.'

And he approached the bed to shelter her with his dressing-gown. But even as he covered her, he saw how blue her lips were, and heard the desperate heaving of her lungs, and was afraid. He had watched death moving over the city all night, and now in his own bedroom, he could feel the same presence.

Rasil died a young woman in her husband's eyes, though she was well into her sixties. And Abram grieved for her all the twenty years left to him.

43

When Diana was thirteen her interests in life were dancing, American jazz and her Katz cousins. All this changed however, after meeting her cousin Kitty, on her way north with Aunt Dorothy a few months after VE day.

All of Diana's Katz cousins were robust and cheerful,

well-dressed in the contemporary local fashions, and most were handsome. But Kitty, at nineteen, was like none of them.

Instead she had a kind of careless grace. Her pale linen suit, tightly belted into her waist, could have been cut for Lauren Bacall; her silk blouse was finely striped as a shirt; and she wore her jacket loose over her shoulders. Her delicate legs and ankles slipped easily into neat, high-heeled sandals and Diana marvelled at them. Her face, too, was astonishing. Green eyes, fine lips, sharp cheekbones. Diana felt a pang of something like envy; and was glad to be in old trousers with a roll-top jumper rather than her own best clothes.

When Betty suggested pointedly that she should go and change, Diana insisted sulkily, 'I *like* being in trousers!'

'So do I,' said her smart cousin, rewarding her with an unexpected smile. 'Please don't bother.'

Betty went off into the kitchen to see to lunch; Dorothy followed, and the two girls were left alone. Diana eyed Kitty cautiously. There were six years between them, and another world.

'Have you come straight from New York?' she asked breathlessly.

New York belonged to an impossible magical continent of plenty, new and shining in Diana's imagination.

'No.' Kitty frowned. 'I spent a few days in London with my father.'

Diana longed to ask what he was like, this Uncle Francis of whom her mother always spoke with such reverence.

It wasn't necessary.

'I suppose he did his best. Took me out to meals, and theatres. Introduced me everywhere. No good, though,' said Kitty.

'What wasn't?' asked Diana after a pause, her curiosity overcoming her nervousness.

'Well, neither of us seems to care, really.'

Kitty shrugged her shoulders.

'I'm going up to Somerville, anyway, in October, so we don't have to sort out where I'm living.'

She saw that Diana had never heard of Somerville, and added kindly enough, 'Up to Oxford. To read English.'

271

Diana absorbed the fact that people who looked like Kitty might go to university.

Kitty began to pace about the room restlessly. 'Do you have a cigarette?'

'Well. I know where they are,' Diana hesitated.

Then she boldly opened the door in the sideboard where her father kept drinks and cigarettes. She had been to it often enough in secret, but not usually when her mother was likely to notice.

Now Kitty tapped the cigarette on her nail, lit it, and drew smoke down deeply into her lungs, while she studied Diana.

'You don't look much like your mother,' she said.

Diana flushed. She would have given a great deal for more feminine features.

'More like Aunt Dorothy. I know. Everyone says so,' she admitted ruefully.

Clearly, Kitty found her tone surprising. She examined her cousin critically, without venturing any opinion for a moment and then said, 'Aunt Dorothy is the most marvellous woman I've ever met. I can't be like her, I know. But I love her more than anyone.'

Diana considered the confession.

For her part she had already felt how easy it would be to be like Dorothy. Now, it no longer seemed a sentence of doom, but an opportunity, even exhilarating on the lips of this vehement girl. And why should she not? Diana knew she could never be gentle like her mother; never serve and tend and sustain as she did. But she could be fierce and free like Dorothy.

'When she was younger, she was the most beautiful woman I ever knew, except for my own mother.'

Diana lowered her eyes. She knew very little about Francis's wife, because her mother had always discussed her in a hushed voice, as if there was some disgraceful secret about her.

'I never met your mother,' she said, a note of inquiry in her voice.

'*Couldn't* have. She was in hospital for years,' said Kitty. 'I only saw her twice myself, and once she attacked me.'

Diana could think of nothing to say.

'Anyway, she's dead now.'

Kitty threw her cigarette into the open fire. 'It's really weird coming back to England.'

Diana nodded, open-eyed, and Kitty added thoughtfully, 'Poor old Pop, he's probably a bit past it, by now.'

'Past?'

'Getting married, I mean. To his girlfriend. Well. Do *you* want to get married?'

'Of *course*.' Diana had no idea it was possible to hope for anything else.

'I don't. Shan't, either.'

Dorothy came into the room at this point and said sharply, 'Nonsense. You don't know what you want yet.'

To Diana's surprise, Kitty did not bridle in any way at Dorothy's rebuke. Instead, she sat down meekly at the table, and from that point on answered every question about her life politely and formally.

It was 1948. Benjy, who had come home to lunch as usual, was mildly hostile to Kitty; but she met his aggression by teasing him and even flirting.

'If I were Jewish,' she said suddenly, 'I'd go to Palestine right off.'

Benjy stared, uncertain in his own mind about her Jewishness as much as anything else. His eyes wandered over to his wife and daughter.

'I've thought of it,' he said. 'The British Army wouldn't have me, but I'm a good fighter. Maybe the Zionists could find a place for me.'

Diana was fired with a wild patriotism. 'Oh, *let's*. Do let's go,' she cried. 'It would be such an adventure.'

'Aye. It would,' said Benjy, drily.

'I hope you will not consider doing anything so daft,' cried Dorothy. She had never been a Zionist, and had no intention of pretending now.

'Of course we shall not,' said Betty, quietly. 'Benjy would never put Diana in danger.'

Kitty's eyes flickered wickedly at that and Diana, too,

273

picked up for the first time how odd it was for her mother to speak of herself as if she only existed as part of her husband and daughter.

'Imagine, though,' Kitty said. 'They took on seven Arab armies.'

'Fighting.' Benjy looked for the word he wanted. 'Well, that's a privilege, my girl. After what happened in Europe.'

At the end of the meal, the two girls were sent off to wash up.

'I like your Dad,' said Kitty.

Diana was pleased, and said nothing.

Kitty gave her a teacloth, and began reflectively to mop the plates in the hot soapy water, which Betty had left ready for them so that the wrong bowls should not be used by mistake.

'Now *Francis*,' said Kitty, 'sometimes I don't understand how Francis keeps going at all. But come along,' Kitty said impatiently. 'Start wiping.'

Diana had indeed been hypnotized into immobility.

'Your father *has* to, I suppose. That's different. There's something gallant about him battling on, really. I don't suppose he specially enjoys it,' said Kitty.

Diana thought about that. 'I think he *does*, though. Enjoy it.'

'Oh, well. Perhaps that's what it is. Francis doesn't enjoy anything much.'

Diana exercised her own first independent act of judgement.

There were things Kitty didn't know, and things Kitty wanted to believe.

The assessment in no way affected the hold Kitty's presence exercised upon Diana's imagination.

Soon after this, Diana began to renew her interest in school. It was an interest that divided her from her Katz cousins, who disliked bookishness. Particularly in girls.

44

It was not long afterwards that Solomon's cleaning woman found the old man sitting upright and dead in an armchair next to the telephone. He was in his dressing-gown and slippers, and had evidently just made ready for bed; there was no sign of pain.

'By heck, that gave me a turn,' she told Benjy, who had driven up to Bootle to see what needed to be done. Francis and Dorothy were both too busy to come immediately; and he didn't want Betty to have the pain of it.

Over the next few days Diana scrutinized her mother closely to see if she was particularly upset. Her eyes reddened once or twice behind her new glasses; but she seemed calm. No one thought it right that Diana should go to the funeral.

One morning, she was wakened by a bellow of fury from her parents' room. Her father had brought a letter up to his wife, and what he read in it had goaded him to a mad rage.

'The old bugger. The mean bugger,' he shouted.

Diana went running in at once to see what had happened.

Her mother was sitting up in bed calmly, drinking the tea Benjy had brought her. A rolled scroll of paper lay on the shiny satin eiderdown.

'We don't need it,' Betty soothed her husband. 'It doesn't matter.'

'It's the *spirit* I mind,' Benjy growled. 'How could he? Why? Fancy leaving everything to the others. And not a penny to you. It's rotten.'

He was genuinely upset and angry.

Diana tried to follow what had happened.

'It's a queer thing, that,' said Benjy, evidently almost awed by the old man's deviousness. 'He never *did* take Dorothy out. Why shouldn't you be there? By heck, it's a *mistake*, that's what it is. Why *shouldn't* you be there?'

'It doesn't matter,' repeated Betty.

She had always known herself disliked, cut off, rejected by Solomon. She smiled. What was new and good was that she had Benjy to care for her.

Diana pieced the situation together gradually. The whole Gordon estate had been divided between Francis and Dorothy. There was no mistake about it, either; because he hadn't changed his mind since the year they sold the house in Prince's Road. The only alteration was a neat codicil leaving a thousand pounds to Diana.

Betty tried to mollify Benjy. 'You see. He thought of the child.'

'Yes. He thought she'd need it. It was *me* he was against, I know that. The old sod. But he'd no right taking it out on you.'

'I'm not hurt by it,' said Betty.

Diana wondered if she was. It was hard to tell if her mother felt pain. She was too brave. Too brave for her own good, thought Diana, with precocious wisdom.

She didn't often think about her mother, but she knew Betty was iller than she admitted.

45

'It's a question of loyalty,' said Betty with unusual firmness. It cost an effort to sit up in bed with the painkiller wearing off and the sun beating in through the high glass windows of the ward. But the pain in her belly was as nothing to the pressure she felt emanating from her sister's presence in the chair next to the bed. Dorothy was her unchanged, indefatigable self.

'Stuff,' she said. 'You need looking after. A holiday. I know *him*.' She meant Benjy.

'No, you don't. You never *have*.'

Betty reddened behind her glasses at the mention of her husband. To her own fury, tears began to run down her cheeks.

'Humph,' said Dorothy gruffly, embarrassed by so much emotion. In all her fifty-two years she'd never seen the like. It was asking for trouble for any two people to be that dependent.

'All I want is to get out of here,' cried Betty desperately.

'They'll want a look. Whatever,' said Dorothy. 'Be sensible. I'll have a word with the houseman and get you into that side ward.'

Betty was glad to be offered the chance of getting out of the sight of the other three ladies in her ward, but she did wish Dorothy had not spoken so that they could hear what she said. They knew she was special, of course. And she didn't like to feel their jealousy focus on her.

Particularly the Chinese girl in the far bed. She had already decided the doctors were treating her as inferior. Her lips curled to imitate the sneer of the doctor. She mimed the superiority of the night sister. Betty was sorry for the Chinese girl. In spite of her animation, she looked dark-eyed and tired. And she was trying to hold on to her two-and-a-half-month-old foetus after two miscarriages. Betty wished her well, and a few tears gathered surreptitiously for herself and Benjy. What a bad choice she had been!

When the visitors had gone, the Chinese girl came across and explained about the piece of jade that she wore round her neck. She was only twenty-seven; her mother-in-law had given it to her for luck and fertility. But with one ovary gone after an ectopic pregnancy, and mysterious pains, she turned down her mouth.

'The doctor will try all she can, but who knows? You look unhappy,' she challenged.

Betty sensed the hunger for disaster in her and denied it superstitiously. The girl had her name wrong and for some reason Betty was glad, as if not knowing her name would put her out of the girl's spell.

It was like not saying out loud the name of the disease. She knew what it was. Cancer. Even inside her head the word sounded like a death sentence.

The daylight hours went quietly, even enjoyably; but when the light clicked off her heart had pounded with terror.

When Benjy came he told her he'd been having strange dreams. He'd been pursued by an angry bird of prey. And he was dressed for warmth in a sheepskin coat, he said, laughing his huge jolly laugh.

'I thought it was after me. Afterwards, I heard the creature swoop down on a lamb. It called out *Mama*, though,' he added, troubled.

She cried thinking of that. He didn't even know what troubled him, she thought. She would never have another child. Never a son, as he must have hoped; didn't all men hope for a son? Whatever happened, they would have to take out the womb. She had been bleeding too badly; it was dangerous. She knew it herself.

She wasn't really afraid of dying except for him.

And her daughter too. Of course. But Diana would be all right, Betty knew that. She had trained her to be as alert and sharp as she could. There was nothing soft in her. Betty knew her husband was more vulnerable.

She smiled at him; she was smiling *only* for him, as he sat at her bedside. She touched his hand. To encourage him. She was only smiling to encourage him.

Benjy lay on his bed unsleeping all night long; he kept up a constant moaning prayer. In the next room, Diana lay awake and listened in terror. She was more afraid for him than her mother in the hospital.

On the day of the operation, Rasil and Harry arrived to help in sustaining Benjy, moving around performing the unfamiliar chores of Betty's carefully run house, as though her spirit made its own demands upon them.

Benjy did nothing. He sat at the blue formica table, muttering, 'Why should it come to her? She was always good. Kind to everyone. Why should it come to her?'

When he cried, his whole face opened with misery, and his daughter couldn't bear it. She had sat at the hospital bed, wide-eyed and dry-eyed, next to her mother. But she could

278

not bear her father's helpless tears and was reduced to weeping with him as she watched those big shoulders shake. The operation was at three in the afternoon. At twelve a doctor had to be called for Benjy. Protesting and praying still, he was lifted into his bed and given some powerful sedative that left him blank-faced and still moaning in his sleep, not quite out of reach even then of what he could not endure.

And some time around one Dorothy arrived. Benjy could still be heard moaning in his sleep. But there was Dorothy. She had once left home to do what she wanted and served her whole life doing it. Even now, she laughed more easily than anyone Diana knew, and perhaps was happier.

'Spinster,' Benjy had always sneered at her, because she answered him back, and would not be put down. 'The trouble with her,' he would say to Diana, 'is she's never had a *man* to knock all that nonsense out of her.'

Ever since her meeting with Kitty, Diana had seen her own resemblance to Dorothy growing in the mirror. Now her father's words frightened her like a curse. She was afraid, in case she too had whatever quality it was her father disliked so intensely, and kept men away and made you lonely for ever.

She'd *always* been afraid of Aunt Dorothy. First *of* her, and then turning *into* her. But the next day she had never been so glad to see anyone in her life. Her father could still be heard moaning in his sleep; Diana was half-crazed with the sound of that, and the slow-moving hands of the clock. She and Aunt Dorothy sat and talked over the blue table together, waiting.

What a clever woman Dorothy was. She didn't try to talk about anything else. She said, 'It depends what they find, love. I've seen it so many times. Sometimes it just comes away like a piece of fungus, and it's over and easy as that. Just wait and see.'

It was Dorothy who answered the telephone. And, in spite of her calm, her hand was so wet the receiver slid about in her fingers and she couldn't hear what the other voice was saying. Diana watched her face for clues.

But it was all right. It was all right. And Diana rushed in

to her father to tell him so. 'It's all right! It's all right! It hasn't spread out like a tree. It's all gone. She'll be fine.'

But he was too heavily sedated to hear her. In his sleep the two lines of pain at each side of his nose were like deep scars; and she kissed him, her poor loving father, and went back into the kitchen. Her aunt said briskly, 'Well, thank God for that. Is there any whisky, do you think?'

And as the two of them sat together she felt a great love for this old tough bird of a woman; just because she was alone and didn't seem lonely. Because she was strong. And Diana knew she would never insult her aunt's spirit with her father's sneers again.

She liked the way Dorothy couldn't be bullied, and even, with a residual sense of treachery, she liked the way she stood up to her father. Wished somewhere that her mother, too, could do that. Knew and accepted why it was more fun talking to Dorothy. Because she'd lived all the way round the world, and because she found boring all the things Diana found boring. And now as Diana looked at her – she was a very handsome woman with ginger hair – she wasn't all that sure how spinsterly a life she'd led. It was her *mother* who looked like a nun; who seemed in getting married to have taken on a discipline of service; and Dorothy who seemed free. Like a lovely wild bird.

Of course, she couldn't let her score points over her father. That was too easy, and her father was clumsy verbally; in every confrontation between them Diana was torn and confused.

She had to be guarded even that afternoon, watching the criticism of her father growing over the blue table between them; she couldn't have that, she couldn't have *that* either. To be dependent – as he was totally dependent – might be tyrannous; but it had a certain human warmth which was worth something too.

Dorothy only pitied Benjy. Poor man. Poor man. Because we're all alone, Diana. We have to be able to stand that. Being alone.

But was that true? Diana wasn't sure then whether she agreed with Dorothy, who was certainly tough as wire. About

280

that strength. Wasn't there something treacherous and cold in it? Was it a saintly strength? Or perhaps both these things were the same.

It was what she came to live by.

46

All her life Betty had been an invisible spirit even in her own house, helper and server first to her father and mother, and then to her husband and daughter. Until her own illness. And then, it was as if she had been waiting all her life for her true strength to become clear.

The illness had been conquered. It was Betty's will that had conquered it, as it seemed to her daughter; and she had thrown all of that will into that fight because she was necessary to her husband. And yet her confrontation with death had changed her, too. She was physically more stringy now; spiritually, more obviously formidable.

She had always helped Benjy to write difficult letters. Now, as she drafted letters to the bank manager, she became thoughtful.

'Do you think I could look at the accounts some time, Benjy?' she asked one day.

'I pay an accountant for that,' he said, surprised. 'You're my wife, not a book-keeper.'

'I just want to see what's going wrong.'

'Nothing is wrong,' he growled. 'How do you mean wrong?'

Betty sighed. 'The letters to the bank,' she reminded him.

He stared at her. 'The books are just a mess of figures. What will you see from that?'

'I don't know till I look.'

'So all right. Look.'

*

He brought home the year's books the next day, and Betty put on her strongest reading glasses and spent the whole morning over them. When Benjy came in for lunch he found a chop and baked potatoes in the oven and his wife still at work.

'So?' He came and stood over her.

'I haven't finished,' she said gravely. 'Tell me, who is this Mr Clarence?'

'Oh. He's a traveller. A bit of a *ganeff*. Well, all commercials fiddle.'

'Yes,' said Betty. 'Well, he got away with quite a bit last year.'

'How much?' asked Benjy, fascinated in spite of himself.

'Up to September . . . ' Betty handed him a piece of paper.

Benjy whistled. 'He's robbing me blind,' he shouted. 'Right. Let me get on the phone. If nothing else, he's got to go.'

'Wait,' said Betty. 'I haven't finished yet.'

Nor had she.

'How is it the accountant saw none of this?' demanded Benjy, as his wife began patiently to analyse the ways he was being cheated by his staff.

'He's looking for different things, I suppose,' she said tactfully.

For two pins Benjy would have got rid of him as well.

But there was more wrong with Benjy's business than that.

One day, Betty came home thoughtfully from a bridge game at the Reisens, and asked her husband, 'Do you think it makes sense to stay in manufacture? Reisen says you can get everything a third cheaper from overseas.'

'What does Abe Reisen know about wood?'

Betty sighed.

'Don't you understand?' pleaded Benjy. 'Abe Reisen has been a middleman all his life. OK. He's right. But I can't be an importer and exporter or whatever he calls himself. I can *make* things. That's what I do.'

'You can't make things other people sell that much cheaper,' said Betty with unexpected firmness.

He knew she was right. People didn't want wooden clothes pegs any more, anyway.

Through the serving hatch, Diana heard the interchange with a kind of mute incredulity.

Benjy's instinct was to stay small, to curl in; to rely only on his own skills, with fewer men. Betty saw he was right. That he couldn't handle the stress of Reisen's deals.

'But I could manage all that,' she suggested tentatively. 'While you are reorganizing yourself.'

'You could, too,' admitted Benjy. 'Maybe you should. But you'd need capital. And we can't borrow against stock, because I've already done that.'

'I know,' Betty laughed. 'But I've a little put away. Enough. If you trust me.'

'You are a *marvel*,' said Benjy with incredulous admiration.

So it was that Benjy Katz became an importer and exporter.

And as if to confirm Betty's new-found confidence in her ability to manipulate the world, her daughter Diana won a scholarship to Cambridge.

1956

47

'How could she do such a terrible thing?' Benjy demanded.

Betty pursed her lips, disapproving herself, and not conniving.

'It's that bloody university.'

Diana had declared she wanted to marry a boy who wasn't Jewish.

'Look at your brother Francis. Didn't he pay enough for his mistake?'

Betty protested the irrelevance of Francis's marriage. In truth, there was little congruence in the situation, quite apart from Vivien's health. The boy Diana had chosen lacked all the advantages of the Gentile world. He had few advantages of any kind that Betty could make out, being ill-dressed, Irish-spoken and altogether vehemently working class.

Betty could see it would have been harder for Diana than it had been for Francis to fit into the English world of Cambridge. She had the voice and manner of her Katz cousins, for all the books she had in her head. What she could not understand was the quality she saw as Diana's obstinacy. Why cling to bits and pieces of Yiddish and the jokes picked up from Len? No wonder if she was found unacceptable.

Diana knew she could explain Cambridge 1956 to her mother as little as her father; and she did not know herself why it gave her courage to remember her father's shrug, and his easy dismissal of criticism. She did not want to learn the vowels of Cheltenham and Roedean.

The question of loyalty was poignant. And not just to her father and mother. It was loyalty to the dead. So many had died in mud and fire for being Jewish. To give it up seemed a gross betrayal.

But Diana felt at home with Jake. She couldn't feel at home

287

with the group of very Orthodox students, who prayed every Saturday morning at the shabby schoolroom of a synagogue in Thompson's Lane. They were as alien to her in their way as the public school children about her.

Into the same schoolroom, on Friday nights, went an attractive, rowdy collection of uncertain believers like herself. There were Socialist talks, Zionist talks, Hebrew songs, and homely evenings. But for the most part the boys were all scientists or lawyers. Arts students held aloof from the Jewish Society.

The world to which Diana aspired was the articulate world of those whose parents were academics or wrote for literary journals. Her Jewishness was no bar to that; but she felt she wasn't sharp or quick enough to enter it. It was Jake who brought her in; Jake, with his Irish wit, who took her in on his arm.

Diana did not try to share her new life with her parents. In the vacations, she moved peaceably about the home, not needing to quarrel with them, using their familiar vocabulary, keeping their rules. Why not? In termtime, she and Jake shared everything: Donne and Hopkins; Eliot; Faulkner and Hemingway. They saw all the student plays, and argued for Beckett and against Ionesco, with anyone who would listen. And Jake acted the part of Jacques in the Marlowe Society main production.

In rehearsal, Diana watched him from the stalls of the ADC with her whole body clenched in her seat as he fooled with his part, mimicking Touchstone, teasing the actress who played Audrey. 'Bear your body seemly.' But as soon as she saw him in front of an audience she relaxed, feeling them warm to him. He was talented, and she was in love with his talent, and the miracle of his willingness to share it with her. No problem there.

So Diana moved away from being Jewish, as she moved away from her mother and father. It didn't fetter her, or worry her.

She was relieved not to have Christianity, really. Her Methodist friends had much more severe crises of conscience. About sex, for instance. The nearest Diana came to a religious crisis was reading Bunyan's *Grace Abounding to Me Most Miserable of Sinners*. She had suddenly asked herself then with horror clutching her heart: What if it's *true*? Who's to say it's not? Look how many people believe it. And had gone around almost mad with the fear of hellfire for a week, until Jake laughed her out of that. Lent her Joyce. Returned her to humour and humanism.

Luckily Jake didn't care too much about the Church.

'I'll convert, if you like,' he said, grinning. 'I've always liked the idea. Numinous feelings. Ethics and no after-life. I'm perfectly serious, honest.'

It wouldn't have helped, of course, as far as the Katz family were concerned.

With a first class degree in Part II Diana's own tentative assessment of the world seemed to be assured. The doors stood open. And if her decision to stay on at university met nothing but black-eyed hostility from her father, she and Jake at least knew what it meant.

Shortly after the tripos results had been posted in the Senate House, Diana decided it was the right time to attempt to make friends with Uncle Francis. It wasn't that she wanted anything from him, exactly; but it often irked her that he had taken no note of her progress, and after all, he was in the same game, as Jake put it. Perhaps she hoped he might be the one member of the family that would understand what she wanted from life.

She went to see him at his publishing house.

There he was, a large, red-faced man with a booming voice and tufts of silver hair, trying to make friends with his niece. Was it her fault it went badly? She still resented those epistles in copper-plate which her mother always treated with such extravagant respect. He mentioned a writer friend whose books Diana hadn't much enjoyed. And she made the mistake of saying so. Cambridge, Cambridge, she thought immediately. She could hear it had come out as a sneer; and her uncle chose to read it that way. He made a huffy reference to Leavis, and his own more liberal days, and that was that. They hadn't hit it off.

Her mother was disappointed. It seemed to Diana that

after that encounter her mother began to treat all her own achievements with a kind of sniff. Reserving her judgement. Qualifying it with the information that after all Francis had not accepted her daughter.

It only caused Diana to redouble her own efforts.

'You'll never do it,' Jake had once tried to explain to her.

'What?'

'Win a place for your mother. In the Gordon family stakes.'

'I don't know what you're talking about,' she insisted, freezing off that painful line of inquiry, meaning she didn't want to know.

Jake looked like Holbein's Wyatt, bearded and handsome, with just enough anger in his small and stony eyes to make him formidable. He was strong and solidly built; and since he never read books with an eye to the tripos, it wasn't surprising that it was Diana who got a first, not he. But Jake never took much account of degrees.

He wasn't an opportunist. He didn't have to be. People wanted him at their parties. When he met useful people he wasn't frightened of them, because he sensed how much they liked him. He was easy to like. Everything fell into his lap.

Liverpool Irish, he liked to call himself. And he liked people to imagine from the jeer in his voice that he'd grown up poor. He had a warm, musical voice that had never tried to lose its northern vowels. But his mother had a good piece of property in Dublin, Diana discovered.

His first book was very successful. Several of the poems were about his father, whom he idolized; and most of the critics who praised it thought he was writing straight out of his own life. It was an invented life, of course; even if, as the marriage wore on, it seemed to Diana that he gradually came to believe in his own fantasy. He found his own style very early, and the words he used were heavy and short like the people in his own family, and he used their solidity to carry the weight of all their lives.

Diana thought he was lucky. She would have liked to write poems herself, and sometimes she felt the excitement of words so intensely that she tried, feeling each word in her mouth like a separate pebble. But it was a secret game; she could not have said why exactly, but she did not want Jake or anyone to see. It was a temptation which she disciplined.

She put her main energy into editing a critical text of a minor Romantic poet who, by an odd coincidence, had recently been published by her Uncle Francis after a century's neglect.

48

Francis had his own troubles. He was in pain.

He had cancelled two weeks in Tuscany because of it, and was irritable with everyone. He did his best, though, to conceal his state from Dorothy when he took her to tea at the Connaught.

She was wearing a pink straw hat and a greeny-grey print dress, as if knowing the tearoom would be precisely that colouring, even to the flowers and the napkins. Francis said as much as he held her chair and took his own.

Her laugh was deeper than he remembered, throaty with cigarettes.

For a while they talked of Kitty; Dorothy saw a good deal of her and Francis did not. He thought his daughter's decision to go from Oxford into nursing was perverse and wasteful, and he blamed Dorothy for it.

'Perhaps. She seems very content,' Dorothy assured him, knowing that wasn't the point.

'She had a literary talent,' he objected, wondering even as he said it how sharp that gift had been. It was Betty's child, evidently, who shared his own passion.

'Yes? Do you think that so important? You aren't looking well,' she said abruptly.

Francis felt his blood mounting in his cheeks with annoyance. What did she expect? Here he was in a hot wet

August stuck in London.

'I suppose you think I should eat less and take more exercise?' he asked. 'The cakes are very good here, by the way.'

'Thank you. I'll have a piece of the strawberry flan. I have no idea about your eating habits,' said Dorothy, unfolding the pink linen napkin and placing it on her knee. 'I think you should have an X-ray.'

Francis continued to spread jam over his teacake, although her words gave him a nasty jolt. He had been losing weight for some time and, aside from the pain, he had recently experienced one or two humiliating symptoms, which he certainly did not want to discuss with her.

'You, on the other hand, are looking splendid,' he parried.

This was true. Dorothy had aged splendidly; and now, just returned from Sark, where she holidayed every year, her skin was tanned almost to teak. With her fine high nose and grey hair she resembled an Indian chieftain.

She laughed at him. 'Don't put me off. I'm worried about you.'

He was embarrassed. They were not close, though she was the only member of the family he ever saw.

'I wish you would not concern yourself.'

'Tell me your other news, then,' said Dorothy patiently.

He shrugged.

'Did they feast you on caviare and champagne in Moscow?' she asked mischievously.

Francis hesitated. 'Moscow was very disturbing,' he admitted. 'But yes, as you imply, I had my share of the fleshpots.'

'Can it really all be true? About Uncle Joe?'

Francis looked at her gravely. 'There was nothing avuncular about Stalin, whatever I once thought,' he told her.

'I expect it was all right for ordinary people,' she suggested.

'Who do you imagine filled his camps? Well, it's true I didn't talk to many. They haven't exactly encouraged the spread of English. And people are scared of talking to foreigners.'

'Were you followed?'

'Of course.'

'And are you going to publish the dissident literature?'

Francis had, as it happened, exactly a decision of that kind on his mind at the moment. It was a delicate question.

'Perhaps.'

'Would you put someone at risk because it was good business?'

'Of course not. What kind of a business do you think I run?'

'I can never make you talk to me about it! How can I tell?' she pointed out.

He made a last effort to wrest back the conversational advantage. 'And you? Now you have retired. How do you look back on all your years of drudgery?'

'Work,' said Dorothy. 'Well, I think it was the most important thing in my life. Finally.'

Francis thought she might say as much, but less cheerfully.

Turning in his chair, he called the waiter for more hot water. The pains had returned to his belly, and he was finding it hard to disguise them.

'Francis,' said Dorothy gently.

He groaned. 'All right, all right,' he said. 'I'll do as you say.'

Francis was admitted to hospital within the fortnight. Cancer of the bowel, the surgeon said. But the prognosis was good. Francis was less grateful to Dorothy than he should have been for pressing action upon him. Aside from the fear of surgery, the details of the operation, and the necessary bag that would hang at his side to serve as an anus, sickened him. Partly for this reason, and partly because he never liked to see visitors when he was off guard, he gave none of his friends any hint of his whereabouts.

His daughter Kitty came to visit him in his small side ward the day before his operation. For a moment, seeing her, Francis was reminded so painfully of Vivien he could not think what to say to her, and there was an awkward silence.

'Tomorrow, is it? Don't worry. He's a very good man,' she said at last.

'I'm sure,' he replied gruffly.

'Do you dream much?' she asked him.

'Not a great deal.' He stared at her. 'Why?'

'They'll give you morphine. You might enjoy it.'

'I don't put much trust in visions,' he said. 'I hope you don't either.'

'What do you believe in?' She was teasing, evidently.

'Oh, the usual things. Civilization. Decency.'

'Parliamentary democracy?' she finished, smiling.

'All that,' he smiled back. 'Old-fashioned of me, I know. But there it is.'

'I just wondered if it was enough.'

Enough, thought Francis recoiling from the momentary intimacy. As if anything was enough.

'It's all there is,' he said bleakly.

And what have you found, he wondered, looking at her eager face. Service, dedication, what? That seems to answer so finely. Vivien's daughter. She was prettier than his niece, he thought. He hadn't liked his niece. There was something aggressive in her. Something of the Katz family perhaps. He wasn't going to pretend to like them. Something jumped-up. Ill-bred. He could not imagine how Betty had produced such a child.

Kitty stood up lightly. 'Time to go, I think.' But she hesitated. 'I didn't know what to bring you. Books seemed silly. Still.' She held one out.

It was a recent biography of Richard Wagner. The choice surprised him. His own musical taste was closer to the baroque and for a moment he wondered if Wagner was a fad of Kitty's generation.

She met his questioning eyes uncertainly. 'I don't know much about opera. You took me once or twice, remember?'

He remembered well. It was *The Marriage of Figaro*, in English moreover, magnificently performed. Kitty had sulked throughout. He was obscurely disappointed to find no greater significance in the choice.

'And nursing, my dear,' he remembered. 'Has that made you happy?'

He could see that it was not something she intended to discuss with him, and shortly afterwards she was gone.

A nurse came in to take a note of what he wanted for supper, and to remind him he must not eat or drink after 10 p.m. He assured her grimly that he was unlikely to forget he was having an operation in the morning.

'Will you want a sleeping pill?'

'I think I will.'

Francis made himself prepare calmly for sleep in an ordinary way but, as he brushed his teeth, and stared into his own familiar flushed face, his thoughts strayed uncomfortably. Two days ago he had watched patients returning on their trolleys from the last session of surgery, their grey, drowned faces against the scarlet bedclothes; an occasional slack and insensible arm attached to a drip.

I'm alone, he thought.

It was how he had lived for the last few years, and he had not disliked it. When he wanted company he went out for it. Otherwise, he had no one to please but himself. When Dorothy suggested they might set up together after her retirement, he had not welcomed the idea.

'I'm too obstreperous for you,' he'd said, and she'd rewarded his honesty with a rare smile.

'We never got on as children,' she agreed.

'You were too bossy then,' he objected.

'Worse now,' she laughed.

All the same, he found himself remembering hopefully that she had promised to visit him at the weekend.

He wanted to see no one whatsoever for several days; his attention was altogether absorbed with the discomforts that followed surgery. At first he was nothing but a body, waiting for the nurses bringing needle and release on their four-hourly rounds; twenty-four hours later, he was restored to a more or less querulous normality.

After one or two false starts, he began to skim through the biography Kitty had brought him; the monstrosity of genius was always fascinating. It was well enough put together; but it chilled him nevertheless. It was not, of course, Wagner's notorious prejudice. More a matter of the Jewish musicians who accepted Wagner's patronage. He had to lay the book aside. Could such servility be excused? Condoned?

Had he been guilty of it himself? Was he not among those cultured Jews who stripped themselves of all the obvious tokens of their race?

Francis could not disperse the chill.

Wagner's unfairness and dishonesty, his insistence on the natural impossibility of a Jewish contribution to German literature was only part of it. There were other echoes.

It was not so long ago that he had come in late on an argument while dining as a guest in Peterhouse.

'As critics, yes. Writers for television certainly. Maybe in prose, one or two. But poets?'

'What about Isaac Rosenberg?'

'Two or three poems, not more.'

Francis realized what was being discussed before the neat young historian and his guest from Oxford recognized him.

'Good evening, sir,' they said then.

And he had hesitated to take them on. The conviction that Jews could only serve the arts at one remove came too close to home. Heine, he might have said. Even Pasternak, in their terms. But he was too conscious of his own role as entrepreneur; he had loved the English language and assimilated the subtlest cadence of it, but he had not written poems. He was too good a case in point. And so he let the matter go.

'A coward, I suppose,' he suggested to Dorothy, telling her, rather to his own surprise, something of what he felt.

She thought about that. 'Not really. They would have collapsed in shame if you'd challenged them.'

'In my thoughts, I mean. Treacherous.' He was too tired to pursue the guilt.

She saw that and wanted to reassure him. 'You're in good shape, you know. Have they explained?'

He nodded.

'I saw Betty at the weekend. She sent her love to you.'

At this an expression flickered over Francis's face for a moment that she could not read.

It had come to him clearly for the first time what he had taken against in Betty's daughter. Diana looked Jewish in a way none of the Gordon family had ever done. He was ashamed at the thought. It left him cold, heartless and isolated.

49

For three years Diana and Jake lived in an enchanted planet of their own, suffused with sexual joy and a sense that everything was going well for them. Jake wrote poems and taught for a language school. Diana wrote up her PhD.

Then, in 1961, came the trial of Adolf Eichmann, and the horror of that daily newsprint bit like acid into Diana's unbelieving mind all year. Of course, she had read the newspapers after the war. She knew the facts. She had seen the photographs. But now, every day, the newsprint in *The Times* brought the truth into her consciousness in a new way.

Now she read as if for the first time what had been done to the Jews of Europe.

The words bit into her. And it was the words more than the pictures; the death marches more than the gas chambers. The horror of children in their fathers' arms, gagged by their fathers' loving hands, because soldiers shot any child that cried. All the strength and stamina and endurance were for nothing, because no one was intended to survive.

The knowledge of the horrors settled like ash into her. She could hardly move about her daily work. From library to college room. And her colleagues read the same newspapers, but the greyness did not enter them. It was something in Europe, long past. Something far off. Nothing that would ever happen to them.

It wasn't just Germans. Diana knew that. It was Poles too, French too. It was *people*. People had done these terrible things. And now she understood what could happen anywhere. Anyone could suffer such things; anyone could make them happen. There was no protection.

She looked at herself among the bones and the mangled bodies; among emaciated racks of ribs she saw herself one of

297

them. She was a victim of the same disaster.

'That's what it *means*, being Jewish,' Diana tried to explain, shaken, to Jake.

'What about the gypsies? God help us all, what about the Poles?' he demanded.

And somehow he knew the words to heal her.

He knew how to lift the sense of being cursed off her.

The following year Diana decided to have a *seder* night. Jake humoured her. Asked her if she had intimations of God. She tried to explain it more soberly. It was to be her gesture of allegiance. It was something she could do, setting out white linen, and using silver candlesticks, buying the sweet Palwin wine of her childhood. It was intended as an act to assert that Hitler had not altogether won.

'If you'll join me,' she asked Jake gruffly, 'it will make a kind of sense.'

'I've always liked candles,' he agreed.

So she invited a few others, to make it more like a family occasion, a young American girl, a boy from Hungary. Then she ordered the *matzot*; bought a Haggadah; spent all day following the recipes for *charoseth* and *kneidlach*.

Jake was impressed and amused.

'All this you need to serve God?' he mimicked the up-turn of a Jewish voice.

She laughed. She was happy. This was something she could do; and she determined to do it with her mother's thoroughness.

Only one thing did she get wrong.

The date.

And what could it mean when Diana, careful Diana, who double-checked every page reference, every footnote without weariness, mistook a date?

'Easily done,' she said sullenly. 'The calendar gave me the first day. I *forgot* you begin with the night before. But it doesn't matter, that was the *idea* of having two *seder* nights. In case people counted wrong. It doesn't matter. The second night is as good as the first.'

And it should have been. But somehow it mattered to

Diana that they'd missed the night most Jews keep. How could she have been so careless? What did it mean?

'You aren't a *joiner* by nature, are you?' asked Jake, unwisely answering the question as she put it to him. 'You don't really want to be part of the tribe at all. Not the living ones, anyway.'

She smiled rather wanly, not wanting to quarrel, needing the evening to go well.

It wasn't altogether a failure.

Diana would have liked to read the Hebrew text; indeed, sonorous voices of her childhood already sounded in her ears. But it was the Hungarian who obliged, for a while. To Jake's delight, he had a light tenor voice, and sang with great verve. And then everyone fell into conversation.

'To have four glasses of wine made compulsory is very endearing,' said Jake. 'Would you think our Lord would have been mildly sloshed, then, at the Last Supper?'

The Hungarian reproved him for the frivolity; so Jake turned his attention to the American girl, who seemed ready to giggle.

The Hungarian shrugged. 'Nothing bad ever happened to them,' he said to Diana, as if to a fellow-European.

Diana froze.

'Were many of your family lost?' she asked, spellbound into that complicity.

'All those who lived in Debreczen,' he shook his head. 'The peasants always hated Budapest, and the Jews in the villages meant Budapest to them. You could say my aunts and uncles died for the Austro-Hungarian Empire.'

He laughed.

The information agitated Diana.

'And you are here to do research on Rilke? How can you? Isn't the German language tainted for you?'

The Hungarian shook his head. 'You forget. How the marriage of German and Jewish culture was of such an amazing fecundity. Think of Kafka.'

And the word *fecundity* stayed with Diana through the evening.

A little drunk, sitting on the bed naked with her slender

neck cupped in his large soft hand, she muttered it to Jake.

'Is that an invitation?' he teased her.

'I can't bear it. Any children I might have. Being hunted down.' She shook her head.

'As Jews?' His eyebrows rose in disbelief.

She nodded.

'Baptize them then,' he suggested.

'I *couldn't*. Don't you *see* how I couldn't? What a treachery that would be?'

He took away his hand and lay back on the bed. 'There are worse things.'

She stared at him wildly. 'Worse? What can have been worse?'

'Hellfire,' he said quietly. 'It took me a time to throw off my own Church, Diana.'

'But I'm talking about something *real*. In the real world.' Diana flared up with anger.

And at first Jake would not be provoked. 'You're a natural Protestant,' he said. 'You think you can get to God on your own. Without Church. Or tribe.' And he wagged his finger drunkenly at her. 'Beware the sin of pride.'

After that, they quarrelled all night.

The quarrel dispersed, but Diana's preoccupations put a distance between them, as she continued to wonder uneasily about God. About Grandpa Abram. And about what to do if she had children. In that shocked, uneasy condition she was unprepared for the arrival of the sixties in Cambridge.

It was true the sixties did not arrive on time. They reached the undergraduate population of Cambridge some time in 1966. And they separated her from Jake, even though, to the amusement of more sophisticated friends, they remained in love with one another.

And faithful.

But the sixties *suited* Jake; just as Diana could find no place in them. He crossed the street from their tiny house in Eltisley Avenue to smoke pot with the students; listened to Captain Beefheart; even tried LSD. And she disliked the whole drug culture; although, as anywhere else, she soon learned to *pass*.

Among the people who flourished in the sweet smell of grass, knowing the language. *Passing*, as a coloured man with a white skin might pass among alien culture. A voyeur among those who took risks. Holding off, all the time.

And still not sleeping around, as people had begun to do so easily, so readily.

'Scared to,' Jake said, unimpressed by her fidelity.

They had quarrelled over that and soon afterwards she began to wonder if what he said meant he was enjoying the new freedoms.

'Look, I'm more interested in the politics of this movement than the sex,' Jake tried to explain.

He had been across to give a reading at the University of Essex and had come back in such a state of exhilaration that Diana at once concluded a woman was responsible.

'No. And again. No,' he said patiently. 'It was *all* the kids. That's all. Marching about and caring.'

'Sounds pretty fascist.'

He thought about that, and, with characteristic honesty, admitted, 'Well. Maybe. If you think *Battleship Potemkin* is fascist.'

'What did you do, march on the vice-chancellor?'

'Something like that.' He sounded rather depressed.

Her gibe had gone home.

And he began to sleep badly.

'Take pills,' she suggested.

The advice made him very angry. 'You just want me to shut up about it. But I warn you, Diana, I'm getting bored. You don't care if I write or not, do you?'

'That's not fair,' she protested.

He laughed.

'I've a nine o'clock lecture,' she pleaded. 'I *must* get back to sleep, Jake.'

'Sleep,' he groaned. 'It's all you think of. You can't *wait* to snuggle into it, can you?'

And he put the light on without ceremony. Diana flinched.

'I'm going to read,' he said.

'Why can't you see that nothing you read now will do

you any good? And you've all tomorrow for it.'

'I've got to put something alive and real into my soul now. But how could you understand that? Do you *need* a soul to do what you do? It's all mechanical. That's why you can get up fresh as a daisy and go straight to it.'

'Jake!'

'And that's all that counts, isn't it? Being able to do that. When did you last have a living thought, Diana? When did you last have *one* living thought you didn't get from a book?'

'Of course I have them,' she muttered thickly.

'All right. Tell me a thought, then. And I'll put the light out.'

'Jake, I'm too exhausted now. Goddamn it, show a bit of mercy.'

'By which you mean, *shut up*! As ever.'

Her heart was banging with a kind of sick fatigue. 'I get ill if I'm tired, Jake.'

'Night after night,' muttered Diana. 'I'm going to be really ill if you go on like this. What are you trying to do?'

'When is the right time, Diana?' Jake demanded.

She was silent.

'In the morning? But that's when you're working. In the evening?'

She got up then, and said shakily, 'I'm going to sleep downstairs.'

Then they looked at one another uneasily, not knowing what to make of her sudden move. The floor below seemed inexpressibly cold and miserable. She didn't want to go. In a way she was afraid to go.

'How is it *my* fault, anyway? I mean what's wrong with you?' she said, still holding the covers.

'It's your fault because you don't care what I do. Just as long as I'm not a nuisance,' said Jake.

He looked so miserable then that she got back into bed and they held one another very close.

'Passion, or your kind of independence,' said Jake. 'You can't have both. Think of the end of an opera like *Jenufa*. Two desperate people turning together, and all that marvellous soaring music – '

'Passion?'

'Exactly. Passion, desperation, *need*. That's the key to it all. *Need*. Now if what's really happening inside all the time is, yes, well, I *love* you darling, but what really matters is what I have to do in the morning – '

'Real life *is* about what you do in the morning,' said Diana.

'No passion in real life, then?'

'I don't accept that polarity,' she argued.

'It's not a question of what you accept. Once you know you can junk the whole thing, once you know you'll survive anyway, how can you talk about *need*? You can't have things that are mutually incompatible.'

'I want both,' she said doggedly.

Of course. Her own life, her own world. And love too. Why not?

'Passion or independence?' said Jake, smiling evilly.

'Look, I'm *made up* of things that are mutually incompatible, according to you,' she flared.

'Yes.'

'Well, does that make me a monster, or what?'

Diana remained in touch with her parents as they aged through the same decade in which she struggled; but she was not close to them. How could she be? They could not have begun to understand the change in her life; would not have believed in the way people lived around her. Ten-year-old marriages shattered; bewildered middle-aged women, who had once longed for freedom, found they had been given it. They also found themselves living alone on a third of the income they had been used to. Some of them had to learn that working for a living was more of a strain than they had expected.

There, at least, Diana felt she had some dignity. She had *always* worked. Desperately as she needed Jake, it wasn't for his financial support. And, for all the tension, she would never have broken with him. But it was strange how that common image of the heart *sinking* so accurately described her physical sensations. What biological meaning could it have? She really felt her heart was a heavy weight in her chest.

Jake spent the last August of their marriage wheezing

with asthma. The attack was unexpected; he'd had nothing more than hay fever before that summer. And he didn't believe the doctors, refused to take the pills, thought back over the year for signs of the malaise of the soul that had brought on this new sickness of the body.

'I've been muffled,' he said. And it *had* been his year of muffled creation. 'These squeezed air sacs. *Muffled*. I'm being silenced,' he said.

So he decided telling the truth would save him, and started telling it explosively to everyone, especially to Diana.

'Living with you, that's all it is. You see, just saying that gets the adrenalin flowing. My soul has been shrivelled up all year. There's the truth. Now who needs Ventolin?' he said.

But the truth had only limited efficacy.

The next night he spent fighting for breath, and she sat up with him and watched the orange street lights on Newnham Road until the sky behind the elms went white, thinking of dying and the way death had suddenly turned its sight upon her whole generation. She thought of friends who had killed themselves approaching forty; and others who had fallen ill, and taken it bravely; of one gone thin and yellow facing colostomy and mutilation. And she knew it was all the same, finally, all the terrors were there in each black silence between Jake's wheezing breath.

Jake. I need you, she thought.

And when the pink light came in through the slats of the window she said, 'Listen, you must get out of this mouldy city. It's killing you. Let's go somewhere where the air is dry.'

So they'd gone to the north of Sicily, where, on Goethe's headland, a friend of Jake's had a primitive hut.

And of course, everything had gone badly.

Every morning Diana woke at six and looked round the toothy, plantless hillside crumbling all round the strip of hotels, and prepared for boredom or quarrels or worse. Jake couldn't do more than ten strokes in the sea without puffing. So by the time the bay had disappeared, and the water was greeny-grey and the bodies of all the visitors still in the sea looked like shadows, she and Jake were ready to lash out at each other, with or without cause.

Every day Diana sat with the yellow *strega* sour in her stomach. And one afternoon, she thought she saw her father from the back; and longed for him so much she ran over to him. Only to find a stranger. She was so struck with the pain of that discovery she mentioned it carelessly to Jake, and he exploded with fury.

'I see what it is now, what protects you. So you don't need me or any man.'

'I need you. I need you,' she protested.

'You don't need anyone's presence. Just some outline of them. Some ghost. That's all. It's your childhood. Your damned, safe, loving childhood. That's how you carry on.'

'You said they enfeebled me,' she argued sullenly.

The break took Diana by surprise.

Jake had been invited to New York and had been away longer than he'd planned. It wasn't so uncommon; but she'd missed him, and wanted him back. So when she heard his voice on the telephone, she was at first too pleased to take in what he was saying.

But soon she was listening hard enough, her mouth dry, and her throat aching.

He had decided to stay in New York. And, yes, there was someone else. No, he didn't want a divorce. Didn't want anything, really. She accepted the information numbly.

It had happened to other people. Now it had happened to her. She was just another casualty in a new war.

Diana straightened her spine and determined to cope.

She went shopping for new clothes and fresh make-up. Had her hair trimmed in London. She saw that she looked bold, unafraid, grown-up.

But Diana had reckoned without time and chance.

50

The following weekend, she heard that her mother, ill all year and visited so rarely, had died in the night.

Her father was out of his mind with grief; and as she set off home with no more than a note to the senior tutor, she could already feel the constraint of an old love forming a web around her.

Through the window of the diesel train Diana saw everything remotely: the fens, flooded with silver water in the grass, the white seabirds settled there, and the fields of wrecked cars. There was a pain in her throat, and she did not know if the pain was for herself, or for her mother.

She gave me her protection, thought Diana, and I never really knew her. She was generous. She could have yoked me to them easily, or let my father do as much, and she refused to do that. Let me go. Yes, it was her will that set me free. So that I didn't have to keep returning, to be checked over, to demonstrate my loyalty, or perform the public duties of a daughter.

Diana changed trains from the Eastern Region to a 125, all orange-cushioned and shining, and lay back numbly in her seat.

I wasn't a very affectionate daughter to her, she thought. And an almost forgotten memory of her mother dabbing lotion on her chicken-pox all one night returned like an image of her lost childhood and that gentle, uncomplaining protection which Diana had accepted so easily.

Her father was blank-eyed with loss. Inconsolable. And incredulous.

'She was ill all year. She wouldn't listen to anyone.'

And again.

'We were so happy. We had everything we wanted.'

Diana believed him. Yet her mother's feelings remained a puzzle to her, as she thought with bewilderment of her patient bustle and easy coping. Was that enough to make sense of a life? Had she been stoical and dutiful? Or had she shared her father's contentment without any restlessness? No way to know now, thought Diana. I should have talked to her more often.

'Where's your Jake?' demanded her father, with a brief return of energy. 'Wasn't your mother worth his time?'

Diana put away the moment of admitting to her own loss. 'He's in New York,' she temporized.

But her father had begun to sob, unheedingly.

And Diana took in the extent of his collapse and the nature of her new responsibilities.

Her mother could protect her no longer.

51

Diana moved her father into the Eltisley Avenue house, even though she knew exactly what constraints she would be accepting. Her spine grew straighter. Her clothes cleaner-cut. Her lips thinner. And one day when she looked into the mirror, she saw that she looked almost as Aunt Dorothy had looked when she visited Diana's home at the time of her mother's illness. But now she accepted the resemblance. She was not bitter. She recognized how much she had the qualities of spinsterhood.

And she refused to settle into being a wife for her father.

'What kind of a life do you lead, my poor Diana?' he asked.

'I'm perfectly happy,' she snapped angrily. 'Happier than most women I know of my age. At least I have self-respect.'

'A woman should have children,' he said obstinately. 'Why don't you divorce that great lobbus of a husband?

Someone else will come along. A nice, normal *yiddisher* boy.'

'Because I don't want to sit home cooking. I'm doing what I care about. You just can't see that, because you can't imagine work being the most important thing in your life. It was always a means to an end to you.'

'So what else is it?'

For some reason, perhaps because of her mother's ill luck, Diana had always feared she would be unable to have children. But she had Katz blood. No rhesus factor. No abnormalities. Except, of course, she was thirty-four. A little strange, perhaps, to check out, in the abstract as it were, whether it was still possible for her to have a child.

Her doctor obviously had the same thought. 'Is it congratulations then, Diana?'

'Nothing like that,' she denied, colouring.

'It must be *something* like that, unless you're expecting God,' he teased her. 'Anyway, you've nothing to worry about, but don't leave it any longer. There's more to having a baby than getting pregnant. Leave it much later and you'll run into trouble. Think of the child.'

Numbly, Diana contemplated the impossibility of making any move at all.

Benjy tried to be useful. Shopping. Or cooking what he remembered of the traditional foods. When she came back from the library she often found him bending over the stove, with a teatowel round his waist to protect himself from the flour and sugar. He didn't believe in using books, of course, and guessed the ingredients, but he usually got it about right.

Only she couldn't give him the praise he wanted. She was too much locked up in her own hurt. And she thought of Grandpa Abram living into his eighties. It made her severe. It made her remote.

Benjy was still a strong man; his shoulders unbowed, and his hair still black, except for his eyebrows. Every morning he dressed as carefully as if he were going off to work. Reluctantly, Diana faced the fact that they could be together for ten years at least.

So she had to lay down ground rules. About who could

come to the house. Stay the night. About being out late in London. Or, worst of all, being at work in the house itself. Not willing to be taken out for lunch. Not wanting to go shopping.

They began to quarrel often and bitterly. Once, Benjy drove off down south in his car in a huff; but he relented halfway to Bournemouth, and phoned to tell her where he would be staying, so she wouldn't worry.

Sometimes he complained to the charwoman, 'I'm not supposed to do *anything*, according to my daughter. Once you're old, she thinks you should just be stuck in a room like an old dog. Well, I'm not finished yet.'

And he wasn't.

He went and sat near the river and watched the trees. And one day he bought himself an easel and paints. And began. At first he was bewildered by his difficulty in making the trees look as if they came up out of the ground. They all lay down flat like a piece of primitive art. Touched, Diana took him to the Fitzwilliam, and what he saw astonished him. He'd no idea there was so much skill in it, he grumbled.

But he didn't give up. He discovered a class in painting at the local college and enrolled there.

To Diana's surprise, he turned out to have talent.

One afternoon, Benjy finished a picture that pleased him so much he went out to buy the wood to frame it. Using old, familiar tools, he cut the wood to size with pleasure. But then felt a grinding pain in his teeth. He had to sit down, and massage his jaw. Diana was out, and when she came back she found him shivering by a radiator and holding a hot water bottle.

Her own heart went cold, looking at him.

The doctor took a long time to come; but when he came, he told her what she already knew. It was a coronary. As the doctor arranged for the ambulance, Diana wanted to burst into tears.

At Addenbrooke's, the staff took a long time to find Benjy's notes; but they attached him to a heart bleeper, and as Diana watched the little tennis ball of white on the telly screen, she looked anxiously for irregularity. It looked OK, she thought.

'Can't you make them get a move on, Diana?' asked Benjy. 'I'm cold.'

She walked over to the young houseman on duty and asked quietly at the same time what the trace said to him. He was tired, she saw, and answered without caution, 'Nothing shows up yet. Can't tell. The papers will be down soon. Wasn't he on steroids?'

'Yes,' she said, her heart sinking.

She had seen her father ill before, and he was usually emotional, hugging her to him with desperate affection, as if taking for granted the depth of her own love and the extent to which she shared his own fear.

Now that she was truly afraid, he seemed strangely cooler.

'Is it all ending, Diana?' he asked.

The dignity of his appraisal stunned her. He was calmly looking into his own death. She didn't know how to meet his courage.

'Nonsense,' she said. 'You're as tough as an old boot.'

He nodded, but she could not tell if he was reassured. She wished she had said something more loving.

A nurse approached him, and she heard him bellow at her, 'No! It's spelled K-A-T-Z. Get my name right!' with such ferocity that for a moment she wondered if she were not exaggerating the danger.

Where did it come from, that courage, and where had she seen it before?

God-given, she thought. It was a blessing that came only to believers.

When they sent her home, she had almost begun to think she was exaggerating.

'Goodnight, Dad,' she said, quite casually.

But the hospital woke her an hour after she had gone to sleep with the news of his death.

For some reason the only person she wanted to talk to about her pain was Jake.

And she heard in his voice from New York that he was a little depressed himself. But he listened to her carefully.

310

'I'm alone too,' he said. 'Never liked it.'

'What happened to the chick?' she asked.

'Buzzed off to Kansas with someone in his teens. I'm getting old for all this swinging about myself.'

She laughed. He could always make her laugh.

And she wanted to say: Come home, darling. I need you. But she couldn't. She waited an expensive minute to see if the invitation would come from him.

It didn't.

'I never let him see I loved him, Jake. When he was lonely and needed it. He thought I didn't care.'

'He'd have known. Anyone could see.'

She knew Jake could hear her grief. Wanted him to hear it.

'Once he'd have known, yes. But not *then*! I didn't mean to be cruel, but I am, Jake. I thought it would go on and on. I had to make some kind of a stand, didn't I?'

'Poor Diana.'

But that wasn't what she wanted. She sniffed. Pulled herself together.

'I could have made *him* happy, anyway,' she said.

Perhaps it was mainly what she wanted to say.

'How's the economy?' he asked. 'Things are closing in on me.'

'Are they?' She didn't understand what he meant.

He sighed. 'Well, I guess it hasn't reached the academic world.'

'I saw your last book.'

'Did you? Sharp of you, that, considering.'

'Oh come on, it wasn't ignored,' she teased him.

'Mm.' He sounded grumpy.

For a while they talked about Benjy. Jake said, 'He must have found it hard. Fitting in.'

'With me, you mean?' she asked shakily.

'Well. And all the rest.'

There was a little more chat, and then she held the purring, useless phone in her hands, and the tears ran freely down her cheeks.

Goodbye, my love, she thought. All love goes with you.

*

311

For a long while after that, Diana consulted no one's wish but her own. Her parents were dead, she had lost Jake, there seemed no point being chaste. And Jake had been wrong about one thing. She needed sex. She found it easily, wherever she chose to, never closely, never intimately, never for long.

'Like a bloody man,' her lovers accused her.

'Well?'

That's how I am, she decided, hardening up. That's how I need to be.

That's how Diana lived.

A huntress; and if not chaste, cold.

She hadn't chosen her own shape, but she accepted it.

52

Diana had always thought of ageing into a distinguished old lady with her mother's approval glowing about her. Now that her mother was dead, the pleasure had gone out of that possibility; and as she now considered the matter, it seemed realistic to admit that the glow had begun to dim even while her mother was alive. So what was there to hope for and look forward to?

It had always been the job of Uncle Francis to bring distinction upon the family, and Diana was not supposed to top his achievement even if her mother had ever admitted the possibility. Even Francis's death had not altered that situation. Perhaps it had even sealed it. Diana could remember the two-column obituary notice in *The Times*, ceremoniously cut out and sent to her, of which her mother had been so proud.

Mean old bugger, thought Diana, he'd never repaid that admiration with anything but faintly patronizing letters.

*

Often now as she dropped into sleep, she found her father waiting for her. Sometimes he appeared quite practically to punish Jake. That was a frequent dream. The simplest. He just lifted Jake up easily, with all that marvellous lout energy he'd never really found a use for, and threw him over a wall. Sometimes he was waiting sadly, with deep brown eyes questioning; and she longed to hurry past the old hand that reached for her.

'Don't forget us altogether, Diana,' he would say.

And sob, so that Diana woke in horror.

One wet June night she was driving along the A45 to a party out in a village. And suddenly she felt: I'm alone. *Alone*. And it made her faint with horror, not because she was afraid something was going to happen to her, just through the knowledge and the pain of it, like the ache of something lost. There was moonlight on the wet grass; and the fields stretched out on either side of her. Empty of life. She had to pull into the kerb and try and analyse why she felt so intense a panic.

After all, she was going to a party, wasn't she? There'd be maybe one hundred and fifty people who would either know her or want to meet her. She'd be introduced proudly. Well-known. Of course. You'll want to meet — . And all through the smiles and the glances of admiration, Diana would know that none of it mattered, and that it was *her* choice, because she had wanted praise, admiration and success more than love. Yet that wasn't quite the regret either. It was more an odd and disturbing *lightness*, as if she had become suddenly aware that no one was coming along with her any more. It had always seemed like such a drag, pulling people along, worrying over them, having to plan their lives as well as her own. And now suddenly there was no one to take along that whole moonlit fen road but herself.

And it didn't seem to have enough weight, that self.

Diana remembered with a mixture of shame and embarrassment how at a party recently she'd wanted to dance, *wanted* to, when they played an old blues. But couldn't. Because she was dressed in a tweedy suit. Because she'd adopted another uniform. And, short of taking off all her

313

clothes, there had been no *way* for her to dance to that music. So she'd left her partner bewildered on the floor, and stood for a long while outside near the lime trees.

I'm forgetting something. I've put something away from me, she puzzled, in her parked car.

And Jake's last drunken words came back to her persuasively.

'Of course you haven't got a way of life of any kind. You can't mix up two families like the ones you come from. You're a monster, a biological *sport.*'

Diana thought of the tombstones in Southport and the earth beneath them; her parents there, as lovingly bonded in death as they had always been in life, and all the questions she had failed to ask, and which could never be answered now.

I wanted to write poems, she thought. And I wanted children. The impulse seemed to have the same tender source.

Once she had been in Jake's bed, asleep at his side, dreaming at his side. There was some minute, helpless crustacean she was trying to protect. It kept slithering out of her fingers, struggling to its own destruction. Any moment it would fall through a grid and be lost for ever. She was weeping in her dream with terror, then she was awake at Jake's side again, with tears still scalding her throat and running down her face. It was grey half-light. Jake stirred and threw a heavy arm over her body.

'Whatever is it?'

'We've lost him,' she said, her words broken with violent sobs.

For a moment, he said nothing as if he had not understood she was talking about their son.

Then she remembered. Of course, they had no children. Jake blamed her for that.

'Have you ever wondered why we don't have kids?' he asked her.

It was just before they split.

'We made a *decision*,' she said rashly.

314

'Who made a decision?'

'We made it together. We talked it through. Oh shit, you must remember that.'

'You made it,' said Jake.

'OK. I made it. I'm not RC so I'm allowed to make that kind of decision. But you *knew* I was making it.'

'But why, Diana? *Why* did you? Decide that.'

How could she explain the pain the decision had given her. It'll be too late soon, she thought. Too late. And the guilt of that overcame her treacherously. Her mother had been so unlucky. To have tried so often and lost so many children in the womb.

Jake had turned away triumphantly.

'If you had any guts, you'd have taken the chance,' he said.

Could she have done that?

Poetry is a risk, too, she thought. To put yourself out. Expose yourself like that. It was an incautious act.

As such, she reflected, it wouldn't have worried her father.

When Diana remembered her father, she thought of joy; his face open with laughter, his delight in buying fruit, flowers, toys, clothes. A profusion of gifts.

Her mother didn't approve of any of it.

'What are you teaching the child? We can't afford to live like that!'

It had always been so easy to cheat her father into extravagance.

'Which do you want? The green dress or the red?' he'd ask.

And she'd sigh, pretending to choose, knowing exactly what would happen.

'Have them both then. Go on, wrap them up,' he'd order the assistant.

And she'd hear her mother draw in a long breath of disapproval. 'You'll have to learn some time, Diana. To cut your coat according to your cloth.'

Which was true. There were two lessons, though, and Diana had found it easier to learn her mother's than her father's.

*

Children and poetry, Diana mused.

Her spirits lifted. Why not? she thought. *Why ever not?*

53

It was a hot September. A line of passengers, waiting to board the Euston train, baked under the shallow curved roof of Lime Street Station. Among them stood Leonard Katz, and a little ahead of him, closer to the barrier, stood a fine, white-haired woman, dressed in a neat linen suit. Her profile seemed to him disturbingly familiar. As he picked up his bag to thrust it on board the restaurant car, Len realized he was following Dorothy.

'My eyes are going. Betty's sister, isn't it?' he asked, uncertainly. They had last met at Betty's funeral.

But she recognized him easily. 'Len. And where are *you* off to?'

'Another *bris*. My fourth grandson. You live in London now, I heard.'

'Most of the year. Since Francis left me his flat. Shall we eat together?'

Len took his seat fairly carefully, because his back played him up on long journeys.

'Bit of arthritis,' he excused himself. 'Let me get you a scotch.'

She nodded, studying his face. 'You look well. What are you doing now?'

'What does an old man do?' he grinned.

'You're alone?'

'I'll stick it out while I can,' Len said thoughtfully. 'Don't fancy being packed off from one to another like Uncle Abram.'

'That old fraud,' said Dorothy.

Len was surprised. 'Uncle Abram? Never.'

'All that religion and he had to borrow money from his own children,' she insisted.

'There are worse things than borrowing money. They all loved him, didn't they?'

Dorothy looked unimpressed. 'He lived on their backs,' she insisted.

Len shrugged. The waiter came to take their order, and attention was diverted to the menu.

'I found Liverpool changed,' she said, after a pause.

'Whole country's changed,' Len agreed. 'I was in Leicester last week. You know, all the houses in Highfields, round the *schule*, are full of West Indians.'

'And how do you feel about that?'

'Wish 'em well, poor sods. What else? Coming in our place. Even if I'm just another white bastard to them. Well, it's not going to be easy for anybody this time round.'

Dorothy eyed him shrewdly. He didn't appear to be particularly prosperous, but he clearly looked after himself well. She said as much.

'Well, I got lucky. It could change. I'm an old man, I take things easy, enjoy life. What about you?'

'In my own way,' said Dorothy judiciously.

FOR THE BEST IN PAPERBACKS, LOOK FOR THE

In every corner of the world, on every subject under the sun, Penguin represents quality and variety—the very best in publishing today.

For complete information about books available from Penguin—including Pelicans, Puffins, Peregrines, and Penguin Classics—and how to order them, write to us at the appropriate address below. Please note that for copyright reasons the selection of books varies from country to country.

In the United Kingdom: For a complete list of books available from Penguin in the U.K., please write to *Dept E.P., Penguin Books Ltd, Harmondsworth, Middlesex, UB7 0DA.*

In the United States: For a complete list of books available from Penguin in the U.S., please write to *Dept BA, Penguin,* Box 120, Bergenfield, New Jersey 07621-0120.

In Canada: For a complete list of books available from Penguin in Canada, please write to *Penguin Books Ltd, 2801 John Street, Markham, Ontario L3R 1B4.*

In Australia: For a complete list of books available from Penguin in Australia, please write to the *Marketing Department, Penguin Books Ltd, P.O. Box 257, Ringwood, Victoria 3134.*

In New Zealand: For a complete list of books available from Penguin in New Zealand, please write to the *Marketing Department, Penguin Books (NZ) Ltd, Private Bag, Takapuna, Auckland 9.*

In India: For a complete list of books available from Penguin, please write to *Penguin Overseas Ltd, 706 Eros Apartments, 56 Nehru Place, New Delhi, 110019.*

In Holland: For a complete list of books available from Penguin in Holland, please write to *Penguin Books Nederland B.V., Postbus 195, NL-1380AD Weesp, Netherlands.*

In Germany: For a complete list of books available from Penguin, please write to *Penguin Books Ltd, Friedrichstrasse 10-12, D-6000 Frankfurt Main 1, Federal Republic of Germany.*

In Spain: For a complete list of books available from Penguin in Spain, please write to *Longman, Penguin España, Calle San Nicolas 15, E-28013 Madrid, Spain.*

In Japan: For a complete list of books available from Penguin in Japan, please write to *Longman Penguin Japan Co Ltd, Yamaguchi Building, 2-12-9 Kanda Jimbocho, Chiyoda-Ku, Tokyo 101, Japan.*